ANTON PAVLOVICH CHEKHOV was born on January 17, 1860, in Taganrog on the Sea of Azov. The son of a small shopkeeper and the grandson of a serf, he had to improve his station in life the hard way. At sixteen, he was left to shift for himself while his father fled with the rest of the family to Moscow to escape a debtors' prison. After finishing school in his native town, Chekhov went to Moscow where, with the aid of a scholarship, he entered the University to study medicine. To help with the family finances, he started publishing tales, anecdotes, jokes and articles. By the time he took his medical degree in 1884, writing had become his main interest and occupation. His literary reputation grew with the publication of the book *Motley Stories*, in 1886. That same year he made the acquaintance of Alexey Suvorin, owner of the newspaper *New Time*, who invited him to contribute longer tales at a higher rate. In 1888 he was awarded the Pushkin Prize for the collection *In the Twilight*. This and the publication of the long story *The Steppe* marked the beginning of Chekhov's recognition as one of Russia's leading young writers. In the years following he produced his first serious full-length play, *Ivanov* (1888), as well as a steady stream of short stories. The first production of his famous play *The Sea Gull* (1896) was a miserable failure. But in 1898 the play was revived at the Moscow Art Theater and proved a resounding success as did the Theater's productions of *The Three Sisters* and *The Cherry Orchard*. In 1901 Chekhov married the actress Olga Knipper. He died of tuberculosis on July 2, 1904.

# Anton Chekhov

# WARD SIX

## and other stories

A New Translation by Ann Dunnigan

With an Afterword by
Rufus W. Mathewson

A SIGNET CLASSIC from
**NEW AMERICAN LIBRARY**
TIMES MIRROR
New York and Scarborough, Ontario
The New English Library Limited, London

SIGNET, SIGNET CLASSICS, MENTOR, PLUME AND MERIDIAN BOOKS
are published *in the United States* by
The New American Library, Inc.,
1301 Avenue of the Americas, New York, New York 10019,
*in Canada* by the New American Library of Canada, Limited,
81 Mack Avenue, Scarborough, Ontario M1L 1M8,
*in the United Kingdom* by The New English Library Limited,
Barnard's Inn, Holborn, London, E.C. 1, England.

*First Printing, September, 1965*

5  6  7  8  9  10  11  12  13

PRINTED IN THE UNITED STATES OF AMERICA

# CONTENTS

# WARD SIX

## I

In the hospital yard there stands a small annex surrounded by a whole forest of burdock, nettles, and wild hemp. The roof is rusty, the chimney half caved in, the porch steps rotted and overgrown with grass, and only a few traces of stucco are left on the walls. The front of the annex faces the hospital and the back looks onto a field from which it is separated by the gray hospital fence topped with spikes. These spikes, the fence, and the annex itself all have that peculiarly desolate, Godforsaken look characteristic of our hospital and prison buildings.

If you are not afraid of being stung by the nettles, come with me along the narrow path leading to the annex, and let us see what is going on inside. Opening the first door, we find ourselves in the entry. Whole mountains of hospital rubbish are piled against the walls and stove. Mattresses, old tattered dressing gowns, underdrawers, blue-striped shirts, utterly useless worn-out boots and shoes—all this litter lying in jumbled, raddled, moldering heaps and giving off a stifling odor.

Lying on top of this rubbish, his pipe invariably clenched in his teeth, is the guard Nikita, an old retired soldier still wearing his rusty army insignia. He has a grim haggard face, a red nose, and bushy eyebrows that make him look like a Russian sheep dog; although small, lean and sinewy, there is nevertheless something authoritative in his bearing, and his fists are powerful. He is one of those diligent, simple-minded, dogmatic, and obtuse individuals who love law and order more than anything else in the world, and as a consequence are convinced that *they* have to be beaten. He distributes blows indiscriminately on the face, chest, or back, in the certainty that there is no other way to keep order here.

Next you come into a large spacious room which occupies the whole building, not counting the entry. The walls are painted a muddy blue, and the ceiling, as in a peasant's chimneyless hut, is black with soot—obviously the stoves here smoke in winter, filling the room with charcoal fumes. The windows are disfigured by an iron grille on the inside. The floor is gray and splintery. The place stinks of sauerkraut, smoldering wicks, bedbugs, and ammonia, and for the first moment this stench gives you the impression that you are entering a menagerie.

The beds in the room are screwed to the floor. Sitting or lying on them are men in blue hospital gowns and old-fashioned nightcaps. These are the lunatics.

There are five of them. Only one is of noble birth, the rest are commoners. The one nearest the door, a tall thin man with a glossy red mustache and eyes red from weeping, sits with his head in his hands staring fixedly into space. He grieves day and night, sighing and shaking his head, and smiling bitterly; he rarely takes part in a conversation and as a rule does not reply to questions; when given food, he eats and drinks automatically. To judge from his agonizing racking cough, his hectic flush and emaciated body, he is in the early stages of consumption.

Next to him is a small, sprightly, exceedingly active old man with a pointed beard and kinky black hair like a Negro's. He spends the day either wandering up and down the ward, going from window to window, or sitting on the bed, his feet tucked under him Turkish style, restlessly whistling like a bullfinch, singing in a low voice, and chuckling. He manifests this same childish gaiety and lively disposition at night when he gets up to say his prayers, that is, to beat his breast with his fists and pluck at the door with his fingers. This is the Jew Moiseika, a hatter who lost his mind twenty years ago when his workshop burned down.

He alone of the inmates of Ward Six is permitted to go out of the building and even out of the hospital yard and into the street. He has enjoyed this privilege for years, probably as an old resident of the hospital, and as a quiet harmless idiot and town buffoon, whose appearance in the streets surrounded by dogs and little boys has long been a familiar sight. Wearing his ragged hospital robe, a ridiculous nightcap and slippers, sometimes barelegged and even naked under his robe, he roams the streets, stopping at house gates and shops, begging a kopeck. He is given kvass in one place, a bit of bread or a kopeck in another, and generally returns to the annex feeling rich and content. Everything he brings back is taken away from him by Nikita for his own use. This the soldier does roughly and in anger, calling on God to witness that he will never again let the Jew go out into the street, that for him there is nothing in the world worse than a breach of regulations.

Moiseika loves doing a good turn. He brings his companions water, covers them up when they are asleep, promises to make them new caps and to bring each of them a kopeck when he goes out, and it is he who spoon-feeds his neighbor on the left, a paralytic. He does not act out of compassion or any sort of humane considerations, but simply in imitation of Gromov, his neighbor on the right, automatically submitting to his influence.

Ivan Dmitrich Gromov, a nobleman of about thirty-three, formerly a court bailiff and provincial secretary, suffers from persecution mania. He either lies curled up in bed or paces back and forth as if taking exercise, but seldom sits down. He is always in a state of agitation and excitement, always under the strain of some vague undefined expectation. The slightest rustle in the entry or shout in the yard is enough to make him raise his head and listen: are they coming for him? Is it him they are looking for? At such times his face expresses the most acute anxiety and repugnance.

I like his broad pale face with its high cheekbones, an unhappy face in which a soul tormented by perpetual struggle and fear is reflected as in a mirror. His grimaces are queer and morbid, but the fine lines drawn on his face by deep and genuine suffering denote sensibility and culture, and there is a warm lucid gleam in his eyes. I like the man himself, always courteous, obliging, and extremely considerate in his treatment of everyone except Nikita. When anyone drops a button or a spoon, he leaps from his bed and picks it up. He always greets his companions with a good morning when he gets up and wishes them good night when he goes to bed.

Apart from his grimacing and being continually overwrought, his madness expresses itself in the following ways. Sometimes in the evenings he wraps his robe around him, and, trembling all over, his teeth chattering, begins rapidly pacing up and down like a man in a high fever. From the way he suddenly stops and looks at his companions it is clear that he wants to say something very important, but evidently realizing that nobody will listen to him or understand him, he impatiently shakes his head and continues pacing. Soon, however, the desire to speak overrules all other considerations, and he lets himself go and talks feverishly, passionately. His speech, as in a delirium, is frenzied, spasmodic, disordered, and not always understandable, yet one detects something singularly fine in the words and in his voice. When he talks, both the lunatic and the man are distinguishable in him. It would be difficult to set down on paper his mad tirade. He discourses on human baseness, on violence vanquishing truth, on the glorious life that one day will appear on earth, on the iron grilles on the windows which constantly remind him of the stupidity and cruelty of the oppressors. It makes for a confused and incoherent potpourri of songs which, though old, have yet to be sung to the end.

## II

Some twelve or fifteen years ago an official by the name of Gromov, a substantial well-to-do man, lived in his own house on the main street of the town. He had two sons: Sergei and Ivan. When Sergei was a fourth-year student he fell ill with galloping consumption and died, and this death was the prelude to a whole series of misfortunes which suddenly rained down upon the Gromov family. Within a week of Sergei's burial the old man was put on trial for forgery and embezzlement, and soon after died of typhus in the prison hospital. The house and all their personal property was sold at auction, and Ivan Dmitrich and his mother were left entirely without means.

When his father was alive, Ivan Dmitrich, who was living in Petersburg where he was a student at the university, received sixty or seventy rubles a month from home and had absolutely no conception of want, but now he was forced to make drastic changes in his life. He had to work from morning to night giving ill-paid lessons and doing copying, and even so he went hungry, as everything he earned was

sent home for the support of his mother. Unable to endure
such a life, he lost heart, his health failed, and he left the
university and went home. Here in the little town where he
had connections, Ivan Dmitrich got work as a teacher in the
district school, but he was unable to get along with his
colleagues, was not liked by his pupils, and soon gave up
teaching. His mother died. He had been out of work for
about six months, living on nothing but bread and water,
when he obtained the position of court bailiff, and he remained in this office till he was dismissed because of ill
health.

Even as a young student he had never appeared to be
robust. Always pale, thin, and subject to colds, he ate little
and slept badly. One glass of wine went to his head and
made him hysterical. Although generally drawn to people,
thanks to his irritable disposition and mistrustfulness, he
never was close to anyone and had no friends. He invariably
spoke with contempt of the townspeople, saying that their
gross ignorance and sluggish animal life was insufferable and
detestable to him. He spoke in a shrill tenor, vehemently,
never without either exasperation and indignation or ecstasy
and wonder—and always sincerely. No matter what one
talked to him about, he always came back to the same thing:
the atmosphere of the town is stifling and dull; the people, all
devoid of higher interests, lead dismal meaningless lives di-
versified only by violence, coarse debauchery, and hypocrisy;
scoundrels are well-fed and well-dressed, while honest men
live from hand to mouth; there is a need for schools, for a
local newspaper with a decent point of view, a theater, public
lectures, solidarity of intellectual forces, and for society to
be made aware of itself, to be aroused. In judging people he
laid the colors on thick, seeing everything as black or white
and recognizing no intermediate shades; mankind was divided
into honest men and scoundrels, and there was no middle
ground. Of women and love he spoke with ardent enthusiasm,
but he had never in his life been in love.

Despite the harshness of his judgments and his nervous
irritability, he was liked in the town and affectionately referred to as Vanya behind his back. His innate refinement,
his complaisance, integrity, and moral purity, together with
his shabby coat, sickly appearance, and family misfortunes,
combined to inspire a kind, warm, melancholy feeling; moreover he was well-educated and well-read; according to the

townspeople there was nothing he did not know and they regarded him as a sort of walking encyclopedia.

He read a great deal. He used to sit in the club, nervously plucking at his beard as he leafed through magazines and books, and from the expression on his face he appeared to be not so much reading as devouring their contents, hardly giving himself time to digest what he read. It makes one think that reading was one of his morbid habits, for he pounced on everything that came to hand with equal avidity, even last year's newspapers and almanacs. At home he always read lying down.

# III

One autumn morning Ivan Dmitrich, his overcoat collar turned up, was splashing through the mud of side streets and back yards on his way to the house of some citizen or other to exercise a writ of execution. In one of the side streets he met two convicts in chains accompanied by four armed guards. Ivan Dmitrich had often encountered convicts and they always aroused in him feelings of compassion and discomfort, but this time he was strangely and unaccountably affected. For some reason he suddenly felt that he too could be clapped in irons and led in this same way through the mud to prison. As he passed the post office on his way home he met a police inspector of his acquaintance who greeted him and accompanied him a few paces down the street, and somehow this aroused his suspicion. At home he was haunted all day by these convicts and soldiers with rifles, and an inexplicable mental anxiety prevented him from reading or concentrating. He did not light his lamp in the evening and at night he was unable to sleep, but kept thinking that he too could be arrested, clapped in irons, and thrown into prison. He knew of no crime in his past and was confident that in the future he would never be guilty of murder, arson, or theft, but was it not possible to commit a crime by accident, without meaning to, and was not calumny too, or even a judicial error, conceivable? Not without reason does the age-old experience of the people teach that no one is safe from the poorhouse or prison. And, legal procedures being what they are today, a miscarriage of justice is not only quite possible but would be nothing to wonder at. People who have an official, professional relation to other men's suffering —judges, physicians, the police, for example—grow so callous in the course of time, simply from force of habit, that even if they wanted to they would be unable to treat their clients in any but a formal way; in this respect they are not unlike the peasant who slaughters sheep and calves in his back yard, oblivious to the blood. And once this formal, heartless attitude has been established, only one thing is needed to make a judge deprive an innocent man of all his rights and sentence him to hard labor: time. Just the time necessary for the observation of certain formalities for which a judge receives his salary—and it is all over. Then try to find justice and protection in this filthy little town two hundred versts from a railroad. And, indeed, is it not absurd even to think of justice when society regards every kind of violence as both rational and expedient, while every act of clemency, such as a verdict of acquittal, provokes an outburst of dissatisfaction and feelings of revenge?

In the morning Ivan Dmitrich got up in a state of dread and with cold sweat on his brow, by now absolutely convinced that he could be arrested at any moment. Since the oppressive thoughts of the preceding day had remained with him so long, he thought it meant there was some measure of truth in them. They certainly could not have entered his mind apropos of nothing.

A policeman walked slowly past the window: that could not be without reason. Two men stopped near the house and stood there in silence. Why had they stopped talking?

And for Ivan Dmitrich there now came days and nights of torture. Everyone who passed his windows or entered the yard seemed to him a spy or a detective. The district police inspector was in the habit of driving down the street in a carriage and pair every day at noon on his way to the police department from his estate on the outskirts of town, but now when he passed, Ivan Dmitrich imagined he was driving unusually fast and that his face wore a rather singular expression: obviously he was rushing to announce the appearance of a dangerous criminal in town. Ivan Dmitrich shuddered at every ring and knock at the gate, was in agony if he came upon a new face at his landlady's, smiled and commenced whistling to show how unconcerned he was whenever he encountered a policeman or gendarme. He lay awake whole nights expecting to be arrested, but would sigh and snore loudly to make the landlady think that he was sleeping, for, of course, if one could not sleep it meant he was tortured by pangs of conscience—what a piece of evidence that would be! Facts and common sense told him that all these fears were absurd and psychopathic, that there was really nothing so terrible about arrest and imprisonment—so long as one's conscience was clear; but the more sensibly and logically he reasoned, the more acute and agonizing his inner anxiety became. He was like the hermit who tried to make a clearing in the virgin forest: the more zealously he wielded his ax, the denser and mightier grew the forest. Realizing at last that it was futile, Ivan Dmitrich gave up reasoning and abandoned himself to terror and despair.

He commenced to avoid people and to live in solitude. His work, distasteful to him before, now became unbearable. He was afraid someone might get him in trouble, might surreptitiously slip a bribe into his pocket and then expose him; or that he himself would accidentally make some error in the official documents that would be tantamount to fraud, or perhaps lose money that did not belong to him. Oddly, his mind had never before been so flexible and inventive as now when he daily contrived a thousand reasons why he should tremble for his freedom and honor; but, on the other hand, his interest in the outside world, and particularly in books, diminished, and his memory noticeably deteriorated.

In the spring, when the snow had melted, two partly decomposed corpses were found in the ravine near the cemetery —an old woman and a little boy, both bearing marks of a violent death. The whole town talked of nothing but these corpses and the unknown murderers. To prevent people thinking it was he who had killed them, Ivan Dmitrich walked about the streets with a smile on his face, and on meeting one of his acquaintances, would assure him, turning pale then flushing, that there was no more reprehensible crime than murdering the weak and defenseless. But this duplicity soon exhausted him, and after some reflection he decided that the best thing for a man in his position to do was to hide in the landlady's cellar. He spent the whole day and night and the following day in the cellar; then, thoroughly chilled, stole back to his room like a thief when it grew dark. He stood motionless in the middle of his room till daybreak, listening. Early in the morning, before sunrise, some workmen came to the landlady's apartment. Ivan Dmitrich knew perfectly well they had come to reset the stove in the kitchen, but fear prompted him to think they were policemen in disguise. He stealthily crept out of the apartment without stopping to put on his hat and coat and, terror-stricken, ran down the street. Barking dogs tore after him, somewhere behind him a man shouted, the wind whistled in his ears, and it seemed to Ivan Dmitrich that all the violence in the world had gathered together in pursuit of him.

He was stopped and brought home, and the landlady was sent for a doctor. Dr. Andrei Yefimych, of whom more later, prescribed cold compresses and laurel water, then sadly shook his head and left, telling the landlady he would not come again, as one ought not to interfere with people going out of their minds.

Since he had not the means to be taken care of at home, Ivan Dmitrich was sent to the hospital, where he was put into the ward for venereal patients. He did not sleep at night, was capricious, and disturbed the other patients; soon, on Andrei Yefimych's orders, he was transferred to Ward Six.

Within a year Ivan Dmitrich was entirely forgotten in the town, and his books, which the landlady had piled in a sledge in the lean-to, were pilfered by small boys.

## IV

Ivan Dmitrich's neighbor on the left, as I have already said, is the Jew Moiseika, and on his right is a peasant so rolling in fat as to be almost spherical, with an inane and totally vacant expression. This inert, gluttonous, slovenly animal, who long ago lost the capacity to think and feel, perpetually exudes a rank, fetid odor.

Nikita, who has to clean up after him, beats him horribly, using all his strength and not even sparing his own fists; and what is awful is not that he is beaten—one can get used to that—but that this stupefied animal does not react to the blows by a sound, a gesture, an expression in the eyes, but merely rocks back and forth like a heavy barrel.

The fifth and last inmate of Ward Six, a former mail

sorter in the post office, is a thin little blond man with a kind but rather sly face. Judging by the clear and merry look in his serene intelligent eyes, he harbors some delightful and important secret. Under his pillow and mattress he keeps something he never shows anyone, not from fear of its being taken away or stolen, but from modesty. Sometimes he goes to the window, turns his back to his comrades, and puts this object on his chest, bending his head to look at it; if you go up to him at such a moment he becomes flustered and quickly snatches it off. But his secret is not hard to guess.

"You may congratulate me," he often says to Ivan Dmitrich. "I have been recommended for the Stanislas second grade with a star. The second grade with a star is given only to foreigners, but for some reason they intend to make an exception in my case," he says with a smile, shrugging his shoulders in bewilderment. "That, I must confess, I did not expect!"

"I know nothing about these things," Ivan Dmitrich declares morosely.

"But you know what I'll get sooner or later?" the former mail sorter continues with a sly wink. "I shall undoubtedly get the Swedish 'Polar Star.' A decoration like that is worth exerting yourself for. A white cross and black ribbon. Very handsome."

Probably in no other place is life so monotonous as in the hospital annex. In the morning the patients, except the paralytic and the fat peasant, wash at a big tub in the entry, drying themselves on the skirts of their dressing gowns; after that they drink tea, which is brought by Nikita from the main building. They are allowed one mugful each. At noon they are given sauerkraut soup and gruel, and in the evening their supper consists of the gruel left over from dinner. In the intervals they lie on their beds, sleep, gaze out the windows, and pace up and down. And so it is every day. Even the former mail sorter talks always of the same decorations.

Rarely is a fresh face seen in Ward Six. The doctor stopped admitting any new lunatics long ago, and people who are fond of visiting insane asylums are few in this world. Once every two months the barber Semyon Lazarich comes to the annex. How he cuts the patients' hair, how Nikita assists him, the consternation into which the inmates are thrown at every appearance of the drunken, grinning barber, are things we shall not speak of.

Apart from the barber no one looks into the ward. The patients are condemned to seeing no one but Nikita day after day.

Of late, however, a rather strange rumor has been spreading through the hospital. It is reported that the doctor has been visiting Ward Six.


# V

A strange rumor!

Dr. Andrei Yefimych Ragin is a remarkable man in his way. He is said to have been very religious in his early youth and to have prepared himself for an ecclesiastical career with the intention of entering the theological academy on finishing high school in 1863; but it seems that his father, a doctor of medicine and a surgeon, was virulent in his ridicule and categorically announced that he would no longer consider him his son if he became a priest. How true this is I do not know, but on more than one occasion Andrei Yefimych himself confessed that he had never felt a vocation for medicine or for the exact sciences in general.

However that may be, after graduating from medical school he did not take Orders. He evinced no special devoutness and was no more like an ecclesiastic at the beginning of his medical career than he is now.

He is heavy, coarse, and boorish in appearance; his face, beard, and flat limp hair, and his rugged, ungainly figure, suggest a gruff, overfed, intemperate tavernkeeper. His stern face is covered with blue veins, the eyes small, the nose red. Being tall and broad-shouldered, with huge hands and feet, he looks as if one blow of his fist would knock the daylights out of a man. But his step is soft, his bearing circumspect and ingratiating, and when he meets anyone in a narrow corridor he is always the first to stop and make way, saying: "Sorry!"—not, as one might expect, in a deep bass, but in a high soft tenor. He has a small tumor on his neck which prevents him from wearing stiff collars, and as a consequence wears only soft linen or cotton shirts. Altogether he does not dress like a doctor. He goes around in the same suit for ten years, and when he does get a new one, which he usually buys in a Jewish shop, it looks just as shabby and rumpled on him as the old one; he receives patients, eats

dinner, and visits friends in the same coat, not out of nig-
gardliness, but out of a complete disregard for his personal
appearance.

When Andrei Yefimych came to our town to take up his
duties, the "charitable institution" was in an appalling state.
One could hardly breathe for the stench in the wards, corridors, and hospital yard. The hospital attendants, the nurses,
and their children all slept in the wards with the patients.
Everyone complained that life was made miserable by cockroaches, bedbugs, and mice. In the surgical section they had
not yet got rid of erysipelas. There were only two scalpels in
the entire hospital, not a single thermometer, and the bath-
tubs were used for storing potatoes. The superintendent, matron, and medical assistant all robbed the patients, and the
old doctor, Andrei Yefimych's predecessor, was said to have
engaged in the illicit sale of hospital alcohol and to have
organized a veritable harem for himself among the nurses
and patients. The townspeople were well aware of these irregularities and even exaggerated them, but took them calmly;
some justified them on the grounds that only peasants and
workingmen went to the hospital, and they had nothing to
complain of since they were considerably worse off at home
—you wouldn't expect to feed them on woodcock! Others
made the excuse that the town was unable to support a
decent hospital without help from the zemstvo; thank God
for any hospital, even a bad one! But the recently formed
zemstvo failed to open a hospital either in the town or in the
district on the grounds that the town already had one.

After inspecting the hospital, Andrei Yefimych came to the
conclusion that it was an infamous institution, highly detrimental to the health of the community. In his opinion the
wisest thing to do would be to discharge the patients and
close the hospital. But for this, he reasoned, something more
than his will would be required, and in any case it would
serve no purpose; if physical and moral impurity were driven
out of one place they would only move to another; one must
wait for it to wither away of itself. Moreover, if the people
had opened the hospital and tolerated it, it meant that they
needed it; superstition and all the rest of life's filth and
abominations are necessary, for in time they are converted
into something useful, as dung into black soil. There is
nothing on earth so fine that its origin is without foulness.

Once he had taken up his duties, Andrei Yefimych did not

appear to be greatly concerned about the irregularities. He only asked the hospital attendants and nurses not to sleep in the wards and installed two cupboards of instruments; but the superintendent and the matron did not change, and the erysipelas in the surgical ward remained.

Andrei Yefimych has an intense love of honesty and reason, but he lacks the will power and self-confidence to organize a reasonable and honest life around him. He is utterly incapable of commanding, forbidding, insisting. It almost seems as if he had taken a vow never to raise his voice or to use the imperative mood. It is hard for him to say: "Give me," or "Bring me"; when he feels hungry he clears his throat and hesitantly says to the cook: "I might have some tea . . ." or: "I might have dinner now . . ." As for telling the superintendent to stop stealing, or dismissing him, or abolishing the sinecure—such things are absolutely beyond him. When people deceive him, flatter him, bring him a deliberately falsified account to sign, Andrei Yefimych turns red as a lobster and feels guilty, but signs it; when the patients complain to him of hunger or the rough treatment of the nurses, he is embarrassed and guiltily mumbles:

"Very well, very well, I'll look into it later. . . . Most likely there is some misunderstanding. . . ."

At first Andrei Yefimych worked assiduously. He received patients daily from morning till dinnertime, performed operations, and even took obstetrical cases. The ladies all said that he was most considerate and an excellent diagnostician, especially of women's and children's diseases. As time went on, however, he became noticeably wearied by the monotony and obvious futility of the work. Thirty patients today, tomorrow thirty-five, the next day forty—and so on, day after day, year after year, but the mortality rate never goes down and the sick never stop coming. To give any real help to forty sick people in the course of a morning is a physical impossibility, and perforce results in fraud. If in a given year you see 12,000 patients, it means, by simple reckoning, that 12,000 people have been deceived. To put the seriously ill in wards and treat them according to the precepts of science is also impossible, for while the precepts exist, there is no science; if, on the other hand, you waive philosophy and pedantically follow the rules as other doctors do, first of all it requires cleanliness and ventilation instead of filth, wholesome nourishment instead of reeking sauerkraut soup, and decent assistants instead of thieves.

And, indeed, why keep people from dying since death is normal, the decreed end for everyone? What if the life of some huckster or official is prolonged by five or ten years? And if one thinks the aim of medicine is the alleviation of suffering by means of drugs, the question inevitably arises: why alleviate it? In the first place, suffering is said to lead to self-perfection, and in the second place, if man learns to ease his suffering with pills and drops he will completely abandon religion and philosophy, wherein till now he has found not only a defense against every adversity, but happiness itself. Pushkin suffered agonies before his death, Heine was a paralytic for years; why, then, should an Andrei Yefimych or a Matryona Savishna be spared illness when their insipid lives would be as empty as an amoeba's were it not for suffering?

Oppressed by such reasoning, Andrei Yefimych grew disheartened and gave up going to the hospital every day.

# VI

This is how he spends his life. Generally, he gets up at eight o'clock, dresses, and eats breakfast. Then he either sits in his study and reads or goes to the hospital. In the dark narrow hospital corridor sit the out-patients waiting to be admitted. Attendants and nurses rush by, their heels clattering on the brick floor; emaciated patients walk by in dressing gowns; corpses and vessels of waste matter are carried out; children cry; and there is a cold draft. Andrei Yefimych knows that for feverish, consumptive, or impressionable patients such conditions are a torture, but what is to be done?

In the consulting room he finds the medical assistant, Sergei Sergeich, a fat little man with a plump, well-washed, clean-shaven face and mild docile manners, wearing a new loose-fitting suit and looking more like a senator than a medical assistant. He has a tremendous practice in the town, wears a white tie, and considers himself more knowledgeable than the doctor, who has no practice at all. In one corner of the consulting room there is a large icon in a case and a heavy icon lamp; near it stands a church candelabra under a dust cover; the walls are hung with portraits of bishops, a view of the Svyatogorsk Monastery, and garlands of dried cornflowers. Sergei Sergeich is religious and loves pomp. The icon was installed at his expense; on Sundays, by his order, one of the patients reads aloud from the Book of Psalms, after which Sergei Sergeich himself makes the rounds of the wards carrying a censer with burning incense.

The patients are numerous and time is short, so the doctor confines himself to a brief examination and administering medications such as volatile ointment and castor oil. Andrei Yefimych sits lost in thought, his cheek resting on his fist, and puts his questions mechanically. Sergei Sergeich is also present; he rubs his hands and occasionally interposes a remark.

"We suffer sickness and want," he says, "because we do not pray to the merciful Lord as we should. Yes!"

Andrei Yefimych does not perform any operations during this time; he long ago got out of the habit, and the sight of blood upsets him now. When he has to open a baby's mouth to look at his throat and the child cries and defends himself with his little fists, the noise makes his head spin and tears come to his eyes. He hastily writes a prescription and motions the mother to take the child away.

He is soon wearied by the timidity and incoherence of the patients, the presence of the pompous Sergei Sergeich, the portraits on the walls, and his own questions, which he has not varied in more than twenty years. After seeing five or six patients he goes, leaving the rest to the assistant.

Andrei Yefimych sits down in his study and begins reading as soon as he gets home, enjoying the thought that, thank God, he no longer has a private practice and nobody will disturb him. He reads a great deal and always with pleasure. Half of his salary is spent on books, and three of the six rooms in his apartment are crammed with old magazines and books. He prefers works on history and philosophy; the only medical publication he subscribes to is *The Physician*, which he invariably starts reading from the back. He reads uninterruptedly for hours at a stretch without tiring, not rapidly and passionately as Ivan Dmitrich had once read, but slowly, with penetration, often dwelling on a passage that pleases or puzzles him. There is always a decanter of vodka near his book, and a salted cucumber or pickled apple lying on the cloth without a plate. Every half hour he pours him-

self a glass of vodka and drinks it down without taking his
eyes from the book, then he feels for the cucumber and takes
a bite.

At three o'clock he circumspectly approaches the kitchen
door, coughs, and says:

"Daryushka, I might have dinner now. . . ."

After a rather poor and badly served dinner, Andrei
Yefimych walks from room to room, his arms folded on his
chest, thinking. The clock strikes four, then five, and he is
still pacing and thinking. From time to time the kitchen
door creaks and Daryushka's sleepy red face appears.

"Andrei Yefimych, isn't it time for your beer?" she anxiously inquires.

"No, it's not time yet . . ." he answers. "I'll wait a bit . . .
I'll wait. . . ."

Toward evening the postmaster, Mikhail Averyanych, comes
in—the only man in the whole town whose company Andrei
Yefimych does not find irksome. Mikhail Averyanych was
once a very rich landowner and cavalry officer, but was
ruined and forced to enter the postal service late in life. He
has a hale and hearty look, luxuriant gray side whiskers, a
loud but pleasant voice, and the manners of a well-bred man.
He is kind and sensitive but irascible. When anyone comes
into the post office and protests, disagrees, or merely starts
an argument, Mikhail Averyanych turns livid, trembles from
head to foot, and in a thunderous voice shouts: "Silence!"
so that the post office has a long established reputation for
being a formidable institution to visit. Mikhail Averyanych
likes and respects Andrei Yefimych for his erudition and
nobility of spirit, but he is haughty toward the rest of the
town's inhabitants, treating them as though they were his
inferiors.

"Well, here I am!" he says, entering the room. "How are
you, my friend? Probably getting sick of me by now, eh?"

"On the contrary, I'm delighted," the doctor replies. "Always glad to see you."

The friends sit down on the sofa in the study and smoke in
silence for a while.

"Daryushka, what about a little beer?" Andrei Yefimych
says.

The first bottle is drunk in the same silence: the doctor
musing, Mikhail Averyanych with the merry, animated look

of a man who has something very interesting to tell. It is always the doctor who begins the conversation.

"What a pity," he says slowly and softly, shaking his head and not looking his friend in the eye (he never looks anyone in the eye), "what a great pity, my dear Mikhail Averyanych, that our town is devoid of people who enjoy an interesting and intelligent conversation, or who are even capable of one. It's an enormous privation for us. Even the educated classes do not rise above triviality; the level of their development, I assure you, is not a bit higher than that of the lower classes."

"Absolutely true. I agree."

"You are aware, of course," the doctor continues in quiet measured tones, "that everything in this world is insignificant and uninteresting except the higher spiritual manifestations of the human mind. It is the mind which draws a distinct boundary line between the animal and man, giving an intimation of the divinity of the latter, and to some degree even compensating him for a nonexistent immortality. From this we may conclude that the intellect is the only possible source of enjoyment. We, however, neither see nor hear any trace of intellect around us—which means we are deprived of enjoyment. True, we have books, but that is not at all the same as living talk and social intercourse. If you will allow me to make a not very apt comparison: books are the printed score, while conversation is the song."

"Absolutely true."

A silence falls. Daryushka comes out of the kitchen and with an expression of blank dejection stands in the doorway listening, her chin propped on her fist.

"Ah!" sighs Mikhail Averyanych, "what can you expect of the present-day mind!"

And he proceeds to tell of how splendid, gay, and interesting life used to be, of how clever the intelligentsia of Russia was then, and what a high value was set on honor and friendship. People used to lend money without promissory notes, and it was considered a disgrace not to extend a helping hand to a friend in need. What campaigns, skirmishes, adventures, what friendships, and what women! And the Caucasus—what a marvelous country! . . . There was the wife of one of the battalion commanders, a strange woman, who used to put on an officer's uniform and drive off into the mountains in the evening alone, without an escort. It was said she had a romance with some prince in one of the native villages.

"Holy Mother!" Daryushka sighs.

"And how we drank! How we ate! What desperate liberals we were!"

Andrei Yefimych listens without hearing; he is lost in thought, sipping his beer.

"I often dream about intelligent people and conversations with them," he suddenly says, interrupting Mikhail Averyanych. "My father gave me an excellent education, but under the influence of the ideas of the sixties, he forced me to become a doctor. I sometimes think that if I had not obeyed him I would now be in the very center of some intellectual movement. I would probably be on the staff of a university. Of course, intellect too is transitory, not immortal, but you know why I have an inclination for it. Life is a miserable trap. As soon as a thinking man reaches maturity and becomes capable of conscious thought, he cannot help feeling that he is in a trap from which there is no escape. When you come to think of it, he has been brought to life from a state of nonexistence against his will, by pure chance. What for? If he tries to find out the meaning and purpose of his existence he either gets no answer or is told all sorts of absurdities; he knocks—no one opens to him; death too comes against his will. And just as men in prison, united by their common misfortune, feel better when they are together, so in life people with a turn for analysis and generalizations do not notice that they are in a trap when they come together and pass the time in the exchange of free and elevating ideas. In this respect the mind is a source of incomparable pleasure."

"Absolutely true."

Without looking his companion in the eye, Andrei Yefimych goes on talking in his soft faltering voice about intellectual people and their conversations, and Mikhail Averyanych listens attentively, agreeing: "Absolutely true."

"But don't you believe in the immortality of the soul?" the postmaster suddenly asks.

"No, my dear Mikhail Averyanych, I do not believe in it, nor do I find grounds for believing in it."

"To tell the truth, I have doubts about it myself. Although, on the other hand, I have a feeling I will never die. Ugh, I think to myself, you old fogy, it's time you were dead! But there is a wee small voice in my soul that whispers: don't believe it, you won't die!"

Soon after nine Mikhail Averyanych leaves. As he stands in the hall putting on his fur coat, he says with a sigh:

"Still, what a hole fate has thrown us into! And the worst of it is, we shall have to die here too. Ugh!"

# VII

After seeing his friend out, Andrei Yefimych sits down at the table and resumes his reading. Not a sound breaks the stillness of the night, and time itself seems to have stopped, to be holding its breath with the doctor over his book, as if nothing exists but this book and the lamp with its green globe. Gradually the doctor's coarse rugged face lights up with a smile of impassioned delight at the workings of the human mind. Oh, why is not man immortal? he thinks. Why these brain centers and their convolutions, why vision, speech, feeling, genius, if all this is destined to go into the ground, ultimately to grow cold together with the earth's crust, and then for millions of years to whirl with it around the sun without aim or reason? Surely it is not necessary, merely for the sake of this cooling and whirling, to draw man, with his superior, almost godlike intelligence, out of oblivion, and then, as if in jest, to turn him into clay.

Metabolism! But what cowardice to console oneself with that substitute for immortality! The unconscious processes that take place in nature are beneath even human stupidity, for in stupidity there is at least consciousness and will, while in these processes there is absolutely nothing. Only a coward whose fear of death is greater than his self-respect can solace himself with the thought that his body will go on living in a blade of grass, a stone, a toad. . . . To see immortality in the transmutation of matter is as strange as to predict a brilliant future for a violin case after a precious violin has been broken and rendered useless.

When the clock strikes, Andrei Yefimych leans back in his chair and closes his eyes to think a little. And, without realizing it, under the influence of the fine ideas gleaned from his book, he casts a glance at his past and at the present. The past revolts him; better not to think of it. And the present is no different. He knows that while his thoughts are whirling around the sun with the earth's cooling crust, in a large building right next to a doctor's apartment people are languishing in disease and filth; someone is perhaps lying awake trying to combat the vermin, someone else has been infected with erysipelas or is moaning because of a bandage that is wound too tight; patients may be playing cards and drinking vodka with the nurses. Twelve thousand people a year are swindled; the entire hospital system is based on theft, wrangling scandal-mongering, favoritism, and gross quackery, exactly as it was twenty years ago, and remains a vicious institution, in the highest degree detrimental to the health of the community. He knows that behind the bars of Ward No. 6 Nikita beats the patients, and that Moiseika goes through the town begging alms every day.

On the other hand, he knows quite well that during the last twenty-five years a miraculous change has taken place in medicine. When he was studying at the university, it had seemed to him that before long medicine would undergo the fate of alchemy and metaphysics, but now, reading about medicine at night moves him, excites his wonder and enthusiasm. What unforeseen brilliance, what a revolution! Thanks to antiseptics, operations are performed which the great Pirogov had considered impossible even *in spe*. Ordinary zemstvo doctors are not afraid to do a resection of the knee joint; only one in a hundred dies from an abdominal operation; gallstones are considered too trivial to write about; syphilis can be completely cured. And what of hypnotism, the theory of heredity, the discoveries of Pasteur and Koch, the statistics of hygienics, and our Russian zemstvo doctors? Psychiatry, with its modern classification of diseases, its methods of diagnosis and treatment, is a veritable Elborus compared with the past. The insane are no longer doused with cold water or put into strait jackets, but are treated humanely, and, according to what one reads in the newspapers, balls and entertainments are arranged for them. Andrei Yefimych knows that with current views and tastes being what they are, an abomination like Ward Six is possible only in a town two hundred versts from a railroad, where the mayor and the members of the town council are all semiliterate tradesmen who regard a doctor as an oracle to be trusted implicitly, even if he pours molten lead down people's throats;

anywhere else the public and the newspapers would have demolished this little Bastille long ago.

"And yet," Andrei Yefimych asks himself, opening his eyes, "what has come of it? Antiseptics, Koch, Pasteur—but the essentials haven't changed in the least. Sickness and mortality remain the same. They organize entertainments and balls for the insane, but they still keep them confined. So it is all futile, senseless, and there is no essential difference between the best Viennese clinic and my hospital."

But mental anguish and a feeling akin to envy disturb his equanimity. This, no doubt, is owing to fatigue. As his heavy head sinks onto the book, he puts his hands over it to make it softer, thinking:

"I am serving a pernicious cause and receiving a salary from the people I deceive. I am dishonest. But, of course, I am nothing of myself, a mere particle in a necessary social evil: all district officials are bad and are paid for doing nothing. . . . Consequently, it is not I who am to blame for my dishonesty, but the times. . . . If I had been born two hundred years later I should have been different."

When the clock strikes three he puts out the lamp and goes to his bedroom. But he does not feel like sleeping.

# VIII

A year or two ago the zemstvo magnanimously decided to contribute three thousand rubles a year toward increasing the town hospital's medical staff till such time as a zemstvo hospital should be opened, and the district doctor, Yevgeny Fyodorych Khobotov, was hired as Andrei Yefimych's assistant. Still a young man—not yet thirty—tall, dark, with broad cheekbones and small eyes, he looks as if his ancestors were of an alien race. He arrived in town without a kopeck, bringing with him only a small trunk and a homely young woman with a baby in her arms whom he called his cook. Yevgeny Fyodorych always wears a forage cap and high boots, and in winter goes around in a sheepskin jacket. He soon made friends with the medical assistant, Sergei Sergeich, and with the treasurer, but for some reason he calls the rest of the staff aristocrats and avoids them. There is only one book in his whole apartment—*Latest Prescriptions of the*

*Viennese Clinic for 1881.* He never visits a patient without taking this book with him. At night he plays billiards at the club, but does not care for cards. In conversation he is very keen on using such expressions as "You're dillydallying," or "Don't try to pull the wool over my eyes."

Twice a week he goes to the hospital, makes the rounds of the wards, and receives out-patients. The complete absence of antiseptics and the practice of blood-cupping arouse his indignation, but he avoids introducing any new methods for fear of offending Andrei Yefimych. He considers his colleague Andrei Yefimych an old fraud, suspects him of being a man of great means, and secretly envies him. He would gladly take his place.

## IX

One spring evening toward the end of March, when the snow had melted and starlings were singing in the hospital garden, the doctor came out to see his friend the postmaster to the gate. At that moment the Jew Moiseika came into the yard, returning with his booty. He was without a cap and wore only low overshoes on his bare feet; in his hand was a little sack with the alms he had collected.

"Give a little kopeck!" he said to the doctor, smiling and shivering with cold.

Andrei Yefimych, who could never refuse, gave him a ten-kopeck piece.

"How awful that is!" he thought, looking at the man's bare legs and thin raw ankles. "And it's so wet."

Moved by a combination of pity and revulsion, he followed the Jew into the annex, looking now at his bald head, now at his ankles. On seeing the doctor enter, Nikita jumped up from a heap of litter and stood at attention.

"Good evening, Nikita," Andrei Yefimych said in his soft voice. "Perhaps you could give that man a pair of boots . . . otherwise he'll catch cold."

"Yes, sir, Your Honor! I'll report it to the superintendent."

"Please do. Ask him in my name. Say I requested it."

The door leading into the ward was open. Ivan Dmitrich lay on his bed propped up on one elbow listening in alarm to the unfamiliar voice; all at once he recognized the doctor. Trembling with rage he leaped up, his face flushed and wrathful, his eyes starting out of his head, and rushed into the middle of the room.

"The doctor has come!" he cried, and burst out laughing. "At last! I congratulate you, gentlemen. The doctor has deigned to visit us! Dirty dog!" he shrieked in a frenzy such as had never before been seen in the ward. "Kill that damned cur! No, killing's too good for him—drown him in the privy!"

Hearing this, Andrei Yefimych looked into the ward and gently asked: "What for?"

"What for?" shouted Ivan Dmitrich, convulsively pulling his robe around him and approaching the doctor with a threatening look. "What for? Thief!" he uttered the word with disgust, then puckered up his lips as if he were about to spit. "Quack! Hangman!"

"Don't get excited," said Andrei Yefimych with a guilty smile. "I assure you, I have never stolen anything, and as for the rest, you are probably greatly exaggerating. I see you are angry with me. Try to compose yourself, I beg you, and tell me calmly: what is it that makes you so angry?"

"Why do you keep me here?"

"Because you are ill."

"Yes, I am ill. But there are dozens, hundreds, of madmen walking around at liberty, simply because you, in your ignorance, are incapable of distinguishing them from the sane. Why, then, must I, and these other unfortunates, be shut up here as scapegoats for all of them? Morally, you, the medical assistant, the superintendent, and the rest of your hospital rabble are immeasurably inferior to every one of us —why then should we be here and not you? Where's the logic?"

"Morals and logic do not enter into it. Everything depends on chance. Those who are put in here, stay here; those who are not, enjoy their liberty, that's all. And there is no morality or logic in the fact that I am a doctor and you are a mental patient—it's pure chance, nothing more."

"I don't understand that twaddle . . ." Ivan Dmitrich said dully, and sat down on his bed.

Moiseika, whom Nikita had not ventured to search in the doctor's presence, had spread out his crusts, bits of paper, and bones on his bed and, still shivering with cold, began talking to himself in Hebrew in a rapid, singsong voice. He probably imagined he had opened a shop.

"Let me out!" said Ivan Dmitrich in a quavering voice.

"I can't."

"But why can't you? Why?"

"Because it is not within my power. Think: what would be the use of my letting you out? You leave—and the townspeople or the police will stop you and bring you back."

"Yes, yes, that's true . . ." Ivan Dmitrich said, rubbing his forehead. "It's awful! What am I to do? Tell me, what?"

His voice and his youthful face, intelligent despite his grimacing, appealed to Andrei Yefimych. He longed to show him some kindness, to soothe him. He sat down on the bed beside him, thought for a moment, and said:

"You ask me what to do? In your position, the best thing you could do would be to run away from here. But, unfortunately, it would be useless. You would be stopped. When society decides to protect itself from criminals, the psychically ill, and other difficult people, it is invincible. There is only one thing left for you: comfort yourself with the thought that your presence here is indispensable."

"It's no good to anyone."

"So long as prisons and insane asylums exist, someone must be put into them. If not you—me; if not me, someone else. Wait for that time, in some distant future, when prisons and insane asylums have ceased to exist, then there will be no bars on the windows, no hospital gowns. Such a time is bound to come sooner or later."

Ivan Dmitrich smiled sardonically.

"You don't mean it," he said, narrowing his eyes. "Gentlemen like you and your right hand, Nikita, have no concern with the future, but you may be sure, my dear sir, that better times will come! I may express myself in a banal way—laugh if you like—but the dawn of a new life is at hand, justice will triumph, and—our day will come! I don't expect to see it, I'll be dead by then, but other men's grandchildren will witness it. I congratulate them with all my heart, and rejoice, rejoice for them! Forward! May God help you, my friends!"

Ivan Dmitrich, his eyes shining, got up, stretched his arms toward the window and went on speaking in an emotional voice.

"From behind these bars I send you my blessing! Long live justice! I rejoice!"

"I see no reason for rejoicing," said Andrei Yefimych, who found Ivan Dmitrich's gesture theatrical, but at the same time very appealing. "There will be no more prisons and lunatic asylums, and justice, as you choose to express it, will triumph, but, you see, the essence of things will not change, the laws of nature will remain the same. People will fall ill, grow old, and die, just as they do now. So, no matter what magnificent dawn illuminates your life, you will, in the end, be nailed up in a coffin and thrown into a pit."

"And immortality?"

"Oh, come now!"

"You don't believe in it; well, I do. Dostoyevsky, or maybe it was Voltaire, said that if there were no God, man would have invented Him. And I firmly believe that if there is no immortality, sooner or later the great human mind will invent it."

"Well said," observed Andrei Yefimych, smiling with pleasure. "It's good that you believe. With such faith one may be well off even sealed up within four walls. But you are an educated man, I see."

"Yes, I attended the university, but I didn't graduate."

"You are a man who knows how to think. In any circumstances you can find solace within yourself. Free and profound thought that strives for an understanding of life, together with a thorough contempt for the vanity of this world—these are two blessings beyond anything man has known. And you can possess them in spite of all the barred windows in the world. Diogenes lived in a barrel, but he was happier than all earthly monarchs."

"Your Diogenes was a blockhead," Ivan Dmitrich remarked sullenly. "Why do you talk to me of Diogenes, and understanding?" All at once he grew angry and sprang up. "I love life—love it passionately! I have a persecution mania, a constant, tormenting fear, but there are moments when I am overwhelmed by a thirst for life, and then I am afraid of losing my mind. I want desperately to live, desperately!"

Pacing back and forth in agitation, he lowered his voice and said:

"In my dreams I am visited by phantoms. I hear voices, music, . . . I seem to be walking through a forest, along a seashore, and I long passionately for the bustle and cares of . . . Tell me, what is new there?" asked Ivan Dmitrich. "What is going on in the outside world?"

"Do you want to hear about our town, or things in general?"

"First tell me about the town, and then about the world in general."

"Well . . . it's insufferably boring in town. . . . There's no one to talk to, no one to listen to. There are no new people. Though, as a matter of fact, a young doctor by the name of Khobotov came to us not long ago."

"I was already here when he came. A boor, isn't he?"

"Yes, a man of no culture. It's strange, you know. . . . Judging from what one hears, there is no intellectual stagnation in the big cities, things are going on, which means there must be real people there, but for some reason, they invariably send us people the like of which you've never seen. It's an unfortunate town!"

"Yes, an unfortunate town!" sighed Ivan Dmitrich, and laughed. "But how are things in general? What do they write about in the newspapers and magazines?"

By now it was dark in the ward, and the doctor rose to his feet and stood telling him about what was being written both abroad and in Russia, and of what was now discernible as the modern trend of thought. Ivan Dmitrich listened attentively, asked questions, then suddenly, as if remembering something horrible, clutched his head and lay down on the bed with his back to the doctor.

"What's the matter?" asked Andrei Yefimych.

"You won't get another word out of me," said Ivan Dmitrich rudely. "Leave me alone!"

"But why?"

"Leave me alone, I tell you! Why the hell do you persist?"

Andrei Yefimych shrugged his shoulders, sighed, and went out. As he passed through the entry, he said:

"You might clean up this place, Nikita. . . . There's a terribly strong odor here!"

"Yes, sir, Your Honor!"

"What a nice young man!" thought Andrei Yefimych, as he returned to his own apartment. "In all the time I've been living here, he's the first man I've been able to talk to. He's capable of reasoning, and is interested in just the right things."

While he was reading, and later in bed, he kept thinking about Ivan Dmitrich, and when he woke up the next morning he remembered that he had made the acquaintance of an intelligent and interesting man and decided to pay him another visit at the first opportunity.

# X

Ivan Dmitrich was lying in the same position as the day before, his head clutched in his hands and his legs drawn up. His face was not visible.

"Good day, my friend," said Andrei Yefimych. "You're not asleep, are you?"

"In the first place, I am not your friend," Ivan Dmitrich articulated into the pillow, "and in the second place, you are wasting your time: you won't get a single word out of me."

"Strange . . ." murmured Andrei Yefimych, somewhat abashed. "We were having such a harmonious talk yesterday, till all at once you took offense and broke off. . . . I must have made some sort of blunder; perhaps I expressed some idea that is not in accord with your convictions. . . ."

"Do you really expect me to believe that?" said Ivan Dmitrich, raising himself slightly and gazing at the doctor with a mocking and at the same time anxious expression; his eyes were red. "You can do your spying and cross-examining some place else—it won't do you any good here. I knew yesterday what you had come for."

"A strange fantasy!" said the doctor with a wry smile. "So, you think I'm a spy?"

"Yes, I do. . . . A spy or a doctor who has been sent to test me—it's all the same."

"Well, you really are a—forgive me—but you are a queer fellow!"

The doctor sat down on a stool near the bed and shook his head reproachfully.

"But let us suppose that you are right," he said. "Let us suppose that I trick you into saying something in order to betray you to the police. You would be arrested and brought to trial. But would you be any worse off in court, or in prison, than you are here? And if you were deported, even if you were to be sentenced to penal servitude, do you think it would be worse than being locked up in this ward? I don't think it would be any worse. . . . What is there for you to be afraid of then?"

Evidently these words had an effect on Ivan Dmitrich. He quietly sat down.

It was between four and five o'clock in the afternoon, the time of day when Andrei Yefimych was generally pacing up and down in his apartment, and when Daryushka would ask if it were not time for his beer. The day was clear and mild.

"I was taking my after-dinner walk and thought I would drop in and see you," said the doctor. "It's a real spring day."

"What month is it now? March?" asked Ivan Dmitrich.

"Yes, the end of March."

"Very muddy outside?"

"No, not very. The garden paths are already visible."

"It would be nice to drive out of town in an open carriage on a day like this," said Ivan Dmitrich, rubbing his red eyes as if he were just waking up, "and then to return home to a warm comfortable study . . . and have a decent doctor cure one's headache. . . . It's been such a long time since I've lived like a human being. And it's so foul here! Unbearably foul!"

He was enervated and languid after the excitement of the day before, and disinclined to talk. His fingers trembled, and it was evident from his face that he had a severe headache.

"There is no difference between a warm comfortable study and this ward," said Andrei Yefimych. "Peace and contentment do not lie outside a man, but within him."

"What do you mean?"

"The ordinary man looks for good or evil in external things: an open carriage, a study, while the thinking man looks for them within himself."

"Go preach that philosophy in Greece, where it's warm and smells of oranges; it's not suited to the climate here. Who was it I was talking to about Diogenes? Was it you?"

"Yes, it was I . . . yesterday."

"Diogenes didn't need a study or a warm room, it was hot there anyhow. He could sleep in a barrel and eat olives and oranges. But you bring him to Russia to live and he'd be begging for a room, and not just in December, but in May. He'd be doubled up with cold."

"No. One can be impervious to cold, as to any other pain. Marcus Aurelius said: 'Pain is the vivid representation of pain: if, with an effort of will, you change this image, reject it, and stop complaining, the pain will disappear.' This is true. The wise man, or even the merely rational, thinking man, is distinguished precisely by his disdain for suffering; he is always content, and nothing ever surprises him."

"Then I must be an idiot, for I suffer, am discontented, and continually surprised at human baseness."

"But that's all to no purpose. If you will reflect on this more often, you will realize how insignificant the external things which agitate us really are. One must strive for comprehension of life—therein lies the true blessing."

"Comprehension . . ." Ivan Dmitrich frowned. "Internal, external . . . I'm sorry, I don't understand this. All I know is that God created me out of warm blood and nerves—yes! And organic tissue, if it is viable, must react to every irritation. And I do react! To pain I respond with tears and outcries, to baseness with indignation, to vileness with disgust. In my opinion this is exactly what is known as life. The lower the organism, the less sensitive it is, and the more feeble its response to irritation; the higher it is, the more receptive, and the more energetic its reactions to reality. How could you not know this? A doctor, and not know such elementary things! For a man to despise suffering, to be always content, to be surprised at nothing, he would have to reach this state—" and Ivan Dmitrich pointed to the fat, bloated peasant, "or else have become so hardened by suffering as to have lost all sensitivity to it, in other words, to have ceased living. You must excuse me, I am neither a sage nor a philosopher," he continued irascibly, "and I understand nothing of such things. I am in no position to argue."

"On the contrary, you argue exceedingly well."

"The Stoics, whose teaching you travesty, were remarkable men, but their philosophy congealed two thousand years ago and has not advanced a particle, nor will it advance, because it is not practical, not vital. Its success was limited to a minority, which spent its time studying and savoring every sort of teaching, but the majority never understood it. A doctrine that preaches indifference to riches and the comforts of life, and contempt for suffering and death, is absolutely incomprehensible to the vast majority, since this majority has never known either riches or comforts; and to despise suffering would mean to despise one's own life, for man's entire existence is made up of sensations of hunger, cold, humiliation, loss, and a Hamlet-like fear of death. In these sensations lies the whole of life: one may be oppressed by it, one may hate it, but not disdain it. And so, I repeat, the teaching of the Stoics cannot possibly have a future; what has gone on from the beginning of time to our own day, as you see, are struggle, sensibility to pain, and a capacity to respond to irritation."

Ivan Dmitrich suddenly lost the thread of his thoughts, stopped, and rubbed his forehead with vexation.

"I wanted to say something very important, but I'm confused," he said. "What was I saying? Yes! This is what I wanted to say: one of the Stoics sold himself into slavery in order to redeem his neighbor. So, you see, a Stoic reacted to an irritant, for in order to perform such a magnanimous act as destroying oneself for the sake of one's neighbor, one must possess a soul capable of indignation and compassion. Here in this prison I've forgotten everything I ever knew, or I would remember something more. . . . And take Christ! Christ responded to reality by weeping, smiling, being sorrowful, wrathful, and even melancholy; He did not go to meet suffering with a smile, nor did He despise death, but prayed in the garden of Gethsemane that this cup would pass from Him."

Ivan Dmitrich laughed and sat down.

"Let us assume that man's peace and contentment are not external, but within him," he said. "And let us assume that we ought to despise suffering and be surprised at nothing. But what right have you to preach this? Are you a sage? A philosopher?"

"No, I'm not a philosopher, but everyone ought to preach it because it makes sense."

"Yes, but I want to know why you consider yourself competent in the matter of comprehension, disdain for suffering, and so on. Have you ever suffered? Have you any idea what suffering is? Allow me to ask: were you ever whipped as a child?"

"No, my parents had an aversion for corporal punishment."

"My father used to thrash me cruelly. He was a stern hemorrhoidal functionary with a long nose and yellow neck. But let's talk about you. In all your life no one has ever laid a finger on you, intimidated you, or beaten you; you're as strong as an ox. You grew up under your father's wing, were educated at his expense, and then immediately got hold of a sinecure. For more than twenty years you have been living in a warm, well-lighted apartment free of charge;

you keep a servant, you have the right to work however you like and as much as you like, or even not to work at all. By nature you are a flaccid, lazy man, and as a consequence have tried to arrange your life so that nothing can disturb you or make you move. You have handed your work over to the medical assistant and the rest of the riffraff, while you yourself sit in peace and warmth, piling up money, reading your books, beguiling yourself with reflections on all sorts of sublime nonsense, and" (Ivan Dmitrich glanced at the doctor's red nose) "drinking. In short, you've never seen life, know absolutely nothing about it, and have only a theoretical acquaintance with reality. And you despise suffering and are surprised at nothing for a very simple reason: your vanity of vanities, external and internal, your contempt for life, suffering, and death, your comprehension and true blessing—all this is a most comfortable philosophy for the Russian sluggard. You see a peasant beating his wife, for instance. Why interfere? Let him beat her, they'll both die sooner or later anyhow; and besides, the one who does the beating wrongs himself, not his victim. Getting drunk is stupid, unseemly; if you drink—you die; and if you don't drink—you die. A woman comes to you with a toothache. . . . Well, what of it? Pain is nothing but the image of pain, and besides, we can't live in this world without sickness, we all die, so run along, my good woman, and don't hinder me from enjoying my thoughts and my vodka. A young man comes to you for advice, he wants to know what to do, how to live; anyone else would stop and think before replying, but you have a ready answer: strive for comprehension, for the true blessing. There is, of course, no answer. . . . We are kept here behind bars, tortured, left to rot, but this is all very fine and rational, because there is absolutely no difference between this ward and a warm comfortable study. A convenient philosophy: you have nothing to do, your conscience is clear, and you feel you're a sage. . . . No, sir, this is not philosophy, not thought, not breadth of vision, but laziness, pretense, mental torpor. . . . Yes!" Ivan Dmitrich grew angry again. "You despise suffering, but if you pinched your little finger in that door, you'd probably start howling at the top of your voice."

"Perhaps I wouldn't howl," said Andrei Yefimych with a gentle smile.

"Oh, no! Look here, if you were suddenly struck down

with paralysis, or, let us say, some insolent fool were to take advantage of his rank and position to insult you publicly, and you knew he could do it with impunity—then you would realize what it means to put people off with your 'comprehension' and 'true blessing'!"

"That's very original," said Andrei Yefimych, rubbing his hands and laughing with pleasure. "I admire your turn for generalizations, and the character sketch you have drawn of me is simply brilliant. I must confess that talking with you gives me the greatest pleasure. Well . . . I've heard you out, now be so good as to listen to me. . . ."

# XI

They went on talking for about an hour, and apparently the conversation made a deep impression on Andrei Yefimych. He commenced going to the annex every day. He went in the mornings, after dinner, and often dusk would find him in conversation with Ivan Dmitrich. At first Ivan Dmitrich was wary of him, suspecting him of some malicious intent, and openly expressed his hostility; then, as he grew accustomed to him, his fractious manner changed to one of condescending irony.

Soon the rumor spread through the hospital that the doctor had taken to visiting Ward Six. No one—not the medical assistant, the nurses, nor Nikita—could understand why he went, why he sat there for hours at a time, what he could be talking about, why he wrote no prescriptions. His conduct seemed strange. Mikhail Averyanych often failed to find him at home, which had never happened before, and Daryushka did not know what to make of it, for the doctor no longer drank his beer at the proper time and sometimes was even late for dinner.

One day—it was by now the end of June—Dr. Khobotov came to see Andrei Yefimych, and, not finding him at home, went to look for him in the yard; there he was told that the old doctor had gone to visit the mental patients. Going into the annex he stopped in the entry, where he overheard the following conversation.

"We shall never agree, and you will never succeed in converting me to your beliefs," Ivan Dmitrich was saying

querulously. "You know nothing of reality, have never suffered, but have only battened on the sufferings of others
like a leech; while I have suffered continually from the
day I was born till now. Therefore, I tell you frankly, I
consider myself superior to you and in all respects more
competent. It is not for you to teach me."

"I have absolutely no intention of converting you to my
beliefs," said Andrei Yefimych gently, regretting that he was
misunderstood. "And that is not the point, my friend. The
point is not that you have suffered and I have not. Suffering
and joy are transitory; never mind them, they do not matter. The point is that we can think; you and I see in each
other men who are capable of thinking and reasoning, and
this creates a bond between us, however different our views.
If you knew, my friend, how sick I am of the general in-
sanity, mediocrity, and stupidity, and what a pleasure it
is to talk to you! You are an intelligent man and I enjoy your
company."

Khobotov opened the door an inch and looked into the
ward; Andrei Yefimych and Ivan Dmitrich, wearing his
nightcap, were sitting side by side on the bed. The insane
man was grimacing, shuddering, and convulsively pulling
his robe around him, while the doctor sat motionless with
bowed head, his flushed face looking helpless and sad.
Khobotov shrugged his shoulders, grinned, and exchanged
glances with Nikita. Nikita too shrugged his shoulders.

The next day Khobotov went to the annex accompanied by
the medical assistant. They both stood in the entry listening.

"Our old man seems to have completely lost his moorings!"
said Khobotov as they left the annex.

"Lord have mercy on us sinners!" sighed the pious Sergei
Sergeich, carefully avoiding the puddles to keep from soiling his highly polished boots. "To tell you the truth, my
dear Yevgeny Fyodorych, I have long been expecting this."

# XII

Andrei Yefimych soon became aware of an atmosphere
of mystery around him. The attendants, nurses, and patients
looked at him inquisitively when they met him and began
whispering when he passed. Masha, the superintendent's

little girl, whom he used to enjoy meeting in the hospital garden, now for some reason ran away when he smilingly approached, wanting to stroke her hair. The postmaster, Mikhail Averyanych, no longer said: "Absolutely true" when listening to him, but muttered: "Yes, yes, yes . . ." in unaccountable confusion, looking at him thoughtfully and sadly; moreover he was always advising his friend to give up vodka and beer, though, being a tactful man, he never spoke of it directly but always in a roundabout way, telling him, for instance, about a certain battalion commander, an excellent man, or about the regimental priest, also a splendid fellow, both of whom, having fallen ill as a result of drinking, made complete recoveries when they gave it up. Two or three times his colleague Khobotov visited him, and he too advised Andrei Yefimych to give up spirituous liquors, recommending, for no apparent reason, that he take bromine drops.

In August Andrei Yefimych received a letter from the mayor requesting his presence on a very important matter. Arriving at the town hall at the appointed time, he found the military commander, the superintendent of the district school, a member of the town council, Khobotov, and a plump blond gentleman with a difficult Polish name, who lived at the stud farm thirty versts from town and was just passing through.

"We have here a deposition that concerns you, sir," said the councilman to Andrei Yefimych, after everyone had exchanged greetings and sat down at the table. "Yevgeny Fyodorych here says that there's not room enough for the dispensary in the main building, and that it ought to be moved into one of the annexes. This, of course, is no problem, it can be moved, but the main consideration is that the annex is in need of repairs."

"Yes, repairs are inevitable," said Andrei Yefimych, after a moment's thought. "If, for instance, the corner annex were to be fitted up as a dispensary, I suppose a minimum of five hundred rubles would be required. A fruitless expenditure."

Everyone remained silent for a while.

"I have already had the honor of reporting to you ten years ago," Andrei Yefimych went on in his soft voice, "that in its present form this hospital represents a luxury beyond the town's means. It was built in the forties, and things were different then. The town spends too much on unnecessary buildings and superfluous personnel. I think that with a different system it would be possible to maintain two model hospitals for the same money."

"Let's have another system, then!" said the councilman briskly.

"I have already had the honor of submitting my opinion: transfer the medical department to the jurisdiction of the zemstvo."

"Yes, transfer the money to the zemstvo and they'll steal it," said the fair-haired doctor, laughing.

"That's what usually happens," agreed the councilman, also laughing.

Andrei Yefimych turned a dull and apathetic eye on the doctor and said:

"We must be fair."

Everyone commenced talking about how boring it was for a decent man to live in such a town. No theater, no music, and at the last club dance there were about twenty women and only two partners for them. The young men did not dance but spent the entire evening swarming around the buffet or playing cards. Andrei Yefimych, without looking at anyone, remarked in his slow quiet way, what a pity, what a great pity it was that the townspeople should squander their life's energy, their hearts and minds, on cards and gossip, and that they should have neither the capacity nor the inclination to spend time in interesting conversation or in reading, should refuse to take advantage of the pleasures of the mind. The mind alone was interesting and remarkable; everything else was base and trivial. Khobotov listened attentively to his colleague and suddenly asked:

"Andrei Yefimych, what is the date today?"

Having received an answer, he and the other doctor, in the tone of examiners who sense their own incompetence, proceeded to ask Andrei Yefimych what day of the week it was, how many days there were in a year, and whether it was true that there was a remarkable prophet living in Ward Six.

In answer to the last question Andrei Yefimych flushed and said:

"Yes, he is ill, but he is an interesting young man."

There were no more questions after that.

When he was putting on his coat in the hall, the military

commander came up to him, put his hand on his shoulder, and said with a sigh:

"It's time for us old fellows to take a rest!"

As he came out of the town hall, Andrei Yefimych realized that this was a committee appointed to investigate his mental condition. Remembering the questions that had been put to him, he blushed, and for the first time bitterly deplored the science of medicine.

"My God," he thought, recalling how the doctors had examined him, "only recently they attended lectures on psychiatry and took their examinations—why then this crass ignorance? They haven't the slightest understanding of psychiatry!"

And for the first time in his life he felt insulted and angry.

That same day, toward evening, Mikhail Averyanych came to see him. Without even taking time to greet him, the postmaster went up to him, took both his hands, and with deep feeling said:

"My dear, dear friend, prove to me that you believe in my genuine affection for you and consider me your friend. ... My dear friend!" and, not letting Andrei Yefimych speak, he went on in great agitation: "I love you for your erudition, for your nobility of soul. Listen to me, my dear. Professional ethics oblige the doctors to hide the truth from you, but I am a soldier, I will be blunt: you are not well! Forgive me, my dear, but this is the truth, and everyone around you noticed it long ago. Dr. Yevgeny Fyodorych has just told me that for the sake of your health it is essential that you have rest and recreation. Absolutely true! Splendid! I am taking a leave of absence in a few days, going away for a change of air. Prove to me that you are my friend and come with me! Come, we'll recapture our youth!"

"I feel perfectly well," said Andrei Yefimych after a moment's thought. "I can't go away. Let me prove my friendship in some other way."

To go somewhere for no reason, without his books, without Daryushka and his beer, suddenly to disturb a routine of life that had been set for twenty years, at first struck him as a wild, fantastic idea. But then he recalled the conversation in the town hall, the feeling of depression he had experienced as he returned home, and the thought of a brief absence from a town where stupid people regarded him as a madman suddenly appealed to him.

"And where exactly do you intend to go?" he asked.

"To Moscow, to Petersburg, to Warsaw. . . . I spent the five happiest years of my life in Warsaw. What an amazing city! Let us go, my dear friend!"

## XIII

A week later it was suggested to Andrei Yefimych that he take a rest—in other words, that he send in his resignation—a suggestion he treated with indifference; and a week after that he and Mikhail Averyanych were sitting in a stagecoach on their way to the nearest railway station. It was cool clear weather, the sky was blue, the air transparent. They covered the two hundred versts to the station in two days, twice putting up for the night. At the posting stations, when they were served tea in glasses that had not been properly washed, or when the horses were not harnessed quickly enough, Mikhail Averyanych became livid and trembled from head to foot. "Silence!" he would shout. "Don't argue!" And in the stagecoach he talked incessantly about his travels in the Caucasus and Poland. What adventures he had had, what encounters! He spoke in a loud voice and with such wide-eyed wonder that it might have been thought he was lying. Moreover he kept breathing into Andrei Yefimych's face and roaring with laughter right next to his ear, which made the doctor extremely uncomfortable and prevented him from concentrating and reflecting.

On the train they traveled third class for the sake of economy, choosing a car for nonsmokers. Half the passengers were quite respectable-looking people. Mikhail Averyanych soon made friends with everyone, moving from one seat to another, saying in a loud voice that no one should travel on these shocking lines. A complete swindle! How different, now, from being on a horse; you cover a hundred versts in a day and feel fresh and healthy afterward. And our crop failure is due, of course, to the draining of the Pinsk marshes. Things are in a bad state everywhere. He got excited, kept talking loudly, and would not let anyone else say a word. His ceaseless chatter interspersed with loud guffaws and vivid gestures wearied Andrei Yefimych.

In Moscow Mikhail Averyanych put on a military jacket

without epaulettes, and trousers with red piping. When he went out he wore a military cap and overcoat, and soldiers in the street saluted him. He now appeared to Andrei Yefimych like a man who has dissipated all the good qualities of the country gentleman and kept only the bad. He liked to be waited on, even when there was no need. A box of matches would be lying in plain sight on the table and he would shout for a waiter to bring him matches; he thought nothing of appearing in his underwear in front of the maid; all servants, even old men, he addressed condescendingly, and called them blockheads and fools when he was in a bad temper. This, Andrei Yefimych knew, was typical of men of his class, but it disgusted him.

The first thing Mikhail Averyanych did was to take his friend to the Iverskaya Chapel. He prayed fervently, bowed to the ground with tears in his eyes, afterward saying with a deep sigh:

"Even if you don't believe, it makes you feel better to pray. Kiss the icon, my dear fellow."

Andrei Yefimych was embarrassed but kissed the icon, while Mikhail Averyanych with shaking head and pursed lips whispered a prayer, the tears welling up into his eyes again.

From there they went to the Kremlin, where they saw the Tsar-cannon and Tsar-bell, and even touched them. They admired the view of the river, visited the Cathedral of the Savior, and the Rumyantsev Museum.

They dined at Tyestov's. Mikhail Averyanych studied the menu a long time, stroking his whiskers and speaking to the waiter in the tone of a gourmet who was very much at home in restaurants.

"Let's see what you're going to feed us today, my good man!"

# XIV

The doctor walked about, looked at things, ate and drank, the whole time feeling nothing but annoyance with Mikhail Averyanych. He longed for a respite, to get away from him, hide from him, but his friend considered it his duty not to let him out of his sight and to provide him with as many distractions as possible. When there was nothing to look at, he entertained him with conversation. Andrei Yefimych bore it for two days, and on the third day announced that he did not feel well and intended to spend the day in the hotel room. His friend said that in that case he would stay in too. He agreed that they needed a rest, otherwise their legs would give out. Andrei Yefimych lay down on the sofa, his face to the wall, and listened with clenched teeth as his friend vehemently assured him that sooner or later France was bound to crush Germany, that Moscow was full of swindlers, that you cannot judge a horse by its points alone. . . . The doctor was conscious of palpitations and a buzzing in his ears, but he could not bring himself to ask his friend to stop talking or to go away. Fortunately Mikhail Averyanych got tired of sitting in a hotel room and went out for a stroll after dinner.

Left alone, Andrei Yefimych gave himself up to a feeling of relief. How good to lie motionless on a sofa, conscious of being alone in the room! True happiness is impossible without solitude. The fallen angel probably betrayed God out of a longing for that solitude which is denied to angels. Andrei Yefimych wanted to think about the things he had seen and heard in the last few days, but he could not get Mikhail Averyanych out of his mind.

"And to think that he asked for leave and came away with me out of friendship and altruism," thought the doctor with vexation. "There's nothing worse than this benevolent guardianship. He's kind, well-meaning, jolly, but there you are—a bore. An insufferable bore! In the same way there are people who never say a word that isn't sensible and good, yet make you feel how stupid they are."

On the days that followed, Andrei Yefimych professed to be ill and did not leave the room. He lay with his face to the wall and suffered agonies while his friend tried to divert him with talk, and found rest only in his absence. He was angry with himself for having come, as well as with his friend, who daily became more garrulous and unconstrained. Andrei Yefimych was completely unsuccessful in his efforts to raise his thoughts to a serious, elevated plane.

"I'm being called to account by that reality Ivan Dmitrich was talking about," he thought, exasperated by his own pettiness. "However, it's all nonsense. . . . I'll get home, and everything will be as before. . . ."

In Petersburg it was the same: he spent whole days lying on the sofa in the hotel room, getting up only to drink beer.

Mikhail Averyanych was in great haste to reach Warsaw.

"My dear man, why should I go to Warsaw?" Andrei Yefimych said in an imploring voice. "Go without me, and let me go home. I beg you!"

"On no account!" protested Mikhail Averyanych. "It's an amazing city. I spent the five happiest years of my life there."

Andrei Yefimych lacked the will to insist on having his own way, and reluctantly went to Warsaw. Here he kept to his room, lay on the sofa, was furious with himself, his friend, and the hotel servants, who stubbornly refused to understand Russian, while Mikhail Averyanych, as usual, was bursting with good health and high spirits and running about town from morning to night looking up old friends. On several occasions he spent the night out. After one such night he returned early in the morning in a violently agitated state, red-faced and disheveled. He paced the room for a long time, muttering to himself, then stopped and said:

"Honor above all!"

After pacing a little longer, he clutched his head and in a tragic voice proclaimed:

"Yes, honor above all! I curse the moment it entered my head to come to this Babylon! My dear friend," he said, turning to the doctor, "you may well despise me: I have gambled and lost! Give me five hundred rubles!"

Andrei Yefimych counted out five hundred rubles and handed them to his friend without a word. The latter, still red with shame and rage, uttered an incoherent and somewhat unnecessary vow, put on his cap, and went out. When he returned two hours later, he threw himself into an armchair, heaved a loud sigh, and said:

"My honor is saved! Let us go, my friend. I don't want to remain another instant in this cursed city. Swindlers! Austrian spies!"

By the time they reached home it was November and the streets lay under deep snow. Dr. Khobotov had taken Andrei Yefimych's place; he was still living in his old apartment,

waiting for Andrei Yefimych to come and vacate the hospital
apartment. The homely woman he called his cook was
already living in one of the annexes.

A new hospital scandal was going around town. It was
said that the homely woman had quarreled with the superintendent, and that he had crawled on his knees before her,
begging her forgiveness.

On the very day of his arrival Andrei Yefimych was obliged to look for a new apartment.

"My friend," the postmaster said to him timidly, "forgive an indiscreet question: what means have you at your
disposal?"

Andrei Yefimych silently counted his money and replied:
"Eighty-six rubles."

"That's not what I meant," Mikhail Averyanych brought
out in embarrassment, having misunderstood the doctor's
answer. "I mean, how much money have you got altogether?"

"But that's what I'm telling you: eighty-six rubles. . . .
I have nothing more."

Although Mikhail Averyanych regarded the doctor as an
honest and upright man, he had always suspected him of
having accumulated at least twenty thousand rubles. Now,
on learning that Andrei Yefimych was a pauper, that he had
absolutely nothing to live on, he burst into tears and threw
his arms around his friend.


# XV


Andrei Yefimych went to live in a little house with three
windows belonging to a woman named Byelova. There were
only three rooms in the house, not counting the kitchen.
The doctor had the two rooms looking onto the street, and
Daryushka, the landlady, and her three children lived in
the third room and kitchen. Occasionally the landlady's lover,
a drunken peasant who raised an uproar that terrified
Daryushka and the children, came to spend the night. When
he arrived, settling himself in the kitchen and demanding
vodka, everyone felt terribly cramped, and the doctor, who
was sorry for the crying children, would take them into his
rooms and make up beds for them on the floor; this gave
him great satisfaction.

He got up at eight o'clock, as always, and after his morning tea sat down to read his old books and magazines. He had no money to buy new ones. Whether it was because the books were old or because of the change in his surroundings, reading no longer fascinated him, in fact, it tired him. To avoid being idle, he drew up a detailed catalogue of his books and glued labels onto the backs of them, finding this painstaking mechanical work more interesting than reading. In some unaccountable way the monotony of the work seemed to lull his thoughts, and, thinking of nothing, the time passed quickly. Even sitting in the kitchen peeling potatoes or picking over buckwheat with Daryushka seemed interesting now. On Saturdays and Sundays he went to church. Leaning against the wall and closing his eyes, he listened to the choir and thought of his father and mother, of the university, and of various religions; he felt soothed and melancholy, and as he left the church regretted that the service had ended so soon.

Twice he went to the hospital to see Ivan Dmitrich and have a talk with him, but on both occasions found him extraordinarily excited and malicious. He demanded to be left in peace, saying that he had long ago grown sick of empty prattle, and asked only one recompense from these damned scoundrels for all the suffering he had undergone —solitary confinement. Was he to be denied this too? Both times as Andrei Yefimych took his leave and wished him good night, Ivan Dmitrich snarled:

"Go to hell!"

Andrei Yefimych could not make up his mind whether to go a third time or not. He wanted very much to go.

In the old days Andrei Yefimych had been in the habit of pacing the floor after dinner and thinking; now he lay on the sofa with his face to the wall till time for evening tea, indulging in petty thoughts which he could not control. He was mortified that after more than twenty years of service he had been granted neither a pension nor a bonus. True, he had not done his work honestly, but all civil servants without exception, whether they had served honestly or not, received pensions. Contemporary justice consists precisely in the fact that rank, orders, and pensions are awarded not for any moral quality or ability, but for service, regardless of what it had been. Why should he alone be an exception? He had absolutely no money. He was ashamed to pass a shop and meet the shopkeeper's eye. Thirty-two rubles were owing for beer. And he owed money to Byelova too. Daryushka had been secretly selling his old clothes and books, and kept telling the landlady that the doctor was expecting to receive a large sum of money very soon.

He was angry with himself for having spent the thousand rubles he had saved on a trip. How useful that thousand rubles would have been now! And it annoyed him that people would not leave him in peace. Khobotov felt obliged to visit his ailing colleague now and then. Everything about the man was repellent to Andrei Yefimych: his sleek face and horribly condescending tone, his high boots, and the way he used the word "colleague"; but what was most revolting was the fact that he considered it his duty to look after Andrei Yefimych and actually believed he was giving him medical treatment. He never came without bringing a bottle of bromine drops and some rhubarb pills.

Mikhail Averyanych also considered it his duty to visit his friend and divert him. He would enter Andrei Yefimych's room with an exaggerated air of familiarity and forced hilarity, immediately assuring him that he was looking splendid today, and that things were obviously on the mend, thank God—from which one could only conclude that he considered his friend's case hopeless. He had not yet repaid the money he had borrowed in Warsaw and was weighed down by a sense of shame, the strain of which caused him to laugh even louder and to try to tell even funnier stories. His anecdotes and stories now seemed endless and were a torture to both Andrei Yefimych and himself.

During his visits Andrei Yefimych usually lay down on the sofa, turned his back, and listened with clenched teeth; he felt layers of scum forming on the surface of his soul, and after each visit the scum seemed to rise higher, as if it were going to choke him.

In an effort to stifle his contemptible feelings he would try to dwell on the thought that sooner or later he, Khobotov, and Mikhail Averyanych would all die, leaving not the slightest imprint on the world. He tried to imagine some spirit flying through space a million years hence, passing over the globe, looking down and seeing nothing but clay and bare rocks. Everything—culture and moral law—would have vanished, leaving not so much as a burdock growing. Of what consequence then was the insignificant Khobotov, the oppressive friendship of Mikhail Averyanych, or his shame before a shopkeeper? It was all trivial, mere nonsense.

But such reasoning no longer helped. Scarcely had he evoked the image of the globe a million years hence than Khobotov in his high boots would appear from behind the bare rocks, or he would hear the forced laughter of Mikhail Averyanych and his embarrassed whisper: "As for that Warsaw debt, my dear friend, I'll pay you back one of these days . . . without fail."

# XVI

One afternoon Mikhail Averyanych came to see Andrei Yefimych after dinner when he was lying on the sofa. Khobotov happened to appear at the same time, with the bromine drops. Andrei Yefimych drew himself up heavily and sat on the sofa supporting himself with both hands.

"Now today, my friend, you have a much better color than you had yesterday. Why, you're fine, just fine! Good for you!"

"It's high time you were improving, my dear colleague," said Khobotov with a yawn. "You're probably getting fed up yourself with all this dillydallying."

"We'll get well!" said Mikhail Averyanych jovially. "We'll live to be a hundred, just see if we don't!"

"I don't know about a hundred, but he's certainly good for another twenty," said Khobotov reassuringly. "You're not so bad, my dear colleague, not so bad. . . . Don't look so despondent. . . . You needn't try pulling the wool over our eyes."

"We'll show you what we're made of!" said Mikhail Averyanych, roaring with laughter and slapping his friend on the knee. "We'll show them yet! Next summer, God willing, we'll dash off to the Caucasus and ride all over those mountains on horseback! Trot-trot-trot! And when we come back from the Caucasus, before you know it, we might even be celebrating a wedding!" Mikhail Averyanych winked slyly. "We'll marry you off, my friend, just see if we don't. . . ."

Andrei Yefimych suddenly felt the scum rise to his throat; his heart was pounding violently.

"How vulgar!" he said, rising abruptly and going to the window. "Don't you realize in what bad taste this is?"

He meant to go on mildly and politely, but he involuntarily clenched his fists and raised them over his head.

"Leave me alone!" he shouted, in an unnatural voice, turning red and shaking from head to foot. "Get out! Both of you—get out!"

Mikhail Averyanych and Khobotov stood up and stared at him, first in bewilderment and then in alarm.

"Get out, both of you!" Andrei Yefimych went on shouting. "Stupid people! Fools! I don't want your friendship—nor your medicine, you blockhead! The vulgarity—sickening!"

Khobotov and Mikhail Averyanych exchanged glances, and backed away to the door and out into the passage. Andrei Yefimych snatched up the bottle of bromine drops and threw it after them; the bottle broke with a crash on the threshold.

"You can go to hell!" he shouted in a tearful voice, running out into the passage. "To hell with you!"

When his visitors had gone, Andrei Yefimych, trembling as though in a fever, lay down on the sofa and kept saying over and over again:

"Stupid people! Fools!"

When he had grown calm, the first thing that occurred to him was that poor Mikhail Averyanych must feel terribly humiliated and heavyhearted, and that all this was appalling. Such a thing had never happened to him before. Where was his intelligence, his tact? Where was his comprehension of things, his philosophical detachment?

He was unable to sleep the whole night from shame and vexation with himself, and in the morning, around ten o'clock, set out for the post office to apologize to the postmaster.

"We'll forget all about it," said Mikhail Averyanych with a sigh; he was deeply moved and pressed his hand warmly. "Let bygones be bygones. . . . Lyubavkin!" he cried in a voice that made the entire postal staff and everyone else in the post office start. "Bring a chair! And you wait!" he shouted at a peasant woman who was holding out a registered letter to him through the grille. "Can't you see I'm busy? . . . We'll forget what's past," he went on affectionately to Andrei Yefimych. "Do sit down, my dear friend."

He sat for a moment in silence, stroking his knees, and then said:

"It never entered my head to take offense. Illness is no joke, I know. The doctor and I were quite alarmed by your attack yesterday, and we had a long talk about you. My dear friend, why do you refuse to take your illness seriously? You can't go on like this. Forgive me, but as a friend I must tell you frankly," Mikhail Averyanych whispered, "you live in the most unfavorable surroundings: it's cramped, dirty, there's no one to look after you, no money for medical treatment. . . . My dear friend, the doctor and I both implore you with all our hearts to take our advice: go to the hospital! The food there is wholesome, and you'll have nursing and treatment. Although Yevgeny Fyodorych, just between you and me, is *mauvais ton*, he is nevertheless knowledgeable, and you can fully rely on him. He gave me his word he would look after you."

Andrei Yefimych was touched by the postmaster's genuine concern, and by the tears which suddenly glistened on his cheeks.

"My most esteemed friend, don't believe it!" he whispered, laying his hand on his heart. "Don't believe them! It's a trick! All that is wrong with me is that in the course of twenty years I have found only one intelligent man in our whole town, and he is mad. I'm not ill, I've simply been caught in a vicious circle from which there is no way out. And it makes no difference to me now what happens."

"Go to the hospital, my dear friend."

"To the hospital or into a pit—it's all one to me."

"Promise me you will obey Yevgeny Fyodorych in everything."

"Very well, I promise. But I repeat: I've been caught in a vicious circle. Now everything, even the most sincere interest of my friends, leads to only one thing—my ruin. I am going to my ruin, and I have the courage to recognize it."

"You will get better, dear friend."

"What's the use of saying that?" said Andrei Yefimych testily. "There are very few men who, toward the end of their lives, do not experience what I'm going through now. When you are told you have something like diseased kidneys or an enlarged heart and you begin to have medical treatment, or when they tell you you're insane, or a criminal, in other words, when people suddenly start paying attention to you, then you know you are caught in a vicious circle from which you will never escape. If you try to get out you will only get in deeper. You had better give up, for there is no human effort that can save you. So it seems to me."

In the meantime people were crowding around the grille. To avoid keeping them waiting any longer, Andrei Yefimych stood up and began taking his leave. Mikhail Averyanych made him repeat his promise and accompanied him to the door.

That same day toward evening Khobotov, in his sheepskin jacket and high boots, unexpectedly made his appearance and, as if nothing had happened, said to Andrei Yefimych:

"I've come on business, my dear colleague. I want to ask you to join me in a consultation, will you?"

Thinking that Khobotov wanted to divert him with an outing, or perhaps give him a chance to earn a little money, Andrei Yefimych put on his coat and hat and went with him. He was glad of the opportunity to expiate his guilt of the day before and be reconciled with him. In his heart he thanked Khobotov, who made no allusion to the incident, evidently trying to spare his feelings. One would hardly have expected such tact from this uncultivated man.

"And where is your patient?" asked Andrei Yefimych.

"In the hospital. I've been wanting to show you this for a long time now. . . . A most interesting case."

They went into the hospital yard, and, skirting the main building, turned toward the annex where the insane were housed. And all this, for some reason, in silence. As they entered, Nikita, as usual, jumped to attention.

"One of the patients here has developed a complication in the lungs," Khobotov said in an undertone when he and Andrei Yefimych were in the ward. "You wait here, I'll be right back. I'm just going to get a stethoscope."

And he went out.

# XVII

It was growing dark. Ivan Dmitrich lay on his bed with his face buried in the pillow; the paralytic sat motionless, quietly weeping and moving his lips. The fat peasant and the former mail sorter were asleep. It was quiet in the ward.

Andrei Yefimych sat down on Ivan Dmitrich's bed and waited. But when half an hour had passed, instead of Khobotov, Nikita came into the ward carrying a dressing gown, underclothes, and slippers.

"Please change your clothes, Your Honor," he said quietly. "This is your cot here," he added, pointing to an unoccupied bed that obviously had just been brought in. "Don't worry, you'll get well, God willing."

Andrei Yefimych understood everything. Without a word he walked over to the bed Nikita had indicated and sat down; when he saw that Nikita stood there waiting, he completely undressed, feeling horribly embarrassed, and put on the hospital clothing. The drawers were much too short, the shirt long, and the dressing gown smelled of smoked fish.

"You'll get well, God willing," Nikita repeated.

He gathered up the doctor's clothes and went out, shutting the door after him.

"It's all the same . . ." thought Andrei Yefimych, modestly drawing the dressing gown around him and feeling that he looked like a convict in his new costume. "It's all the same . . . whether it's a frockcoat, a uniform, or this robe, it's all the same. . . ."

But what about his watch? And the notebook he kept in his side pocket? His cigarettes? Where had Nikita taken his clothes? Now, perhaps, he would never again, till the day of his death, put on trousers, a waistcoat, and boots. All this seemed strange, even incomprehensible, at first. But Andrei Yefimych was convinced even now that there was no difference between Byelova's house and Ward No. 6, that everything in this world was nonsense, vanity of vanities; and yet his hands trembled, his feet were cold, and the thought that Ivan Dmitrich would soon get up and see him in a hospital robe filled him with dread. He stood up, took a few steps, and sat down again.

Half an hour passed, an hour, and he was sick to death of sitting there; was it really possible to live a day, a week, even years, the way these people lived? Here he had been sitting, getting up and taking a few steps, and sitting down again; he could go and look out the window, walk about once more—and then what? Just sit there like a graven image and think? No, that was hardly possible.

Andrei Yefimych lay down, but immediately got up and wiped the cold sweat from his brow with his sleeve, feeling as he did so that his whole face smelled of smoked fish. He commenced pacing again.

"It's some sort of misunderstanding . . ." he said with a gesture of bewilderment. "I must speak to them, there's some misunderstanding. . . ."

Just then Ivan Dmitrich woke up. He sat up, his cheeks propped on his fists. He spat. Glancing apathetically at the doctor, for a moment he appeared not to understand, then the expression on his sleepy face became mocking and spiteful.

"Aha! So they've locked you up too, my dear!" he said in a hoarse drowsy voice, screwing up one eye. "Delighted! First you sucked other people's blood, now they'll suck yours. Splendid!"

"It's some sort of misunderstanding . . ." mumbled Andrei Yefimych, frightened by Ivan Dmitrich's words; he shrugged his shoulders and repeated: "a misunderstanding of some sort. . . ."

Ivan Dmitrich spat again and lay down.

"This accursed life!" he snarled. "And what makes it so mortifying, so galling, is that life will end, not in any recompense for suffering, not with an apotheosis, as it does in an opera, but in death; a couple of attendants will come, take the corpse by the arms and legs, and drag it down to the cellar. Ugh! Well, it doesn't matter. . . . Our day will come in the next world. I'll come back here as a ghost and haunt these swine. I'll make their hair turn gray."

Moiseika returned from one of his walks, and, seeing the doctor, held out his hand and said:

"Give a little kopeck!"

# XVIII

Andrei Yefimych walked to the window and looked out at the field. It was growing dark, and on the horizon at the right rose a cold livid moon. Not far from the hospital fence, some two hundred yards, stood a tall white building surrounded by a stone wall. It was the prison.

"So this is reality!" thought Andrei Yefimych, and he became terrified.

The moon was terrifying, and the prison, and the spikes

in the hospital fence, and the distant flames of the bone-black plant. He heard a sigh behind him; turning, he saw a man with stars and decorations sparkling on his chest, who was smiling and slyly winking. And this too was terrifying.

Andrei Yefimych assured himself that there was nothing singular about the moon or the prison, that people who were mentally sound wore decorations, and that in time everything would rot and turn to clay, but he was suddenly overwhelmed with despair, and, clutching the iron grille of the window with both hands, tried with all his might to shake it. But the bars were strong and did not yield.

Then, in an effort to shake off his terror, he went over to Ivan Dmitrich's bed and sat down.

"I've lost courage, dear friend," he murmured, trembling and wiping away the cold sweat. "I've lost courage."

"Try philosophizing," said Ivan Dmitrich derisively.

"My God, my God. . . . Yes, yes. . . . You were once pleased to say that while there is no philosophy in Russia, everyone philosophizes, even the little nobodies. But what harm does their philosophizing do anyone?" Andrei Yefimych's voice sounded as if he were on the verge of tears, as if he wanted to arouse Ivan Dmitrich's pity. "So why this malevolent laugh, dear friend? And why shouldn't these little people philosophize when they have no other satisfaction? . . . For an intelligent, cultured, proud, freedom-loving man, made in the image of God, to have no alternative to becoming a doctor in a stupid, dirty little town, and spending his whole life applying leeches and mustard plasters! The quackery, narrowness, vulgarity! Oh, my God!"

"You're babbling nonsense. If being a doctor repels you, you could have gone into one of the ministries."

"No, no, there's nothing one can do. We are weak, my friend. . . . I used to be indifferent, I reasoned confidently, soundly, but at the first rude touch of life I lost courage . . . collapsed. . . . We are weak. . . . We are miserable creatures. . . . And you too, my friend. You are intelligent, well-born, you imbibed noble impulses with your mother's milk, but you had hardly embarked on life when you became exhausted and fell ill. . . . Weak, weak! . . ."

With the onset of evening, something other than fear and a sense of ignominy had begun to gnaw at Andrei Yefimych. At last he realized that he was longing for his beer and cigarettes.

"I'm going out, my friend," he said. "I'll tell them to give us some light. . . . I can't stand this. . . . I'm not equal to it. . . ."

Andrei Yefimych went to the door and opened it, but Nikita instantly jumped up and barred his way.

"Where are you going? None of that, none of that!" he said. "It's time you were in bed!"

"But I'm only going out for a minute, just to walk a little in the yard," said Andrei Yefimych, panic-stricken.

"Impossible, not allowed! You know that yourself."

Nikita slammed the door and leaned his back against it.

"But what difference will it make if I go out?" Andrei Yefimych asked, shrugging his shoulders. "I don't understand! Nikita, I must go out!" he said in a trembling voice. "I absolutely must!"

"Don't cause any disorder, now, that's bad," Nikita warned him.

"What in God's name is going on!" screamed Ivan Dmitrich, suddenly jumping up. "What right has he to prevent anyone from going out? How dare they keep us here? The law states quite clearly that no one can be deprived of freedom without a trial. It's coercion! Tyranny!"

"Of course, it's tyranny!" said Andrei Yefimych, encouraged by Ivan Dmitrich's clamor. "I want to go out, I must! He has no right to stop me! Let me out, I tell you!"

"Do you hear, you dumb brute?" shouted Ivan Dmitrich, pounding on the door with his fists. "Open the door, or I'll break it down! Butcher!"

"Open it!" shouted Andrei Yefimych, shaking all over. "I insist!"

"Keep it up!" answered Nikita from the other side of the door. "Go on, keep it up!"

"Go and call Yevgeny Fyodorych, at least. Tell him I ask him to please come here . . . for a minute!"

"He'll come tomorrow without being called."

"They'll never let us out!" Ivan Dmitrich was saying meanwhile. "They'll let us rot here! Oh, Lord, can it be that there is no hell in the next world, and that these scoundrels will be forgiven? Where is justice? Open the door, you beast, I'm suffocating!" he cried in a hoarse voice, and threw himself against the door. "I'll beat my brains out! Murderer!"

Nikita quickly opened the door, and using both hands and his knee, roughly knocked Andrei Yefimych to one side,

then drew back his fist and punched him in the face. Andrei
Yefimych felt as though a huge salty wave had broken over
his head and was dragging him back to his bed; there was,
in fact, a salty taste in his mouth, probably blood from his
teeth. Waving his arms as if trying to emerge, he caught
hold of somebody's bed, and at that moment felt two more
blows from Nikita's fists in his back.

Ivan Dmitrich screamed loudly. He too was evidently
being beaten.

Then all was quiet. The moon shed its pale light through
the bars, and on the floor lay a shadow that looked like a net.
It was terrible. Andrei Yefimych lay still, holding his breath,
waiting in terror to be struck again. He felt as if someone
had taken a sickle, thrust it into his body, and twisted it
several times in his chest and bowels. He bit the pillow and
clenched his teeth with pain; and all of a sudden out of the
chaos there clearly flashed through his mind the dreadful,
unbearable thought that these people, who now looked like
black shadows in the moonlight, must have experienced this
same pain day in and day out for years. How could it have
happened that in the course of more than twenty years
he had not known, had refused to know this? Having no
conception of pain, he could not possibly have known it, so
he was not guilty, but his conscience, no less obdurate and
implacable than Nikita, made him turn cold from head to
foot. He jumped up, wanting to shout at the top of his lungs,
to rush out and kill Nikita, Khobotov, the superintendent,
the medical assistant, and then himself, but no sound came
from his mouth and his legs would not obey him; gasping
for breath, he tore at his dressing gown and the shirt over
his chest, ripped them, and fell back on the bed unconscious.

# XIX

The next morning his head ached and there was a buzzing
in his ears; he felt ill in every part of his body. The memory
of his weakness the day before caused him no shame. He
had been cowardly, frightened even of the moon, and had
frankly expressed thoughts and feelings he had never suspected in himself; for instance, the notion that lack of satis-

faction led the ordinary man to philosophize. But nothing mattered to him now.

He neither ate nor drank, but lay motionless and silent.

"It doesn't matter . . ." he thought, when he was questioned. "I won't answer. . . . It doesn't matter."

After dinner Mikhail Averyanych came bringing a quarter of a pound of tea and a pound of fruit candies. Daryushka also came and stood by the bed for an hour with an expression of dumb grief on her face. And Dr. Khobotov visited him. He brought a bottle of bromine drops and ordered Nikita to fumigate the ward.

Toward evening Andrei Yefimych died of an apoplectic stroke. He first suffered violent chills and nausea; something loathsome seemed to permeate his entire body even to his finger tips; it rose from his stomach to his head and flooded his eyes and ears. Everything turned green before him. Andrei Yefimych realized that the end had come and remembered that Ivan Dmitrich, Mikhail Averyanych, and millions of others believed in immortality. And what if they were right? But he felt no desire for immortality, and gave it only a momentary thought. A herd of reindeer, about which he had been reading the day before, extraordinarily beautiful and graceful, ran by him; a peasant woman held out a registered letter to him. . . . Mikhail Averyanych said something. . . . Then all was gone, and Andrei Yefimych lost consciousness forever.

Attendants came, picked him up by the arms and legs, and carried him into the chapel. There he lay on a table, his eyes open, with the moon shining down on him through the night.

In the morning Sergei Sergeich came, and after piously praying before the crucifix, closed the eyes of his former chief.

Andrei Yefimych was buried the following day. Only Mikhail Averyanych and Daryushka were at the funeral.

1892

# THE DUEL

# I

It was eight o'clock in the morning—the time when the officers, local officials, and visitors customarily bathed in the sea after the hot stifling night and then went to the pavilion to drink coffee or tea. Ivan Andreich Layevsky, a thin, blond young man of twenty-eight, wearing slippers and the official cap of the Ministry of Finance, found a number of acquaintances on the beach when he came down to bathe, among them his friend Samoilenko, the army doctor.

Fat and paunchy, with a large, closely cropped head, no neck, a red face, big nose, shaggy black eyebrows and gray whiskers, and speaking moreover in a raucous military bass, this Samoilenko made the unpleasant impression of a gruff bully on every newcomer, but two or three days after the first encounter one began to think his face extraordinarily kind, appealing, even handsome. In spite of his awkwardness and rough manner, he was a mild man, infinitely kind, good-natured, and obliging. He was on familiar terms with everyone in town, lent everyone money, doctored everyone, made matches, patched up quarrels, and arranged picnics at which he broiled shashlyk and made a very tasty soup of gray mullets; he was always bustling about asking favors for someone, and always delighted about something. The general opinion was that he had no faults and suffered from only two weaknesses: first, he was ashamed of his own kindness and tried to disguise it with a surly expression and an assumed gruffness, and second, he liked having the medical assistants and soldiers address him as "Your Excellency," although his rank was only that of a civil councilor.

"Answer one question for me, Aleksandr Davidych," Layevsky began, when they were shoulder deep in the water. "Suppose you had fallen in love with a woman, had lived with her, say, for over two years, and then, as often happens, fell out of love and commenced feeling she was a stranger to you. How would you act in such a case?"

"Very simple. Go, dear lady, wherever you please—and that's that."

"That's easy to say! But if she has no place to go? A lone woman, with no relatives, not a kopeck to her name . . . and who can't work . . ."

"Well, then? Toss her a lump sum of five hundred or give her twenty-five a month—and that's that. Very simple."

"Even supposing you have the five hundred, or the twenty-five a month . . . the woman I'm speaking of is a cultivated woman, and proud. Could you really bring yourself to offer her money? And in what guise?"

Samoilenko was about to answer, but at that moment a big wave covered them both, broke on the beach and rattled back over the pebbles. The two friends came out onto the shore and began dressing.

"Of course, it's difficult living with a woman you don't love," said Samoilenko, shaking the sand out of his boot. "But you have to look at it humanely, Vanya. If it happened to me, I wouldn't even let her see that I no longer loved her, I'd go on living with her the rest of my life."

He suddenly caught himself, ashamed of what he had said, and added:

"But for all I care, women might as well not exist. The hell with them!"

When they had dressed they went to the pavilion.

Here Samoilenko was very much at home and even had his own tableware. Every morning he was brought a tray on which there was a cup of coffee, a tall cut glass filled with water and ice, and a small glass of cognac; he first drank the cognac, then the hot coffee, then the ice water, which must have been delightful, for afterward his eyes seemed to melt and, smoothing his whiskers with both hands, he would gaze out to sea and say:

"An astoundingly magnificent view!"

After a long night spent in futile, melancholy thoughts which kept him from sleeping and intensified the sultriness and gloom of the night, Layevsky felt shattered and listless. And he felt no better for his dip and the coffee.

"Let's go on with our talk, Aleksandr Davidych," he said. "I won't make a secret of it, I'll tell you frankly, as a friend: things are going badly with Nadyezhda Fyodorovna and me . . . very badly! Forgive me for discussing my private affairs with you, but I simply must talk about it."

Samoilenko, foreseeing what was coming, lowered his eyes and commenced drumming on the table with his fingers.

"I've lived with her for two years and have ceased to love her," Layevsky continued, "or, more accurately, I have realized that there never was any love. . . . These two years have been—a delusion."

Layevsky had a habit of carefully examining the pink palms of his hands, biting his nails, or pinching his cuffs while talking, and he was doing it now.

"I know perfectly well you can't help me," he said, "but I'm telling you because for miserable misfits like me the only salvation is in talking. I have to generalize about everything I do, I have to find an explanation and justification for my absurd life in someone else's theories, in literary types, in the notion, for instance, that we noblemen are degenerating, and so on. . . . Last night, for example, I kept consoling myself by thinking: Ah, how right Tolstoy was, how inexorably right! And that made me feel better. Yes, my friend, he's really a great writer! No matter what you say. . . ."

Samoilenko, who had never read Tolstoy, but intended every day to read him, was embarrassed and said:

"Yes, all the other authors write from imagination, while he writes straight from nature. . . ."

"My God," sighed Layevsky, "how we have been mutilated by civilization! I fell in love with a married woman; and she fell in love with me. . . . In the beginning there were kisses, quiet evenings, vows; there was Spencer, and ideals, and common interests. . . . What a deception! We were actually running away from her husband, but we lied to ourselves and said we were running away from the emptiness of our cultural lives. This is how we pictured our future: to begin with, in the Caucasus, while we were getting to know the place and the people, I would don a civil servant's uniform and enter the service; then, at our leisure, we would find a plot of land and toil in the sweat of our brows, plant a vineyard, fields, and so on. If it had been you or that zoologist of yours, von Koren, you would have lived with Nadyezhda Fyodorovna for thirty years perhaps, and left your heirs a rich vineyard and three thousand acres of maize, but I felt like a bankrupt from the first day. The heat is unbearable, the town dull, deserted; you go out into the country and under every bush and stone you feel there are venomous insects, scorpions, snakes, and beyond the fields —mountains, desert. Alien people, alien nature, a pitiful culture—all this, brother, is not so easy as strolling along the Nevsky in a fur coat arm in arm with Nadyezhda Fyodorovna, dreaming of the sunny South. Here the struggle is not with life but with death, and what kind of fighter am I? A miserable neurasthenic, self-indulged. . . . From the very first I knew that my ideas about a vineyard and a life of toil were not worth a damn. As for love, I can tell you that living with a woman who has read Spencer and has followed you to the ends of the earth is no more interesting than living with any Anfisa or Akulina. There's the same smell of ironing, of powder, of medicines, the same curl papers every morning, the same self-deception. . . ."

"You can't keep house without ironing," said Samoilenko, blushing at Layevsky's speaking to him so openly about a lady he knew. "You're out of sorts today, Vanya, I can see that. Nadyezhda Fyodorovna is a fine woman, well-educated, and you—you're a man of the greatest intelligence. . . . Of course you're not married," Samoilenko went on, darting a glance at the neighboring tables, "but that's not your fault, and besides, one ought to be above such prejudices, and rise to the level of modern ideas. I believe in free love myself, yes. . . . But in my opinion, once you've lived together you ought to stay together for the rest of your lives."

"Without love?"

"Now let me explain something to you," said Samoilenko. "Eight years ago we had an old fellow, an agent, here—a man of the greatest intelligence. And this is what he used to say: the chief thing in married life is patience. Do you hear, Vanya? Not love, but patience. Love can't last long. You've been in love for two years, and now, evidently, your domestic life has reached a period when, in order to keep your equilibrium, so to speak, you have to exercise all your patience. . . ."

"You may believe your old agent, but to me his advice

is . . . nonsense. The old fellow was a hypocrite: he was able to exercise patience by treating the person he didn't love as an object, something indispensable to his discipline, but I haven't fallen that low yet; if I want to exercise patience I'll buy myself some dumbbells or an unruly horse, and leave human beings in peace."

Samoilenko ordered white wine with ice. When they had each drunk a glass, Layevsky suddenly asked:

"Tell me, please, what does softening of the brain mean?"

"It's . . . how can I explain it to you? . . . It's a disease in which the brain becomes softer . . . as if it were dissolving."

"Curable?"

"Yes, if the disease is not neglected. Cold showers, cantharides . . . Well . . . and certain internal remedies . . ."

"Oh . . . So you see the position I am in. I can't live with her: I simply cannot. When I'm with you I can philosophize about it and smile, but at home I am utterly depressed. I am so appalled that if I were told, let us say, that I should have to live with her for another month, I think I'd put a bullet in my head. And at the same time it's impossible to leave her. She's alone, can't work, neither she nor I have any money. . . . What would become of her? Whom could she turn to? There's nothing I can think of. . . . Come, tell me: what am I to do?"

"Hm-m . . ." Samoilenko growled, not knowing what to answer. "Does she love you?"

"Yes, she loves me, since at her age and with her temperament she wants a man. It would be as hard for her to give me up as it would be to give up her powder, or her curl papers. I'm an integral, indispensable, part of her boudoir."

Samoilenko was embarrassed.

"You're out of sorts today, Vanya," he said. "You probably haven't slept."

"Yes, I slept badly. . . . Altogether I feel vile. My head is empty, my heart is numb, it's a kind of weakness. . . . I must get away!"

"Where to?"

"Up north. To the pines and the mushrooms, to people, ideas. . . . I'd give half my life to be bathing right now in some little stream in the province of Moscow or Tula, to feel chilly, you know, and then to wander about for a few hours with even the worst student, talking and talking. . . . And the scent of hay! Do you remember? And evenings, walking in a garden and hearing the sound of a piano in the house, hearing a train pass. . . ."

Layevsky laughed with pleasure; tears came to his eyes, and to hide them he reached over to the next table for matches.

"I haven't been in Russia for eighteen years," said Samoilenko. "I've forgotten what it's like. In my opinion, there's no place in the world more magnificent than the Caucasus."

"There's a painting by Vereshchagin in which a group of men condemned to die are languishing at the bottom of a deep well. To me your magnificent Caucasus looks exactly like that well. If I were offered my choice of being a chimney sweep in Petersburg or a prince here, I'd take the chimney sweep."

Layevsky fell into a reverie. Looking at his stooped figure, his eyes fixed on one spot, his pale, perspiring face and sunken temples, his gnawed fingernails, and the slipper that dangled from his foot revealing a badly darned sock, Samoilenko was filled with pity and, probably because he reminded him of a helpless child, asked:

"Is your mother living?"

"Yes, but we're not on good terms. She couldn't forgive me for this affair."

Samoilenko was fond of his friend. He looked upon Layevsky as a good fellow, a student, a straightforward man with whom one could drink, laugh, and talk without reserve. What he was able to understand about him he heartily disliked. Layevsky drank a great deal and at the wrong times, gambled, despised his work, lived beyond his means, often used indecent expressions in conversation, wore slippers in the street, and quarreled with Nadyezhda Fyodorovna in the presence of others—and this Samoilenko did not like. But the fact that Layevsky had once been a student of philology, subscribed to two thick magazines, often talked so cleverly that only a few people understood him, and was living with an educated woman—all this Samoilenko did not understand but liked, and he considered Layevsky his superior and respected him.

"Just one more detail," said Layevsky, shaking his head. "Only this is between you and me; I'm keeping it from Nadyezhda Fyodorovna for the time being, so don't make a slip in front of her. . . . Day before yesterday I received a letter telling me her husband had died of softening of the brain."

"May the kingdom of heaven be his . . ." sighed Samoilenko. "Why are you keeping it from her?"

"To show her that letter would simply mean: let's go to church and get married. First we must clarify our relations. When she's convinced that we can't go on living together, I'll show her the letter. It will be safe then."

"Do you know what, Vanya?" said Samoilenko, and his face suddenly took on a mournful, pleading look, as if he were about to ask something absolutely delightful and was afraid of being refused. "Marry her, my dear boy!"

"Why?"

"Fulfill your obligation to that splendid woman! Her husband has died, this is the hand of Providence showing you what to do!"

"But don't you understand, you queer fellow, that this is impossible? To marry without love is as base and unworthy as to serve Mass without believing."

"But it is your duty!"

"Why is it my duty?" Layevsky asked irritably.

"Because in taking her away from her husband you assumed a responsibility."

"But I'm telling you in plain Russian: I don't love her!"

"All right, there's no love, but you can respect her, show her consideration. . . ."

"Respect her, show her consideration . . ." Layevsky repeated mockingly; "you'd think she was an abbess. . . . You're a poor psychologist and physiologist if you think that living with a woman you have only to show her respect and consideration. The most important thing for a woman is the bedroom."

"Vanya, Vanya. . . ." Samoilenko was embarrassed.

"You're an elderly child, you theorize; I'm a young old man and practical, and we shall never understand each other. We'd better drop this conversation. Mustafa!" Layevsky shouted to the waiter. "How much do we owe?"

"No, no!" the doctor was dismayed. "I'm paying for this. I ordered. Charge it to me!" he shouted to Mustafa.

The friends got up and walked in silence along the esplanade. When they reached the boulevard they stopped and shook hands in farewell.

"You're very spoiled, my friend," Samoilenko sighed. "Fate

has sent you a young, beautiful, cultivated woman—and you renounce her, while I—if God were to give me some lopsided old woman—so long as she was kind and affectionate—I'd live with her in my own little vineyard and——" He caught himself and said: "And the old witch could at least look after the samovar for me."

After taking leave of Layevsky, he continued along the boulevard. When, ponderous, majestic, with a stern expression on his face, he walked down the boulevard in his snow-white tunic and superbly polished boots, thrusting out his chest on which was displayed the Vladimir Cross on a ribbon, he was very much pleased with himself and felt that the whole world was looking at him with pleasure. Glancing from side to side without turning his head, he decided that the boulevard was most satisfactorily laid out, that the young cypresses, eucalyptuses, even the ugly, sickly palms, were very handsome and would in time give abundant shade, and that the Circassians were an upright and hospitable people.

"Strange that Layevsky doesn't like the Caucasus," he thought, "very strange."

Five soldiers carrying rifles saluted him as they passed. The wife of an official was walking along the opposite pavement with her schoolboy son.

"Marya Konstantinovna, good morning!" he called out to her, with a pleasant smile. "Have you gone to bathe? Ha-ha-ha! . . . My respects to Nikodim Aleksandrovich!"

He walked on, still smiling pleasantly, till, catching sight of one of his medical assistants approaching, he suddenly frowned, stopped him, and asked:

"Is there anyone in the infirmary?"

"No one, Your Excellency."

"Eh?"

"No one, Your Excellency."

"Good. Carry on. . . ."

Swaying majestically, he made for a lemonade stand kept by a full-bosomed old Jewish woman who pretended she was a Georgian, and said to her in a voice loud enough to command a regiment:

"Be so good as to give me some soda water."

# II

Layevsky's coldness to Nadyezhda Fyodorovna expressed itself chiefly in the fact that everything she said or did seemed to him a lie or the equivalent of a lie, and everything he read against women and love seemed to apply perfectly to himself, to Nadyezhda Fyodorovna and her husband. When he reached home she was sitting at the window, already dressed, her hair done, and with a preoccupied expression on her face was drinking coffee and leafing through a thick magazine. He thought that drinking coffee was not a sufficiently remarkable event to warrant such a preoccupied expression, and that she had wasted her time on a fashionable coiffure, since there was no one here to attract and no occasion for it. In the magazine, too, he saw a lie. She had dressed and arranged her hair, he thought, in order to appear beautiful, and she was reading in order to appear intelligent.

"Will it be all right if I go bathing today?" she asked.

"Why not? I don't suppose it will cause an earthquake one way or the other. . . ."

"No, I only asked in case the doctor should be vexed."

"Well, then, ask the doctor. I'm not the doctor."

At this moment what Layevsky disliked above all in Nadyezhda Fyodorovna was her bare white neck with the little curls at the nape, and remembering that when Anna Karenina had stopped loving her husband what she disliked most was his ears, he thought: "How true! How true!" Feeling weak and empty-headed, he went to his study, lay down on the sofa, and covered his face with a handkerchief to keep the flies from bothering him. Oppressive, sluggish thoughts, all about the same thing, crawled through his mind like a long wagon train on a dank autumn evening, and he fell into a drowsy, despondent state. He felt guilty toward Nadyezhda Fyodorovna and her husband, guilty of the husband's death. He felt guilty toward his own life, which he had ruined, and toward the world of high ideas, learning, and work, and this wonderful world seemed real and possible, not here on this shore where hungry Turks and lazy Abkhazians roved, but there, in the north, where there were operas, theaters, newspapers, and every kind of intellectual activity. One could be honest, intelligent, high-minded, and pure only there, not here. He reproached himself for having no ideals, no guiding principles in his life, although now, at least, he had a vague understanding of what this meant. Two years ago when he fell in love with Nadyezhda Fyodorovna, it seemed to him that he had only to join his life to hers, go to the Caucasus, and he would be saved from the vulgarity and emptiness of his life; now he was just as certain that he had only to forsake Nadyezhda Fyodorovna and go to Petersburg to have everything he wanted.

"To get away!" he muttered, sitting up and biting his fingernails. "To get away!"

He imagined himself boarding the steamer, then having lunch, drinking cold beer, conversing with the ladies on deck, and later taking the train at Sevastopol and setting off. Long live freedom! Stations flash by, one after the other, the air grows colder, sharper, birch trees begin to appear, fir trees . . . Kursk, Moscow. . . . In the station restaurants there is cabbage soup, mutton with kasha, sturgeon, beer, in short— no more Asiaticism, but Russia, the real Russia. The passengers in the train talk of trade, the new singers, the Franco-Russian *entente;* on all sides there is a feeling of vital, spirited cultural and intellectual life. . . . Faster, faster! Now, at last the Nevsky, Great Morskaya Street, and then Kovensky Lane where he had lived as a student, and the dear gray sky, the drizzling rain, the drenched cabmen. . . .

"Ivan Andreich!" someone called from the next room. "Are you at home?"

"I'm here," Layevsky replied. "What do you want?"

"Papers!"

Layevsky languidly got up, yawned, and with a feeling of giddiness shuffled into the next room in his slippers. One of his young colleagues was standing in the street at the open window laying out some government documents on the window sill.

"Right away, my friend," Layevsky said softly and went to look for the inkstand; returning to the window he signed the papers without looking at them and said: "It's hot!"

"Yes. Are you coming in today?"

"I doubt it . . . not feeling very well. Tell Sheshkovsky I'll drop in and see him after dinner."

The clerk left. Layevsky again lay down on the sofa and began thinking:

"And so I must weigh all the circumstances and consider. . . . Before leaving here I ought to pay my debts. I owe about two thousand rubles . . . and have no money. . . . Of course, that's not important; part I'll pay now, somehow or other, the rest I'll send later from Petersburg. The chief thing is Nadyezhda Fyodorovna. . . . First of all we must clarify our relations. . . . Yes."

After a while he wondered if it would not be better to go to Samoilenko for advice.

"I could go," he thought, "but of what use would it be? I'd again say something out of place about boudoirs, women, about what's honest or dishonest. What the devil is the use of talking about what's honest or dishonest when I must make haste to save my life, when I am suffocating in this cursed bondage and killing myself? One must finally come to the realization that to go on living such a life as mine is so vile and cruel as to make everything else seem petty, insignificant. To get away!" he muttered, sitting down again. "To get away!"

The desolate seashore, the ravening heat, the monotony of the hazy lilac-colored mountains, everlastingly the same, everlastingly solitary and silent, overwhelmed him with despair, seemed to lull him to sleep and enervate him. Perhaps he was a very clever, talented, remarkably honest man; perhaps if he were not hedged in on all sides by sea and mountains he might become a superlative zemstvo leader, a statesman, an orator, publicist, a great man. Who knows? If so, was it not stupid to discuss whether it was honest or dishonest for a gifted and useful man—a musician or an artist, for instance—to break through a wall and dupe his jailers in order to escape from prison? Anything is honest for a man in such a position.

At two o'clock Layevsky and Nadyezhda Fyodorovna sat down to dinner. When the cook served them a rice and tomato soup, Layevsky said:

"Every day the same thing. Why not have cabbage soup?"

"There is no cabbage."

"Strange. At Samoilenko's they have cabbage soup, and at Marya Konstantinovna's they have cabbage soup. I alone, for some reason, am obliged to eat this sugary slop. This is really impossible, darling."

As with the great majority of husbands and wives, in the early days Layevsky and Nadyezhda Fyodorovna never got through a single dinner without whims and scenes, but ever since Layevsky had decided he no longer loved her, he had tried to give in to her in everything, always spoke gently and politely, smiled, and called her "darling."

"This soup tastes like licorice," he said, smiling; he made an effort to appear affable, but he was unable to restrain himself and said: "No one in this house looks after the housekeeping. . . . If you're so sick, or so busy reading, then let it go and I'll look after the kitchen."

In the past she would have replied: "Go ahead," or: "I see you want to make a cook out of me," but now she only glanced timidly at him and blushed.

"Well, and how do you feel today?" he asked tenderly.

"Today I'm all right. Oh, there's just a little weakness. . . ."

"You must take care of yourself, darling. I'm awfully worried about you."

Nadyezhda Fyodorovna had, in fact, some sort of illness. Samoilenko said it was undulant fever and gave her quinine; the other doctor, Ustimovich—a tall, lean, unsociable man who sat at home during the day, and in the evening, his hands clasped behind him holding his cane upright against his back, walked slowly up and down the sea front coughing —was of the opinion that she had a female complaint and prescribed hot compresses. In the past, when Layevsky loved her, Nadyezhda Fyodorovna's illness had excited his fear and pity; now he saw something false even in her illness. Her sallow, sleepy face, the apathetic gaze and yawning which always followed her attacks of fever, the way she lay wrapped in a plaid looking more like a little boy than a woman, and the fact that her room was close and smelled bad—all this, to his mind, destroyed the illusion and was an argument against love and marriage.

For the second course he was served spinach with hardboiled eggs, while Nadyezhda Fyodorovna, as an invalid, had *kisel* with milk. First she kept touching it with her spoon, her expression preoccupied, then she languidly commenced eating it and sipping the milk; when he heard her swallowing, Layevsky was seized with such an overwhelming aversion for her that it made his scalp crawl. Although he realized that such a feeling would be insulting even to a dog, he was annoyed, not with himself, but with her for arousing this feeling in him, and he understood why lovers sometimes murder their mistresses. He, of course, would not kill her, but if he had been on the jury now he would have acquitted the murderer.

"*Merci*, darling," he said after dinner, kissing her on the forehead.

He went back to his study and paced back and forth for five minutes, looking askance at his boots, then sat down on the sofa and muttered:

"To get away, to get away! To clarify our relations and get away!"

He lay down and again it occurred to him that the death of Nadyezhda Fyodorovna's husband might be his fault.

"To blame a man for falling in or out of love is stupid," he assured himself as he lay there cocking his legs in order to pull on his boots. "Love and hatred are beyond our control. As far as her husband is concerned, it may be that indirectly I was one of the causes of his death, but, then again, is it my fault that I fell in love with his wife and she with me?"

He got up, and when he had found his cap set out to visit his colleague Sheshkovsky, at whose apartment the government clerks met every day to play vint and drink cold beer.

"My indecision reminds me of Hamlet," thought Layevsky on the way. "How true Shakespeare's observation! Ah, how true!"


# III

To relieve the boredom, and out of sympathy for the plight of newcomers without families who, because of the absence of hotels in the town, had no place to dine, Dr. Samoilenko maintained a sort of table d'hôte. At this time he had only two boarders: a young zoologist, von Koren, who had come to the Black Sea to study the embryology of the jellyfish, and Deacon Pobyedov, only recently graduated from the seminary and assigned to the town to carry out the duties of the old deacon, who had gone away for a cure. They paid twelve rubles a month each for dinner and supper, and Samoilenko had made them give their word that they would appear promptly at two o'clock for dinner.

Von Koren was generally the first to arrive. He would sit down in the drawing room without a word, take an album from the table, and carefully examine the faded photographs of unknown men in full trousers and top hats and ladies in crinolines and lace caps; Samoilenko remembered only a few of them by name, and of those he had forgotten he used to say with a sigh: "Splendid fellow, a man of the greatest intelligence!" When he had gone through the album, von Koren would take a pistol from the shelf, screw up his left eye and take deliberate aim at a portrait of Prince Vorontsev, or he would stand before the mirror studying his swarthy face and big forehead, his black hair, kinky as a Negro's, his shirt of dun-colored cotton printed with huge flowers like a Persian rug, and the wide leather belt he wore instead of a waistcoat. This contemplation of his own image gave him almost more satisfaction than examining the photographs or the expensively mounted pistols. He was quite pleased with his face, his beautifully trimmed beard, and his broad shoulders —unmistakable evidence of his excellent health and strong constitution. He was satisfied, too, with his dashing get-up, from the necktie matching his shirt to his tan shoes.

While von Koren was looking through the album and standing before the mirror, Samoilenko, without his coat or waistcoat, his collar open, excited and bathed in perspiration, was bustling about the kitchen and pantry tables preparing a salad, a sauce, meat, or cucumbers and onions for a cold soup, meanwhile glaring fiercely and from time to time brandishing a knife or spoon at the orderly who was helping him.

"Hand me the vinegar!" he ordered. "That's not the vinegar—it's the olive oil!" he shouted, stamping his feet. "Where are you going now, you hyena?"

"For the butter, Your Excellency," replied the panic-stricken orderly in a cracked tenor.

"Be quick! It's in the cupboard! And tell Darya to put some dill in the jar of cucumbers! Dill! Cover the sour cream, you dim-wit, or the flies will get into it!"

The whole house seemed to reverberate with his cries. At ten or fifteen minutes before two, the deacon arrived, a young man of twenty-two, thin, long-haired and beardless, with a barely perceptible mustache. Coming into the drawing room he crossed himself before the icon, smiled, and held out his hand to von Koren.

"Hello," said the zoologist coldly. "Where have you been?"

"On the wharf catching chub."

"Oh, of course. . . . It would appear, Deacon, that you are never going to settle down to work."

"Why should I? Work is not a bear, it won't run away to the woods," said the deacon, smiling and thrusting his hands into the deep pockets of his cassock.

"There's no one to flog you!" sighed the zoologist.

Another fifteen or twenty minutes passed, and still they were not called to dinner, but they could hear the orderly running back and forth between the kitchen and pantry, his boots clattering on the floor, and Samoilenko shouting:

"Put it on the table! What are you doing with it? Wash it first!"

Famished, the deacon and von Koren commenced tapping their heels on the floor, like spectators in a theater expressing their impatience. At last the door was opened and the harassed orderly announced that dinner was ready. In the dining room they were met by a hectic, ill-humored Samoilenko, steaming from the heat of the kitchen. He gave them a frenzied glance; then, with a look of dread, lifted the lid of the soup tureen and served them each a plateful, and only after he was convinced that they were eating with relish and enjoying it did he give a sigh of relief and settle himself in his deep armchair. His face grew languid, unctuous. . . . Unhurriedly he poured himself a glass of vodka and said:

"To the health of the younger generation!"

Following his conversation with Layevsky, despite his excellent frame of mind, Samoilenko had felt a certain heaviness of spirit the whole day; he was sorry for Layevsky and wanted to help him. When he had drunk a glass of vodka before the soup, he sighed and said:

"I saw Vanya Layevsky today. The man's having a hard time getting along. On the material side things are not very encouraging, but what's even worse is the psychological— he can't cope with it. I feel sorry for the lad."

"There's someone I do not feel sorry for!" said von Koren. "If that charming fellow were drowning I'd take a stick and give him a push: drown, brother, drown!"

"That's not true. You wouldn't do such a thing!"

"What makes you think I wouldn't?" The zoologist

shrugged his shoulders. "I'm just as capable of a good deed as you are."

"Drowning a man—that's a good deed?" asked the deacon, and he laughed.

"Layevsky—yes."

"I think the soup lacks something," said Samoilenko, trying to change the subject.

"Layevsky is positively pernicious—he's as dangerous to society as the cholera microbe," continued von Koren. "It would be doing a service to drown him."

"It does you no credit to express yourself in such a way about your neighbor. Tell me: what is it you hate him for?"

"Let's not talk nonsense, Doctor. To hate and despise a microbe would be silly, but indiscriminately to regard everybody one meets as one's neighbor—thank you very much, that simply means one is lacking in judgment, renouncing true relationships, washing one's hands, in short. I consider your Layevsky a scoundrel. I don't conceal it, and I am absolutely scrupulous in treating him as such. Well, you consider him your neighbor—you embrace him, then; your looking on him as your neighbor means that you have the same relationship to him as you have to the deacon and to me—which is none at all. You are equally indifferent to everyone."

"To call a man a scoundrel!" mumbled Samoilenko, frowning with distaste. "That is so wrong I can't even find words for it!"

"People are judged by their actions," von Koren continued. "Now, judge for yourself, Deacon. . . . I'm going to tell you about him. The career of this Mr. Layevsky will be unrolled before your eyes like a long Chinese scroll, and you can read it from beginning to end. What has he done in the two years that he had been living here? Let us add it up on our fingers. First, he taught the inhabitants to play vint; two years ago this game was unknown here, now everyone plays it from morning till late at night—even the women and young boys. Second, he taught the inhabitants to drink beer, which was also unknown here, and they are further indebted to him for an acquaintance with the various kinds of vodka, so that blindfolded they can distinguish Koshelev's vodka from Smirnov No. 21. Third, the men here used to make love to other men's wives clandestinely, on the same impulse that makes thieves steal in secret instead of openly; adultery was considered something one would be ashamed to make a public display of. Layevsky, however, has shown himself a pioneer in this respect: he lives openly with another man's wife. Fourth . . ."

Von Koren quickly finished his soup and handed the plate to the orderly.

"I understood Layevsky from the very first month of our acquaintance," he went on, addressing the deacon. "We arrived here at the same time. People like him are very keen on friendship, intimacy, solidarity, and all that sort of thing, because they always want company for vint, drinking, and eating; besides, they are garrulous and need an audience. We became friends—that is, he wandered in every day, prevented me from working, and indulged in confidences concerning his mistress. From the first I was struck by his extraordinary mendacity, which absolutely sickened me. As a friend, I remonstrated with him, asked him why he drank so much, why he lived beyond his means and incurred debts, why he did nothing, read nothing, had so little culture, so little knowledge—and in answer to all my questions he would smile bitterly and say: 'I'm a failure, a superfluous man,' or: 'What do you expect from us, old man, the dregs of the serf-owning class?' or: 'We're degenerating. . . .' Or he'd start a long rigmarole about Onegin, Pechorin, Byron's Cain, Bazarov, of whom he would say: 'They are our fathers in spirit and in flesh.' So we are to understand that it's not he who is to blame that government packets lie unopened for weeks at a time, that he drinks and gets others drunk; it's Onegin, Pechorin, Turgenev who are to blame for inventing the failure and the superfluous man. The cause of his extreme profligacy and shamelessness, you see, lies not in himself but somewhere outside, in space. And so—an ingenious trick!—it is not he alone who is dissolute, false, and vile, but we. . . . 'We of the eighties'; 'we indolent, nervous offspring of the serf-owning class'; 'civilization has mutilated us. . . .' In short, we are to understand that such a great man as Layevsky is great even in his downfall; that his licentiousness, ignorance, and slovenliness constitute a natural historical phenomenon, sanctified by inevitability; that the causes of it are universal, elemental, and that we should burn a candle before Layevsky, since he is the destined victim of the age, of the spirit of the times, of heredity, and so forth. All the officials and ladies used to Oh and Ah listening to him, and it took me a long time to figure out what sort of person I was dealing with: a cynic, or a clever sharper. Such types as he, superficially intellectual, with a smattering of education, and a great deal of talk about their own nobility, know how to pose as extraordinarily complex natures."

"Stop it!" Samoilenko flared up. "I will not have a very noble man spoken ill of in my presence!"

"Don't interrupt, Aleksandr Davidych," said von Koren coldly, "I'm about to finish. Layevsky is a fairly uncomplicated organism. Here is his moral skeleton: in the morning—slippers, bathing, coffee; then till dinnertime—slippers, a constitutional, conversation; at two o'clock—slippers, dinner, wine; at five o'clock—bathing, tea, liquor, followed by vint and lies; at eight o'clock—supper, liquor, and after midnight—bed and *la femme*. His existence is confined within this narrow program like an egg in a shell. Whether he walks, sits, writes, is angry or happy, it all comes to nothing but drinking, cards, slippers, and women. Women play a dominant, a fatal, role in his life. He says himself that he was in love at the age of thirteen. When he was a first-year student he lived with a lady who had a beneficial influence on him and to whom he is indebted for his musical education. In his second year he bought a prostitute from a brothel and raised her to his own level, that is, took her as his mistress; she lived with him for six months and then ran away—back to the brothel—and her flight caused him no little mental anguish. Alas, his suffering was so acute that he had to leave the university and spend two years at home doing nothing. But this was all for the best. At home he became intimate with a widow who advised him to give up the study of law and take up philology. And so he did. On completing his studies he fell passionately in love with his present—what's her name?—married woman, and had to run away with her to the Caucasus—for the sake of his ideals, so he says. . . . If not today, tomorrow, he'll get tired of her and run off to Petersburg—again for the sake of his ideals."

"What do you know about it?" growled Samoilenko, glaring wrathfully at the zoologist. "You'd better eat your dinner."

Boiled mullet with Polish sauce was served. Samoilenko gave each of his boarders a whole fish and poured the sauce himself. Two minutes passed in silence.

"Woman plays a considerable role in the life of every man," said the deacon. "There's nothing you can do about it."

"Yes, but to what degree? For each of us woman is mother, sister, wife, friend, but for Layevsky she's everything, while being nothing but a mistress. She—that is, cohabitation with her—is the joy and purpose of his life; he is cheerful, sad, bored, disillusioned, because of women; if life is disagreeable—a woman is to blame; if a new life dawns, new ideals are discovered—here again, look for the woman. . . . The only literary works or paintings that give him any satisfaction are those in which a woman figures. Ours is a poor age, in his opinion, inferior to the forties and the sixties only because we do not know how to abandon ourselves blindly to the passion and ecstasy of love. These voluptuaries must have a special growth in their heads, like a sarcoma, which compresses the brain and governs their whole psychology. Observe Layevsky when he is sitting anywhere in company. You will notice that when some general question is raised in his presence—about cells, for example, or instinct—he sits apart and neither speaks nor listens; he looks pained, disenchanted, nothing interests him, it's all insipid, insignificant, but as soon as you begin talking about the male and female—about how the female spider devours the male after fertilization, for instance—his eyes burn with curiosity, his face brightens; the man comes to life, in short. All his thoughts, however noble, lofty, or indifferent, have one and the same focal point. You walk down the street with him and pass a donkey, for instance . . . 'Tell me, please,' he asks, 'what would happen if you mated a donkey with a camel?' And his dreams! Has he ever related his dreams to you? Magnificent! He either dreams that he is married to the moon, or that he is called up before the police and sentenced to cohabit with a guitar. . . ."

The deacon burst into peals of laughter; Samoilenko frowned furiously, screwing up his face in an effort not to laugh, but he was unable to restrain himself and guffawed.

"It's all a lie!" he said, wiping the tears from his eyes. "I swear to you, it's a lie!"

# IV

The deacon was very easily amused, laughing at every trifle till he got a stitch in his side and was helpless with laughter. He seemed to enjoy being with people only because they had something ridiculous about them and could be given comical nicknames. Samoilenko he had nicknamed "the tarantula," the orderly "the drake," and he was in ecstasies when one day von Koren called Layevsky and Nadyezhda Fyodorovna "the macacos." Listening to anyone speak he would peer eagerly into his face without blinking, and one could see his eyes fill with mirth and his face grow tense in anticipation of the moment when he could let himself go, rocking with laugher.

"He is a corrupt and perverse type," the zoologist continued, and the deacon, expecting him to say something funny, kept his eyes riveted to his face. "It's a rare thing to encounter such insignificance. His body is flabby, weak, and old, while his intellect in no respect differs from that of some shopkeeper's fat wife who does nothing but gobble and guzzle, sleep on a featherbed, and keep her coachman as a lover."

The deacon once more burst into laughter.

"Don't laugh, Deacon," said von Koren. "It's stupid, actually. I should have paid no attention to his insignificance," he continued, after waiting for the deacon to stop laughing, "I should have passed him by, if he were not so harmful and dangerous. His harmfulness lies first of all in the fact that he is successful with women and therefore threatens to leave descendants, in other words, to present the world with a dozen Layevskys just as feeble and perverse as himself. Secondly, he is in the highest degree contaminating. I've already told you about his vint and beer. In another year or two he will win over the entire Caucasian coast. You know how the masses, especially their middle stratum, believe in intellectuality, a university education, an aristocratic manner, and literary language. No matter what abomination he had committed, they would all think it quite fine and proper, since he is an intellectual, a liberal, and a university man. What's more, as a failure, a superfluous man, a neurasthenic, and victim of the times, anything is permitted him. He's a charming fellow, a good sort, and so genuinely tolerant of human weaknesses; he's complaisant, affable, accommodating, and not proud; you can drink with him, use foul language, gossip. . . . The masses, always inclined to anthropomorphism in religion and morals, love best those demigods who have the same weaknesses as themselves. Consider, then, what a broad field he has for contamination! Besides, he's a clever hypocrite, not a bad actor, and he knows which side his bread is buttered on. Just take his tricks and sophistries, his attitude to civilization, for instance. He has scarcely even sniffed at civilization, and yet: 'Ah, how we have been mutilated by civilization! Ah, how I envy those savages, those children of nature, who know nothing of civilization!' We are to understand, you see, that at one time, in the days of yore, he was wholeheartedly devoted to civilization, in service to it, comprehended it through and through, but that it has exhausted, disillusioned and deceived him; he is Faust, you see, a second Tolstoy. . . . And as for Schopenhauer and Spencer, he treats them like little boys, paternally clapping them on the shoulder: 'Well, what do you say, old boy?' He hasn't read Spencer, of course, but how charming he is when he says of his lady, with light, casual irony: 'She's read Spencer!' And everyone listens to him and no one cares to realize that this charlatan hasn't the right to kiss the sole of Spencer's foot, much less speak of him in that tone! To undermine civilization, authority, other men's holy of holies, to sling mud at them and facetiously wink at them only to justify and hide one's own weakness and moral poverty, is possible only for a very vain, low, despicable creature."

"I don't know what you expect of him, Kolya," said Samoilenko, now looking at the zoologist with guilt rather than with anger. "He's just like everybody else. He's not without his weaknesses, of course, but he keeps abreast of contemporary ideas, he's in the service, being of use to his country. Ten years ago there was an old fellow serving here as agent, a man of the greatest intelligence. . . . Now this is what he used to say——"

"Never mind, never mind!" the zoologist interrupted. "He serves the government, you say. But how does he serve it? Are things any better because of his coming here—are the officials more punctual, more honest, more polite? On the contrary, with his authority as a cultivated university man, he simply sanctions their debauchery. He is punctual only on the twentieth of the month when he collects his salary; the rest of the time he shuffles about the house in slippers trying to look as if he were doing the Russian government a great kindness by living in the Caucasus. No, Aleksandr Davidych, don't defend him. You're insincere from start to finish. If you really loved him and considered him your neighbor, first, you would not be indifferent to his weaknesses, and then you would not indulge him but would try, for his own sake, to render him harmless."

"Meaning?"

"Render him harmless. Since he's incorrigible, there is only one way to render him harmless. . . ." Von Koren drew his finger across his throat. "Or he might be drowned," he added. "In the interests of humanity and in their own interests, such people ought to be exterminated. Without fail."

"What are you saying?" Samoilenko mumbled, getting up and staring in amazement at the calm, cold face of the zoologist. "Deacon, what is he saying? Why, are you in your right mind?"

"I don't insist on the death penalty," said von Koren. "If it has proved prejudicial, then devise something else. If Layevsky cannot be exterminated, then isolate him, ostracize him, put him on common labor. . . ."

"What are you saying?" Samoilenko was horrified. "With pepper, with pepper!" he cried in a tone of despair, seeing the deacon about to eat the stuffed eggplant without pepper. "You, a man of the greatest intelligence, what are you saying? To put our friend, a proud, educated man, on common labor!"

"If he's proud and tries to resist, put him in chains!"

Samoilenko was unable to utter a word and only twitched his fingers. At the sight of his stunned and really ridiculous face, the deacon burst into laughter.

"Let's stop talking about it," said the zoologist. "Just remember one thing, Aleksandr Davidych: primitive man was spared such types as Layevsky by natural selection and the struggle for existence, which our culture has considerably weakened—and we ought to see to the extermination of the weak and worthless ourselves; otherwise, when the Layevskys multiply, civilization will perish and mankind will completely degenerate. And it will be our fault."

"If people have to be drowned and hanged," said Samoilenko, "then to hell with your civilization, to hell with mankind! To hell with it! Now this is what I have to say to you: you are a very learned man, a man of the greatest intelligence, the pride of your country—but the Germans have ruined you. Yes, the Germans! The Germans!"

Since leaving Dorpat, where he had studied medicine, Samoilenko had rarely seen a German, and had not read a single German book, but in his opinion, every evil of politics or science stemmed from Germans. Where he had got this notion he himself could not have said, but he held to it firmly.

"Yes, Germans!" he repeated once more. "Let's go and have some tea."

The three men stood up, put on their hats, and went out into the front garden, where they sat in the shade of a chestnut tree, pear trees, and pale maples. The zoologist and the deacon sat on a bench near a little table, while Samoilenko sank into a wicker armchair with a broad sloping back. The orderly brought tea, jam, and a bottle of syrup.

It was very hot, above ninety degrees in the shade. The sultry air was heavy, motionless, and a long spiderweb hung limply suspended from the chestnut tree to the ground without stirring.

The deacon took up the guitar, which always lay on the ground by the table, tuned it, and in a high voice softly sang:

*Round the tavern table stood the seminary lads . . .*

then immediately fell silent because of the heat; he mopped his brow and gazed up at the blazing blue sky. Samoilenko dozed; he was enervated and intoxicated by a delightful after-dinner drowsiness which quickly took possession of his whole body; his arms dangled, his eyes shrunk, his head sank onto his breast. He looked at von Koren and the deacon with tearful tenderness and mumbled:

"The younger generation . . . luminary of science . . . lamp of the church. . . . Before we know it . . . this long-skirted hallelujah will spring up into a bishop . . . if we don't watch out we'll be kissing his little hand. . . . Well . . . God willing . . ."

Soon a snore was heard. Von Koren and the deacon finished their tea and went out into the street.

"Are you off to the wharf again to catch chub?" asked the zoologist.

"No, it's too hot."

"Come along to my place. You can wrap a parcel and make a copy of something for me. And, incidentally, we can have a talk about what you are to do. You must work, Deacon. You can't go on like this."

"What you say is reasonable and logical," said the deacon, "but my idleness finds its excuse in the circumstances of my present life. You yourself know that the uncertainty of a person's situation definitely contributes to a state of apathy. Only God knows whether I have been sent here temporarily or permanently; I am living in uncertainty, while my wife is vegetating at her father's and missing me. And, I confess, my brain is devitalized by the heat."

"That's all nonsense," said the zoologist. "You can get used to the heat and you can get used to being without the deaconess. You ought not to indulge yourself. You must take yourself in hand."

# V

Nadyezhda Fyodorovna went to bathe in the morning; behind her walked Olga, her cook, carrying a pitcher, a copper basin, towels, and a sponge. Two unknown steamers with dirty white funnels, evidently foreign freighters, stood at anchor in the roadstead. Men dressed in white and wearing white shoes walked along the wharf shouting loudly in French and receiving answers from the ships. There was a lively ringing of bells in the little town church.

"Today is Sunday!" Nadyezhda Fyodorovna remembered with satisfaction.

She felt completely well and was in a gay, holiday mood. Wearing a new loose-fitting dress made of pongee silk, and a large straw hat with a broad brim bent sharply down over her ears so that her face appeared to be looking out from a little basket, she fancied she looked very charming. She was thinking that in the whole town there was only one young, beautiful, well-educated woman—herself, and that she alone knew how to dress inexpensively but with elegance and taste. This dress, for example, had cost only twenty-two rubles, and yet how charming it was! In the whole town she alone knew how to be attractive, and there were a great many men who for this reason could not help being envious of Layevsky.

She was glad that Layevsky had been cold to her lately, guardedly polite, even insolent and rude at times; in the past she had responded to all his vagaries, his cold, contemptuous, or strange, incomprehensible looks, with tears, reproaches, and threats to leave him or to starve herself to death; now she only blushed, looked guiltily at him, and was glad he did not treat her with affection. She would have found it preferable, even more agreeable, if he had abused or threatened her, since she felt completely guilty toward him. First she felt guilty for not sympathizing with his dreams of a life of labor, for the sake of which he had given up Petersburg and come here to the Caucasus, and she was certain that this was precisely the reason he had been angry with her of late. She had thought that coming to the Caucasus she would find a secluded little nook on the shore, a cozy little garden with shade, birds, rivulets, where she could plant flowers and vegetables, raise ducks and chickens, entertain the neighbors, nurse the poor peasants and distribute little books among them; but the Caucasus had turned out to be nothing but bare mountains, forests, and huge valleys, where the heat was extreme and one had to spend a great deal of time and effort to find a place to settle, where there were no neighbors of any kind, and one might even be robbed. Layevsky had been in no hurry to find a piece of land; she was glad of that, and there seemed to be a tacit agreement between them never to mention the life of labor. He was silent, she thought, because he was angry with her for being silent.

In the second place, without his knowledge she had bought various trifles to the value of three hundred rubles in Achmianov's shop during these two years. She had bought them bit by bit—dress goods, a piece of silk, a parasol— and imperceptibly the debt had grown.

"I'll tell him about it today," she decided, but instantly realized that in his present frame of mind this would hardly be a suitable time to talk to Layevsky about debts.

In the third place, she had on two occasions received a visit from Kirilin, the police inspector, in Layevsky's absence: once in the morning when Layevsky had gone to bathe, and another time at midnight when he was playing cards. Thinking about it Nadyezhda Fyodorovna blushed and glanced back at the cook as if fearing her thoughts had been overheard. The long, insufferably hot and tedious days, the beautiful languorous evenings, the stifling nights, this whole life when from morning to night one had no idea how to spend the useless hours—not to mention her fixed idea that she was the youngest, most beautiful woman in the town and was wasting her youth—and the fact that Layevsky himself, though honest and idealistic, was forever the same, always shuffling about in his slippers, biting his nails, boring her with his caprices—all led, little by little, to her being possessed by desire, and, like a mad woman, she thought of nothing else day and night. In her breathing, her glances, her tone of voice, her walk, she felt only desire; the murmur of the sea told her she must love, as did the evening darkness, and the mountains, too. . . . And when Kirilin began paying court to her, she had neither the wish nor the will to resist and could not help surrendering to him.

The foreign steamers and the men in white now for some reason prompted her to think of a vast hall; mingled with the sound of French, a waltz strain began to throb in her ears, and her breast quivered with inexplicable joy. She wanted to dance, to speak French. . . .

There was nothing so dreadful about her infidelity, she cheerfully reflected. Her heart had no part in it; that she still loved Layevsky was clear from the fact that she was jealous of him, felt sorry for him, and missed him when he was away. Actually Kirilin had turned out to be only so-so, a bit coarse, though handsome; but it was all over with him now, and there would be nothing more. What had been was past, it was nobody's business, and even if Layevsky were to find out he wouldn't believe it.

There was only one bathing cabin for women on the shore; the men bathed in the open. On entering it, Nadyezhda Fyodorovna found a middle-aged woman, Marya Konstantinovna Bityugova, the wife of an official, and her daughter Katya, a fifteen-year-old schoolgirl; both were sitting on a bench undressing. Marya Konstantinovna was a kind, effusive, tactful individual who spoke in a drawling voice full of pathos. She had been a governess till the age of thirty-two, when she had married Bityugov, an extremely meek, bald-headed little man, who combed his hair over his temples. She was still in love with him, jealous of him, blushed at the word "love," and assured everyone that she was exceedingly happy.

"My dear!" she exclaimed ecstatically on seeing Nadyezhda Fyodorovna, and her face took on an expression her friends called "almond-oily." "How delightful, dear, that you have come! We can bathe together—this is enchanting!"

Olga quickly threw off her dress and chemise and began to undress her mistress.

"It's not as hot today as yesterday, is it?" said Nadyezhda Fyodorovna, shrinking from the rough touch of the naked cook. "Yesterday I almost died of the heat."

"Oh, my dear, yes! I nearly suffocated myself. Would you believe it, I bathed three times yesterday—think of it, my dear, three times! Nikodim Aleksandrych was actually worried!"

"Is it possible to be so ugly," Nadyezhda Fyodorovna wondered, looking at Olga and the official's wife; she glanced at Katya and thought: "The girl's figure is not bad."

"Your Nikodim Aleksandrych is very charming," she said. "I'm simply in love with him."

"Ha-ha-ha! That's enchanting!" said Marya Konstantinovna with a forced laugh.

Freed of her clothing, Nadyezhda Fyodorovna felt a desire to fly. And it seemed to her that if she were to wave her arms she would surely soar upward. When she was undressed she noticed Olga looking scornfully at her white body. Olga, a young soldier's wife, living with her lawful husband, considered herself a better woman than her mistress, and superior to her. Nadyezhda Fyodorovna also felt that Marya Konstantinovna and Katya did not respect her and were afraid of her. It was unpleasant, and in order to raise herself in their estimation she said:

"At home in Petersburg now, life in the summer villas is at its height. My husband and I have so many friends! We really ought to go and visit them."

"Your husband, I believe, is an engineer, isn't he?" inquired Marya Konstantinovna timidly.

"I am speaking of Layevsky. He has a great many friends. But, unfortunately, his mother, a proud aristocrat, is not very intelligent . . ."

Without finishing the sentence, she flung herself into the water. Marya Konstantinovna and Katya followed her.

"The world is so full of prejudices," continued Nadyezhda Fyodorovna, "that life is not so easy as it seems."

Marya Konstantinovna, who had been a governess in aristocratic families, was an authority on social matters, and said:

"Oh, yes! Would you believe it, my dear, at the Garatynskys' it was absolutely required that one dress for lunch as well as for dinner, so that in addition to my salary, I got something extra for my wardrobe, just like an actress."

She was standing between Nadyezhda Fyodorovna and Katya, as if to shield her daughter from the water that washed the former.

Through the open door, which gave directly onto the sea, they saw someone swimming a hundred feet from their bathing place.

"Mama, it's our Kostya!" said Katya.

"Oh—oh!" cackled Marya Konstantinovna in dismay. "Oh, Kostya!" she shouted. "Come back! Come back!"

Kostya, a fourteen-year-old boy, making a display of his courage before his mother and sister, plunged and swam farther out, then, exhausted, he made haste to return, and it was apparent from the strained and serious expression on his face that he was unsure of his strength.

"The trouble one has with these boys, my dear!" said Marya Konstantinovna, growing calm. "Before you know it, he'll break his neck. Ah, my dear, how delightful, and yet how difficult, to be a mother! One is afraid of everything!"

Nadyezhda Fyodorovna put on her straw hat, threw herself into the water and swam out to sea. After swimming about thirty feet she turned on her back. The sea was visible as far as the horizon, and she could see the steamers, the people on the shore, the town, and all this, together with the sultry heat, the limpid, tender waves, excited her, whispering to her that she must live, live. . . . A sailboat, sharply cleaving the waves and air, bore swiftly past her; the man sitting at the tiller looked at her and she found it pleasant to be looked at.

After bathing, the ladies dressed and walked off together.

"I have a fever every other day, and yet I don't get thin," said Nadyezhda Fyodorovna, licking the salt from her lips and smiling in response to the bows of her acquaintances. "I've always been plump, and now I believe I'm plumper than ever."

"That, my dear, is constitutional. If, like me, for instance, one isn't inclined to plumpness, then nothing you eat will help. But you've soaked your hat, my dear."

"It doesn't matter, it will dry."

Nadyezhda Fyodorovna again saw the men in white who were walking on the wharf and speaking French, and again for some reason joy stirred in her breast and she remembered dimly a large hall in which she had once danced, or of which, perhaps, she had only dreamed. And something in the depths of her soul vaguely, faintly, whispered to her that she was a petty, common, cheap, worthless woman. . . .

Marya Konstantinovna stopped at her gate and invited Nadyezhda Fyodorovna to come in for a while.

"Do come in, my dear," she said in an imploring voice, and with a look compounded of hope and agony: maybe she would refuse and not come in!

"With pleasure," agreed Nadyezhda Fyodorovna. "You know how I love visiting you!"

And she went into the house. Marya Konstantinovna made her sit down, gave her coffee and sweet rolls, then showed her photographs of her former charges, the Garatynsky girls, who were married now. She also showed her Kostya's and Katya's examination grades, which were not very good, but which she tried to put in a better light by sighing and lamenting about how difficult the lessons were in the high school. . . . She was very attentive to her guest, and, though sorry for her, was tormented by the thought that her being there might have a bad influence on her children's morals, and she was glad that her Nikodim Aleksandrych was not at home. Since, in her opinion, all men liked "those women," Nadyezhda Fyodorovna might have a bad influence even on Nikodim Aleksandrych.

While talking to her visitor, Marya Konstantinovna kept recalling that there was to be a picnic that evening and that von Koren had urgently requested that it not be mentioned to the macacos—meaning Layevsky and Nadyezhda Fyodorovna—but she accidentally blurted it out, then blushed and in her confusion said:

"I hope you are coming too!"

# VI

They had arranged to drive seven versts out of town on the road south and stop near a fishing lodge at the confluence of two streams, the Black River and the Yellow River, there to cook fish soup. They set out shortly after five. Samoilenko and Layevsky drove at the head of the party in a charabanc; behind them, in a carriage drawn by three horses, came Marya Konstantinovna, Nadyezhda Fyodorovna, Katya, Kostya, and the basket of provisions and crockery. In the next carriage rode the police inspector Kirilin, young Achmianov, the son of the merchant to whom Nadyezhda Fyodorovna owed three hundred rubles, and opposite them, huddled up on a little seat with his feet tucked under him, sat Nikodim Aleksandrych, a neat little man with his hair combed over his temples. In the rear drove von Koren and the deacon with a basket of fish at his feet.

"To the r-r-right!" shouted Samoilenko at the top of his voice whenever they came upon a nomad cart or an Abkhazian riding a donkey.

"In two years, when I shall have got the means and the people together, I'll set out on an expedition," von Koren was saying to the deacon. "I shall follow the coast from Vladivostok to the Bering Straits, and from the Straits to the mouth of the Yenisei. We'll chart a map, study the flora and fauna, and make detailed geological, anthropological, and ethnographical investigations. It's up to you whether you come with me or not."

"It's impossible," said the deacon.

"Why?"

"I'm not free, I'm a married man."

"The deaconess will let you go. We'll provide for her. Better still, if you would persuade her, for the common good, to take the veil; that would make it possible for you yourself to take vows and join the expedition as a priest. I can arrange this for you."

The deacon was silent.

"Do you know your theology well?" asked the zoologist.

"Rather badly."

"Hm-m. . . . I can't give you any pointers on that score, be-

90

cause I'm not up on theology myself. You give me a list of the books you need and I'll send them to you from Petersburg this winter. You'll also need to read the writings of religious travelers; there happen to be some good ethnologists among them, as well as men with a thorough knowledge of Oriental languages. When you've familiarized yourself with their methods, you'll find it easier to set to work. And you needn't waste your time while waiting for the books; you come to me and we'll study the compass and go over meteorology. All this is indispensable."

"That's all very well . . ." the deacon murmured, and laughed. "But I was trying to get a place for myself in Central Russia, and my uncle the archpriest promised to help me. If I go with you, I'll have troubled him for nothing."

"I don't understand your hesitation. If you continue to be an ordinary deacon, obliged to serve only on holidays and on the remaining days do nothing but rest from your labors, in ten years you'll be exactly what you are now—with the addition of a beard and mustache; whereas if at the end of those same ten years you return from the expedition, you'll be a different man, you'll be enriched by the consciousness of having done something."

Shrieks of terror and delight came from the ladies' carriage. They were driving along a road hollowed out of what was literally the edge of an overhanging cliff, and it seemed to all of them that they were racing along the shelf of a high wall and about to drop into the abyss. On the right stretched the sea, on the left an uneven brown wall with black splotches and red veins, and above them climbed bushy evergreens, which bent down as though gazing at them in fear and curiosity. A minute later there were more screams and laughter as they drove under a huge overhanging rock.

"I don't know why the devil I'm coming with you," said Layevsky. "How stupid and vulgar! I want to go north, to get away, escape, and here I am, for some reason, going on this idiotic picnic."

"But look at that view!" said Samoilenko as the horses turned to the left and the valley of the Yellow River came into view, the river itself turbid, raging, yellow and glittering.

"I see nothing fine in that, Sasha," retorted Layevsky. "To be constantly in ecstasies over nature, it seems to me, indicates a poverty of imagination. Compared to what my imagination can give me, all these rivulets and rocks are mere rubble—nothing more."

The carriages were now going along the river bank. The high mountainous banks gradually converged, the valley narrowed, and a gorge appeared ahead; the craggy mountain around which they were driving had been heaped up by nature out of huge rocks that crushed one another with such force that Samoilenko involuntarily groaned at each glimpse of them. The beautiful, somber mountain was cleft in places by narrow crevices and gorges which breathed dampness and mystery on the passers-by; through the gorges other mountains could be seen, brown, pink, lilac, either smoky or bathed in brilliant light. From time to time, as they passed a gorge, they heard the sound of water falling from the heights and splashing on the rocks.

"Ah, these damned mountains!" sighed Layevsky. "I'm so sick of them!"

Where the Black River fell into the Yellow River, its inky waters staining the yellow and grappling with it, the Tartar Kerbalai's fishing lodge stood on the side of the road with the Russian flag on its roof and a chalked sign: PLEASANT LODGE. There was a little garden enclosed by a wattle fence, with tables and benches, and from a brambly thicket rose a solitary cypress, dark and beautiful.

Kerbalai, a brisk Tartar in a blue shirt and white apron, stood in the road bowing low to the arriving carriages, his hands clasped over his stomach, his glistening white teeth displayed in a smile.

"Greetings, Kerbalai!" Samoilenko shouted to him. "We're going to drive on a little farther. Bring along the samovar and some chairs. And be quick!"

Kerbalai nodded his shaved head and said something that only those in the last carriage could hear: "We've got trout today, Your Excellency."

"Bring them, bring them!" von Koren said to him.

The carriages came to a stop about five hundred yards from the lodge. Samoilenko chose a small meadow strewn with stones convenient for sitting on, where a tree blown down in a storm lay with upturned shaggy roots and dry yellow needles. Here a frail log bridge had been thrown across the river and on the bank directly opposite a little shed for drying maize stood on four low stakes, recalling the fairy tale hut on chicken legs. A little ladder led down from the door.

The first impression they all had was that they would never make their way out of there. On all sides, wherever they looked, the mountains loomed menacingly above them, and from the direction of the lodge and its lone dark cypress the evening shadows rushed in upon them, making the narrow, sinuous valley narrower and the mountains higher. They could hear the rumbling of the river and the ceaseless chirring of crickets.

"Enchanting!" said Marya Konstantinovna, sighing ecstatically. "Look, children, just see how splendid it is! What stillness!"

"Yes, it really is splendid," agreed Layevsky, who liked the view and for some reason suddenly grew melancholy as he looked at the sky and then at the blue smoke rising from the chimney of the lodge. "Yes, splendid," he repeated.

"Ivan Andreich, give us a description of the view!" said Marya Konstantinovna tearfully.

"What for?" asked Layevsky. "The impression is better than any description. When the wealth of colors and sounds that everyone receives from nature by direct impression is prattled about by writers it is garbled and unrecognizable."

"Is that so?" von Koren coldly inquired, choosing for himself the largest of the rocks near the water and trying to clamber up and sit on it. "Is that so?" he repeated, staring Layevsky in the face. "And *Romeo and Juliet*? Or Pushkin's *Ukrainian Night*? Nature ought to come and bow down at their feet."

"Perhaps so . . ." Layevsky concurred, too lazy to reason and contradict him. "However," he added after a pause, "what is *Romeo and Juliet* basically? Beautiful, poetic, sacred love—the roses under which the rot is hidden. Romeo was the same sort of animal as everyone else."

"No matter what one talks to you about, you always bring it down to——" von Koren glanced at Katya and broke off.

"Bring it down to what?" asked Layevsky.

"Someone says to you, for example: 'What a beautiful bunch of grapes!' and you say: 'Yes, but how ugly when it is chewed up and digested in the stomach!' Why say it? It's hardly news, and is . . . altogether a peculiar way to behave."

Layevsky knew that von Koren did not like him, and for this reason was afraid of him; he felt that everyone was constrained in his presence, and as if someone were standing behind his back. He walked away without answering and was sorry he had come.

"Gentlemen, quick march—brushwood for the fire!" commanded Samoilenko.

They scattered in all directions, and no one was left but Kirilin, Achmianov, and Nikodim Aleksandrych. Kerbalai brought chairs, spread a rug on the ground, and set out several bottles of wine. Police Inspector Kirilin, a tall, good-looking man who wore an overcoat over his tunic in all weathers, was like every young chief of police, with his haughty bearing, pompous gait, and guttural, rather rasping voice. He had a dull, sleepy expression, as though he had just been awakened against his will.

"What's that you've brought, you swine?" he asked Kerbalai, deliberately articulating every word. "I ordered *kvarel*, and what have you brought, you ugly Tartar? Well, what?"

"We have plenty of wine of our own, Yegor Alekseich," Nikodim Aleksandrych politely and timidly observed.

"What of it? I want to have my wine, too. I'm participating in this picnic, and I presume I have a perfect right to contribute my share. I pre-sume! Bring ten bottles of *kvarel!*"

"Why so many?" Nikodim Aleksandrych wondered, knowing that Kirilin had no money.

"Twenty bottles! Thirty!" shouted Kirilin.

"Never mind, let him," whispered Achmianov to Nikodim Aleksandrych. "I'll pay for it."

Nadyezhda Fyodorovna was in a gay, mischievous mood. She felt like leaping, laughing, shouting, teasing, flirting. In her inexpensive cotton dress printed with blue pansies, her red shoes, and the same straw hat, she felt as though she were quite small, simple, light and airy as a butterfly. She ran out onto the rickety little bridge and gazed into the water for a minute in order to feel giddy, then shrieking and laughing, ran to the drying shed on the other side; and she fancied that all the men, even Kerbalai, were admiring her. When, in the rapidly falling darkness, the trees blended with the mountains, the horses with the carriages, and lights began to glimmer in the windows of the lodge, following a path that wound between the rocks and bramble bushes, she climbed up the mountain and sat down on a stone. The campfire was burning below. The deacon, his sleeves rolled up, was tending the fire, his long black shadow radiating out

from it as he threw on brushwood and stirred the caldron
with a spoon tied to a long stick. Samoilenko, his face
copper red, was fussing about the fire as he did in his own
kitchen, and frantically shouting:

"Where's the salt, my friend? I suppose you've forgotten
it? Why are you all sitting there at your ease like land-
owners, while I do everything alone?"

Layevsky and Nikodim Aleksandrych were sitting side by
side on the fallen tree, looking pensively into the fire. Marya
Konstantinovna, Katya, and Kostya were taking plates and
cups and saucers out of a basket. Von Koren, with folded
arms and one foot on a rock, was standing at the edge of the
bank lost in thought. Patches of red from the fire mingled
with the shadows, ran along the ground near the dark
human figures, quivered on the mountainside, the trees, the
bridge, and drying shed; across the river the steep hollowed-
out bank was completely illuminated, its reflection flickering
in the stream where the rushing, turbulent water tore it into
fragments.

The deacon went for the fish that Kerbalai was cleaning
and washing on the bank, but stopped halfway and looked
about him.

"My God, how beautiful!" he thought. "People, rocks,
fire, twilight, a misshapen tree—nothing more, and yet how
beautiful!"

Strangers appeared on the opposite bank near the drying
shed. Because of the flickering light and the smoke drifting in
that direction, it was impossible to make them out all at
once, but there were momentary glimpses of a shaggy cap
and gray beard, a blue shirt, a man clothed in rags from
shoulder to knee with a dagger across his stomach, a swarthy
young face with black brows as thick and bold as if they had
been drawn in charcoal. Five of them sat in a circle on the
ground, the remaining five went into the drying shed. One,
standing in the doorway with his back to the fire and his
hands behind him, was relating something which must have
been very interesting, for when Samoilenko put more brushwood on the fire and it flared up, scattering sparks and bright-
ly lighting the drying shed, two sober faces with absorbed
expressions could be seen looking out of the door, while
the men on the ground turned to listen to the story. A little
later those sitting in the circle commenced softly singing
something slow and melodious like Lenten church music.

. . . As he listened to them, the deacon imagined how things would be for him in ten years on his return from the expedition—a young missionary-priest, an author with a name and splendid past, he would be made an archimandrite, then a bishop; he would serve Mass in a cathedral; wearing a golden miter and the medallion of the Virgin Mary, he would come into the ambo, bless the people with the triple and the double candelabra, and proclaim: "Look down from heaven, O Lord, and behold, and visit the vineyard which Thy right hand hath planted!" And the angelic voices of the children would sing in response: "Holy Lord——"

"Deacon, where's that fish?" Samoilenko's voice rang out.

As he went back to the fire, the deacon imagined a church procession going along a dusty road on a hot July day; the peasants in front, the men carrying the banners, the women and young girls, the icons; behind them the boy choir and the sexton with his face tied up and a straw in his hair; next, in proper order, he, the deacon, and behind him the priest wearing his calotte and carrying a cross, followed by a crowd of peasants, women, and boys, raising a dust; and in the crowd the deaconess and the priest's wife wearing kerchiefs on their heads. The choir singing, children howling, quail calling, larks trilling. . . . Now they stop, sprinkle holy water on the herd. . . . They go on, and, kneeling, pray for rain. Then lunch and conversation. . . .

"And that too is good . . ." thought the deacon.


# VII


Kirilin and Achmianov made their way up the mountain path. Achmianov dropped behind and waited, while Kirilin went on to Nadyezhda Fyodorovna.

"Good evening!" he said, giving a salute.

"Good evening."

"Yes-s!" said Kirilin, gazing thoughtfully at the sky.

"Why 'yes'?" asked Nadyezhda Fyodorovna after a brief silence, having noticed that Achmianov was watching them.

"So, it seems," the officer articulated deliberately, "that our love has withered before it bloomed, so to say. How am I supposed to take this? Is it some sort of coquetry on your part, or do you consider me a nincompoop whom you can treat as you please?"

"It was a mistake! Leave me alone!" Nadyezhda Fyodorovna said sharply, looking at him in dismay on this superbly beautiful evening, and wondering whether there could really have been a moment when this man was attractive to her and intimate with her.

"So!" Kirilin said; he stood in silent thought for a few minutes before saying: "Well? We'll wait until you are in a better mood, and, meanwhile, I make so bold as to assure you that I am a gentleman, and I do not permit anyone to doubt it. You can't trifle with me! *Adieu!*"

He saluted and walked off, picking his way between the bushes. Shortly afterward Achmianov irresolutely approached.

"It's a beautiful evening!" he said with a slight Armenian accent.

He was not bad looking, dressed fashionably, and behaved simply, like a well-bred youth, but Nadyezhda Fyodorovna did not like him because she owed his father three hundred rubles; she was vexed that a shopkeeper should be invited to the picnic, vexed that he should approach her, particularly on this evening when her heart was so pure.

"The picnic is quite a success," he remarked, after a pause.

"Yes," she agreed, and then, as though suddenly reminded of her debt, casually added: "Oh, you can tell them in your shop that Ivan Andreich will drop in one of these days and pay the three hundred . . . or whatever it is."

"I'd be willing to give another three hundred just so you wouldn't mention that debt every day. Why so prosaic?"

Nadyezhda Fyodorovna laughed; the amusing thought had occurred to her that if she were willing, and sufficiently immoral, in one minute she might free herself of her debt. If, for instance, she were to turn the head of this handsome young fool! How amusing, how absurd and wild it would be, really! And she had a sudden desire to make him fall in love, to fleece him, then to throw him over and see what would happen.

"Allow me to give you a bit of advice," Achmianov said timidly. "I beg you to beware of Kirilin. He is saying dreadful things about you everywhere."

"I'm not interested in knowing what every fool says of me," Nadyezhda Fyodorovna replied coldly, and she was seized with anxiety; the amusing thought of playing with this handsome young man suddenly lost its charm.

"We must go down," she said. "They are calling."

Down below the fish soup was ready. It was ladled into plates and eaten with the ritual solemnity displayed only on picnics, and everyone agreed that it was exceedingly delicious and that they had never eaten anything so good at home. As is also customary on picnics, adrift in a mass of napkins, parcels, and superfluous greasy papers tossed about in the breeze, no one knew which glass or which piece of bread was whose; they poured wine on the rug and on their own laps, spilled salt, and though it was dark all around them and the fire had burned low, everyone felt too lazy to get up and throw wood on it. They all drank wine, even Kostya and Katya were given half a glass each. Nadyezhda Fyodorovna drank one glass, then another; she got a little drunk and forgot about Kirilin.

"A sumptuous picnic, a delightful evening," said Layevsky, cheered by the wine. "But I prefer a fine winter to all this. 'His beaver collar silvered by hoarfrost . . .'"

"Each to his own taste," observed von Koren.

Layevsky felt uncomfortable: the heat of the fire was beating on his back, but on his breast and face—von Koren's hatred; this animosity, coming as it did from a clever, decent man, and behind which there no doubt lay some valid cause, humiliated and unnerved him, and, not having the strength to oppose it, he said in an ingratiating tone:

"I am passionately fond of nature, and I regret that I am not a naturalist. I envy you."

"Well, I feel neither envy nor regret," said Nadyezhda Fyodorovna. "I don't understand how it is possible for anyone to be seriously occupied with bugs and beetles when people are suffering."

Layevsky shared her opinion. He was totally ignorant of the natural sciences and consequently could never reconcile himself to the authoritative tone and profoundly learned air of those who concerned themselves with the antennae of ants and the claws of cockroaches, and it always irked him that on the basis of these antennae and claws and a certain protoplasm (which for some reason he pictured in the form of an oyster) they should undertake to solve questions involving the origin and life of man. But he detected a

lie in Nadyezhda Fyodorovna's words, and for the sole purpose of contradicting her said:

"It's not a question of beetles but of deductions."

# VIII

It was late, almost eleven o'clock, by the time they began
settling themselves in the carriages to go home. The only
ones missing were Nadyezhda Fyodorovna and Achmianov,
who were on the other side of the river, chasing each other
and shouting with laughter.

"Hurry up, my friends!" called Samoilenko.

"Ladies should not be given wine," said von Koren in a low
voice.

Layevsky, exhausted by the picnic, by von Koren's animosity, and his own thoughts, went to meet Nadyezhda Fyodorovna, and when she seized both his hands and put her
head on his breast, breathless, laughing, feeling happy, gay,
and light as a feather, he stepped back and said severely:

"You are behaving like a . . . cocotte."

It came out so harshly that he instantly felt sorry for her.
On his angry, weary face she read hatred, pity, and annoyance with himself, and all at once her heart sank. She
realized that she had gone too far, had been too free and
easy in her behavior, and, chagrined, feeling heavy, fat,
coarse, and drunk, she climbed into the first empty carriage she came to with Achmianov. Layevsky got in with
Kirilin, the zoologist with Samoilenko, the deacon with the
ladies, and the caravan set off.

"Now you see what the macacos are like . . ." von Koren
began, wrapping himself in his cloak and closing his eyes.
"You heard: she doesn't care to occupy herself with bugs
and beetles, because people are suffering. That's the way all
macacos judge us. A slavish cunning breed, terrorized by the
knout and the fist for ten generations, it quakes and burns
incense to brute force, which is the only thing that moves it;
but just admit a macaco to a free state where there is no
one to take it by the scruff of the neck, and there it
shows itself and makes itself known. Look how bold it is at
art exhibitions, museums, theaters, or when it passes judgment on science: it bristles, rears up on its hind legs, and is

abusive and critical. . . . It is invariably critical—that's the mark of the slave! You will notice, men in the liberal professions are more often abused than swindlers—that's because three quarters of society consists of just such macacos. It never happens that a slave holds out his hand to you and sincerely thanks you for your work."

"I don't know what you expect!" said Samoilenko, yawning. "The poor thing, in all simplicity, was trying to have an intellectual conversation with you and you have to draw conclusions from it. You are angry with him for some reason, and with her by association. And she's a lovely woman!"

"Oh, come now! An ordinary kept woman, dissolute and vulgar. Listen, Aleksandr Davidych, when you meet a simple peasant woman who isn't living with her husband, and does nothing but titter and giggle, you tell her to get out and work. Why are you so timid and fearful of speaking the truth in this case? Just because Nadyezhda Fyodorovna is kept by an official instead of by a sailor?"

"What am I supposed to do," Samoilenko flared up, "beat her, or something?"

"Don't truckle to vice. We damn vice only behind its back, but that's like concealing an insulting gesture in your pocket. I'm a zoologist, or sociologist, which is the same thing, and you are a physician. Society believes in us; we are obligated to point out to it the dreadful harm threatening both present and future generations by the existence of ladies like this Nadyezhda Ivanovna."

"Fyodorovna," Samoilenko corrected him. "And what is society supposed to do?"

"Society? That's its affair. In my opinion, the surest and most direct method is force. She ought to be dispatched to her husband *manu militari,* and if the husband won't have her, she ought to be consigned to penal servitude or sent to a workhouse."

"Ugh!" sighed Samoilenko; he remained silent for a while and then softly asked: "A few days ago you said that people like Layevsky ought to be exterminated. . . . Tell me, if it were . . . let us suppose that the state or society commissioned you to exterminate him, could you . . . bring yourself to do it?"

"My hand would not tremble."

# IX

On arriving home, Layevsky and Nadyezhda Fyodorovna
went into their dark, stuffy, dreary rooms. Both were silent.
Layevsky lit a candle, while Nadyezhda Fyodorovna, without
taking off her hat and cloak, sat down and raised her mournful, guilty eyes to him.

He realized that she was expecting him to make some
sort of statement, but a statement would be boring, useless,
and exhausting, and he was conscience-stricken because he
had lost control and spoken rudely to her. He happened to
feel in his pocket the letter which every day he had been
meaning to read to her, and he thought that if he showed
this letter to her now it would divert her attention to another
channel.

"It's time to clarify our relations," he thought. "I'll give
her the letter. What is to be will be."

He took out the letter and handed it to her.

"Read it. It concerns you."

Having said this, he went to his study and lay down on the
sofa in the dark without a pillow. Nadyezhda Fyodorovna read
the letter and it seemed to her that the ceiling was falling
and the walls closing in on her. It grew suddenly dark,
and she felt hemmed in and frightened. She quickly crossed
herself three times and murmured: "Lord, give him peace . . .
Lord, give him peace. . . ."

Then she burst into tears.

"Vanya!" she called. "Ivan Andreich!"

There was no answer. Thinking that Layevsky had come
in and was standing behind her chair, she sobbed like a
child, saying:

"Why didn't you tell me he was dead? I wouldn't have
gone on the picnic, I wouldn't have laughed so frightfully.
. . . Those men were saying such awful things to me. What
a sin, what a sin! Save me, Vanya, save me. . . . I have been
mad. . . . I am ruined. . . ."

Layevsky heard her sobbing. He felt it was unbearably
stifling, and his heart was beating violently. In despair he
got up, stood in the middle of the room, then groped his
way in the dark to an armchair near the table, and sat down.

"This is a prison," he thought. "I must get away . . . I can't bear it. . . ."

It was too late to go and play cards and there were no restaurants in the town. He lay down again, covering his ears so he would not hear her sobbing, and suddenly he remembered that he could go to Samoilenko's. To avoid walking past Nadyezhda Fyodorovna, he slipped out the window, climbed over the garden fence, and continued down the street. It was dark. A steamer had just arrived, a big passenger ship, judging by its lights. . . . He heard the clatter of the anchor chain. A red light was moving swiftly from the shore toward the ship: it was the customs boat.

"The passengers are asleep in their cabins," thought Layevsky, envying other people's peace of mind.

The windows of Samoilenko's house were open. Layevsky peered through one, then another: it was dark and still inside.

"Aleksandr Davidych, are you asleep?" he called. "Aleksandr Davidych!"

There was a cough and an alarmed cry:

"Who's there? What the devil?"

"It's I, Aleksandr Davidych. Forgive me."

A moment later a door was opened; there was the soft glow of the icon lamp and Samoilenko's huge figure appeared all in white, with a white nightcap on his head.

"What do you want?" he asked drowsily, breathing heavily and scratching himself. "Wait a minute, I'll unlock the door."

"Don't trouble, I'll come in by the window. . . ."

Layevsky climbed through the window, went up to Samoilenko, and seized him by the hand.

"Aleksandr Davidych," he said in a trembling voice, "save me! I implore you, I solemnly entreat you, understand me! My position is agonizing. If it goes on for so much as another day or two I shall strangle myself . . . like a dog!"

"Wait a minute. . . . What exactly are you talking about?"

"Light a candle."

"Oh . . . oh . . ." sighed Samoilenko, lighting a candle. "My God, my God. . . . It's past one, my friend."

"Forgive me, but I cannot stay at home," said Layevsky, feeling greatly relieved by the candle and Samoilenko's presence. "You are my best, my only, friend, Aleksandr Davidych. . . . All my hopes rest in you. For God's sake, whether you feel like it or not, save me! No matter what happens, I must get away from here. Lend me some money!"

"Oh, my God, my God . . ." sighed Samoilenko, scratching himself. "I'm just falling asleep when I hear a whistle, a steamer arriving, and then you. . . . Do you need much?"

"Three hundred rubles at least. I must leave her a hundred, and I need two hundred for the trip. . . . I already owe you about four hundred, but I'll send it all to you . . . all. . . ."

Samoilenko clutched both his whiskers in one hand, took a wide stance, and pondered.

"So . . ." he mumbled irresolutely. "Three hundred. . . . Yes. . . . But I haven't got that much. I'll have to borrow it from someone."

"Borrow it, for God's sake!" said Layevsky, seeing from Samoilenko's face that he wanted to help him and undoubtedly would give him the money. "Borrow it, and I'll pay it back without fail. I'll send it from Petersburg as soon as I get there. You can set your mind at rest on that score. I'll tell you what, Sasha," he said, growing more animated, "let's have some wine!"

"Well . . . all right."

They went into the dining room.

"And what about Nadyezhda Fyodorovna?" asked Samoilenko, setting three bottles and a plate of peaches on the table. "Surely she's not going to remain here?"

"I'm going to arrange everything, everything will be arranged," said Layevsky, feeling an unexpected surge of joy. "Later I'll send her money and she will join me. . . . When she gets there we will clarify our relations. To your health, friend."

"Wait," said Samoilenko. "Drink this first. . . . This is from my vineyard. This bottle is from Navaridze's vineyard, and this one from Akhatulov's. . . . Try all three and tell me frankly. . . . Mine seems to have a touch of acidity. Eh? Don't you think so?"

"Yes. You have comforted me, Aleksandr Davidych. Thank you. . . . I feel better."

"Do you find it acid?"

"God only knows, I don't know. But you are a splendid, wonderful man!"

Looking at his pale, excited, kind face, Samoilenko recalled von Koren's opinion that such people ought to be exterminated, and Layevsky seemed to him a weak, defenseless child whom anyone could injure and destroy.

"And make peace with your mother when you get there," he said. "It's not right."

"Yes, yes, without fail."

They were silent for a while. When they had finished the first bottle, Samoilenko said:

"You ought to make it up with von Koren, too. You are both fine, highly intelligent men, and you glare at each other like wolves."

"Yes, he's a fine and very clever man," Layevsky agreed, now ready to praise and forgive everyone. "He is a remarkable man, but it's impossible for me to get along with him. No! Our natures are too different. I have an indolent, weak, submissive nature; perhaps, in a good moment, I might extend my hand to him, but he would turn away from me . . . with contempt."

Layevsky sipped his wine, paced up and down, then, standing in the middle of the room, continued:

"I understand von Koren very well. His is a tough, indomitable, despotic nature. You've heard him, he talks continuously about an expedition, and it's not empty talk. What he wants is the wilderness and moonlight nights: all around him in little tents under the open sky his sick and hungry Cossacks, bearers, guides, doctor, priest, are sleeping, all exhausted by the arduous march; he alone does not sleep, but sits like Stanley on his camp stool, feeling himself the sovereign of the wilderness and master of these people. He goes on and on, and in the end he perishes himself, but still remains the monarch and despot of the desert, for the cross above his grave can be seen by caravans thirty—forty —miles away, and he dominates the desert. I regret that this man is not in the army. He would have made a splendid military leader—capable of drowning his cavalry in a river and making a bridge of the corpses. And in war hardihood of that sort is more necessary than any sort of fortification or strategy. Oh, I understand him very well! Tell me, why is he throwing himself away here? What does he want here?"

"He's studying marine fauna."

"No. No, brother, no!" sighed Layevsky. "A scientist traveling on the steamer told me that the Black Sea was poor in fauna and that in its depths, thanks to an abundance of hydrogen sulfide, organic life is out of the question. All serious zoologists work in the biological stations at Naples or Villefranche. But von Koren is independent and obstinate: he works on the Black Sea because nobody else is working here; he broke with the university, doesn't care to know other scientists or his colleagues, because he is a despot first and only afterward a zoologist. And, you'll see, something will come of him. Even now he has dreams of returning from his expedition and smoking out the intrigue and mediocrity in our universities and bringing the scientists to their knees. Despotism is just as powerful in science as it is in the army. And he's spending his second summer in this stinking little town because he would rather be first in a village than second in a town. Here he's a king, an eagle; he has everyone under his thumb and oppresses them with his authority. He keeps a tight hand on everyone, interferes in other people's affairs, everything is useful to him and everyone fears him. I'm slipping out of his clutches, he feels it and hates me. Hasn't he told you I ought to be exterminated or consigned to hard labor?"

"Yes," laughed Samoilenko.

Layevsky laughed too and drained his glass.

"Even his ideals are despotic," he said, laughing and biting into a peach. "Ordinary mortals, if they are working for the common good, have their neighbor in mind: me, you, in short, mankind. To von Koren people are—numskulls, nonentities, too insignificant to be the purpose of his life. He works—he'll go on that expedition and break his neck —not out of love for his neighbor, but for the sake of such abstractions as humanity, future generations, an ideal race of men. He is concerned with the improvement of the human race, and in this connection we are only slaves to him, cannon fodder, beasts of burden; some of us he would exterminate or consign to hard labor, others he would pinion with discipline, like Arakcheyev, forcing us to get up and go to bed to the sound of drums, posting eunuchs to watch over our chastity and morals, commanding that anyone who steps out of the circle of our narrow, conservative morality be shot; and all this in the name of improving the human race. And what is this human race? An illusion, a mirage. . . . Despots have always been visionaries. I understand him very well, my friend. I appreciate him and do not deny his importance: it's men like him that keep the world going; if it were left to us alone, for all our kindheartedness and good intentions, we'd do with it just what those flies are doing to that picture. Yes."

Layevsky sat down beside Samoilenko and with genuine feeling said:

"I am a futile, insignificant, fallen man! The air I breathe, this wine, love, life in fact, I have bought with lies, laziness, and cowardice. To this day I have deceived others and myself; I have suffered for it, and my suffering was cheap and vulgar. I bow low before von Koren's hatred, because at times I hate and despise myself."

Layevsky again paced the room in agitation, and said:

"I'm glad that I see my faults clearly, that I am conscious of them. This will help me to reform and become a different man. My dear fellow, if you only knew how passionately and with what anguish I thirst for my own regeneration. And I swear to you I'll be a man! I will! I don't know whether it's the wine speaking in me or whether it really is so, but it seems to me that it has been a long time since I have had such pure lucid moments as I've had with you just now."

"It's time to sleep, brother . . ." said Samoilenko.

"Yes, yes. . . . Forgive me. I'm going now."

Layevsky bustled about the furniture and windows looking for his cap.

"Thank you," he muttered, sighing. "Thank you. . . . Kindness and a good word are better than charity. You have given me new life."

He found his cap, stopped, and looked guiltily at Samoilenko.

"Aleksandr Davidych!" he said in a pleading voice.

"What is it?"

"Let me spend the night here, my friend!"

"You're welcome to. . . . Why not?"

Layevsky lay down on the sofa and went on talking to the doctor for a long time.

## X

A few days after the picnic Marya Konstantinovna unexpectedly called on Nadyezhda Fyodorovna, and without greeting her or taking off her hat, threw her arms around her and pressed her to her bosom, saying in great excitement:

"My dear, I am so distressed and shocked! Yesterday our dear, sweet doctor told my Nikodim Aleksandrych that he had heard your husband passed away. Tell me, my dear . . . tell me, is it true?"

"Yes, it's true, he's dead," replied Nadyezhda Fyodorovna.

"That's dreadful, dreadful, my dear! But there's no evil without good. Your husband was no doubt a marvelous, wonderful, saintly man, and such men are more needed in heaven than on earth."

Every little line and dot on Marya Konstantinovna's face was quivering as if tiny needles were jumping under her skin; she smiled her almond-oily smile, and, panting with enthusiasm, said:

"And so you are free, my dear. Now you can hold up your head and look people boldly in the eye. From now on God and man will bless your union with Ivan Andreich. It's enchanting! I'm trembling with joy, I can find no words. My dear, we'll give you away. . . . Nikodim Aleksandrych and I are so fond of you, you will allow us to give our blessing to your pure, lawful union. When, when do you think of being married?"

"I haven't even thought about it," said Nadyezhda Fyodorovna, freeing her hands.

"That is not possible, dear. You have thought about it, you have!"

"No, I really haven't," said Nadyezhda Fyodorovna, laughing. "Why should we get married? I don't see any necessity for it. We'll go on living as before."

"What are you saying!" Marya Konstantinovna was horrified. "For God's sake, what are you saying!"

"Getting married wouldn't make things any better. On the contrary, it would make them worse. We should lose our freedom."

"My dear, my dear, what are you saying!" exclaimed Marya Konstantinovna, stepping back and clasping her hands. "You're not rational! Come to your senses! You must settle down!"

"What do you mean, settle down? I haven't lived yet, and you tell me to settle down!"

Nadyezhda Fyodorovna reflected that she really had not

lived. As soon as she had completed her studies at the institute she married a man she did not love, then she ran away with Layevsky and had been living the whole time with him on this dull, desolate shore, always in the expectation of something better. Was that life?

"Yet I ought to be married . . ." she thought, but, remembering Kirilin and Achmianov, she blushed and said: "No, it's impossible. Even if Ivan Andreich got down on his knees and begged me, I still would refuse."

Marya Konstantinovna sat on the sofa in silence for a moment, grave, mournful, and gazing fixedly into space, then she got up and coldly announced:

"Good-bye, my dear! Forgive me for having troubled you. Although it is not easy for me, I am obliged to tell you that from this day all is over between us, and in spite of my profound respect for Ivan Andreich, my door is closed to you!"

She uttered these words with such solemnity that she herself was overwhelmed by it; her face commenced quivering again and assumed her soft, almond-oily expression; holding out both her hands to Nadyezhda Fyodorovna, who was embarrassed and dismayed, she said in an imploring voice:

"My dear, allow me, if only for one minute, to be your mother or your older sister! I will be as candid as a mother with you."

Nadyezhda Fyodorovna's heart was filled with such warmth, joy, and self-pity that it was as if her mother had actually risen from the dead and were standing before her. She impulsively embraced Marya Konstantinovna, pressing her face to her shoulder. They both began to weep, sitting down on the sofa again and sobbing for several minutes without looking at each other, unable to utter a single word.

"My dear child," began Marya Konstantinovna, "I shan't spare you, I'm going to tell you some hard truths."

"Do, for God's sake, do!"

"Trust me, my dear. Remember, I was the only one of all the local ladies to receive you. I was horrified by you from the very first day, but I didn't have the heart to treat you with contempt, as everyone else did. I suffered for dear, good, Ivan Andreich, as if he were my own son—a young man in a strange place, inexperienced, weak, without a mother—and I was worried, dreadfully worried. . . . My husband was opposed to making his acquaintance, but I persuaded him . . . convinced him. . . . We began receiving Ivan Andreich, and with him, you, of course, otherwise he would have been insulted. I have a daughter, a son. . . . You understand, the tender mind, the pure heart of a child. . . . 'Whoso offendeth one of these little ones' . . . I received you, but I trembled for my little ones. Oh, when you are a mother you will understand my fears. And everyone was surprised at my receiving you—you will forgive me—like a respectable woman, and insinuated to me that . . . well, naturally, gossip, innuendoes. . . . In the depths of my soul I condemned you, but you were unfortunate, pathetic, wayward, and I ached with pity for you."

"But why? Why?" asked Nadyezhda Fyodorovna. "What did I do to anyone?"

"You are a dreadful sinner. You broke the vow you made to your husband at the altar. You seduced a splendid young man, who, had he not met you, might perhaps have taken a lawful life companion, someone from a good family in his own circle, and he would have been like everyone else now. You have ruined his youth. Don't speak, don't speak, my dear! I will not believe that it's the man who is to blame for our sins. It is always the woman's fault. Men are frivolous in these matters, they live by their heads not their hearts, there's so much they don't understand, while a woman understands everything. It all depends on her. To her much is given, and from her much is required. Oh, my dear, if she had been more foolish than man, or weaker, God never would have entrusted her with the upbringing of little boys and girls. And then, my dear, casting aside all shame, you embarked on the path of sin; any other woman in your position would have hidden herself away, would have sat at home behind closed doors, would have been seen only in the temple of God, pale, dressed all in black, and weeping, and everyone would have said with genuine compassion: 'Lord, this erring angel is returning to Thee. . . .' But you, my dear, forgot all modesty and lived openly, waywardly, as if proud of your sin; you frolicked, you laughed, and watching you I trembled in dread, fearing that a thunderbolt from heaven would strike our home when you visited us. Don't speak, don't speak, my dear!" cried Marya Konstantinovna, observing that Nadyezhda Fyodorovna was about to say something. "Trust me, I will not deceive you, I will not conceal one single truth from your soul's gaze.

Listen to me, my dear. . . . God marks the great sinner, and you have been marked. Just remember, your style of dress has always been appalling!"

Nadyezhda Fyodorovna, who had always had the highest opinion of the way she dressed, stopped crying and looked up in surprise.

"Yes, appalling!" continued Marya Konstantinovna. "Anyone could judge your behavior from the showiness and gaudiness of your attire. People all laughed and shrugged their shoulders looking at you, and I suffered, suffered. . . . And forgive me, my dear, but you are not clean in your person. When we met in the bathhouse, you made me shudder. Your outer clothing is passable, but your petticoat, your chemise . . . my dear, I blush! And no one ever ties poor Ivan Andreich's necktie properly, even from his linen and boots one can see there's no one at home to look after the poor boy. You know, darling, he's always hungry, and naturally, if no one at home sees to the samovar and the coffee, one is bound to spend half one's salary in the pavilion. Your house is dreadful, simply dreadful! No one else in the whole town has flies, but you can't get rid of them, your plates and saucers are black with them. Just look at the windows, and the tables—they're covered with dust, dead flies, glasses. . . . Why should there be glasses here? Why, my dear, at this hour of the day hasn't your table been cleared? And one is embarrassed to go into your bedroom: underclothes flung about everywhere, your various rubber things hanging on the wall, basins standing about. . . . My dear! A husband ought to know nothing of these things, and a wife ought to appear before him as immaculate as a little angel! I wake up every morning at daybreak and wash my face with cold water so my Nikodim Aleksandrych won't see me looking sleepy."

"All that is not worth bothering about," sobbed Nadyezhda Fyodorovna. "If only I were happy, but I'm so unhappy!"

"Yes, yes, you are very unhappy!" sighed Marya Konstantinovna, barely able to keep from bursting into tears. "And terrible grief awaits you in the future! A solitary old age, illness, and then you will have to answer to the Last Judgment. . . . Dreadful, dreadful! Now fate itself holds out a helping hand to you, and you foolishly thrust it aside. Get married, get married quickly!"

"Yes, I must, I must," said Nadyezhda Fyodorovna. "But it's impossible!"

"Why?"

"It's impossible! Oh, if you only knew!"

Nadyezhda Fyodorovna had an impulse to tell her about Kirilin, and about the evening before when she had met the handsome young Achmianov on the wharf and the insane, ridiculous idea of getting rid of her debt had occurred to her; it had been very amusing, but she returned home late in the evening feeling corrupt and irrevocably fallen. She did not know herself how it had happened. And she longed to swear to Marya Konstantinovna that she would pay back the debt, but her sobbing and her shame prevented her from speaking.

"I'm going away," she said. "Ivan Andreich may remain here, but I'm going away."

"Where?"

"To Russia."

"But how will you live there? Why, you have nothing."

"I'll do translations or . . . or open a little bookshop. . . ."

"Don't be fantastic, my dear. You need money for a bookshop. Well, I'll leave you now. You calm yourself and think things over, and tomorrow come and see me in a gay mood. That will be enchanting! Well, good-bye, my little angel. Let me kiss you."

Marya Konstantinovna kissed Nadyezhda Fyodorovna on the forehead, made the sign of the cross over her, and quietly withdrew. It was growing dark; Olga was lighting the fire in the kitchen. Still crying, Nadyezhda Fyodorovna went into the bedroom and lay down on the bed. She commenced to run a high fever. Without getting up she took off her clothes, crumpling them at her feet, and curled up in a ball under the blanket. She was thirsty, but there was no one to give her anything to drink.

"I'll pay it back!" she said to herself, and in her delirium she imagined she was sitting beside a sick woman, whom she recognized as herself. "I'll pay it back. It would be stupid to think that for money I . . . I'll go away and send him the money from Petersburg. First one hundred . . . then another hundred . . . then another. . . ."

It was late at night when Layevsky came in.

"First one hundred," Nadyezhda Fyodorovna said to him, "then another hundred. . . ."

"You ought to take some quinine," he said, thinking: "To-morrow is Wednesday, the steamer leaves, and I won't be on it. That means I'll have to stay here till Saturday."

Nadyezhda Fyodorovna got up on her knees in bed.

"I didn't say anything just now, did I?" she asked, smiling and screwing up her eyes at the candlelight.

"No, nothing. We shall have to send for the doctor in the morning. Go to sleep."

He took a pillow and went to the door. From the time he definitely made up his mind to go away and leave Nadyezhda Fyodorovna, she had begun to arouse feelings of guilt and pity in him; he was slightly ashamed in her presence, as he might have been in the presence of an old or sick horse that he had decided to kill. He stopped in the doorway and glanced back at her.

"I was irritated at the picnic and spoke rudely to you. Forgive me, for God's sake."

After saying this, he went to his study, lay down, and was unable to fall asleep for a long time.

The next morning when Samoilenko, decked out for an official holiday in full-dress uniform with epaulettes and decorations, came out of Nadyezhda Fyodorovna's bedroom after taking her pulse and looking at her tongue, Layevsky, who was standing on the threshold, anxiously asked him:

"Well, what about it? Well?"

His face expressed fear, extreme anxiety, and hope.

"Calm yourself, it's nothing dangerous," said Samoilenko. "The usual fever."

"That's not what I mean," Layevsky frowned with impatience. "Did you get the money?"

"My dear friend, forgive me," whispered Samoilenko, glancing back at the door, embarrassed. "For God's sake, forgive me! No one has any money to spare, and so far I've collected only five or ten rubles here and there—a hundred and ten in all. I'm going to talk to someone else today. Be patient."

"But Saturday is the last day!" whispered Layevsky, trembling with impatience. "By all that's holy, get it before Saturday! If I don't leave here Saturday, then nothing will be of any use to me, nothing! I don't understand how it is that a doctor can have no money!"

"Lord, Thy will be done!" whispered Samoilenko hastily and vehemently, and there was even a catch in his voice.

"They've taken everything I've got, they owe me seven thousand, and I'm in debt everywhere. Is it my fault?"

"But you will get it by Saturday? Yes?"

"I'll try."

"I implore you, my friend! So long as the money is in my hands by Friday morning!"

Samoilenko sat down and wrote a prescription for quinine in a solution of *kalii bromati,* and infusion of rhubarb, and tincture of *gentianae aquae foeniculi*—all in one mixture, then he added rose syrup so it would not taste bitter, and left.

# XI

"You look as if you were coming to arrest me," said von Koren, seeing Samoilenko enter his room in full-dress uniform.

"I was just passing by and thought: Why not drop in and pay my respects to zoology?" said Samoilenko, sitting down at the big table which the zoologist himself had knocked together out of plain boards. "Greetings, holy father!" he nodded to the deacon, who was sitting by the window copying something. "I'll only stay a moment and then run along and see about dinner. It's time. . . . I'm not disturbing you?"

"Not in the least," replied the zoologist, laying out on the table slips of paper covered with fine handwriting. "We've been busy copying."

"So. . . . Oh, Good Lord, Good Lord . . ." sighed Samoilenko; he cautiously drew from the table a dusty book on which there was a dead, dried-up phalanger and said: "Just picture some little green beetle going about its business and suddenly meeting a devil such as this on the road. I can imagine the terror it would feel!"

"Yes, I suppose so."

"Is it equipped with venom to defend itself from enemies?"

"Yes, for defense and attack."

"Well, well, well. . . . Everything in nature is efficient and accountable," sighed Samoilenko. "Only here's what I do not understand. You're a man of the greatest intelligence; explain it to me, please. There are, as you know, certain small beasts no bigger than rats, pretty to look at, but mean and vicious as can be, let me tell you. Suppose one of these little beasts is running through the woods, sees a bird, catches it, and devours it. He goes on, and sees a little nest of eggs in the grass; he doesn't feel like gobbling them up, he's full; nevertheless, he bites into one and knocks the others out of the nest with his paw. . . . He ruins and destroys every creature in his path . . . crawls into others' burrows, digs up anthills, cracks open snails. . . . If he encounters a rat, he attacks it; if he catches sight of a little snake or a mouse, he strangles it. And he goes on like this the whole day. Now, tell me, what's the use of such a beast? Why was it created?"

"I don't know what beast you are talking about," said von Koren, "probably one of the insectivores. Well, what about it? The bird was caught because it was careless; the nest of eggs was destroyed because a bird was not skillful, but built the nest badly and failed to camouflage it. The frog very likely had some imperfection in its coloring, otherwise it would not have been seen, and so on. Your little beast destroys only the weak, the unskilled, and careless, in short, those with defects which nature does not see fit to transmit to posterity. Only the more clever, cautious, strong, and developed survive. In this way, without suspecting it, your little beast serves the great end of perfecting creation."

"Yes, yes, yes. . . . By the way, brother, lend me a hundred rubles, will you?"

"Certainly. There are some very interesting types among the insectivores. The mole, for example, which is considered useful because it destroys harmful insects. They tell of a certain German who sent Emperor Wilhelm I a moleskin coat, and the Emperor is said to have had him reprimanded for destroying so many useful animals. Yet the mole is in no way less cruel than your little beast, besides which it does a great deal of damage to the fields."

Von Koren unlocked a cashbox and took out a hundred-ruble note.

"The mole has a powerful thorax, like the bat," he continued, as he locked the cashbox, "highly developed bones and muscles, and a remarkably well-armed jaw. If it had the dimensions of an elephant, it would be an all-destroying, invincible animal. It's interesting that when two moles meet underground, they both begin digging a platform, as if by agreement. This platform is required for their battle, and when they have finished digging it, they embark on a fierce struggle, fighting till the weaker one falls. Here's a hundred rubles for you," said von Koren, lowering his voice, "but only on condition that you are not borrowing it for Layevsky."

"And what if it were for Layevsky!" Samoilenko flared up. "What business is it of yours?"

"I cannot give it to you for Layevsky. I know you like lending people money. You'd give it to the brigand Kerim if he asked you, but, forgive me, I cannot support you in this bent."

"Yes, I am borrowing it for Layevsky!" said Samoilenko, standing up and brandishing his right arm. "Yes! For Layevsky! And nobody, not the devil himself, has a right to tell me how I should dispose of my own money. You don't care to lend it to me? Is that it?"

The deacon burst out laughing.

"Don't start simmering, be reasonable," said the zoologist. "Lavishing favors on Mr. Layevsky is, in my opinion, as senseless as watering weeds or luring locusts."

"And in my opinion, we are obliged to help our neighbor!" cried Samoilenko.

"In that case, help that hungry Turk lying there under the fence! He's a workingman and more useful, more necessary, than your Layevsky. Give him that hundred-ruble note, or donate a hundred rubles to my expedition!"

"Are you giving it to me or not, I ask you?"

"Tell me frankly: what does he want the money for?"

"It's no secret. He has to go to Petersburg on Saturday."

"So that's it!" von Koren drawled. "Ah-ha! Now we understand. And is she going with him, or how is it to be?"

"She's staying here for the present. He's going to settle his affairs in Petersburg and send her the money, then she'll go."

"Very clever!" said the zoologist. "Clever. Well contrived."

He quickly walked up to Samoilenko and stood face to face with him, looking him in the eye, and asked:

"Tell me frankly: he's tired of her, isn't he? Tell me: he's tired of her, isn't he?"

"Yes," murmured Samoilenko, beginning to perspire.

"How disgusting!" said von Koren, his face expressing his

revulsion. "One of two things, Aleksandr Davidych: either you are in the plot with him, or, excuse my saying so, you are a simpleton. Is it possible you don't realize that he's taking you in like a child, in the most unconscionable way? Why, it's as clear as day that he wants to get rid of her, wants to abandon her here. She'll be on your neck and—also clear as day—you'll have to send her to Petersburg at your own expense. Is it possible that your fine friend has so blinded you with his merits that you can't see the simplest things?"

"That's just conjecture," said Samoilenko.

"Conjecture? Then why is he going away alone instead of taking her with him? And why—just ask him this—why doesn't he send her ahead and then follow? The cunning rogue!"

Crushed by sudden doubts and suspicions about his friend, Samoilenko all at once lost heart and took a milder tone.

"But that's not possible!" he said, remembering the night Layevsky had spent at his house. "He suffers so!"

"And what of it? Thieves and incendiaries suffer too!"

"Even supposing you are right . . ." said Samoilenko, wavering. "Let us assume . . . Still, he is a young man, and in a strange place . . . a student. . . . We've been students, too, and there's no one here but us to come to his aid."

"To help him commit an abomination simply because you and he were at the university at different times, where both of you did absolutely nothing—what nonsense!"

"Wait, let's discuss it cooly. It might be possible, I think, to arrange it like this. . . ." Samoilenko pondered, twitching his fingers. "I will give him the money, you see, but make him promise on his word of honor that within a week he will send Nadyezhda Fyodorovna money for the trip."

"And he'll give you his word of honor, he'll even shed a few tears and believe it himself, but what is his word of honor worth? He won't keep it, and in a year or two, when you meet him on the Nevsky Prospect walking arm in arm with a new love, he will justify himself by saying that he has been mutilated by civilization, that he's cut from the same pattern as Rudin. Drop him, for God's sake! Get away from all that filth, and stop digging in it with both hands!"

Samoilenko thought for a moment and said resolutely:

"But I'll still give him the money. As you wish, but I'm

not capable of refusing a man simply on the basis of conjecture."

"That's fine. Why don't you kiss him, too?"

"Give me the hundred rubles, then," Samoilenko requested timidly.

"I won't give it to you."

A silence followed. Samoilenko was completely crestfallen; his face took on a guilty, shamefaced, ingratiating expression, and it was strange to see this pitiful, childishly embarrassed countenance on a huge man wearing epaulettes and medals.

"The local bishop goes around his diocese on horseback instead of in a carriage," said the deacon, laying down his pen. "His appearance sitting on a horse is touching in the extreme. His simplicity and modesty are filled with Biblical grandeur."

"Is he a good man?" asked von Koren, glad to change the subject.

"How could it be otherwise? Would he have been consecrated a bishop if he were not good?"

"You find some very good and gifted men among bishops," said von Koren. "Only it's a pity that many of them have a weakness for imagining themselves statesmen. One busies himself with Russification, another criticizes the sciences. That's not their business. They'd do better to look into the consistory more often."

"A layman cannot judge a bishop."

"Why not, Deacon? A bishop is a man the same as I."

"The same but not the same," said the deacon, offended, and he took up his pen. "If you were the same, you would have been blessed with grace, and would yourself have been a bishop; but as you are not a bishop it means you are not the same."

"Don't be silly, Deacon," said Samoilenko dejectedly. "Listen, here's what I've devised," he said, turning to von Koren. "Don't give me that hundred rubles. You'll be boarding with me for three months before the winter, so let me have the money in advance."

"I won't do it."

Samoilenko blinked his eyes and turned crimson. He mechanically drew the book with the phalanger on it toward him, then got up and picked up his hat.

Von Koren felt sorry for him.

"What's the use of trying to live and do business with such people!" he said, kicking some paper into a corner in his indignation. "You must understand that this is not kindness, not love, but cowardice, profligacy, poison! What's gained by reason is ruined by your flabby, good-for-nothing hearts! When I was ill with typhoid as a schoolboy, my aunt, out of sympathy, gave me pickled mushrooms to eat, and I nearly died. Both you and my aunt need to understand that love for man is not in the heart, the pit of the stomach, or the loins, but right here!"

Von Koren tapped himself on the forehead.

"Take it!" he said, flinging the hundred-ruble note at Samoilenko.

"You don't have to lose your temper, Kolya," said Samoilenko mildly as he folded the bill. "I understand you perfectly, but . . . put yourself in my position."

"You're an old woman, that's what you are!"

The deacon roared with laughter.

"Listen, Aleksandr Davidych, one last request!" said von Koren vehemently. "When you give that scoundrel the money, do it on condition that he either takes his lady with him or sends her on ahead, otherwise don't give it to him. There's no need to stand on ceremony with him. Tell him! And if you don't, I give you my word I'll go to his office and throw him downstairs, and I'll have nothing further to do with you. Now you know!"

"Why not? To go with her or send her on ahead will be more convenient for him," said Samoilenko. "He'll even be glad. Well, good-bye."

He took his leave complaisantly and went out, but before shutting the door behind him, he glanced back at von Koren, made a terrible face, and said:

"It's the Germans who've ruined you! Yes! The Germans!"

# XII

The next day, Thursday, Marya Konstantinovna was celebrating her son Kostya's birthday. Everyone was invited to come for a pie at noon, and for chocolate in the evening. When Layevsky and Nadyezhda Fyodorovna arrived, the zoologist, who was already in the drawing room drinking chocolate, asked Samoilenko:

"Have you spoken to him?"

"Not yet."

"See that you don't stand on ceremony. I cannot understand the insolence of these people! They know perfectly well how this family looks on their cohabitation, yet they worm their way in here."

"If one paid attention to every prejudice," said Samoilenko, "one could go nowhere."

"Do you mean to say that the repugnance of the masses for illicit love and licentiousness is prejudice?"

"Of course. Prejudice and hostility. When soldiers see a loose woman they laugh and whistle, but just ask them what they themselves are."

"They don't whistle without cause. The fact that these women strangle their illegitimate children and go to prison for it, that Anna Karenina threw herself under a train, that in the villages they tar their gates, that, without being aware of it, what appeals to us in Katya is her purity, that everyone of us dimly feels a need for pure love—even while knowing that there is no such thing—can all this be prejudice? This, my dear friend, is the only thing that has survived from natural selection, and if it were not for this obscure force regulating relations between the sexes, the Layevskys of the world would be showing you how to live and the human race would degenerate within two years."

Layevsky came into the drawing room, greeted everyone, and smiled ingratiatingly as he shook hands with von Koren. He waited for a favorable moment before saying to Samoilenko:

"Excuse me, Aleksandr Davidych, I must have a word with you."

Samoilenko got up, put his arm around Layevsky's waist, and they went into Nikodim Aleksandrych's study.

"Tomorrow is Friday . . ." said Layevsky, biting his nails. "Have you got what you promised?"

"I've only got two hundred and ten. I'll get the rest today or tomorrow. Don't worry."

"Thank God! . . ." sighed Layevsky, so overjoyed that his hands began to tremble. "You have saved me, Aleksandr Davidych, and I swear to you, by God, by my happiness, by anything you like, that I will send you this money as soon as I arrive. And my old debt, too."

"See here, Vanya . . ." Samoilenko began, turning red as he buttonholed him. "Forgive me for meddling in your private affairs, but . . . why don't you take Nadyezhda Fyodorovna with you?"

"You're a funny fellow—how could I? One of us absolutely has to stay, otherwise my creditors would start clamoring. I owe the shops seven hundred rubles, if not more. Just wait, I'll send them the money, I'll pay them off, and then she can leave."

"I see. . . . But why shouldn't you send her on ahead?"

"Oh, my God, how can I?" Layevsky was horrified. "She's a woman, what could she do there alone? What does she know about things? It would only be a delay and an unnecessary waste of money."

"Reasonable . . ." thought Samoilenko, then, recalling his conversation with von Koren, he looked down and said gruffly:

"I can't agree with you. Either you take her with you or send her on ahead, otherwise . . . otherwise I won't give you the money. These are my last words. . . ."

He backed away, lurching into the door, and went out to the drawing room, flushed and overcome with confusion.

"Friday . . . Friday . . ." thought Layevsky, as he returned to the drawing room. "Friday . . ."

He was handed a cup of chocolate. He burned his lips and tongue with the scalding liquid, still thinking: "Friday . . . Friday . . ."

He could not get the word "Friday" out of his head; he thought of nothing but Friday, and the only thing that was clear to him—not in his head, but somewhere in the region of his heart—was that on Saturday he would not be leaving. Before him stood Nikodim Aleksandrych, fastidiously neat, his hair combed over his temples, saying:

"Have something to eat, please do. . . ."

Marya Konstantinovna showed her guests Katya's school report, saying in a drawling voice:

"School is terribly, terribly hard these days! They expect so much. . . ."

"Mama!" Katya groaned, not knowing where to hide herself she was so embarrassed by all the praise.

Layevsky too looked at the report and praised it. Scripture,

Russian language, conduct, the A's and B's danced before his eyes, mingling with the persistent thought of Friday, the carefully combed hair on Nikodim Aleksandrych's temples, and Katya's red cheeks, all of which produced an effect of such vast, insuperable boredom that he could barely keep from shrieking with despair, and he asked himself: "Can it really be possible that I am not leaving?"

Two card tables were placed side by side and they sat down to play postman. Layevsky sat down with them.

"Friday . . . Friday . . ." he thought, smiling and taking a pencil out of his pocket. "Friday . . ."

He wanted to consider his situation, but he was afraid to think. It frightened him to realize that the doctor had caught him in a deception which he had so long and so carefully concealed from himself. Whenever he thought of the future he managed to control his thoughts. He would get on a train and go, thereby solving the problem of his life—and beyond that he did not think. Like a dim, distant light in a field, the thought occasionally flickered in his mind that sometime in the remote future, somewhere in one of the side streets of Petersburg, in order to break with Nadyezhda Fyodorovna and pay all his debts, he would have to resort to a little lie; but he would lie only once, and then a whole new life would begin. And this was right: at the cost of one little lie, he would purchase a great truth.

Now, however, when by his refusal the doctor had bluntly hinted at a deception, he began to realize that he would have to lie not only in the remote future, but today, tomorrow, and a month from now, perhaps even to the end of his life. In fact, in order to get away he would have to lie to Nadyezhda Fyodorovna, to his creditors, and his superiors; then, in order to get money in Petersburg, he would have to lie to his mother, telling her he had broken with Nadyezhda Fyodorovna, and his mother would not give him more than five hundred rubles, which meant that already he had deceived the doctor, for he would not be in a position to send him the money soon. Afterward, when Nadyezhda Fyodorovna came to Petersburg, he would have to resort to a whole series of deceptions, both large and small, in order to separate from her; again a loathsome life of tears, boredom, remorse, and, of course, no new life whatsoever. Deception, nothing more. A whole mountain of lies rose before him. To leap over it in one bound instead of lying piecemeal, he would have to make up his mind to take extreme measures: for instance, to get up without a word, take his cap, and leave at once, without money and without explanation; but Layevsky felt that he was incapable of this.

"Friday, Friday . . ." he thought. "Friday . . ."

They were writing little notes, folding them in two, and putting them into Nikodim Aleksandrych's old top hat; when a sufficient number of notes had accumulated, Kostya, acting the part of the postman, walked around the table delivering them. The deacon, Katya, and Kostya, who had all received amusing notes, were trying to write even funnier ones, and were beside themselves with delight.

"We must have a little talk," Nadyezhda Fyodorovna read in the note she received.

She exchanged glances with Marya Konstantinovna, who gave her an almond-oily smile and nodded her head.

"What is there to talk about?" Nadyezhda Fyodorovna wondered. "If you can't tell everything, there's no use talking."

Before going out for the evening she had tied Layevsky's necktie for him, and this trivial act had filled her soul with tenderness and melancholy. The expression of anxiety on his face, his pallor, his distraught glances, and the incomprehensible change that had taken place in him lately, added to the fact that she was keeping a dreadful, vile secret from him and that her hands had trembled as she knotted his tie— all this seemed to tell her that they would not be together very much longer. She gazed at him as at an icon, thinking: "Forgive me, forgive me. . . ."

Across the table from her sat Achmianov, never taking his black lovesick eyes off her; stirred by passion, she was ashamed, and afraid that even anguish and sorrow would not prevent her from yielding to impure desires, if not today, tomorrow—and that like a confirmed drunkard she would not have the strength to stop herself.

She decided to go away in order to put an end to this life, ignominious to herself and humiliating to Layevsky. She would tearfully implore him to let her go, and if he opposed her she would leave him in secret. She would not tell him what had happened; let his memory of her remain pure.

"I love, love, love you . . ." she read. It was from Achmianov.

She would live in some remote place, work, and send

Layevsky money, embroidered shirts, and tobacco—"from an unknown"—returning to him only in old age, or if he fell dangerously ill and needed a nurse. When, in his old age, he learned the reasons for her refusal to be his wife and for leaving him, he would appreciate her sacrifice and forgive her.

"You have a long nose." That must be from the deacon or Kostya.

Nadyezhda Fyodorovna imagined how, in parting from Layevsky, she would embrace him warmly, kiss his hand, and swear that all, all her life she would love him, and then, living in obscurity among strangers, every day she would think that somewhere there was a friend, someone she loved, a pure, noble, lofty man who cherished a pure memory of her.

"If tonight you do not set a time for our meeting, I assure you on my honor, I shall take measures. You don't treat decent people like this, and you'd better realize it." The note was from Kirilin.

# XIII

Layevsky received two notes; he opened one and read: "Don't go away, my friend."

"Who could have written that?" he wondered. "Not Samoilenko, of course. And not the deacon, he doesn't know I intend to leave. Could it be von Koren?"

The zoologist was bent over the table drawing a pyramid. It seemed to Layevsky that his eyes were smiling.

"Samoilenko must have blabbed," Layevsky thought.

The other note, written in the same disguised handwriting with tails and curlicues said: "Someone will not be leaving on Saturday."

"A stupid gibe," thought Layevsky. "Friday, Friday . . ."

He felt something rise in his throat. He adjusted his collar and coughed, but instead of a cough a laugh burst from his throat.

"Ha-ha-ha!" he went on. . . . "Ha-ha-ha!" What am I laughing at, he wondered. "Ha-ha-ha!"

He tried to restrain himself and to cover his mouth with his hand, but his chest and throat were choked with laughter, and his hand refused to obey him.

"But how stupid this is!" he thought, rocking with laughter. "Have I gone out of my mind?"

The laughter rose higher and higher till it turned into something resembling the yelp of a spaniel. Layevsky tried to get up from the table, but his legs would not respond, and his right hand, strangely out of control, danced on the table, convulsively clutching and crumpling the little pieces of paper. He saw the looks of astonishment, Samoilenko's serious frightened face, the zoologist's eyes, full of cold contempt and loathing, and realized that he was in hysterics.

"How deplorable, how shameful!" he thought, feeling the warm tears on his face. "Oh, oh, what a disgrace! This has never happened to me. . . ."

They grasped him under the arms and, supporting his head from behind, led him out; a glass glittered before his eyes, knocked against his teeth, and water spilled on his chest; he was in a small room in the middle of which stood two beds side by side, both covered with clean snow-white spreads. He fell onto one of them sobbing.

"It's all right, it's all right . . ." said Samoilenko. "These things happen. . . . These things happen. . . ."

Cold with fear and foreseeing something dreadful, Nadyezhda Fyodorovna stood by the bed, her whole body trembling, and asked:

"What's wrong with you? What is it? For God's sake, speak. . . ."

"Can Kirilin have written him something?" she wondered.

"It's nothing . . ." said Layevsky, laughing and crying. "Go away . . . darling."

His face expressed neither hatred nor revulsion, which meant he knew nothing. Somewhat reassured, Nadyezhda Fyodorovna went back to the drawing room.

"Don't worry, my dear!" said Marya Konstantinovna, sitting down beside her and taking her hand. "It will pass. Men are just as weak as we poor sinners. You are both going through a crisis . . . it's quite understandable. Well, my dear, I am waiting for your answer. Let's have a little talk."

"No, we can't talk. . ." said Nadyezhda Fyodorovna, listening to Layevsky's sobbing. "I feel miserable. . . . Please let me go home."

"What's this, what's this, my dear?" cried Marya Konstantinovna in alarm. "You surely don't think I would let you go without supper? We'll have a bite and then you can be off."

"I'm so miserable . . ." whispered Nadyezhda Fyodorovna, clutching the arm of a chair with both hands to keep from falling.

"An attack of infantile eclampsia!" said von Koren cheerfully, as he came into the drawing room, but seeing Nadyezhda Fyodorovna, he was disconcerted and went out.

When his hysterics were over, Layevsky sat on the strange bed thinking:

"What a disgrace, bawling like a slut! I must have been ridiculous and revolting. I'll leave by the back way. . . . But that would make it appear that I took my hysterics seriously. I ought to treat it as a joke. . . ."

He sat there for a while, looking into the mirror, then went back to the drawing room.

"Well, here I am!" he said, smiling; he was agonizingly embarrassed, and felt that the others were embarrassed by his presence. "Such things will happen," he said, as he sat down. "I was sitting here and all of a sudden, you know, I felt a terrible shooting pain in my side . . . unbearable, my nerves couldn't stand it and . . . and it led to that silly business. This nervous age of ours—there's no help for it!"

At supper he drank wine and talked, sighing spasmodically and from time to time rubbing his side as if to show that he still felt the pain. He could see that no one except Nadyezhda Fyodorovna believed him.

Between nine and ten they went for a walk on the boulevard. Nadyezhda Fyodorovna, fearing that Kirilin would speak to her, tried to stay close to Marya Konstantinovna and the children. Weak with misery and fear and knowing she would have a fever, she was so exhausted she could hardly move her legs, but she did not go home because she felt certain she would be followed by Kirilin or Achmianov, or both. Kirilin walked behind her with Nikodim Aleksandrych, and kept singing in an undertone:

"I do not al-lo-ow anyone to tri-ifle with me! I do not al-low it!"

They turned off the boulevard, walking toward the pavilion and then along the shore, where they watched the phosphorescent sea for a long time while von Koren gave them an explanation of phosphorescence.

# XIV

"Why, it's time for my vint. . . . They're waiting for me," said Layevsky. "Good night, my friends."

"Wait, I'll go with you," said Nadyezhda Fyodorovna, taking his arm.

They said good-bye to the company and walked on. Kirilin also took his leave, saying he was going in the same direction, and went with them.

"What is to be, will be . . ." thought Nadyezhda Fyodorovna. "So be it. . . ."

It seemed to her that all her bad memories had left her head and were walking beside her, breathing heavily in the darkness, while she, like a fly that had fallen into an ink-well and was barely able to crawl along the pavement, was besmirching Layevsky's arm and side with black. If Kirilin were to do anything wrong, she thought, it would be she alone who would be to blame. There was a time when no man would have spoken to her as Kirilin had done, and it was she herself who had put an end to that time, snapped it like a thread, destroyed it irrevocably—and whose fault was it? Drunk with her own desires, she had smiled at a perfect stranger, probably for no other reason than that he was tall and well-built; after two meetings she had tired of him and dropped him, and did not that, she thought, give him the right to treat her as he pleased?

"I'll say good-bye to you here, darling," said Layevsky, stopping. "Ilya Mikhailych will see you home."

He bowed to Kirilin and walked quickly across the boulevard and down the street to Sheshkovsky's, where there were lights in the windows, and they heard the gate bang behind him.

"And now, if you please, I'd like to make myself clear," Kirilin began. "I'm not some little boy, some Achkasov, Lachkasov, or Zachkasov. . . . I demand serious attention."

Nadyezhda Fyodorovna's heart beat violently. She did not answer.

"The sudden change in your attitude to me I at first put down to coquetry," Kirilin went on. "Now, however, I see that you simply don't know how to treat a gentleman. You merely wanted to trifle with me, as you're doing with that Armenian brat, but I am a gentleman, and I insist on being treated as such. And so, I am at your service. . . ."

"I feel so miserable . . ." said Nadyezhda Fyodorovna, and she began to cry, turning away to hide her tears.

"I'm miserable too, but what of it?"

Kirilin remained silent for a moment and then, in distinct and measured tones, said:

"I repeat, madam, that if you do not give me a rendezvous this evening, I will make a scandal this very night."

"Let me go this evening," said Nadyezhda Fyodorovna, not recognizing her own voice, it was so weak and pitiful.

"I ought to teach you a lesson. . . . You must excuse my rough tone, but I am obliged to teach you a lesson. Yes . . . I regret to say, you must be given a lesson. I demand two meetings: tonight and tomorrow. After tomorrow you will be entirely free, and can go where you like and with whom you like. Tonight and tomorrow."

Nadyezhda Fyodorovna reached her gate and stopped.

"Let me go," she whispered, trembling all over and unable to see anything before her eyes but his white tunic. "You are right, I'm to blame, but let me go . . . I beg you. . . ." She touched his cold hand and shuddered. "I implore you. . . ."

"Alas!" sighed Kirilin. "Alas! It is not my plan to let you go, but to teach you a lesson, to make you understand. . . . And what's more, madam, I have too little faith in women."

"I'm so miserable. . . ."

Nadyezhda Fyodorovna listened to the steady roar of the sea, looked at the star-strewn sky, and longed to put a sudden end to all the abominable sensations of life with its sea, stars, men, fever. . . .

"Only not in my house," she said coldly. "Take me somewhere else."

"We'll go to Miuridov's. That's best."

"Where is that?"

"Near the old rampart."

She walked rapidly down the street and turned into a side street leading to the mountains. It was dark. Here and there a strip of light from a window fell across the pavement, and she felt like a fly that kept crawling into an inkwell, then out into the light. Kirilin followed her. At one point he stumbled, almost fell, and started laughing.

"He's drunk," thought Nadyezhda Fyodorovna. "It's all the same . . . all the same. . . . So be it."

Achmianov too was not long in taking his leave of the company; he followed Nadyezhda Fyodorovna, intending to ask her to go for a boat ride. When he reached her house he peered over the fence: the windows were wide open but there were no lights.

"Nadyezhda Fyodorovna!" he called.

A moment passed; he called again.

"Who's there?" It was Olga's voice.

"Is Nadyezhda Fyodorovna at home?"

"No. She hasn't come in yet."

"Strange. . . . Very strange . . ." thought Achmianov, beginning to feel uneasy. "She was on her way home. . . ."

He walked down the boulevard and turned into the street where he could see Sheshkovsky's windows. Layevsky was sitting at a table without his coat, looking intently at his cards.

"Strange . . . strange . . ." Achmianov muttered to himself; and, recollecting Layevsky's hysterics, he felt ashamed.

"If she's not at home, where is she?"

He walked back to her house and looked at the dark windows.

"It's a trick, a trick . . ." he thought, remembering that when they had met at the Bityugovs' at noon she had promised to go out in a boat with him in the evening.

The windows were dark in the house where Kirilin lodged, and a policeman was asleep on a bench at the gate. Looking at the windows and the policeman, suddenly everything became clear to Achmianov. He made up his mind to go home, but again found himself near Nadyezhda Fyodorovna's house. He felt his head burn with jealousy and humiliation, and, sitting down on the bench, took off his hat.

The church clock struck the hour only at noon and midnight. Shortly after it had struck midnight, there was a sound of hurried footsteps.

"Tomorrow evening, then, at Miuridov's!" Achmianov heard, and recognized Kirilin's voice. "At eight o'clock. Till then."

Nadyezhda Fyodorovna appeared near the fence. Not noticing Achmianov on the bench, she passed him like a shadow, opened the gate, and went into the house without closing it. In her own room she lit a candle and hastily undressed, but instead of going to bed she fell on her knees before a chair, encircling it with her arms and pressing her head against it.

It was past two when Layevsky came home.

# XV

Having made his decision to lie, not all at once, but little by little, Layevsky went to Samoilenko's the next day between one and two in the afternoon to ask for the money that would enable him to leave on Saturday without fail. After his attack of hysterics, which had added an acute sense of shame to his already depressed state of mind, it was unthinkable that he should remain in the town. If, however, Samoilenko were to insist on his conditions, he would agree to them, take the money, and the next day, at the very moment of departure, say that Nadyezhda Fyodorovna had refused to go; by that time he could easily convince her that it was all being done for her benefit. On the other hand, if Samoilenko, who was obviously under von Koren's influence, absolutely refused to give him the money, or proposed some new conditions, then he would leave that evening on a cargo ship, or even a sailing vessel, for New Athos or Novorossisk, send his mother an abject telegram, and stay there till she sent him the money to travel.

When he arrived at Samoilenko's he found von Koren in the drawing room. The zoologist had just come in for dinner and, as usual, was leafing through the album, scrutinizing the ladies and gentlemen in lace caps and top hats.

"How ill-timed!" thought Layevsky on seeing him. "He might interfere. . . . Good afternoon!"

"Good afternoon!" von Koren replied, without looking up.

"Is Aleksandr Davidych at home?"

"Yes. In the kitchen."

Layevsky went to the kitchen, but, seeing from the door that Samoilenko was busy with the salad, he went back to the drawing room and sat down.

He had always felt ill at ease in the zoologist's presence, and now he was afraid the conversation might turn on his attack of hysterics. More than a minute passed in silence. Von Koren suddenly raised his eyes to Layevsky and asked:

"How do you feel after yesterday?"

"Splendid!" Layevsky replied, flushing. "Actually, you know, it wasn't anything very much. . . ."

"Until yesterday I had assumed that only women had hysterics, so at first I thought that what you had was St. Vitus's dance."

Layevsky smiled ingratiatingly and thought:

"How tactless of him. He knows perfectly well how mortifying it is to me. . . . Yes," he said aloud, still smiling, "it was a ridiculous performance. I've been laughing about it all morning. The curious thing about an attack of hysterics is that you know it's absurd, at heart you are laughing, but at the same time you start sobbing. In our neurotic age we are all slaves to our nerves; they are our masters, and do as they will with us. In this respect civilization has done us a disservice. . . ."

As he talked he found it very disconcerting to have von Koren gravely and attentively listening to him, his eyes unblinking and intent, as though studying him; and he was vexed with himself for the ingratiating smile which, in spite of his dislike for von Koren, he was unable to remove from his face.

"Though I must confess," he continued, "there were more immediate reasons for the attack, and fairly basic ones too. My health has been exceedingly shaky of late. When you add to that the boredom, and being continually short of money . . . the lack of people and general interests . . . I've been in a tight spot."

"Yes, your situation is critical," said von Koren.

These calm cold words, in which there was something between a sneer and an uninvited prophecy, offended Layevsky. He recalled the zoologist's eyes the evening before, full of contempt and loathing; for a moment he could not speak, and when he did he was no longer smiling.

"And where do you get your information about my situation?"

"You just spoke of it yourself, and your friends take such a warm interest in you that one hears of nothing but you all day long."

"What friends? Samoilenko, I presume?"

"Yes, he too."

"I must ask Aleksandr Davidych, and my friends in general, to be less concerned about me."

"Here comes Samoilenko now; do ask him to be less concerned about you."

"I don't understand your tone," muttered Layevsky, and all at once he felt as if he had only just realized that the zoologist hated and despised him, was jeering at him, was his bitterest, most implacable enemy.

"Save that tone for somebody else," he said in a low voice, incapable of speaking loudly because of the hatred that suddenly gripped his chest and throat as the urge to laugh had gripped it yesterday.

Samoilenko came in without his coat, red-faced and perspiring from the stifling kitchen.

"Oh, you're here!" he said. "Greetings, my dear boy. Have you had dinner? Don't stand on ceremony: tell me, have you had dinner?"

"Aleksandr Davidych," said Layevsky, getting up, "when I appealed to you on a certain personal matter, it stands to reason that I did not release you from the obligation of being discreet and of respecting another man's confidence."

"What's this?" Samoilenko was dumfounded.

"If you haven't the money," continued Layevsky, raising his voice and shifting from one foot to the other in his agitation, "then don't give it, refuse it, but why announce in every back street that my situation is critical, and so on? I can't endure the sort of benevolence or good turn where there's a ruble's worth of talk and a kopeck's worth of help! You may boast of your benevolence as much as you please, but no one gave you the right to betray my confidence!"

"What confidence?" asked Samoilenko, puzzled and beginning to grow angry. "If you came here to be abusive, you'd better clear out and come back later."

He remembered the rule that when angry with anyone, mentally to count to a hundred, and he began counting rapidly.

"I beg you not to trouble yourself about me!" Layevsky went on. "Disregard me. And whose business is it what I do and how I live? Yes, I want to go away! Yes, I get into debt, drink, and am living with another man's wife! I'm hysterical and vulgar, and not so profound as some people —but whose business is that? Respect a man's privacy!"

"Excuse me, my friend," said Samoilenko, having counted up to thirty-five, "but——"

"Respect other people's privacy!" Layevsky interrupted him. "This continual talk on someone else's account, the oh-ing and ah-ing, the perpetual shadowing and eavesdropping, this friendly sympathy . . . to hell with it! They lend me money and make conditions as if I were a schoolboy! They treat me like God knows what! I don't want anything!" Layevsky shouted, reeling with emotion and fearing he might have another attack of hysterics. "This means I won't leave Saturday," flashed through his mind. "I don't want anything!" he went on. "All I ask is to be spared this supervision. I'm not a child, and I'm not a lunatic, and I ask you to release me from this surveillance!"

The deacon came in, and, seeing Layevsky pale, waving his arms about, and addressing this strange speech to the portrait of Prince Vorontsov, he stopped at the door transfixed.

"This constant prying into my soul," continued Layevsky, "is an insult to my dignity as a man, and I ask these volunteer detectives to stop their spying. I've had enough!"

"What did you . . . what did you say?" asked Samoilenko; after counting up to a hundred and turning purple, he now walked up to Layevsky.

"I've had enough!" Layevsky repeated, breathing heavily and snatching up his cap.

"I am a Russian physician, a nobleman, and a civil councilor!" said Samoilenko, articulating deliberately. "I have never been a spy, and I allow no one to insult me!" he shouted in a strident tone, emphasizing the last word. "Shut up!"

The deacon, who had never seen the doctor so majestic, so puffed up, flushed, and fierce, covered his mouth and ran out into the entry where he rocked with laughter.

As though in a fog, Layevsky saw von Koren get up, put his hands in his trouser pockets, and stand in an attitude of expectancy, waiting to see what would happen next; this calm air struck Layevsky as insolent and insulting to the highest degree.

"Kindly take back what you said!" shouted Samoilenko.

Layevsky, no longer remembering what he had said, replied:

"Leave me in peace! I don't want anything! All I ask is

that you and all the other Germans of Jewish extraction leave me alone! Otherwise I shall take steps! I will fight!"

"Now it's clear," said von Koren, coming out from behind the table. "Mr. Layevsky wants to divert himself with a duel before his departure. I can give him that satisfaction. Mr. Layevsky, I accept your challenge."

"Challenge?" Layevsky articulated softly, going up to the zoologist and looking with hatred at his swarthy forehead and curly hair. "Challenge? So be it! I hate you! Hate you!"

"Delighted. Tomorrow morning as early as possible near Kerbalai's. The details to your liking. And now, clear out!"

"I hate you!" said Layevsky in a low voice, breathing heavily. "I have hated you a long time. A duel! Yes!"

"Get him out of here, Aleksandr Davidych, or I'll leave," said von Koren. "He might bite me."

Von Koren's cool tone calmed the doctor; he seemed to recover himself and come to his senses with a start; putting his arms around Layevsky's waist he drew him away from the zoologist, mumbling affectionately in a voice that shook with emotion:

"My friends. . . . My dear, good . . . You lost your tempers, that's enough, now . . enough. . . . My friends. . . ."

At the sound of that soft, friendly voice, Layevsky felt that something unheard-of and monstrous had just happened to him, like nearly being run over by a train; he all but burst into tears, and with a gesture of despair ran from the room.

"To feel that you are hated, to expose yourself in the most pitiful, contemptible, helpless way to the man who hates you—my God, how deplorable!" he thought shortly afterward, as he sat in the pavilion feeling as if his body had suffered a blight from the hatred of which he had just been the object. "How gross it is, my God!"

Cognac and cold water lifted his spirits. He had a vivid mental image of von Koren's calm supercilious face, his eyes the day before, his ruglike shirt, white hands, and voice, and a heavy, passionate, ravening hatred churned in his breast, clamoring for satisfaction. He mentally struck von Koren to the ground and trampled on him. Recalling in the most minute detail all that had happened, he wondered how he could have smiled ingratiatingly at that insignificant man, and how, in general, he could value the opinions of petty and entirely unknown people who lived in an inconsequential town which, it appeared, was not even on the map, and which not one respectable person in Petersburg had ever heard of. If this miserable little town were to sink into the earth or burn down, a telegram conveying the news would be read in Russia with no more interest than an advertisement for the sale of second-hand furniture. Whether he killed von Koren tomorrow or let him remain alive was all the same, equally futile and uninteresting. To shoot him in the arm or leg, wound him, then laugh at him, and let him go like an insect with a broken leg that struggles in the grass, to let him, in his dumb misery, disappear in the crowd of those as insignificant as himself . . .

Layevsky went to Sheshkovsky, told him all about it, and asked him to be his second; then they both went to the head of the postal-telegraph office to ask him to be the other second, and stayed to have dinner with him. At dinner there was a great deal of joking and laughing, Layevsky making fun of his almost total inability to shoot, calling himself a royal archer and William Tell.

"This gentleman is in need of instruction . . ." he said.

After dinner they sat down to cards. As he played and drank wine, Layevsky thought to himself that a duel was stupid and absurd inasmuch as it never settled the question but only complicated it, and yet it was sometimes unavoidable. In the present case, for instance, one certainly couldn't take von Koren to court. And the impending duel was good in that it would make it impossible for him to remain in town. He got slightly drunk, enjoyed the game, and felt extremely well.

But when the sun had set and it grew dark he was overcome with anxiety. It was not fear of death, for as he was having dinner and playing cards he for some reason felt confident that the duel would come to nothing; it was fear of something unknown which was to take place tomorrow morning for the first time in his life, and fear of the approaching night. . . . He knew that the night would be long and sleepless, that he would have to think not only of von Koren and his hatred, but also of that mountain of lies he had to get through and which he had neither the strength nor the ability to dispense with. It was as though he had suddenly fallen ill; he instantly lost all interest in cards and in people, commenced fidgeting, and asked to be allowed to go home. He was eager to get into bed, to lie perfectly still and prepare his thoughts for the night. Sheshkovsky and the postal official accompanied him home and then went on to von Koren's to discuss the arrangements for the duel.

Near his own apartment Layevsky met Achmianov. The young man was breathless and excited.

"I've been looking for you, Ivan Andreich!" he said. "I beg you to come quickly. . . ."

"Where?"

"A gentleman you don't know wants to see you . . . on very important business. He urgently begs you to come for a minute. He wants to speak to you about something. It's a matter of life and death for him. . . ."

In his excitement Achmianov spoke with a strong Armenian accent.

"Who is this man?" asked Layevsky.

"He asked me not to mention his name."

"Tell him I'm busy. Tomorrow, if it's convenient . . ."

"Impossible!" Achmianov was aghast. "He wants to tell you something which is very important for you . . . very important! If you don't come, something dreadful will happen!"

"Strange," murmured Layevsky, unable to understand why Achmianov was so excited and what mystery there could be in this dull, superfluous little town. "Strange . . ." he repeated doubtfully. "However, let's go. It's all the same."

Achmianov quickly walked on ahead and Layevsky followed. They went down the street and turned into an alley.

"What a bore this is," said Layevsky.

"In a moment, in a moment . . . we're almost there."

Near the old rampart they went down a narrow alley between two fenced-in vacant lots, and through a large yard to a rather small house.

"This is Miuridov's house, isn't it?" asked Layevsky.

"Yes."

"But why we have come through these back yards I don't understand. We might have come by way of the street. It's nearer."

"Never mind, never mind. . . ."

Layevsky also found it strange that Achmianov led him to the back entrance, motioning him to go in quickly and not to speak.

"This way, this way . . ." said Achmianov, cautiously

opening the door and going into the entry on tiptoe. "Quickly, quickly, I beg you. They might hear."

He listened, drew a deep breath, and said in a whisper:

"Open that door and go in. . . . Don't be afraid."

Layevsky, bewildered, opened the door and went into a low-ceilinged room with curtained windows. There was a candle on the table.

"What do you want?" asked someone in the next room. "Is that you, Miuridov?"

Layevsky turned, went into the other room, and there saw Kirilin and Nadyezhda Fyodorovna side by side.

He did not hear what was said to him, but staggered back and reached the street without knowing how he got there. His hatred for von Koren, his anxiety—all vanished from his soul. As he went home he kept waving his right hand awkwardly and looking attentively at his feet, trying to walk where it was smooth. At home in his study he paced back and forth, rubbing his hands and twitching his shoulders and neck as if his jacket and shirt were too tight; then he lit a candle and sat down at the table. . . .

# XVI

"The humanities, of which you speak, will satisfy the human mind only at such time as they are led to converge with the exact sciences and progress side by side with them. Whether they will meet under a microscope, or in the soliloquies of a new Hamlet, or in a new religion, I do not know, but it is my belief that the earth will be covered with a crust of ice before it happens. The most enduring and vital of all humanitarian doctrines is, of course, the teachings of Christ; but look how variously they are interpreted! Some teach that we should love our neighbor, with the exception of soldiers, criminals, and lunatics: the first they permit to be killed in war, the second to be isolated or executed, and the third they forbid to marry. Other interpreters teach us to love all our neighbors without exception, making no distinction between the pluses and the minuses. According to their teachings, if a consumptive, a murderer, or an epileptic seeks your daughter in marriage—give her to him; if cretins make war on the physically and mentally healthy

—offer your heads. This preaching of love for love's sake, like art for art's sake, would lead in the end to the complete extinction of mankind, thereby perpetrating the most grandiose crime that has ever been committed on earth. The interpretations are exceedingly numerous, and since they are so numerous, the serious mind is not satisfied with any one of them and hastens to add its own. Therefore, never put a question, as you say, on philosophical or so-called Christian grounds: by so doing you simply further remove the question from a solution."

The deacon listened attentively to the zoologist, thought a moment, and then asked:

"Was the moral law, which is natural to every man, invented by philosophers, or did God create it together with the body?"

"I don't know. But this law is to such a high degree common to all peoples and all ages that I feel it ought to be recognized as being organically connected to man. It was not invented, but existed, and will continue to exist. I don't say that it will one day be seen under a microscope, but its organic connection has been manifestly proven: serious affections of the brain and all so-called mental diseases show themselves first, so far as I know, in a perversion of the moral law."

"Very well. So it follows that just as our stomach tells us to eat, so our moral sense bids us love our neighbor. Right? But our physical nature, through self-love, opposes the voice of conscience and reason, and this gives rise to many brain-racking questions. To whom are we supposed to turn for the solution of these problems, if you forbid our putting them on philosophical grounds?"

"Turn to what little exact science we have. Trust to the evidence and the logic of facts. True, it is scanty, but on the other hand, it is less vacillating and diffuse than philosophy. The moral law, let us assume, requires that you love people. Well? Love ought to include the removal of everything which one way or another is injurious to man, that threatens him with danger, either in the present or the future. Both our knowledge and the evidence tell us that the morally and physically abnormal are a threat to humanity. If this is so, then combat those who are abnormal. And if you are incapable of raising them to the level of normality, you must have the strength and the ability to render them harmless—that is, to exterminate them."

"In other words, love consists in the strong overcoming the weak."

"Precisely."

"But, you know, it was the strong who crucified our Lord Jesus Christ," said the deacon vehemently.

"The fact of the matter is that He was not crucified by the strong, but by the weak. Human culture has grown feeble and strives to nullify both the struggle for existence and natural selection, hence the rapid increase of the weak and their predominance over the strong. Imagine that you have succeeded in instilling—in a crude and elementary form—humanitarian ideas in bees. What would the result be? The drones, who ought to be killed, would remain alive, would eat up the honey, defile and overpower the bees—and the result would be the predominance of the weak over the strong and the degeneration of the latter. The same thing is happening now with humanity: the weak are oppressing the strong. Among savages, who so far remain untouched by culture, the strongest, wisest, and most moral takes the lead; he is chief and master. While we, who are cultured, crucified Christ and go on crucifying Him . . . which shows there is something lacking in us. . . . And this something we must renew in ourselves, or there will be no end to these errors."

"But what is your criterion for distinguishing the strong from the weak?"

"Knowledge and evidence. The tubercular and the scrofulous are recognized by their diseases, the immoral and the insane by their acts."

"But, after all, mistakes can be made!"

"Yes, but there's no use being afraid of wetting your feet when a flood is threatening."

"That's philosophy," laughed the deacon.

"Not at all. You're so corrupted by your seminary philosophy that you see nothing but fog in everything. The abstract sciences with which your young head is stuffed are called abstract because they abstract your mind from what is obvious. Look the devil straight in the eye, and if he is the devil, then say he's the devil, and don't go crawling to Kant or Hegel for explanations."

The zoologist paused for a moment and then went on:

"Twice two is four, and a stone's a stone. Tomorrow, now,

we have a duel. You and I will say it's stupid, absurd, that dueling has outlived its time, that there is no essential difference between the aristocratic duel and a drunken brawl in a tavern; nevertheless, we shall not abstain, we shall go and fight. So there is a force stronger than reason. We cry out that war is pillage, barbarism, atrocity, fratricide; we cannot look upon blood without fainting; but just let the French or the Germans insult us and we instantly feel our spirits rise, and with the greatest sincerity start shouting 'Hurrah!' and rush at the enemy; you will invoke God's blessing on our weapons, and our valor will arouse general, and what's more, sincere, enthusiasm. Again it follows that there is a force, which, if not higher, is stronger than ourselves and our philosophy. We can no more stop it than we can stop that cloud moving in from the sea. Don't be hypocritical, don't thumb your nose at it, and don't say: 'Oh, it's stupid! Oh, it's old-fashioned! Oh, it's not in accord with Scripture!' but look it straight in the eye, acknowledge its rational validity, and when, for instance, it is about to annihilate a rotten, scrofulous dissolute breed, don't interfere, with your pills and citations from your misunderstood Gospels. In Leskov we read of the conscientious Danila, who finds a leper on the outskirts of the town and feeds and warms him in the name of Christ and of love. If that Danila had really loved people, he would have dragged the leper as far as possible from the town, flung him into a pit, and gone on to serve the healthy. Christ, I hope, taught us a rational, intelligent, and practical love."

"What a funny fellow you are!" laughed the deacon. "Since you don't believe in Christ, why do you mention Him so frequently?"

"Yes, I do believe. But in my own way, of course, not in yours. Ah, Deacon, Deacon!" laughed the zoologist; he put his arm around his waist and gaily said:

"Well, what about it? Are you coming to the duel with us tomorrow?"

"My Orders do not permit it, otherwise I should come."

"What do you mean—Orders?"

"I have been ordained. I am in a state of grace."

"Oh, Deacon, Deacon," repeated von Koren, laughing. "I love talking to you."

"You say you have faith," said the deacon. "What kind of faith is that? Why, I have an uncle, a priest, who has such faith that in a time of drought, when he goes out in a field to pray for rain, he takes his umbrella and leather coat with him so he won't get wet on the way back. Now, that's faith! When he talks about Christ, a light radiates from him, and all the peasants, men and women, can be heard sobbing. He could turn that cloud back and put all those forces you talk of to flight. Yes . . . faith moves mountains."

The deacon laughed and clapped the zoologist on the shoulder.

"That's how it is . . ." he went on. "Here you are always teaching, sounding the depths of the sea, sorting out the weak and the strong, writing books, challenging people to duels—and everything remains as it was; but let some feeble old man with the holy spirit stammer just one word, or let a new Mohammed come galloping out of Arabia with a scimitar, and everything will be turned upside down; not one stone will be left standing on another in Europe."

"Well, Deacon, that's in the lap of the gods."

"Faith without works is dead, but works without faith— even worse, nothing but a waste of time, that's all."

The doctor appeared on the esplanade; seeing the deacon and the zoologist he went up to them.

"I believe everything is settled," he said, breathlessly. "Govorovsky and Boiko will be the seconds. They'll set out at five in the morning. How it has clouded over," he said, looking at the sky. "You can't see a thing. It's going to rain any minute."

"You're coming with us, I hope?" von Koren asked.

"No, God help me, I'm upset enough as it is. Ustimovich will go instead of me. I've already spoken to him."

There was a flash of lightning far out at sea followed by a hollow peal of thunder.

"How stifling it is before a storm!" said von Koren. "I'll bet you've already been to Layevsky's and wept on his bosom."

"Why should I go to him?" replied the doctor, disconcerted. "What next!"

Before sunset he had walked several times up and down the street and boulevard hoping to meet Layevsky. He was ashamed of his outburst and of the sudden rush of kindness that had followed it. He wanted to apologize to Layevsky in a jocular tone, scold him, reassure him, and tell him that dueling was a survival of medieval barbarism, but that

Providence itself had led them to this duel as a means of reconciliation: the next day both, being splendid men and of the greatest intelligence, after an exchange of shots would appreciate each other's nobility and become friends. But he had not encountered Layevsky.

"Why should I go to him?" Samoilenko repeated. "I didn't insult him, he insulted me. Tell me, please, why did he attack me? What harm had I done him? I walk into the drawing room, and suddenly, without rhyme or reason: Spy! How do you like that! Tell me, what started it? What had you said to him?"

"I told him his position was hopeless. And I was right. Only honest men or scoundrels can find a solution for every situation; but for someone who wants to be at the same time honest and a scoundrel, there is no solution. However, it's eleven o'clock, gentlemen, and we must get up early tomorrow."

There was a sudden gust of wind, raising the dust along the esplanade, whirling it into eddies, and drowning the sound of the sea with its roar.

"A squall!" said the deacon. "We'd better go, or our eyes will be filled with dust."

As they left, Samoilenko, clutching his cap, said with a sigh: "I probably won't sleep tonight."

"Don't agitate yourself," said the zoologist. "You can set your mind at rest: the duel will come to nothing. Layevsky, very chivalrously, will fire into the air—he can do nothing else—and I, very likely, shan't fire at all. To be arrested on Layevsky's account, and lose time—the game's not worth the candle. By the way, what is the penalty for dueling?"

"Arrest, and in the case of your opponent's death, imprisonment for up to three years."

"In the fortress of St. Peter and St. Paul?"

"No, in a military prison, I believe."

"Still, this fine fellow should be taught a lesson."

Lightning flashed over the sea behind them, illuminating the mountains and rooftops. Near the boulevard the friends parted. When the doctor had disappeared into the darkness and the sound of his footsteps had died away, von Koren called after him:

"Let's hope the weather won't interfere tomorrow!"

"It probably will! Please God it may!"

"Good night!"

"What about the night? What did you say?"

It was hard to hear over the thunder and the roar of wind and sea.

"Nothing!" the zoologist shouted and hurried home.


# XVII

> . . . and in my mind, oppressed with anguish,
> Crowd multitudes of grievous thoughts;
> In silence memory unfurls
> Its lengthy scroll before me.
> With loathing reading there my life
> I quake and curse and bitterly lament.
> But all the bitter tears I shed
> Will never wash away those lines.
>
> —PUSHKIN


Whether they killed him tomorrow or made a mockery of him—that is, left him his life—he was ruined in any case. Whether this dishonored woman killed herself from shame and despair or dragged out her pitiful existence—she was ruined in any case. . . .

So thought Layevsky as he sat at his table late in the evening still rubbing his hands. The window suddenly blew open with a bang; a violent wind rushed into the room and papers flew off the table. Layevsky closed the window and bent down to pick up the papers. He was aware of a new sensation in his body, a kind of awkwardness he had not felt before, and his own movements were unfamiliar to him; he walked without confidence, thrusting out his elbows and twitching his shoulders, and when he sat down at the table he immediately commenced rubbing his hands again. His body was no longer supple.

On the eve of death one ought to write to one's nearest relations. Thinking of this, he took up his pen and with a trembling hand wrote: "Mother."

He wanted to write and ask his mother, in the name of the merciful God in whom she believed, to give shelter and a little warmth and kindness to the unfortunate woman he had dishonored, who now was solitary, impoverished, and weak; to forget and forgive everything, everything, everything, and by her sacrifice to atone, at least in part, for her son's terrible sin; but remembering his mother, a stout, heavily built old woman in a lace cap, going out into the garden in the mornings followed by some hanger-on with the lapdog, remembering her proud haughty face and the way she imperiously shouted at the gardener and the servants, he scratched out the word he had written.

There was a flash of lightning in all three windows, followed by a deafening peal of thunder that began with a dull rumble and ended in a crash so violent that the windowpanes rattled. Layevsky got up, went to the window, and pressed his forehead against the pane. Outside there was a violent, magnificent storm. On the horizon white ribbons of lightning repeatedly flashed from the clouds into the sea, illuminating the huge black waves in the distance. He saw lightning on the right and on the left, and it undoubtedly was flashing above the house too.

"A storm!" whispered Layevsky; he felt a desire to pray to someone or to something, if only to the lightning or the clouds. "Dear storm!"

He recalled how as a child he had always run bareheaded into the garden when there was a storm, two fair-haired little girls with blue eyes chasing after him, and how they were drenched by the rain; the little girls would laugh with delight, but when there was a loud clap of thunder, they trustingly huddled up to the little boy, as he crossed himself and made haste to repeat: "Holy, holy, holy . . ." Oh, where have they gone, in what sea have they drowned, those early buds of a fair, pure life? He no longer feared a storm nor loved nature; he had no God; all the trusting little girls he had ever known had been ruined by him and his contemporaries; in his entire life he had never planted one tree nor grown a single blade of grass in his own garden; surrounded by living things, he had never saved so much as a fly, but had only destroyed, ruined, lied, and lied. . . .

"What in my past was not evil?" he asked himself, trying to clutch at some bright memory, as a man falling over a precipice clutches at a bush.

School? The university? But that was a sham. He had been a poor student and had forgotten what little he had learned. His service to his country? That too had been a sham, for he did nothing in the service, received a salary for no reason, and outrageously swindled the state without being prosecuted. He had had no need for truth, and had never sought it; his conscience, spellbound by evil and lies, had slept or kept silent; like an alien, or someone brought to Earth from another planet, he had taken no part in the common life of men, had been indifferent to their sufferings, ideas, religions, teachings, quests, and struggles; he had never said a kind word to anyone, nor written a single word that was not useless and commonplace; he had never done the least thing for others, but had eaten their bread, drunk their wine, stolen their wives, lived on their thoughts, and, to justify his parasitic life both to them and to himself, had always assumed a rather pretentious air, as if he were above them. Lies, lies, and more lies. . . .

The vivid memory of what he had seen that night at Miuridov's caused him unbearable disgust and anguish. Kirilin and Achmianov were loathsome, but they only continued what he had begun; they were his accomplices and disciples. He had taken a young, weak woman, who trusted him more than a brother, and, depriving her of husband, friends, and country, had brought her here—into this heat, and fever, and tedium; day in and day out, like a mirror, she was bound to reflect his idleness, viciousness, and lying—that was all she had to fill her weak, listless, pitiful existence; then he had grown sick of her, and, lacking the courage to leave her, had further enmeshed her in a web of lies. . . . These men had done the rest.

Layevsky sat down at the table, then walked to the window again; put out the candle, then lighted it again. He cursed himself aloud, wept, cried out, and asked forgiveness; several times he rushed to the table and wrote: "Mother."

Except for his mother he had no relations or close friends, but how could his mother help him? And where was she? He wanted to run to Nadyezhda Fyodorovna, fall at her feet, and beg her forgiveness; but she was his victim, he was as afraid of her as if she were dead.

"My life is ruined!" he muttered, rubbing his hands. "Why am I still alive, my God! . . ."

He had cast his own dim star out of the sky, and it had fallen, leaving no trace in the nocturnal darkness; it would not appear again in the sky, for life is given but once, never to return. If it had been possible to recover the past days and years, he would have replaced the lies with truth, the idleness with work, the boredom with joy; he would have restored purity to those he had robbed of it, would have

found God and righteousness; but that was as impossible as
to restore the fallen star to the sky. And because it was impossible, he was in despair.

When the storm was over, he sat by the open window and
calmly thought of what lay before him. Von Koren would
probably kill him. The man's clear cold philosophy of life
permitted the annihilation of the worthless and effete; if
it wavered at the decisive moment, the hatred and aversion
that Layevsky inspired in him would come to his aid. But
if he missed his aim, or, to mock his despised opponent,
merely wounded him or fired into the air, what could he do
then? Where could he go?

"To Petersburg?" he asked himself. "But that would mean
to begin anew the old life I've been cursing. And the man
who, like a bird of passage, seeks salvation in a change of
place, will find nothing: the whole world is the same for
him. Seek salvation in people? In whom and how? There is
no more salvation in Samoilenko's kindness and generosity
than there is in the deacon's laughter or von Koren's hatred.
One must look for salvation only in one's self, and if it
is not found there, why waste time?—one must kill oneself,
that's all. . . ."

There was the sound of a carriage. It was growing light.
The carriage passed, then turned, its wheels screaking on
the wet sand, and stopped near the house. There were two
men in it.

"Wait, I'll be there in a moment!" he said to them from
the window. "Surely it's not time yet?"

"Yes. Four o'clock. By the time we get there . . ."

Layevsky put on his overcoat and cap, put cigarettes in his
pocket, and stood irresolutely; it seemed to him that there
was something more to be done. In the street the seconds
were talking in low voices, the horses snorted, and these
sounds in the damp early morning, when everyone was asleep
and the sky was barely beginning to grow light, filled his
soul with a desolate feeling like a presentiment of evil. He
hesitated for a moment, then went into the bedroom.

Nadyezhda Fyodorovna lay stretched out on the bed,
wrapped from head to foot in a steamer rug; she did not
stir, and her whole appearance, especially her head, reminded him of an Egyptian mummy. Looking at her in silence, Layevsky mentally asked her forgiveness, and thought
that if heaven was not empty and there really was a God,

then He would save her; and if there was no God, then let her perish, there was no reason for her to live.

All at once she started and sat up in bed. Lifting her pale face and gazing in horror at Layevsky, she asked:

"Is it you? Is the storm over?"

"It's over."

And then she remembered; putting both hands to her head, she shuddered all over.

"How miserable I am!" she exclaimed. "If you only knew how miserable I am! I expected you to kill me," she went on, half closing her eyes, "or turn me out of the house into the rain and storm, but you keep delaying . . . delaying . . ."

He impetuously embraced her, and covered her hands and knees with kisses; when she murmured something, trembling at the recollection of the past, he stroked her hair, and looking into her face, he realized that this unhappy, sinful woman was the one person close to him, the only one whom nobody could replace.

When he left the house and got into the carriage, he knew that he wanted to come back alive.

# XVIII

The deacon got up, dressed, took his thick gnarled walking stick and quietly left the house. It was dark, and for the first few minutes he was unable to see even the white stick as he walked down the street; there was not a star in the sky and it looked as if it would rain again. A smell of wet sand and sea was in the air.

"Let's hope the Chechens don't attack," thought the deacon, as he listened to the loud and lonely echo of his stick tapping in the stillness of the night.

By the time he had left the town he was able to see both the stick and the road; dim spots appeared here and there in the sky and soon a star peeped out, timidly winking its single eye. Walking along the high rocky coast, the deacon could not see the water below; the sea slumbered, its unseen waves breaking indolently, sluggishly, on the shore, as if sighing: Ouf! And how slowly! One wave broke and the deacon counted eight steps before the next; six steps, then a third. As before, nothing was visible in the darkness, but one could hear the drowsy languid drone of the sea and sense the infinitely remote and inconceivable time when God moved over chaos.

The deacon felt apprehensive. He wondered if God would punish him for keeping company with unbelievers and even going to watch them duel. The duel would be trifling, bloodless, and absurd, but nonetheless a heathen spectacle at which it was thoroughly improper for a clergyman to be present. He stopped, wondering whether or not to turn back. But an intense, feverish curiosity withered his doubts and he went on.

"Even though they are unbelievers, they're good people and they will be saved," he reassured himself. "They're bound to be saved!" he said aloud, lighting a cigarette.

By what standard should one measure a man's worth in order to judge him rightly? The deacon thought of his enemy, the inspector of the clerical school, who believed in God, lived a chaste life, and did not fight duels, but who used to feed him bread with sand in it, and once had almost torn off his ear. If human life was so unwisely arranged that everyone in the school could respect and pray for the health and salvation of this cruel dishonest man who stole government flour, was it then just to shun men like von Koren and Layevsky simply because they were unbelievers? The deacon tried to resolve this question, but the recollection of how ridiculous Samoilenko had looked yesterday interrupted his train of thought. What a good laugh they would have tomorrow! The deacon pictured himself hiding behind a bush and watching, and tomorrow, when von Koren began boasting at dinner, he, the deacon, would laughingly recount all the details of the duel.

"And how do you know all this?" the zoologist would ask.

"I just do! I stayed at home, but I know."

It would be fine to write about the duel in a comic vein. His father-in-law would read it and laugh; a good story, written or told, was meat and drink to his father-in-law.

The valley of the Yellow River opened out ahead. The stream was wider and more fierce after the rain, and instead of murmuring, as before, it roared. Dawn was beginning to break. The gray misty morning, the clouds racing to the west to overtake the thunderhead, the mountains girded with mist, and the wet trees, all struck the deacon as ugly and wrathful. He washed in the stream, said his morning prayers, and felt a longing for the tea and hot buns with

sour cream that were served at his father-in-law's table every
morning. He thought of the deaconess and "The Days Beyond Recall" which she played on the piano. What sort of
woman was she? The deacon had been introduced, betrothed,
and married to her all in one week; he had lived with her
less than a month when he was ordered here, so that he had
not yet found out what she was like. All the same, he
rather missed her.

"I must write her a few lines . . ." he thought.

The rain-soaked flag on the fishing lodge hung limp, and
the lodge itself, with its wet roof, looked darker and lower
than before. A nomad cart stood at the door; Kerbalai with
two Abkhazians and a young Tartar woman in full trousers, probably his wife or daughter, were carrying sacks
of something out of the house and putting them in the
cart, the bottom of which was covered with maize straw.
Near the cart stood a pair of donkeys, their heads lowered.
When the sacks had been put into the cart, the Abkhazians
and the Tartar woman began covering them with straw, and
Kerbalai hurriedly harnessed the donkeys.

"Smuggling, no doubt," thought the deacon.

There was the fallen tree with the dried needles, and there
the black patch where the camp fire had been. He remembered every detail of the picnic: the fire, the singing of the
Abkhazians, his sweet dreams of the religious procession and
of becoming a bishop. . . . The Black River had grown
blacker and broader from the rain. The deacon cautiously
crossed the frail little bridge, now touched by the crests of
the muddy water, and climbed the ladder to the drying shed.

"A splendid mind!" he thought of von Koren as he
stretched out on the straw. "A fine mind, God grant him
health. Only there's something cruel about him. . . ."

Why did he and Layevsky hate each other? Why were
they going to fight a duel? If they had known the poverty he
had known since childhood, if they had grown up among
ignorant, hard-hearted, grasping, coarse and ill-mannered
people who grudged you a crust of bread, spat on the floor
and belched at dinner and at prayers; if, from childhood, they
had not been spoiled by pleasant surroundings and a select
group of friends, how they would have reached out to each
other, how readily forgiven one another's shortcomings,
valuing what was good in the other. Why, there were so few
even outwardly decent people in the world! True, Layevsky

was flighty, dissipated, and strange, but, after all, he didn't steal, didn't spit loudly on the floor, or abuse his wife, saying: "You'll eat till you burst, but you won't work"; nor would he beat a child with harness reins, nor feed his servants putrid salt meat—surely this was reason enough to treat him with forbearance? Besides, he was the first to suffer from his failings, like a sick man from his sores. Instead of being induced, either by boredom or some sort of misunderstanding, to look for degeneracy, extinction, heredity, and other such incomprehensible things in one another, would it not be better to stoop a little lower and direct their hatred and anger to where whole streets were groaning with gross ignorance, greed, impurity, cursing and screaming? . . .

The sound of a vehicle interrupted the deacon's thoughts. He looked out the door and saw a carriage with three men in it: Layevsky, Sheshkovsky, and the head of the postal-telegraph office.

"Stop!" said Sheshkovsky.

All three got out of the carriage and looked at one another.

"They're not here yet," said Sheshkovsky, shaking off the mud. "Well? Let's get the lay of the land and find a suitable spot. There isn't room to turn around here."

They went farther up the river and soon vanished from sight. The Tartar coachman sat in the carriage, his head on one shoulder, and fell asleep. After waiting ten minutes, the deacon came out of the drying shed, took off his black hat to avoid being noticed, looked about, then crouched down and began making his way between the bushes and rows of maize along the bank; he was sprinkled with big drops of water from the trees and maize; everything was wet.

"What a shame!" he muttered, picking up his wet, muddy skirt. "Had I known, I wouldn't have come."

Before long he heard voices and caught sight of three men; Layevsky, with hunched shoulders and hands in his sleeves, was pacing rapidly to and fro in a small glade; his seconds stood on the bank rolling cigarettes.

"Strange . . ." thought the deacon, not recognizing Layevsky's gait. "He looks like an old man."

"What bad manners!" said the postal official, looking at his watch. "It may be all very cultured and fine to be late, but to my way of thinking, it's swinish."

Sheshkovsky, a stout man with a black beard, stood listening.

"They're coming!" he said.

# XIX

"I'm seeing it for the first time in my life! How glorious!" said von Koren, as he appeared in the glade with both arms outstretched to the east. "Look: green rays!"

In the east, from behind the mountains, rose two green streaks of light, which were, in fact, beautiful. The sun was rising.

"Good morning!" the zoologist continued, nodding to Layevsky's seconds. "I'm not late, am I?"

Behind him came his seconds, Boiko and Govorovsky, two very young officers of identical height in white tunics, and the gaunt unsociable Dr. Ustimovich, carrying a parcel of some sort in one hand, the other, as usual, holding his walking stick stretched along his back. He set the parcel on the ground, put the other hand behind his back, and commenced pacing up and down the glade.

Layevsky felt the weariness and awkwardness of a man who is perhaps soon to die, and is for that reason the object of general interest. He wanted to be killed as quickly as possible or else taken home. For the first time in his life he was seeing the sunrise; the early morning, the green rays of light, the dampness, and the people in wet boots, all seemed to have nothing to do with his life, they were superfluous and embarrassed him; none of it had anything to do with the night he had lived through, or with his thoughts and feelings of guilt, and he would gladly have left without waiting for the duel.

Von Koren was noticeably excited and trying to hide it, pretending that nothing interested him so much as the green rays. The seconds were confused and exchanged glances as though asking one another why they were there and what they were to do.

"I assume there's no point in going farther, gentlemen," said Sheshkovsky. "This place will do."

"Yes, of course," von Koren agreed.

A silence followed. Ustimovich, who had been pacing, suddenly made an abrupt turn to Layevsky and said in a low voice, breathing in his face:

"They probably haven't had time to inform you of my terms. Each side pays me fifteen rubles, and in the event of a death, the survivor pays the whole thirty."

Layevsky had met the man before, but only now for the first time did he clearly observe his dull eyes, bristling mustache, and wasted consumptive neck: a usurer, not a physician! His breath had a disagreeable meaty smell.

"What people there are in the world!" thought Layevsky, and replied: "Very well."

The doctor nodded and commenced pacing again; clearly, he did not need the money, but asked for it simply out of animosity. Everyone felt it was time to begin, or to finish what had been begun, but instead of either beginning or ending they walked about or stood and smoked. The young officers, who were present at a duel for the first time in their lives, and had very little confidence in this civilian—and, to their way of thinking, pointless—duel, were scrutinizing their tunics and smoothing their sleeves. Sheshkovsky went up to them and said:

"Gentlemen, we must make every effort to prevent this duel from taking place. They ought to be reconciled." He turned red and continued: "Yesterday Kirilin came to see me, bemoaning the fact that Layevsky had found Nadyezhda Fyodorovna with him . . . and all that sort of thing."

"Yes, we know about that too," said Boiko.

"Well, you see now . . . Layevsky's hands are trembling, and all that sort of thing. . . . He wouldn't even be able to lift a pistol. Fighting with him would be as inhuman as fighting with a man who is drunk or who has typhus. If a reconciliation cannot be arranged, we ought to postpone the duel, perhaps. . . . It's a hellish business. I don't even want to look at it."

"You should talk to von Koren."

"I don't know the rules of dueling, damn it all, and I don't want to; he may think Layevsky's a coward and has sent me to talk to him. Well, let him think what he likes, I'll speak to him."

Sheshkovsky irresolutely turned, walking toward von Koren with a slight limp, as though his foot had gone to sleep, his whole figure the picture of indolence as he moved toward him, clearing his throat.

"There's something I must say to you, sir," he began, looking intently at the flowers on the zoologist's shirt. "This is confidential. . . . I don't know the dueling rules, damn it all, and I don't care to; I'm speaking not as a second, and all that sort of thing, but as a man, and so on."

"Yes. Well?"

"When the seconds propose a reconciliation, generally nobody listens to them; it's regarded as a formality. Pride and all that. But I humbly beg you to observe Ivan Andreich. He is not in a normal state today, not in his right mind so to speak, he's pitiful. He has had a misfortune. I can't endure gossip——" Sheshkovsky reddened and glanced around, "but in view of the duel, I find it necessary to inform you that last night, at Miuridov's, he found his lady with . . . a certain gentleman."

"How revolting!" muttered the zoologist; he turned pale, knit his brows, and spat loudly: "Tfoo!"

His lower lip began to tremble and he walked away from Sheshkovsky; then, as if he had unexpectedly tasted something bitter, once again loudly spat, and for the first time that morning turned a look of hatred on Layevsky. His excitement and awkwardness had passed; he threw back his head and in a loud voice said:

"Gentlemen, what are we waiting for, I should like to know? Why don't we begin?"

Sheshkovsky exchanged glances with the officers and shrugged his shoulders.

"Gentlemen!" he said loudly, addressing no one in particular. "Gentlemen! We propose a reconciliation!"

"Let's get the formalities over with as quickly as possible," said von Koren. "Reconciliation has already been discussed. Now what is the next formality? Make haste, gentlemen, time will not wait."

"All the same, we insist on a reconciliation," said Sheshkovsky in the guilty tone of a man obliged to interfere in the affairs of others; he flushed, put his hand on his heart, and continued: "Gentlemen, we see no grounds for associating the affront with a duel. The offenses we occasionally inflict on one another through human weakness have nothing to do with dueling. You are university men, cultivated, and doubtless you yourselves see nothing in a duel but an obsolete and hollow formality, and all that sort of thing. We look on it in the same way, otherwise we shouldn't have come, as we cannot countenance people shooting one another in our presence, and so on." Sheshkovsky wiped the perspiration from his face and went on: "Put an end to your misunderstanding, gentlemen, shake hands, and let us go home and drink the cup of peace. On my word, gentlemen!"

Von Koren did not speak. Layevsky, seeing that he was looking at him, said:

"I have nothing against Nikolai Vassilyevich. If he considers me to blame, I am ready to apologize."

Von Koren was outraged.

"It is obvious, gentlemen," he said, "that you would like to see Mr. Layevsky return home a magnanimous and chivalrous figure, but I am unable to afford you and him this satisfaction. And there was no need for you to get up early and drive ten versts out of town to drink the cup of peace, have a bite to eat, and explain to me that a duel is an obsolete formality. A duel is a duel, and there is no reason to make it any more false and stupid than it already is. I want to fight!"

A silence followed. Boiko took a pair of pistols out of a box: one was given to von Koren and one to Layevsky, after which there was a certain confusion, momentarily amusing to the zoologist and the seconds. It appeared that not one of them had ever been present at a duel before, and nobody knew exactly how they ought to stand or what the seconds were supposed to say and do. But then Boiko remembered, and with a smile commenced explaining.

"Gentlemen, who remembers how it is described in Lermontov?" asked von Koren, laughing. "In Turgenev, too, Bazarov exchanges shots with someone. . . ."

"What is there to remember?" said Ustimovich impatiently, and he stopped pacing. "Measure the distance—that's all."

And he took three steps, as if to demonstrate how the measuring ought to be done. Boiko counted off the paces and his companion drew his saber and scratched a mark on the ground to indicate the boundaries at either end.

There was complete silence as the opponents took their places.

"Moles," recalled the deacon, who was sitting in the bushes.

Sheshkovsky said something, Boiko explained something again, but Layevsky did not hear, or rather heard, but did not understand. When the time came, he cocked the pistol and raised the cold heavy weapon with the barrel pointing upward. He forgot to unbutton his overcoat, and it felt very tight in the shoulder and under the arm, and he lifted his arm as awkwardly as if his sleeve were made of tin. Remembering the hatred he had felt the day before for that swarthy brow and curly hair, he thought that even then, in a moment of intense hatred and anger, he could not have shot a man. Fearing that the bullet might somehow hit von Koren by accident, he raised the pistol higher and higher, and he felt that this ostentatious magnanimity was tactless and not at all magnanimous, but he could not do otherwise. Looking at von Koren's pale face and mocking smile, it was clear that he had been certain from the very beginning that his adversary would fire into the air, and Layevsky thought that now, thank God, everything would be over, that he had only to squeeze the trigger harder. . . .

His shoulder jerked violently from the kick of the pistol; a shot rang out, followed by an echo in the mountains: pah-tah!

Von Koren too had cocked his pistol; he glanced in the direction of Ustimovich, who continued his pacing, hands behind his back, paying no attention to anything.

"Doctor," said the zoologist, "be so good as to stop moving to and fro like a pendulum. You distract my vision."

The doctor stood still. Von Koren took aim at Layevsky.

"Finished!" thought Layevsky.

The barrel of the pistol, aimed directly at his face, the expression of hatred and contempt in von Koren's stance and his whole body, the murder that was about to be committed by a decent man in broad daylight in the presence of other decent men, the stillness, and the unknown power that compelled Layevsky to stand still and not run—how mysterious, how incomprehensible and terrible it all was! The time it took von Koren to aim seemed longer than a night to Layevsky. He looked imploringly at the seconds; they were motionless and pale.

"Fire, and be quick!" thought Layevsky, feeling that his pale, quivering face must arouse even greater hatred in von Koren.

"Now I shall kill him," thought von Koren, aiming at Layevsky's forehead and fingering the trigger. "Yes, I shall certainly kill him. . . ."

"He'll kill him!" A despairing cry was heard from somewhere very near.

At that moment the shot rang out. Seeing Layevsky standing in the same spot, still on his feet, everyone looked in the direction of the cry and saw the deacon. He was standing in the maize on the opposite bank, pale, his wet hair sticking to his forehead and cheeks, completely drenched and muddy, waving his wet hat and smiling somewhat strangely. Sheshkovsky laughed for joy, burst into tears, and walked away. . . .

# XX

Shortly afterward von Koren and the deacon met near the little bridge. The deacon, excited and breathing heavily, avoided looking von Koren in the eye.

"It looked to me as if you intended to kill him . . ." he mumbled. "How contrary to human nature that is! How completely unnatural."

"And how did you get here?" asked the zoologist.

"Don't ask!" replied the deacon with a gesture of despair. "The Evil One tempted me, saying: 'Go, go on. . . .' So I came, and almost died of fright there in the maize. But now, thank God, thank God . . . I am highly pleased with you . . ." he mumbled. "And old Grandpa-Tarantula will be pleased. . . . It's funny, really funny! Only I beg you most urgently not to tell anyone I was here, or I may get it in the neck from the authorities. They'll say: 'The deacon was a second.' "

"Gentlemen!" said von Koren. "The deacon asks you not to tell anyone you saw him here. The consequences might be unpleasant."

"How contrary to human nature!" said the deacon. "Kindly forgive me, but the expression on your face made me think you were surely going to kill him."

"I was very much tempted to put an end to that scoundrel," said von Koren, "but you shouted so close at hand that I missed my aim. However, the whole procedure is revolting to anyone not used to it, and it has worn me out, Deacon. I feel utterly exhausted. Let us go. . . ."

"No, you must allow me to go on foot. I shall have to get dry, for I'm wet through and chilled."

"As you wish," said the exhausted zoologist in a weary tone, and he got into the carriage and closed his eyes. "As you wish. . . ."

While they were walking around the carriages and taking their places, Kerbalai stood in the road, his hands clasped over his stomach, bowing low and showing his teeth; he thought the gentlemen had come to enjoy nature and drink tea, and could not understand why they were getting into their carriages.

They set out in absolute silence, leaving only the deacon standing near the lodge.

"Come lodge, drink tea," he said to Kerbalai. "Me want eat."

Kerbalai spoke perfectly good Russian, but the deacon thought the Tartar would understand him better if he spoke to him in broken Russian.

"Give omelette, give cheese. . . ."

"Come, come, Father," said Kerbalai bowing. "There is cheese, there is wine. . . . Eat whatever you like."

"How do you say 'God' in Tartar?" the deacon asked as he went into the lodge.

"Your God and my God are the same," said Kerbalai, not understanding him. "God is the same for all, only people are different. Some are Russians, some are Turks, some are English—all kinds of people, but God is one."

"Very good. If all men worship the same God, then why do you Muslims look upon Christians as your eternal enemies?"

"Why are you angry?" asked Kerbalai, clasping his hands over his stomach. "You are a priest, I am a Muslim—you say you want to eat, I give you food. . . . Only the rich decide which is your God and which is mine, to the poor it is all the same. Eat, if you please."

While this theological discussion was taking place in the lodge, Layevsky was driving home, remembering how dreadful it had been for him to leave at dawn, when the road, the rocks, and mountains were dark and wet and an unknown future lay before him as terrifying as a bottomless abyss; while now the raindrops clinging to the grass and stones sparkled like diamonds in the sun, nature smiled joyously, and the dreadful future had been left behind. He looked at Sheshkovsky's morose, tear-stained face, at the two carriages ahead in which von Koren, his seconds, and the doctor rode, and he felt as if they were all returning from a graveyard, where they had just buried an unbearably difficult man who had been a burden to everyone.

"It's all over," he thought of his past as he cautiously stroked his neck with his fingers.

On the right side of his neck near the collar there was a small swelling, the length and breadth of his little finger; it was painful, as if a hot iron had grazed his neck. This was a contusion caused by the bullet.

Later, when he reached home, there stretched before him a long, strange, sweet day, as misty as slumber. Like a man released from prison or a hospital, he stared at long-familiar objects and marveled that tables, windows, chairs, the light, the sea, all stirred in him a keen, childish delight, such as he had not known for many many years.

Nadyezhda Fyodorovna, pale and haggard, could not understand his gentle voice and unfamiliar bearing; she hurriedly told him everything that had happened to her. . . . It seemed to her that he scarcely heard and did not understand, and that if he knew everything he would curse her, kill her; but he listened, stroking her face and hair, and looked into her eyes.

"I have no one but you . . ." he said.

Then they sat in the garden for a long time, huddled together, saying nothing, or dreaming aloud in brief, broken phrases of a future happy life, and it seemed to him that he had never before spoken at such length or so eloquently.

## XXI

More than three months had passed.

The day set by von Koren for his departure had come. A cold heavy rain had been falling since early morning, a northeast wind was blowing, and the waves rose high on the sea. It was said that the steamer could hardly put into the roadstead in such weather. According to the schedule, it should have arrived at ten in the morning, but von Koren, who had gone down to the shore at midday and again after dinner, saw nothing through his binoculars except gray waves and rain curtaining the horizon.

Toward the end of the day the rain ceased and the wind dropped perceptibly. Von Koren had become reconciled to the thought of not getting away that day, and had settled down to play chess with Samoilenko, but when it grew dark the orderly announced that there were lights on the sea and a rocket had been seen.

Von Koren made haste. He put his satchel over his shoulder, embraced Samoilenko and the deacon, and, though there was not the slightest necessity, went through all the rooms again, then said good-bye to the cook and the orderly and went out into the street feeling that he had forgotten something, either at the doctor's or at his own apartment. He and Samoilenko walked down the street side by side, followed by the deacon carrying a small trunk, and last of all the orderly with two suitcases. Only Samoilenko and the orderly could make out the dim lights on the sea; the others peered into the darkness seeing nothing. The steamer stood at a distance offshore.

"Faster, faster!" von Koren hurried them. "I'm afraid it will leave!"

As they passed the little house with three windows into which Layevsky had moved shortly after the duel, von Koren could not refrain from glancing at the window. Layevsky sat bent over a table writing, his back to the window.

"It's amazing," said the zoologist softly, "how he has buckled down!"

"Yes, one may well be amazed," sighed Samoilenko. "He sits like that from morning till evening, just sits and works. He wants to pay off his debts. And, brother, he lives worse than a pauper."

There was a momentary silence. The zoologist, the doctor, and the deacon stood at the window watching Layevsky.

"And he never got away from here, poor fellow," said Samoilenko. "Do you remember what an effort he made?"

"Yes, he has certainly buckled down," repeated von Koren. "His marriage, the way he works all day long for a crust of bread, a certain new expression in his face and even in his walk—it's all so extraordinary that I don't know what to call it."

The zoologist took Samoilenko by the sleeve and continued with emotion in his voice:

"Tell him and his wife that when I left I was full of admiration for them, and wished them all the best . . . and ask him, if it is possible, not to think ill of me. He knows me. He knows that if I could have foreseen this change in him I might have become his best friend."

"Go in and say good-bye."

"No. It's awkward. . . ."

"Why? God knows, you may never see him again."

The zoologist reflected and said:

"That's true."

Samoilenko tapped lightly on the window. Layevsky started and looked around.

"Vanya, Nikolai Vassilyevich wants to say good-bye to you," said Samoilenko. "He's about to leave."

Layevsky got up from the table and went into the entry to open the door. Samoilenko, von Koren, and the deacon went into the house.

"I can only stop for a minute," the zoologist began, taking off his galoshes in the entry and already regretting that he had given way to his feelings and come in uninvited. "I feel as if I were intruding," he thought, "and it's stupid."

"Forgive me for disturbing you," he said, following Layevsky into the room, "but I'm just leaving, and I felt like seeing you. God knows whether we shall ever meet again."

"I'm delighted. . . . Please sit down," said Layevsky, and he awkwardly placed chairs for his guests as if he were trying to bar their way, then stood in the middle of the room rubbing his hands.

"Too bad I didn't leave my witnesses outside," thought von Koren, and resolutely said: "Don't bear me ill will, Ivan Andreich. To forget the past is, of course, impossible, it's too painful, and I have not come here to apologize or to contend that I was blameless. I acted in good faith and have not altered my convictions since. . . . It's true, as I now see to my great joy, that I was mistaken about you, but, you see, one can stumble even on a smooth road, such is our human fate: if one does not err in the main, one errs in the particulars. Nobody knows the real truth."

"No, nobody knows the truth . . ." said Layevsky.

"Well, good-bye . . . God give you all the best."

Von Koren held out his hand to Layevsky, who pressed it and bowed.

"Don't bear me ill will," said von Koren. "My greetings to your wife, and tell her I very much regret that I could not say good-bye to her."

"She is at home."

Layevsky went to the door of the next room and said:

"Nadya, Nikolai Vassilyevich wants to say good-bye to you."

Nadyezhda Fyodorovna came in; she stopped near the door and glanced shyly at the visitors. She looked guilty and apprehensive, holding her hands like a schoolgirl who is being reprimanded.

"I am going away now, Nadyezhda Fyodorovna," said von Koren, "and I've come to say good-bye."

She held out her hand uncertainly and Layevsky bowed.

"How pitiful they both are!" thought von Koren. "This life of theirs has cost them dear."

"I shall be in Moscow and Petersburg; is there anything I can send you?" he asked.

"Well . . ." Nadyezhda Fyodorovna glanced anxiously at her husband. "I don't think there's anything. . . ."

"No, nothing . . ." said Layevsky, rubbing his hands. "Our regards."

Von Koren did not know what more could or should be said, although as he came in he thought he would say a great deal that would be warm, good, important. He silently shook hands with Layevsky and his wife, and left them with a heavy feeling.

"What people!" said the deacon in an undertone, as he walked behind them. "My God, what people! Verily the right hand of God hath planted this vine. Lord, Lord! One vanquishes thousands, another tens of thousands. Nikolai Vassilyevich," he said in exaltation, "you know, today you have conquered the greatest of man's enemies—pride!"

"Come now, Deacon! What sort of conquerors are we! Conquerors vanquish eagles, but he's a pitiful figure, timid, crushed, bowing like a Chinese manikin, and I . . . it makes me sad. . . ."

They heard steps behind them. It was Layevsky coming to see him off. The orderly was on the wharf with the two suitcases, and at a little distance stood four boatmen.

"It's really blowing . . . brrr!" said Samoilenko. "There must be quite a gale at sea—oh, oh! You're going at a bad time, Kolya."

"I'm not afraid of seasickness."

"That's not the point. . . . I only hope these idiots don't capsize the boat. You ought to have gone out in the agent's sloop. Where is the agent's sloop?" he shouted to the oarsmen.

"It's gone, Your Excellency."

"And the customs boat?"

"It's gone too."

"Why didn't they announce it?" Samoilenko grew angry. "Blockheads!"

"It doesn't matter, don't worry . . ." said von Koren. "Well, good-bye. God keep you."

Samoilenko embraced von Koren and made the sign of the cross over him three times.

"Don't forget us, Kolya. . . . Write. . . . We'll expect you next spring."

"Good-bye Deacon," said von Koren, shaking hands with

him. "Thanks for your company and all the good talk. Think about the expedition."

"Lord, yes! To the ends of the earth!" laughed the deacon. "Do you think I'm opposed to it?"

Von Koren made out Layevsky in the dark and held out his hand without speaking. The oarsmen were now standing below holding the boat, which was beating against the piles, though the jetty screened it from the heavy sea swell. Von Koren descended the ladder, jumped into the boat, and sat at the tiller.

"Write!" Samoilenko shouted to him. "Take care of yourself!"

"Nobody knows the real truth," thought Layevsky, turning up the collar of his overcoat and thrusting his hands into his sleeves.

The boat swiftly left the wharf for the open sea. It disappeared into the waves only to reappear, coming up out of a deep hollow onto a high crest, so that the men and even the oars were distinguishable. For every three yards that the boat advanced, it was hurled back two.

"Write!" shouted Samoilenko. "Why the devil do you have to go off in such weather!"

"Yes . . . nobody knows the real truth . . ." thought Layevsky, gazing with longing at the dark turbulent sea. "The boat is thrown back; she makes two paces forward and one back, but the oarsmen persevere, they row indefatigably and are not afraid of the high waves. The boat goes on and on; now it's out of sight, but in half an hour the boatmen will see the steamer lights distinctly, and in an hour they'll be alongside its ladder. So it is in life. . . . In the search for truth men make two paces forward and one back. Mistakes, suffering, and the tedium of life force them back, but the thirst for truth and a stubborn will drives them on and on. And who knows? Perhaps they will arrive at the real truth. . . ."

"Good-by-y-ye!" shouted Samoilenko.

"There's not a sign of them," said the deacon. "Happy journey!"

A light rain began to fall.

1891

# A DULL STORY

## (From the Notebook of an Old Man)

## I

There lives in Russia a certain Honored Professor Nikolai Stepanovich, privy councilor and knight, who has received so many decorations, both Russian and foreign, that when he has occasion to wear them all, his students call him "the icon stand." He moves in the most aristocratic circles, and, for the last twenty-five or thirty years at least, there has not been a single eminent scholar with whom he has not been intimately acquainted. Now there is no one for him to be friends with, but if one speaks of the past, the long list of his distinguished acquaintances comes to an end with such names as Pirogov, Kalenin, and the poet Nekrasov, all of whom gave him the warmest and most sincere friendship. He is an honorary member of the faculty of every Russian university and of three universities abroad. And so forth and so on. All this, and a great deal more that might be said, constitutes what is called my "name."

This name of mine is well known. Every educated man in Russia is familiar with it, and abroad it is never mentioned in a lecture hall without adding the words "celebrated and esteemed." It is one of the few fortunate names which it is considered bad taste to take in vain, to abuse in public or in print. And that is as it should be. After all, my name is closely connected with the concept of a man who is famous, richly endowed, and unquestionably useful. I am as hardworking and persevering as a camel, and this is important; and I am gifted, which is even more important. Furthermore —and it may as well be said—I am an honest, well-bred, unassuming fellow. I have never poked my nose into

163

literature or politics, never sought popularity by entering
into polemics with ignoramuses, never made speeches at
banquets or over the graves of my colleagues. . . . All things
considered, my academic name is without blemish and beyond reproach. A fortunate name.

The bearer of this name, which is to say myself, appears to
be a man of sixty-two, bald, with false teeth and an in-
curable tic. My person is as drab and ugly as my name is
illustrious and beautiful. Both my head and my hands shake
from weakness, my neck, as Turgenev says of one of his
heroines, is like the finger board of a double bass, my chest
is hollow, my shoulders narrow. When talking or lecturing,
my mouth twists to one side, and when I smile my face is a
mass of hoary, cadaverous wrinkles. There is nothing imposing about my miserable figure, except perhaps when I
undergo a seizure of my tic, at which time a rather peculiar
expression comes over my face that must suggest to anyone
looking at me the grimly imposing thought: "This man, apparently, has not long to live."

I can still lecture fairly well; as in the past, I am able
to hold the attention of my listeners for two consecutive
hours. My fervor, humor, and command of language make
the defects of my voice pass almost unnoticed, despite the
fact that it is dry, cracked, and makes me sound like a cant-
ing Pharisee. But I write badly. That segment of my brain
which directs the faculty of writing refuses to work. My
memory is impaired, there is a lack of sequence in my
thoughts, and when I set them down on paper it always seems
to me that I have lost the knack of integrating them; the construction is monotonous, the sentences timid and insipid. I
frequently write what I do not mean, and by the time I come
to the end I have forgotten the beginning. Often I forget
the simplest words and am continually forced to waste a
great deal of time and energy trying to avoid superfluous
phrases and unnecessary parenthetical clauses—both obvious signs of the decline of my mental processes. And it is
remarkable that the simpler the letter, the greater the strain
to write it. I feel far more fluent and intelligent writing a
scientific article than a letter of congratulation or a report.
And another thing: I find it easier to write in German or
English than in Russian.

As regards my present way of life, I must note first of all
insomnia, from which I have been suffering of late. If I were

asked what now constitutes the chief and fundamental feature of my existence, I should answer: insomnia. As was my custom in the past, I undress and go to bed precisely at midnight. I fall asleep almost at once, but around two o'clock wake up feeling as if I had not slept. I have to get out of bed, light the lamp, and for an hour or two I pace the floor or contemplate the long-familiar photographs and pictures on my walls. When I tire of walking about, I sit down at my table. I sit motionless, thinking of nothing, desiring nothing; if a book lies before me, I automatically move it closer, and without any interest start reading it. In this way, quite mechanically and in a single night, I read an entire novel with the strange title *What the Swallow Sang*. I sometimes occupy my mind by counting to a thousand, or conjure up the face of one of my colleagues and try to recall in what year and in what circumstances he joined the faculty. I like listening to sounds. Two doors away, my daughter Liza sometimes mutters rapidly in her sleep; or my wife crosses the drawing room with a candle in her hand, invariably dropping the matchbox on the floor; or a warped cupboard creaks; or the lamp may suddenly begin to hiss, and these sounds for some reason move me.

Not to sleep at night is to be conscious every minute that you are not normal, and for this reason I wait with impatience for morning to come, for daytime, when I have a right not to sleep. Many tedious hours pass before the cock crows in the yard. He is my first bearer of good tidings. As soon as I hear him I know that in an hour the hall porter will wake up and, coughing irascibly, come upstairs to fetch something. And gradually a pale light will appear in the windows, voices will be heard in the street. . . .

My day begins with the appearance of my wife. She comes into the room in her petticoat, before her hair has been done, but already washed and smelling of flower-scented eau de Cologne; she looks as if she had come in by chance, and invariably says exactly the same thing.

"Excuse me, I've come only for a minute. . . . Have you had another bad night?"

Then she puts out the lamp, sits down at the table, and begins talking. I am no prophet, but I know in advance what she will say. Every morning the same thing. As a rule, following her anxious inquiries about my health, she abruptly brings up the subject of our son, an officer serving in Warsaw. We send him fifty rubles after the twentieth of every month—and this serves as our chief topic of conversation.

"Of course, it's hard for us," sighs my wife, "but until he is definitely on his feet, it is our duty to help him. The boy is in a strange place, his pay is low. . . . However, if you like, we can send him forty rubles next month instead of fifty. What do you think?"

Daily experience might have taught my wife that our expenses are not reduced by talking about them, but she is impervious to experience, and regularly, every morning, talks about our son, tells me that the price of bread, thank God, has gone down, while sugar has gone up two kopecks—and all with an air of conveying news.

I listen, automatically saying yes to everything, and, probably because I have not slept, I am possessed by strange and futile thoughts. I gaze at my wife in childish wonder. Bewildered, I ask myself: is it possible that this corpulent, ungainly old woman with the dull expression that comes of petty concerns and anxiety over her daily bread, with eyes dimmed by the perpetual brooding on debt and want, and who is capable of talking only of expenses, who smiles at nothing but lowered prices—is it really possible that this woman was once the slender Varya whom I so passionately loved for her fine clear mind, her pure soul, her beauty, and, as Othello loved Desdemona, "that she did pity me"? Is it possible that this is my wife Varya, who once bore me a son?

I gaze intently at the puffy face of this clumsy old woman, searching for my Varya in her, but nothing remains of the past except her anxiety over my health and her manner of calling my salary "our salary," and my cap "our cap." It is painful for me to look at her, but I try to humor her by letting her talk as much as she likes, saying nothing even when she criticizes people unjustly, or nags me for not publishing a textbook and not having a private practice.

Our conversations always end in the same way. Suddenly my wife is dismayed at remembering that I have not had my tea.

"What am I thinking of sitting here?" she exclaims, getting up. "The samovar has been on the table for ever so long, and here I sit chattering. Good heavens, how forgetful I'm becoming!"

She goes quickly to the door, then stops and says:

"You know, don't you, that we owe Yegor five months'

wages? I don't know how many times I've told you that it doesn't do to let the servants' wages lapse. It's much easier to pay ten rubles every month than fifty rubles every five months!"

Once outside the door, she stops again to say:

"There's nobody I pity as I do our poor Liza. Studying at the conservatory the child is constantly in good society, and just look at the way she's dressed! It's a disgrace to appear in the street in such a fur coat. If she were anyone else's daughter it wouldn't matter, but everyone knows her father is a famous professor, a privy councilor!"

And having reproached me with my rank and reputation, she at last goes. This is how my day begins. And it does not improve as it goes on.

While I am drinking my tea, my daughter Liza comes into the room in her fur coat and hat, carrying her music, and ready to go to the conservatory. She is twenty-two years old but looks younger, a handsome girl, rather like my wife in her youth. Kissing me tenderly on the forehead, then dropping a kiss on my hand, she says:

"Good morning, Papa! Are you well?"

As a child she was very fond of ice cream, and I often took her to the confectioner's. Ice cream was for her the gauge of excellence in everything. If she wanted to praise me, she would say: "Papa, you are creamy!" One little finger was called pistachio, another cream, another raspberry, and so on. When she used to come to my room to say good morning, I would take her on my knee, kiss her fingers, and say: "Cream . . . pistachio . . . lemon . . ."

And I still kiss Liza's fingers in memory of those days, murmuring:

"Pistachio . . . cream . . . lemon . . ." but it isn't the same. I am cold as ice, and feel ashamed. When my daughter comes to me and touches my forehead with her lips, I start as if a bee had stung me, and with a forced smile turn my face away. Ever since I began suffering from insomnia, the thought sticks in my brain like a nail: my daughter often sees me, an elderly and celebrated man, blush painfully because of owing money to my footman; she sees how my anxiety over petty debts forces me to drop my work and spend hours pacing the floor and thinking—yet why is it she has never once come to me in secret and whispered: "Father, here is my watch, my bracelets, my earrings, my dresses—

pawn them, you need money" . . . ? How is it, when she sees that her mother and I put ourselves in a false position in an effort to hide our poverty, that she does not relinquish the luxury of studying music? I would not accept her watch, her bracelets, the sacrifice of her lessons—God forbid! That is not what I want.

And this brings me to the thought of my son, an officer in Warsaw. He is an intelligent, honest, sober fellow. But that is not enough for me. I think that if I had an old father, and knew that there were moments when he was mortified by his poverty, I should give up my commission and hire myself out as a workman. Such thoughts about my children are poisoning me. And what good are they? Only a narrow-minded or embittered man harbors feelings of rancor against ordinary human beings because they are not heroes. But enough of this.

At a quarter to ten I must go and give a lecture to my dear boys. I dress and set off on a road I have known for thirty years, a road that has a history for me. There is the big gray house with the chemist's shop: here at one time stood a little house in which there was an alehouse, and it was in this alehouse that I thought out my dissertation and wrote my first love letter to Varya. I wrote it in pencil on a sheet of paper with the heading "Historia morbi." Over there is the grocer's shop, at one time kept by a little Jew who sold me cigarettes on credit, later by a stout woman who was fond of students because "every one of them has a mother," and now by a redheaded merchant, a stolid man who sits drinking tea out of a copper teapot. And here are the gloomy university gates, which have long been in need of repair, the bored yardman in his sheepskin, the broom, the heaps of snow. . . .

Such gates cannot produce a very salutary impression on a fresh young boy from the provinces who imagines that a temple of learning must really be a temple. In a history of Russian pessimism a prominent place among the predisposing causes would have to be given to the generally dilapidated state of university buildings, the gloominess of their corridors, the grimy walls, inadequate light, the dismal aspect of the staircases, cloakrooms, and benches. . . .

And there is our park. It seems to have grown neither better nor worse since my student days. I have never liked it. It would be far more sensible if, instead of emaciated lime trees, yellow acacias, and skimpy cropped lilacs, there were tall pines and great oaks. The student, whose state of mind in the majority of cases is influenced by his surroundings, should see before him only what is lofty, powerful, elegant. . . . The Lord preserve him from sickly trees, broken windowpanes, gray walls, and doors covered with torn oilcloth.

When I come to the wing where I work, the door is thrown open and I am met by my old fellow worker, contemporary, and namesake, the doorman Nikolai. As he lets me in, he clears his throat and says: "A frost, Your Excellency!" Or, if my fur coat is wet: "Rainy, Your Excellency!" Then he runs ahead of me to open all the doors on my way. In my office he carefully helps me off with my coat, and while doing so always manages to give me some item of university news. Thanks to the intimacy existing between all the university doormen and porters, he knows everything that goes on in all four faculties, the chancellor's office, the rector's study, and the library. There is nothing he does not know. When there is news such as the resignation of the rector or one of the deans, I hear him in conversation with a young watchman naming all the candidates for the position, explaining that this one would not be approved by the minister, that one would himself refuse the post, then going into fabulous details about certain mysterious documents received in the chancellor's office, secret conversations said to have been held between the minister and one of the trustees, and so on. Apart from such details, he almost always turns out to be right. If you want to know in what year someone defended his dissertation, joined the university staff, retired, or died, you have only to draw on the vast memory of this veteran, and he will tell you the year, the month, and the day, and will further supply you with every detail of the circumstances accompanying the event. His is the memory of one who loves.

He is the guardian of university traditions. Having inherited from his predecessors a store of legends pertaining to university life, he has added to this wealth treasures of his own, amassed during years of service, and, should you wish, can relate many a tale, both long and short. He can tell of extraordinary sages who knew all there is to know, of remarkable workers who could go for weeks without sleep, of innumerable martyrs and victims of science; and good always triumphs over evil in these stories, the weak vanquish the strong, the wise man the fool, the humble the proud, the young the old. . . . There is no need to take all these legends and marvels at face value, but filter them, and the essentials remain: our splendid traditions and the names of the real heroes, recognized as such by all.

In our society all that is known of the academic world is summed up in anecdotes about the extraordinary absent-mindedness of old professors and a few witticisms variously ascribed to Gruber, myself, and Babukin. For the educated public this is not very much. If it loved science, learned men, and students as Nikolai does, our literature would long ago have been enriched by epics, biographies, and sayings, all of which, unfortunately, it now lacks.

After telling me the news, Nikolai's face takes on a solemn expression and we proceed to business. If an outsider were to hear how freely Nikolai uses our terminology, he might think him a scientist in disguise. As a matter of fact, rumors about the erudition of university watchmen are greatly exaggerated. It is true that Nikolai is familiar with more than a hundred Latin terms, knows how to put a skeleton together, occasionally prepares certain equipment, amuses the students with some lengthy scientific quotation, but such a relatively simple thing as the circulation of the blood, for instance, is as obscure to him today as it was twenty years ago.

Seated at a table in my office, bent low over a book or laboratory apparatus, is my prosector, Pyotr Ignatyevich, a modest, hard-working, but rather mediocre individual of thirty-five, already grown bald and paunchy. He works from morning till night, reads masses of material, and remembers absolutely everything he reads, which makes him worth his weight in gold to me; apart from this, he is a draft horse, in other words, a learned clod. The characteristic features of the draft horse, which distinguish him from the man of talent, are narrowness of vision and an extremely circumscribed specialization; outside his specialization he is as simple as a child.

I recall coming into my office one morning and saying: "Think what a misfortune! They say Skobelev is dead!" Nikolai crossed himself, but Pyotr Ignatyevich turned to me and asked: "Who's Skobelev?" Another time, somewhat earlier, I told him that Professor Perov had died. And my good Pyotr Ignatyevich asked: "What was his field?"

I believe that Patti herself might sing into his ear, a horde of Chinese invade Russia, or an earthquake occur, and he would not turn a hair, but would go on placidly squinting into his microscope. In a word, what's Hecuba to him? I'd give anything to see how this dry stick sleeps with his wife.

Another characteristic: his fanatical faith in the infallibility of science, and, above all, in anything written by a German. He is confident of himself and of his demonstrations, knows his goal in life, and is entirely immune to the doubts and disillusionments that turn a gifted man's hair gray. A slavish reverence for authority and a total lack of any need for independent thought. Hard to shake his convictions, and impossible to quarrel with him. How can you argue with a man who is firmly convinced that medicine is the very best of sciences, doctors the very best of men, and medical traditions the very best of all traditions that exist? Only one imperfect tradition has survived—the wearing of a white tie by doctors. For the scientist, for any educated man in fact, there can be only university traditions as a whole, with no differentiation between medicine, law, and so on, but you would have a hard time getting Pyotr Ignatyevich to agree with this; he would argue with you till doomsday.

His future is quite clear to me. He will do a few hundred impeccable dissections in the course of his lifetime, write numerous arid but tolerable papers, and make a dozen conscientious translations, but he will never set the world on fire—that requires imagination, originality, intuition, none of which he has. To put it briefly, he is not the master, but the servant, of science.

Pyotr Ignatyevich, Nikolai, and I speak in undertones. We are not quite at ease. Hearing the murmur of a sea of voices behind the door in the lecture hall gives rise to a peculiar feeling. In thirty years I have not grown accustomed to this sensation and experience it every morning. I nervously button my frockcoat, ask Nikolai unnecessary questions, lose my temper. . . . Anyone would think I was afraid, but this is not fear, it is something else, something I can neither put a name to nor describe.

I needlessly look at my watch and say: "Well? Time to go in."

And we proceed in the following order: Nikolai goes first, carrying the apparatus or the charts, I follow him, and after me trudges the draft horse, with humbly hanging head; or, when required, a cadaver is carried in on a stretcher, followed by Nikolai, and so on. At my appearance the students rise, sit down again, and the sea of sound instantly subsides. A calm ensues.

I know what I am going to lecture on, but not how, nor where I shall begin and end. There is not a single ready-made phrase in my head. But I have only to look at my audience (ranged before me in the amphitheater) and pronounce the stereotyped phrase: "At our last lecture we stopped at . . ." and a long sequence of sentences pours from my soul—and I'm off!

I speak with irrepressible rapidity and fervor; there is no power on earth that can stem the flow of my speech. To lecture well, that is, with profit to your listeners and without boring them, requires not talent alone but experience and skill; you must have a thorough grasp of your subject and be in absolute control of your own powers and your audience. In addition to all this, you must keep your wits about you and never lose sight of the point in question for an instant.

A good conductor, conveying a composer's ideas, does twenty things at once: he follows the score, waves his baton, keeps an eye on the singers, makes a sign to the drums, the French horn, and so on. It is the same with me when lecturing. I see a hundred and fifty faces before me, each one different from the others, three hundred eyes staring into my face. My aim is to conquer this many-headed Hydra. If, at every moment I am lecturing, I have a clear conception of the degree of its attention and the measure of its comprehension, it is in my power. My other adversary resides within myself—it is the infinite variety of forms, phenomena, and laws, a great many of them conditioned by my own and others' thoughts.

At all times I must have the skill to pluck from this mass of material what is most important and essential and, keeping pace with my own speech, to present my thoughts in a form that is both accessible to the monster's mind and effective in rousing its interest; at the same time I must see to it that my ideas are presented not as they come to me, but in the order required for a proper composition of the picture I wish to paint.

Moreover, I endeavor to make my style literary, with sentences as simple and elegant as possible, and definitions brief and exact. I continually have to remind myself that I have only an hour and forty minutes at my disposal. In short, I must be scientist, teacher, orator, all in one, and woe is me if the orator gets the upper hand of the teacher and scientist, or vice versa!

You lecture for a quarter of an hour, a half hour perhaps, and you begin to notice that the students are staring at the ceiling or at Pyotr Ignatyevich; one fumbles for his handkerchief, another shifts to a more comfortable position, a third smiles at his own thoughts. . . . This means that attention is flagging. Measures must be taken. At the first suitable opportunity I introduce a pun. All hundred and fifty faces smile broadly, eyes sparkle merrily, and a momentary murmur of the sea is heard. . . . I join in the laughter. Attention is revived and I can go on.

No scientific debate, no sort of game or entertainment, has ever given me so much pleasure as lecturing. Only then have I been able to abandon myself entirely to a passion, to have realized that inspiration is not an invention of the poets, but is real. And it seems to me that Hercules, after the most piquant of his exploits, never knew such voluptuous exhaustion as I have experienced after every lecture.

That is how it used to be. Now I experience nothing but torture when I lecture. Before half an hour has passed I begin to feel an overwhelming weakness in my legs and shoulders; I sit down, but am not accustomed to lecturing sitting down; a moment later I get up and go on, then sit down again. My mouth is dry, my voice grows husky, my head swims. . . . In an effort to conceal my condition from my audience I sip water, cough, blow my nose as if troubled by a cold, make irrelevant puns, and end by announcing the recess sooner than I ought to. But it is chiefly shame that I feel.

My conscience and my mind both tell me that the best thing I could do would be to deliver a farewell lecture to the boys, say my last word, give them my blessing, and yield my place to a younger, stronger man. But—God forgive me—I have not the courage to follow the dictates of my conscience.

Unfortunately, I am neither a philosopher nor a theologian. I know quite well that I have no more than six months to live; it would seem that now I ought to be concerned primarily with the mystery beyond the grave, with the visions that may visit me in my sepulchral sleep. But for some reason my soul declines to face these questions, though my mind acknowledges them as all-important. Now, on the threshold of death, the only thing that interests me is what interested me twenty or thirty years ago—science. Even as I breathe my last, I shall go on believing that science is the most important, most beautiful, most essential thing in the life of man, that it always has been and always will be the highest manifestation of love, that by means of it alone will man conquer nature and himself. It may be that this belief is naive and fundamentally incorrect, but I cannot help believing as I do, and for me to overcome this belief of mine would be impossible.

But this is not the point. I only ask indulgence for my weakness, and that it be understood that to sever a man from his professorship and pupils, when to him the destiny of bone marrow is of more interest than the ultimate purpose of the universe, would be tantamount to nailing him up in his coffin before he is dead.

Sleeplessness, and the consequent strain of trying to combat my increasing weakness, have caused something strange to happen to me. In the middle of a lecture tears suddenly choke me, my eyes begin to smart, and I have a passionate, hysterical desire to stretch out my arms and break into a loud lament. I feel like crying out in a loud voice that I, a famous man, have been sentenced by fate to capital punishment, that in six months or so another man will be holding sway in this lecture hall. I want to cry out that I have been poisoned; new thoughts, never before known to me, have poisoned the last days of my life and even now are stinging my brain like mosquitoes. At such moments my situation seems to me so horrifying that I want my listeners to be horrified, to leap from their seats panic-stricken, and rush to the exit with a desperate shriek.

It is not easy to get through such moments.

## II

After the lecture I stay at home and work. I read journals, monographs, prepare my next lecture, and occasionally write something. I do not work uninterruptedly, as I am obliged to receive visitors.

The bell rings. A colleague has come to discuss a professional matter. He comes in, hat and stick in hand, holds them both out to me, and says:

"I've come only for a minute, only a minute! Sit down, *collega*! I just want a couple of words with you!"

We begin by trying to show each other how extraordinarily polite we are, and how absolutely delighted to see each other. I offer him a chair, he offers me a chair; we cautiously pat each other on the back, make tentative buttonholing gestures, as if trying to reach out to one another but afraid of burning our fingers. We both laugh, although nothing amusing has been said. Once seated, we lean toward each other and begin talking in subdued voices. However sincere our relations, we cannot refrain from gilding our conversation in the most Celestial Chinese manner: "as you have so justly observed," or "as I have once before had the honor to inform you," and never fail to laugh at each other's witticisms, no matter how unfortunate they may be. Our business concluded, my colleague abruptly rises, and, with a wave of his hat in the direction of my work, takes his leave. Again we start laughing and patting one another. I accompany him into the hall where I help him on with his coat, while he does his utmost to forestall this superlative honor. Then, when Yegor opens the front door for him, my friend assures me I will catch cold as I make a show of accompanying him out to the street. When at last I return to my room, my face goes on smiling—from inertia, I suppose.

A little later there is another ring. Someone is a long time removing his things and clearing his throat. Yegor announces that a student wishes to see me. I tell him to ask him to come in. A moment later a young man of pleasing appearance enters. For a year now there have been strained relations between this young man and me: he makes a deplorable showing on my examinations and I give him the lowest mark. Every year there are about seven of these young hopefuls whom, to use their language, I "kick out" or "flunk." Those of them who fail the examinations because of illness or inability, as a rule bear their cross with fortitude and do not try to bargain with me; the ones who do try, and who come to my house for this purpose, are the self-confident, easygoing types whose failure perhaps spoils their appetites or interferes with their regular attendance at the

opera. I make allowances for the former, but the latter I
pitch into throughout the entire year.

"Sit down," I say to my visitor. "What have you to say?"

"Excuse me for troubling you, professor . . ." he begins,
stammering and not looking me in the eye. "I wouldn't have
ventured to trouble you if it had not been for . . . Well,
I've been up for your examinations five times now, and . . .
and failed. I beg of you, please be so good as to give me a
passing mark, because . . ."

The argument that all idlers produce in their own favor
is the same: they have passed all their other examinations
brilliantly and failed only mine, which is particularly sur-
prising inasmuch as they have always studied my subject
most assiduously and know it so very well, and if they have
failed it must be owing to some unaccountable misunderstanding.

"Excuse me, my friend," I say to my visitor. "I cannot
give you a passing mark. Go and read up on the lectures
again, then come back, and we shall see."

A pause. I have an inclination to torment a student who
prefers beer and opera to science, and remark with a sigh:

"In my opinion, the best thing for you to do now is to
give up medicine altogether. If, with your abilities, you cannot manage to pass the examination, it is evident that you
have neither the vocation nor the desire to become a doctor."

The face of this sanguine young man lengthens.

"Excuse me, professor," he says with a laugh, "but that
would be odd, to say the least. After studying for five years,
to suddenly—give up!"

"Not at all! Better to have lost five years than to spend
the rest of your life in an occupation that doesn't appeal
to you."

But the next moment I feel sorry for him and hasten
to add: "However, you know best. Well, then, do a little
studying and come back."

"When?" the young idler asks in a hollow voice.

"Whenever you like. Tomorrow if you are ready."

In his good-natured eyes I read: "I can come all right,
but you'll flunk me again, and you know it, you swine!"

"Of course," I add, "it won't make you any more erudite
to take my examination another fifteen times, but it will
develop your character. That's something to be thankful for."

A silence follows. I get up and wait for my visitor to go,

but he stands staring at the window, plucking at his beard and thinking. This becomes boring.

The voice of this sanguine young man is agreeably mellow, his eyes intelligent and mocking, but his genial face looks a little blowzy from frequent indulgence in beer and prolonged repose on the sofa; no doubt he could tell me a great many things about the opera, the company he keeps, his amorous adventures, but, unfortunately, such conversations are hardly appropriate, or I should gladly have listened.

"Professor! I give you my word of honor that if you pass me, I'll . . ."

When matters reach the word of honor stage, I wave my hands and sit down at my desk. The student ponders for a moment and says dejectedly:

"In that case, good-bye. . . . Excuse me. . . ."

"Good-bye, my friend. Good luck to you."

He irresolutely goes out to the hall, slowly puts on his coat, and leaves, probably still pondering. Having dismissed me from his thoughts with: "That old devil!" he goes off to some miserable restaurant to drink beer and eat dinner, then home to sleep. Peace to thy ashes, honest toiler!

A third ring. In comes a young doctor wearing a new black suit, gold-rimmed spectacles, and, of course, a white tie. He introduces himself. I invite him to sit down and ask what I can do for him. This young priest of science begins by telling me, not without emotion, that he passed his doctor's examination this year, and now has only to write his dissertation. He would like to work with me, under my guidance, and would be infinitely obliged if I would supply him with a subject for his thesis.

"I should be happy to be of service to you, *collega*," I say, "but let us come to an understanding as to the meaning of a dissertation. The word is generally taken to mean a work that is the product of independent creative effort. Is that not so? Anything written on another man's theme and under his guidance is called something else. . . ."

The aspirant makes no reply. I become incensed and jump up from my chair.

"Why is it that you all come to me, I'd like to know?" I shout angrily. "Do you think I keep a shop? I'm not dealing in themes. For the thousandth time, I ask you all to leave me in peace! Excuse me if I seem rude, but after all, I'm fed up with this!"

The aspirant continues to remain silent, but a faint flush appears in the region of his cheekbones. His face expresses a profound respect for my great name and learning, but his eyes reveal his contempt for my voice, my pitiful figure, and my nervous gestures. In my anger I impress him as being merely odd.

"I don't keep a shop!" I repeat angrily. "And this is an amazing thing! Why don't you want to be independent? Why is freedom so odious to you?"

I go on and on, and he says not one word. Gradually I calm down and, of course, give in. He gets his theme from me, though it's not worth much, writes—under my supervision—a dissertation that will be of no use to anyone, and defends it in a dreary debate to receive a degree that will be of no use to him.

The bell goes on ringing endlessly, but I shall confine myself to describing the first four callers. When it rings for the fourth time, I hear familiar footsteps, the rustle of a dress, a voice I love. . . .

Eighteen years ago a friend of mine, an oculist, died, leaving a seven-year-old daughter, Katya, and about sixty thousand rubles. In his will he appointed me her guardian. She lived with us till she was ten, then was sent to boarding school and was at home only during the summer holidays. I had no time to look after her upbringing, took notice of her only sporadically, and consequently can say very little about her childhood.

My earliest memory concerning her, and one that I hold dear, is the extraordinary trustfulness she displayed on coming into my home, and later in allowing herself to be treated by doctors—a trustfulness that always lit up her little face. She might be sitting apart, with a bandaged cheek, but she never failed to take a lively interest in whatever was going on around her; whether she watched me writing or leafing through a book, my wife bustling about the house, the cook peeling potatoes, or the dog frolicking, her eyes invariably expressed the same thought: "Everything that happens in this world is wise and wonderful." She was extremely curious and loved talking to me. Sometimes she would sit at the table opposite me, following my movements and asking questions. She wanted to know what I was reading, what I

did at the university, whether I was not afraid of dead
bodies, what I did with my salary.

"Do the students fight at the university?" she would ask.

"Yes, darling, they do."

"And do you make them stand in the corner?"

"I do."

And she thought it so funny that university students
fought and were made to stand in the corner that she burst
out laughing. She was a gentle, patient, good child. More
than once I saw something taken away from her, saw her
unjustly punished, or her curiosity left unsatisfied; at such
times a look of sadness mingled with the invariable expression of confidence in her face—but that was all. I did not
know how to defend her, but when I saw her sadness, I
felt like drawing her close to me and consoling her like an
old nurse: "My dear little orphan!"

I also remember that she loved dressing nicely and sprin-
kling herself with perfume. In this respect she was like me.
I too like fine clothes and good scent.

I regret that I had neither the time nor the inclination
to follow the rise and development of what became Katya's
ruling passion from the time she was fourteen or fifteen
years old. I refer to her ardent love for the theater. When
she came home from boarding school for the summer, there
was nothing she talked of with such eagerness and pleasure
as plays and actors; she wore us out with her incessant
chatter about the theater. My wife and children would not
listen to her. I was the only one who had not the heart to
deny her my attention. When she felt a desire to share her
enthusiasm with someone, she would come into my study
and in a beseeching voice say to me:

"Nikolai Stepanych, do let me talk to you about the theater!"

I would point to the clock and say: "I'll give you half an
hour—go ahead!"

Soon she was bringing home dozens of pictures of actors
and actresses she adored, later she tried her hand at amateur theatricals, and finally, when she had finished school,
she came to me and announced that she was born to be an
actress.

I never shared Katya's enthusiasm for the theater. In my
opinion, if a play is good, you don't need actors to produce

the desired effect: just reading it is enough. And if the play is poor, then no acting can make it good.

In my youth I often went to the theater, and now my family takes a box twice a year and carries me off for an "airing." This, of course, does not entitle me to be a judge of the theater, so I will say very little about it. In my opinion, the theater is no better today than it was thirty or forty years ago. Now as then I can never find a decent glass of water in the corridors or foyers. The cloakroom attendants, as in the past, fine me twenty kopecks for my coat, though there would seem to be nothing reprehensible in wearing warm clothes in winter. Also as in the past, and for no reason whatsoever, music is played during the intermissions, which adds something new and uncalled-for to the impression made by the play, and men still go to the buffet to drink. If there is no progress to be seen in these minor matters, it would be futile to look for it in the essentials.

When an actor, cloaked from head to foot in theatrical traditions and conventions, tries to recite a simple ordinary monologue like "To be or not to be" with the inevitable hissing and contortions of the body, or when he tries to convince me by every means that Chatsky—who spends all his time talking with fools and is in love with a fool—is an exceedingly clever man, and that *Woe from Wit* is not a dull play, then the stage smells of the same routine that bored me forty years ago, when I was regaled with classical wailing and breast-beating. And I leave the theater every time a greater conservative than I entered it.

The credulous and sentimental public may be persuaded that the theater in its present form is a school, but anyone who is acquainted with a school in its true sense will not swallow that bait. I do not know how it will be fifty or a hundred years from now, but in its present condition the theater can serve as nothing but entertainment. And this entertainment is far too costly for us to go on enjoying it. It robs the state of thousands of gifted, healthy young men and women who, if they had not dedicated themselves to the theater, might have been good doctors, farmers, schoolteachers, officers; it robs the public of its evening hours—the best time for intellectual work and conversations with friends. Not to mention the financial waste or the moral damage inflicted on the spectator by seeing murder, adultery, and slander erroneously interpreted on the stage.

Katya, however, was of quite a different opinion. She assured me that the theater, even in its present state, was superior to the lecture hall, to books, to everything in the world. It was a force uniting within itself all the arts, and actors were its missionaries. No art or science by itself was capable of exercising so positive and powerful an effect on the human spirit as the stage, and it was not without reason that even a mediocre actor was more popular than the greatest scientist or painter. No other public activity was able to afford such gratification and enjoyment as the theater.

One fine day Katya joined a theatrical troupe and went away, to Ufa, I believe, taking with her a large sum of money, a multitude of rainbow-tinted hopes, and a very aristocratic view of her work.

Her first letters, written on the road, were wonderful. I read them and was simply amazed that those small sheets of paper could contain so much youth, purity of spirit, and blessed innocence, combined with a subtle, practical judgment that would have done credit to a first-class masculine mind. The Volga, nature, the towns she visited, her companions, her failures and successes, were not so much described as celebrated; every line breathed the confidence I was accustomed to reading in her face—but with all that, there were countless grammatical errors and scarcely any punctuation whatsoever.

Before six months had passed, I received a highly poetical, rapturous letter beginning with the words: "I have fallen in love." The letter was accompanied with a photograph of a clean-shaven young man in a broad-brimmed hat and a plaid flung over one shoulder. The letters that followed were as marvelous as before, but punctuation marks began to make their appearance, mistakes in grammar disappeared, and there was a strong smack of masculinity about them.

Katya now wrote about how splendid it would be to build a big theater somewhere on the Volga, by forming a partnership, of course, and attracting the wealthy merchants and shipowners to the enterprise; there would be plenty of money, the box office receipts would be enormous, actors would work on a cooperative basis. . . . This might be all very well, I told myself, but such schemes could originate only in the mind of a man.

However that may have been, for a year and a half everything seemed to go well: Katya was in love, believed in her work, and was happy; but then I commenced to notice obvious signs of a decline. It began with her complaining to me of her companions—this was the first and most ominous symptom; if a young scientist or writer begins his career by complaining bitterly of scientific or literary men, it is a sure sign that he is enervated and not fit for his work. Katya wrote that her comrades failed to attend rehearsals and never knew their parts, that the absurdity of the plays produced and the way the actors conducted themselves on the stage showed the utmost contempt for the audience; that in the interests of box office receipts, which was all they talked of, dramatic actresses degraded themselves by singing chansonettes, tragedians sang comic songs making fun of deceived husbands and the pregnancy of unfaithful wives, and so on. In fact, it was a wonder the provincial theater had survived and could still maintain itself in this meager and corrupt vein.

In reply I sent Katya a long and, I must confess, boring letter. Among other things I wrote:

"I have not infrequently had occasion to have long talks with old actors, men of the very highest principles, who have been good enough to bestow their affection on me; from my conversations with them I could see that their occupation is governed not so much by their own reason and choice as by fashion and the disposition of the public; the best of them in their time have been obliged to play not only in tragedies, but in operettas, French farces, and pantomimes, and in every case they have been equally certain that they were getting ahead and being of use. So, as you see, the root of the evil must be sought not in the actor, but deeper, in the art itself, and in the attitude of society to it."

This letter of mine only irritated Katya, and she replied:

"We are talking at cross purposes. I was not writing to you about the high-principled men who bestowed their affection on you, but about a band of adventurers who have no principles whatever—a horde of savages who have gone on the stage only because they wouldn't have been accepted anywhere else, and who call themselves artists out of sheer insolence. Not one of them is talented; they are a lot of mediocrities, drunkards, schemers, and backbiters. I cannot tell you how bitter it makes me to see that the art I love so much has fallen into the hands of people I detest; how bitter, too, that the best men view this evil only from a distance, not caring to come closer, and instead of taking one's part, write heavy-handed commonplaces and utterly superfluous sermons. . . ."

And so on in the same style.

A short time elapsed, and I received the following letter:

"I have been brutally deceived. I cannot go on living. Dispose of my money as you see fit. I have loved you as my father and my only friend. Good-bye."

And it turned out that *he* too belonged to the "horde of savages." Later I gathered from certain hints that there had been an attempt at suicide. It appeared that Katya had tried to poison herself. She must have been seriously ill after this, for the next letter I received was from Yalta, where in all probability she had been sent by a doctor. Her last letter contained a request to send her a thousand rubles as quickly as possible, and ended with the words:

"Forgive me if my letter is gloomy. Yesterday I buried my child."

After living in the Crimea for nearly a year, she returned home.

She had been away for about four years, and during all that time, I must admit, I had played a strange and not very admirable role with regard to her. Earlier, when she announced her intention of going on the stage, when she wrote me of her love, had periodic fits of extravagance and demanded that I send her now a thousand, now two thousand rubles, then wrote me of her wish to die and later of the death of her child, on each occasion I had lost my head, and my concern for her fate was expressed only in thinking about her and writing long boring letters. And yet, I had taken the place of her father, and loved her like a daughter!

Now Katya lives not half a verst from me. She has rented a five-room apartment and installed herself quite comfortably in a style all her own. If anyone were to paint a picture of her surroundings, the predominant mood of the painting would have to be indolence. Soft couches and soft ottomans for an indolent body, soft rugs for indolent feet, pale, drab, faded colors for indolent eyes, for the indolent soul a profusion of cheap fans strewn over the walls along with trivial pictures in which originality of execution prevails over content, an abundance of little tables and shelves covered with utterly useless worthless objects, and anomalous scraps of material in place of curtains. . . . All this in combination with an avoidance of bright colors, symmetry, and space, reveals not only laziness, but a perversion of natural taste. Katya lies on a couch for whole days reading—mostly novels and short stories. She goes out of the house only once a day, in the afternoon, to come and see me.

I go on working and Katya sits not far from me on the sofa, wrapped in a shawl as if she were cold. Either because I am fond of her, or because I grew accustomed to her frequent visits when she was a little girl, her presence does not prevent me from concentrating. From time to time I mechanically ask her a question and she gives me a brief reply; or, to relax for a moment, I turn and watch her dreamily looking through a medical journal or newspaper. At such moments I observe that her face has lost its former trusting look. Her expression is cold, apathetic, abstracted, like the faces of travelers who have had to wait a long time for a train. She still dresses beautifully and simply, but has grown careless; it is clear that her dress and hair owe something of their appearance to her habit of lolling in rocking chairs or lying about on couches all day. And she has lost her curiosity and never asks questions, as if, having experienced everything in life, she no longer expects to hear anything new.

About four o'clock there begin to be sounds of activity in the hall and drawing room. This means that Liza has come back from the conservatory and brought some of her girl friends with her. We hear them playing the piano, singing a note or two, and laughing; in the dining room Yegor is setting the table with a clatter of dishes.

"Good-bye," says Katya. "I won't go in and see them today. They must excuse me. I have no time. Come and see me."

I go to the door with her and she inspects me severely from head to foot, remarking with vexation:

"You keep getting thinner and thinner! Why don't you consult a doctor? I'm going to see Sergei Fyodorovich and ask him to have a look at you."

"There's no need, Katya."

"I can't understand what your family can be thinking of! They're a fine lot, I must say!"

She pulls on her coat with a jerk, and two or three hairpins, as usual, fall from her carelessly arranged hair. She is

too lazy or in too great a hurry to set it to rights and
clumsily pushes the falling curls under her hat and leaves.

When I go into the dining room, my wife asks:

"Wasn't that Katya with you just now? Why didn't she
come in to see us? That's really very odd. . . ."

"Mama!" Liza says to her reproachfully. "If she doesn't
care to come in, let her go. We don't have to go down on
our knees to her."

"Well, in any case, it's very rude. To sit there in the study
for three hours and never give a thought to us! But then,
she must do as she pleases, of course."

Both Varya and Liza hate Katya. This hatred is incomprehensible to me; one would probably have to be a woman
to understand it. I am ready to swear that of the hundred
and fifty young men I see every day in my lecture hall, and
of the hundreds of elderly men I meet in the course of the
week, hardly one could be found who would be able to
comprehend this hatred and repugnance for Katya's past—
for the fact that she bore a child out of wedlock, for the illegitimate child itself; and at the same time I cannot think
of a single woman or girl of my acquaintance who, con-
sciously or unconsciously, would not harbor the same feeling. And this is not because women are any purer or more
virtuous than men: after all, purity and virtue are not very
different from vice if they are tinged with malice. I simply
attribute it to the backwardness of women. The melancholy
feeling of compassion and the pangs of conscience experienced by the modern man at the sight of misfortune is to
my mind far greater proof of culture and moral development than hatred and disgust. Modern women are just as
lachrymose and callous as were women in the Middle Ages.
And in my opinion those who advocate giving women the
same education as men are right.

My wife also dislikes Katya for having been an actress,
for her ingratitude, her pride, her eccentricity, for all those
countless vices that one woman can always find in another.

Besides the family and two or three of Liza's girl friends,
her admirer and suitor, Aleksandr Adolfovich Gnekker, is
dining with us. He is a fair-haired young man, not over
thirty, of medium height, stout, broad-shouldered, with red-
dish whiskers and a little waxed mustache that gives his
smooth plump face a doll-like expression. He wears an extremely short jacket, a flowered waistcoat, checked trousers

that are very wide at the top, very narrow at the bottom, and tan shoes without heels. He has the bulging eyes of a crayfish, wears a tie that looks like the tail of a crayfish, and it seems to me that this young man even gives off a smell of crayfish soup. He visits us daily, but no one in the family knows anything about his origins, where he was educated, or what he lives on. He neither plays nor sings, but has some connection with music and singing, sells mysterious grand pianos to mysterious customers, goes frequently to the conservatory, is acquainted with all the celebrities, and has something to do with concerts; his judgments on music are delivered with great authority, and I observe that everyone is eager to agree with him.

Rich people always have their hangers-on, and it is the same with the arts and sciences. I don't suppose that any one of the arts or sciences anywhere in the world is free from such "foreign bodies" as this Mr. Gnekker. I am not a musician, and perhaps I am mistaken about Gnekker, whom, moreover, I hardly know, but the air of authority, the dignity with which he stands at the piano and listens when anyone plays or sings, look very suspicious to me.

You may be a gentleman a hundred times over, and a privy councilor, but nothing can save you from that atmosphere of middle-class vulgarity which courting, matchmaking, and weddings insinuate into your home and state of mind. I can never reconcile myself, for instance, to the expression of triumph on my wife's face whenever Gnekker visits us, or to the bottles of Lafitte, port, and sherry that are brought out, only on his account, so that he may see for himself the lavish and luxurious scale on which we live. Nor can I endure the staccato laugh that Liza has picked up at the conservatory, or her way of screwing up her eyes when there are men present. But above all I cannot for the life of me understand why it is that a creature who is utterly alien to my habits, my profession, my whole way of life, who is totally different from the sort of people I like, should come to my house every day, and dine with me every day. My wife and the servants whisper mysteriously that "he is a suitor," but I still can't make out why he should be here; his presence arouses in me the same perplexity I should feel if they were to set a Zulu next to me at the table. And it also seems strange to me that my daughter, whom I am accustomed to look on as a child, should love that necktie, those eyes, those pudgy cheeks. . . .

In the old days I would either enjoy my dinner or be indifferent to it; now it induces in me nothing but boredom and irritation. Ever since I became an "Excellency" and was made a dean of faculty, my family has, for some reason, found it necessary to make a complete change in our menu and dining habits. Instead of the simple dishes I was in the habit of eating when I was a student and in practice, I am now fed soup puree with some sort of stalactites floating in it, and kidneys in Madeira sauce. My rank and fame have deprived me forever of cabbage soup and little savory pies, of goose with apple sauce, of bream with buckwheat. They also have deprived me of the housemaid Agasha, a garrulous laughter-loving old woman in whose place the pompous dull-witted Yegor now serves dinner with a white glove on his right hand. The intervals between courses are shorter, but seem inordinately long because of being so empty. Gone is the gaiety of the old days, the spontaneous talk, the jokes and laughter, all the mutual affection and joy that used to animate my wife and children when we came together at the table. For a busy man like me, dinner was a time of relaxation and reunion, and for my wife and children a festivity—brief, it is true, but bright and gay—when they knew that for half an hour I belonged, not to science and my students, but to them alone. Gone forever the feeling of exhilaration from one glass of wine, gone Agasha, buckwheat and bream, and the uproar that greeted every little dinner table drama such as the cat and dog fighting under the table, or Katya's bandage falling into the soup.

To describe our dinners nowadays would be as unappetizing as to eat them. Along with her usual worried look, my wife's face wears an expression of triumph and ostentatious dignity. She glances uneasily at our plates and says: "I see you don't like the meat. Tell me: you really don't care for it, do you?" And I have to reply: "There's nothing to be concerned about, my dear, the meat is delicious." Then she says: "You're always trying to spare my feelings, Nikolai Stepanych, and you never tell me the truth. . . . And why is Aleksandr Adolfovich eating so little?" This goes on throughout the entire meal. Liza breaks into her staccato laugh and screws up her eyes. I look from one to the other, and only now, at the dinner table, does it become clear to me that

long ago their inner lives slipped from my control. I feel as
if there had once been a time when I lived in my own
home with a real family, and that now I am dining in the
home of an unreal wife, looking at an unreal Liza. A
startling change has taken place in both of them; somehow
I failed to observe the long process that produced this change
—no wonder I am unable to understand it. Why did the
change take place? I do not know. Perhaps the real trouble
is that God did not endow my wife and daughter with the
same strength He gave to me. Since childhood I have accustomed myself to resist external influences, have steeled
myself against them; such catastrophes as fame, high rank,
the transition from mere sufficiency to living beyond one's
means, acquaintance with celebrities and so on, have scarcely touched me. I have remained intact and unharmed; but
all this has fallen like an avalanche on my wife and daughter, weak and undisciplined as they are, and has crushed
them.

Gnekker and the young ladies discuss fugues, counterpoint, singers, pianists, Bach, and Brahms, while my wife—
lest she be suspected of musical ignorance—smiles sympa-
thetically and murmurs: "Delightful! . . . Really? . . . You
don't say so! . . ." And Gnekker gravely eats, gravely jests,
and listens condescendingly to the young ladies' remarks.
Every now and then he has an urge to speak bad French,
and then, for some reason, he finds it necessary to call me
"*Votre Excellence.*"

And I am morose. Evidently they put me under constraint
and I put them under constraint. Never before have I had
any personal experience of class antagonism, but now I am
tormented by the thought that someone outside my own circle should be sitting here as my daughter's suitor. His presence has a bad influence on me in another respect. Generally,
when I am alone or in the society of people I like, I never
think of my own achievements, or if I should happen to give
them a momentary thought, they appear as trifling as if I
had become a qualified scientist only yesterday; but in the
company of people like Gnekker they seem to tower like
mountain peaks that disappear into the clouds, while down
below the Gnekkers are shuffling about, barely visible to the
naked eye.

After dinner I return to my study and smoke a pipe, the
only one of the entire day, sole relic of my former filthy

habit of smoking from morning to night. While I am smoking my wife comes in and sits down to have a talk with me. And, as in the morning, I know beforehand what the conversation will be.

"I must talk to you seriously, Nikolai Stepanych," she begins. "It's about Liza. . . . Why don't you show any interest?"

"In what?"

"You pretend not to notice anything . . . it's not right. It's simply impossible to go on being so unconcerned. . . . Gnekker has intentions with regard to Liza. . . . What do you think about it?"

"That he is no good, I cannot say, because I don't know him, but that I do not like him—I've already told you a thousand times."

"This is impossible . . . impossible. . . ."

She gets up and paces the floor in agitation.

"It's just impossible to take that attitude to such a serious matter. . . ." she says. "When it's a question of your daughter's happiness, all personal considerations should be set aside. I know you don't like him. . . . Very well, then . . . suppose we refuse him now, break it off—how can you be sure that Liza will not hold it against us for the rest of her life? Suitors are not so plentiful nowadays, goodness knows, and it may very well happen that no one else will turn up. . . . He's terribly in love with Liza, and as far as I can see she likes him too. . . . Of course, he has no settled position, but that can't be helped. Please God, in time he'll get established somewhere. He comes of a good family and is rich."

"Where did you learn that?"

"He told me. His father has a big house in Kharkov and an estate in the neighborhood. So, you see, Nikolai Stepanych, you absolutely must go to Kharkov."

"What for?"

"You can make inquiries. . . . You know some of the professors there, they'll help you. I'd go myself, but I am a woman. I can't. . . ."

"I am not going to Kharkov," I say glumly.

My wife is appalled; an expression of extreme anguish comes over her face.

"For God's sake, Nikolai Stepanych!" she implores me,

sobbing. "For God's sake, relieve me of this burden! I am suffering!"

It pains me to look at her.

"Very well, Varya," I say kindly. "I'll go to Kharkov if you want me to, and do all that you wish."

She presses her handkerchief to her eyes and goes off to her room to cry. I am left alone.

Soon a lamp is brought in. The armchairs and lampshade cast the same old tiresome shadows on the walls and floor, and the sight of them makes me feel as though night had come and now my accursed insomnia would begin. I lie down on the bed, get up and walk about the room, lie down again. . . . As a rule it is after dinner, at the approach of evening, that my nervous tension reaches its highest pitch.

I begin crying for no reason, and bury my head in the pillow. At such moments I am afraid someone may come in, afraid I may suddenly die; I am ashamed of my tears, and something altogether unendurable prevails in my soul. I feel that I can no longer bear the sight of my lamp, my books, the shadows on the floor; I cannot bear the sound of the voices coming from the drawing room. Some incomprehensible, unseen force is violently pushing me out of the house. I leap up, hastily put on my hat and coat, and go out, taking every precaution not to be observed by any member of the household. But where am I to go?

The answer to this question has long been in my mind: to Katya.

# III

I generally find her lying on a Turkish couch or sitting on an ottoman reading. When she sees me, she raises her head languidly, sits up, and holds out her hand.

"Lolling about as usual . . ." I say, after pausing to recover my breath. "It's bad for you. You ought to find something to do!"

"Hm?"

"I say you ought to find something to do."

"What? There's nothing a woman can do but be a simple worker or an actress."

"Well? If you can't be a worker, then be an actress."

She says nothing.

"You ought to get married," I say, half in jest.

"There's no one to marry. And no reason to, either."

"You can't live like this."

"Without a husband? A lot that matters! I could have as many men as I like, if that were what I wanted."

"That's ugly, Katya."

"What's ugly?"

"What you just said."

Seeing that she has upset me, and wishing to smooth over the disagreeable impression she has made, Katya says:

"Come with me. Come . . . this way. . . . Here."

She leads me into a cozy little room, and, pointing to a writing table, says:

"There you are. . . . I prepared this for you. You shall work here. Come every day and bring your work. They don't let you work in peace at home. Will you work here? Would you like to?"

Not to wound her by refusing, I tell her that I will and that I like the room very much. Then we sit down in the comfortable little room and begin talking.

Warm cozy surroundings and the presence of a sympathetic person no longer arouse in me the feeling of gratification they once did, but are a powerful incentive to grumbling and complaining. I somehow feel that if I fret and indulge in a little self-pity, I will feel better.

"Things are in a bad way with me, my dear," I begin, sighing deeply. "Very bad."

"What's the matter?"

"You see, dear, it's like this. . . . The highest and most sacred prerogative of kings is the right to pardon. And I have always felt myself a king, for I have made unlimited use of this right. I have never judged, but have always been indulgent, showering my pardons right and left. Where others have protested or expressed indignation, I have merely counseled and persuaded. All my life I have endeavored to make my company tolerable to my family, students, colleagues, and servants. And this attitude of mine, I know, has been edifying to those around me. But I am no longer a king. Something worthy only of a slave is going on inside me: evil thoughts prowl through my mind day and night, and my soul is a hotbed of feelings such as I have never known before. I feel hatred, contempt, indignation, resentment, fear. I have grown excessively severe, exacting, irritable, discourteous, suspicious. Things that in the old days would have provoked no more than a pun or a good-natured laugh, now evoke dark feelings in me. Even my sense of logic has undergone a change: in the old days it was only money I despised, now I harbor feelings of bitterness not with regard to money, but the rich, as if they were to blame; in those days I detested tyranny and violence, now I detest the men who practice it, as if they alone were guilty, and not every one of us who is incapable of bringing out the best in one another. What is the meaning of this? If these thoughts and feelings have arisen from a change in my convictions, then what has caused the change? Can the world have grown worse and I better, or is it that I have been blind till now, and indifferent? If the change results from a general decline of my mental and physical powers—I am a sick man, you know, losing weight every day—then my situation is indeed pitiable: it means my new ideas are abnormal, morbid, that I ought to be ashamed of them and consider them of no importance. . . ."

"It has nothing to do with illness," Katya interrupts me. "It's simply that your eyes have been opened, that's all. You have seen what you refused to see before. In my opinion, what you ought to do first of all is to break with your family and go away."

"You're talking nonsense."

"You no longer care for them, why be a hypocrite? And is that what you call a family? Nonentities! If they died today, tomorrow no one would miss them."

Katya despises my wife and daughter as much as they hate her. In these days one can hardly speak of people having a right to despise one another, but if one looks at it from Katya's point of view, and acknowledges the existence of such a right, one can see that she has just as much right to despise my wife and Liza as they have to hate her.

"Nonentities!" she repeats. "Have you had dinner today? How is it they didn't forget to call you to the table? How is it they still remember your existence?"

"Katya!" I say sternly. "I want you to stop talking like this."

"Do you think I enjoy talking about them? I'd be happier not even knowing them. Listen to me, dear: give it all up and go away. Go abroad. The sooner the better."

"What nonsense! And what about the university?"

"Give that up too. What's the university to you? It makes no sense. You've been lecturing there for thirty years, and where are your students now? How many of them are well-known scientists? Just count them! It doesn't require a good and talented man to increase the number of doctors who exploit ignorance and pile up hundreds of thousands of rubles for themselves. You are not needed."

"My God, how bitter you are!" I exclaim, appalled. "How bitter! Stop, or I shall leave. I don't know how to reply to such harshness."

The maid comes in and summons us to tea. When we sit down before the samovar our conversation, I am glad to say, changes. Having poured out my complaints, I now feel like indulging in another weakness of old age—reminiscing. I tell Katya about my past, and, to my great astonishment, recount incidents that I had not suspected still lived in my memory. And she listens to me with sympathy, with pride, with bated breath. I am particularly fond of telling her of how I once studied at the seminary, and how I dreamed of going to the university.

"Sometimes I would walk in our seminary garden," I tell her, "and if a breeze brought me the sound of singing and the whine of an accordion from some distant tavern, or if a troika flew by the seminary wall with bells jingling, that alone was enough to make me feel a rush of joy surging, not just in my breast, but in my stomach, in my arms and legs. . . . I would listen to the accordion, to the receding sound of bells, and imagine myself a doctor—painting pictures for myself one better than another. And, as you see, my dreams came true. I have had more than I dared to dream of. For thirty years I have been an admired professor, I have had splendid comrades, have enjoyed a notable fame. I have loved, married for passionate love, had children. In short, looking back, I see my whole life as a beautiful composition, the work of a master. Now it remains for me not to spoil the finale. And this requires that I die like a man. If death is, in fact, a peril, then it must be met in a manner worthy of a teacher, a scientist, and a citizen of a Christian country: with courage and an untroubled soul. But I am spoiling the finale. Drowning, I run to you with a plea for help, and you say to me: drown, that is what you ought to do."

The doorbell rings. Katya and I both recognize the ring and say:

"That must be Mikhail Fyodorovich."

And, indeed, a minute later, in comes my friend, the philologist Mikhail Fyodorovich, a tall, well-built, clean-shaven man of fifty, with thick gray hair and black eyebrows —a good man and an excellent comrade. He comes of an old aristocratic family of rather talented, successful men, who have played important roles in the history of literature and education. He himself is talented, intelligent, and highly cultivated, but rather strange. We are all, to a certain extent strange, we all have our eccentricities, but there is something exceptional in his strangeness, something that is apt to give his friends cause for concern. I know several among them who are unable to see his good qualities just because of this strangeness.

He comes in slowly, drawing off his gloves, and says in his velvety bass:

"Good evening. Having tea? Splendid! It's infernally cold."

He sits down at the table, takes a glass of tea, and immediately begins talking. The thing that is most characteristic about his manner of speaking is a perpetually jocular tone, a blend of philosophy and drollery that reminds one of Shakespeare's gravediggers. He speaks only of serious matters, but never seriously. His judgments are always harsh and cutting, but his mild smooth facetious manner takes the sting out of his abuse and one soon grows accustomed to it. He comes every evening with half a dozen university anecdotes, which he generally begins relating as soon as he sits down at the table.

"Good Lord!" he sighs, with an ironical twitch of his eyebrows. "What clowns there are in this world!"

"Tell us . . ." says Katya.

"As I was coming out of my lecture this morning, I met that old idiot N. N—— on the staircase. He was coming along with that horsy chin of his stuck out, looking, as usual, for someone to listen to his complaints about his migraine, his wife, or the students who stay away from his lectures. 'Oh, he's seen me,' I thought, 'I'm done for, now I am in for it. . . .' "

And so on in the same vein. Or he will begin by saying: "Yesterday I attended a lecture for the general public given by our friend Z. Z——. I am really amazed that our alma mater—tell it not in Gath—risks making a public display of such simpletons as that Z. Z——, Europe's great dunce! You could comb the continent, I've no doubt, and not find another like him. He lectures, if you can imagine it, as if he were sucking a lollypop: smack-smack-smack. . . . He gets cold feet, loses his place in the manuscript, and his poor little thoughts crawl at the speed of a bishop on a bicycle—and the worst of it is that you have absolutely no idea what he is trying to say. The boredom is ghastly, even the flies expire. It can only be compared to our annual gathering in the auditorium for the traditional commencement address, God help us!"

Then an abrupt transition.

"Three years ago—Nikolai Stepanovich here will remember—it fell to me to deliver that address. It was hot, stifling, my uniform cut me under the arms—simply deadly! I spoke for half an hour, an hour, an hour and a half, two hours. . . . 'Thank God,' I thought, 'only ten more pages.' But since the last four pages were entirely superfluous, I counted on leaving them out. 'That,' thought I, 'leaves only six.' But then what do you think? I happened to glance up and there before me in the front row sat a general wearing some sort of decoration, and next to him a bishop. The poor devils were numb with boredom, absolutely goggle-eyed from trying to keep awake and at the same time to look attentive, and as if they understood my lecture and enjoyed it. 'Well,' I thought, 'if you like it so much, you shall have it!' And just for spite, I read the last four pages too."

When he talks, only his eyes and eyebrows seem to smile, a characteristic of ironical people. And at such times there is no trace of malice or hatred in his eyes, but a good deal of wit and that foxy sort of slyness which is seen only in the faces of very observant people. While I am speaking about his eyes, I may as well mention another peculiarity I have observed. When he accepts a glass from Katya, listens to her remarks, or watches her if she happens to leave the room for a moment, there is something gentle, something pure and beseeching in his glance. . . .

The maid removes the samovar and puts a large piece of cheese on the table with some fruit and a bottle of Crimean champagne, a rather poor wine that Katya grew fond of while living in the Crimea. Mikhail Fyodorovich takes two packs of cards from the whatnot and begins playing patience.

He contends that certain varieties of patience require great concentration and sagacity, but that does not prevent him from diverting himself with conversation the whole time he is playing. Katya follows the game attentively, helping him more by her facial expressions than by anything she says. She never drinks more than two small glasses of wine in the course of the evening. I sip a quarter of a tumbler, and the rest of the bottle is left to Mikhail Fyodorovich, who can drink a great deal without ever getting drunk.

We settle a variety of questions over patience, questions for the most part of a higher order and touching on the subject nearest our hearts—science.

"Science, God knows, has become obsolete," says Mikhail Fyodorovich, speaking in measured tones. "Its song is sung. Yes. . . . Humanity has already begun to feel the need of replacing it with something else. It sprang from the soil of superstition, was nourished by superstition, and is now as much the quintessence of superstitition as its defunct grandams, alchemy, metaphysics, and philosophy. And what, actually, has it given to mankind? The difference between learned Europeans and the Chinese, who get along without science, is trifling, purely external. The Chinese know nothing of science, but what have they lost?"

"Flies know nothing of science either," I say, "but what does that prove?"

"There is no need to get angry, Nikolai Stepanych. After all, I am only saying it here among ourselves. . . . I am more circumspect than you think; I have no intention of saying such things in public—God forbid! The mass of humanity cherishes the superstition that science and art are superior to agriculture, commerce, handicrafts. Our sect is maintained by this superstition, and it is not for us to destroy it. God forbid!"

As the game goes on, the younger generation is hauled over the coals too.

"Our present-day populace has degenerated," sighs Mikhail Fyodorovich. "Not to speak of ideals and all that sort of thing, but if, at least, they were capable of work and rational thought! In fact, it's a case of 'Sadly I gaze upon this generation.' "

"Yes, they have degenerated terribly," Katya agrees. "Tell me, have you had a single outstanding student in the last five or ten years?"

"I don't know about our other professors, but I can't think of any among mine."

"In my time I have seen a great many of your students and young scientists, and many actors too . . . well, I have never been so fortunate as to meet—I won't say a hero or a man of talent—even a merely interesting man. They are all colorless, mediocre, puffed up with pretentions. . . ."

These conversations about degeneration never fail to produce the same effect upon me: I feel as though I had accidentally overheard some unpleasant talk about my own daughter. Sweeping accusations based on such threadbare commonplaces, such bugaboos as degeneration, lack of ideals, and references to the glorious past, are offensive to me. Any imputation, even when made in the presence of ladies, ought to be formulated with the utmost exactness, otherwise it is not an accusation but idle vilification, and unworthy of decent people.

I am an old man, I have been teaching for thirty years, and I see neither degeneration nor an absence of ideals, and I do not find that the present is any worse than the past. My doorman Nikolai, whose experience in the matter is worth something, says that present-day students are neither better nor worse than those of the past.

If I were asked what it is I do not like in my students today, I should not be able to answer at once, nor to say very much, but I should be quite specific. I know their defects, and consequently have no need to resort to vague generalities. I do not like their smoking, drinking, and marrying late, nor the fact that they are so unconcerned, at times even so callous, as to tolerate want in their midst and to neglect paying up their arrears in the Students' Aid Society. They do not know other languages, and express themselves incorrectly in their own. Only yesterday one of my colleagues, a professor of hygienics, complained to me that he is obliged to lecture twice as long as he should because of their poor knowledge of physics and complete ignorance of meteorology. They readily succumb to the influence of the latest authors, even when they are by no means the best, but they are utterly indifferent to the classics such as Shakespeare, Marcus Aurelius, Epictetus, or Pascal, and it is this inability to distinguish the great from the inferior that more than anything else betrays their lack of practical intelligence. All complicated questions of a more or less social character (demographic problems, for instance) they solve by resorting to subscription lists rather than by means of scientific investigation and experiment, although these methods are entirely at their disposal and most appropriate to the purpose. They gladly become house physicians, assistants, laboratory technicians, externs, and are willing to stay in these positions till the age of forty, although independence, a sense of freedom, and personal initiative are no less necessary in science than, say, in art or commerce. I have plenty of pupils and listeners, but no assistants or successors, and consequently, while I am fond of them, touched by them, I am not proud of them, and so forth and so on. . . .

Such shortcomings, however numerous, give rise to pessimism or abuse only in the pusillanimous and the timid; they are all of an adventitious and transitory nature, entirely dependent on circumstances; in ten years or so they inevitably will have disappeared or have given place to other, new defects, which in their turn will alarm the fainthearted. The students' sins frequently vex me, but this vexation is nothing compared with the joy I have experienced in the course of thirty years of talking with them, lecturing to them, observing their attitudes and comparing them to those outside their circles.

Mikhail Fyodorovich continues his obloquy, Katya listens, neither of them realizing into what depths the apparently innocent diversion of criticizing their neighbors is gradually leading them. They do not perceive how a simple conversation is degenerating by degrees into mockery and jeering, how they are both stooping to a form of slander.

"Laughable types one meets," says Mikhail Fyodorovich. "Yesterday I went to see our friend Yegor Petrovich, and there I found one of your medicos, a third-year sciolist, I believe. What a face . . . in the Dobrolyubov style . . . deep thought chiseled on the brow. We got into a conversation. 'Well, young man, quite a stir!' I said. 'I read that some German or other, I forget his name, has obtained a new alkaloid, idiotine, from the human brain.' And what do you think? He believed me, and his face was the picture of respect, as if to say: See what we fellows can do! And the other day I went to the theater. I took my seat, and there, just in front of me in the next row, sat a couple of individuals, one apparently a member of our clan, a law student, the other, a shaggy-looking fellow, a medico. The latter

drunk as a lord. His attention to the stage—zero. Just sat
there dozing and nodding, but the minute an actor embarked on a loud monologue, or even raised his voice, he
started, nudged his companion, and said: 'What's he saying?
Is it elevating?' 'Yes,' the law student replied. 'Sublime!
Bra-vo-o!' the medico roared. 'Su-bli-i-me! Bravo-o!' The
stupid sot, you see, goes to the theater not for art but for
uplift. He craves the sublime."

Katya listens, laughing. There is something strange about
her laugh: she catches her breath in quick rhythmic gasps,
very much as if she were playing a concertina, and nothing
in her face expresses mirth except her nostrils. I am depressed
and do not know what to say. At last, beside myself, I flare
up, leap from my chair, and shout:

"Stop it! Why do you sit there like a couple of toads,
poisoning the air with your breath? That's enough!"

And without waiting for them to finish their malicious
talk, I prepare to leave. It's time, in any case—nearly eleven.

"I'll stay a little longer," says Mikhail Fyodorovich. "May
I, Yekaterina Vladimirovna?"

"Of course."

"*Bene.* Then perhaps we can have another little bottle."

They both accompany me into the hall with candles, and
as I put on my overcoat Mikhail Fyodorovich says:

"You've grown terribly thin and old lately, Nikolai Stepanovich. What's the matter with you? Are you ill?"

"Yes, somewhat."

"And he won't consult a doctor," Katya puts in glumly.

"But why don't you consult someone? How can you go on
like this? The Lord helps those who help themselves, my
dear fellow. My regards to your family, and my apologies
for not having gone to see them. In a day or two, before I
go abroad, I'll drop in to say good-bye, I really will! I'm
leaving next week."

I go away from Katya's feeling irritated, alarmed by the
talk of my illness, and dissatisfied with myself. After all, I
ask myself, why not consult one of my colleagues? And I
immediately picture to myself how, after examining me, he
would walk to the window in silence, think for a moment,
then turn to me, and, in an effort to prevent me from reading
the truth in his face, casually say:

"So far I see nothing special, *collega*, nevertheless, I

would advise you to discontinue your work. . . ." Thereby
depriving me of my last hope.

And who is without hope? Now, when I make my own
diagnosis and prescribe for myself, I can occasionally hope
that I am deceived by my own ignorance, that I am mistaken
about the albumin and sugar that I find, about my heart,
about the edema I have twice observed in the morning;
when, with the zeal of a hypochondriac, I look through the
textbooks on therapy, changing my medication daily, I keep
thinking I shall stumble on something comforting. It's all
very petty.

Whether the heavens are covered with clouds or bright
with a moon and stars, each time I look up on my way
home in the evenings I think that soon death will come for
me. It would seem that at such moments my thoughts would
be deep as the sky, clear, momentous. . . . But no! I think
about myself, my wife, Liza, Gnekker, my students, about
people in general; my thoughts are mean, petty; I try to
delude myself, and at these times my attitude to life might
be expressed in the words of the celebrated Arakcheyev, who
in one of his personal letters writes: "Everything good in this
world has something bad in it, and the bad always outweighs
the good." In other words, everything is vile, there is nothing
to live for, and the sixty-two years that I have already lived
are to be considered lost. Catching myself in such thoughts,
I try to persuade myself that they are fortuitous, transitory,
not deeply rooted; but the next moment I think:

"If that is so, then what draws you to those two toads
every evening?"

And I make a vow never to go to Katya's again, though I
know quite well that I shall go the next day.

As I ring my doorbell, and afterward going up the stairs,
I feel that now I have no family and have no desire for
one. Clearly the new Arakcheyev thoughts are not fortuitous and transitory, but dominate my whole being. Conscience-stricken, depressed, sluggish, barely able to move my
limbs, and feeling as though a ton had been added to my
weight, I get into bed and drop off to sleep.

And then—insomnia. . . .

# IV

With the advent of summer life changes.

One fine morning Liza comes into my room and says:

"Come, Your Excellency. Everything is ready."

My Excellency is led into the street, seated in a cab, and driven off. Having nothing better to do, I read signboards backward. The tavern sign "traktir" comes out Ritkart. A good name for a baroness—Baroness Ritkart. Driving along an open field we pass a cemetery, which makes absolutely no impression on me, though I know I shall soon be lying in it, through a wood, then more fields. Nothing of interest. After a two hours' drive, My Excellency is conducted into a summer cottage and installed in a room on the ground floor —a rather small but cheerful room with light blue wallpaper.

The night, as usual, is sleepless, but in the morning, not having to wake up and listen to my wife, I lie in bed. I do not sleep, but remain in that drowsy, half-conscious state in which you know you are not asleep, but dreaming. At noon I get up and sit at my table out of habit; now, instead of working, I amuse myself with French novels sent to me by Katya. It would, of course, be more patriotic to read Russian writers, but I must confess I have no particular liking for them. With the exception of two or three of our older writers, all contemporary writing strikes me as being not so much literature as some sort of home industry existing for no other reason than that it is being encouraged, even though its products enjoy no great success. The very best of these home products can hardly be called remarkable, and any sincere praise of them must be qualified by a "but"; and this holds true for all those literary novelties I have read in the last ten or fifteen years: not one is remarkable, not one exempt from a "but." Clever, edifying, but no talent; or talented, edifying, but not clever; or, finally, talented, clever, but not edifying.

I don't say that these French works are all edifying, talented, and clever. They don't satisfy me either. But they are less boring than Russian books, and it is not unusual to find in them the prime element of creative work—a sense of personal freedom, something that is lacking in Russian writers. I cannot recall a single one of our modern works in which the author has not taken pains from the very first page to involve himself in all sorts of conventions and covenants with his conscience. One is afraid to speak of nudity; another ties himself hand and foot with psychological analysis; a third feels he must have a "warm attitude toward humanity"; a fourth pads his book with descriptions of nature—whole pages of it—so he won't be suspected of tendentiousness. . . . One is bent on being the bourgeois at all costs, another on being the aristocrat, and so on. There is design, there is caution and a certain shrewdness, but neither the freedom nor the courage to write as one pleases, and consequently no creativeness.

All this applies to what is known as belles-lettres.

When it comes to serious articles by Russian writers on such subjects as sociology, art, and so on, I avoid reading them out of sheer timidity. In my childhood and early youth I had a fear of doormen and ushers, a fear which I retain to this day. I am still intimidated by them. It is said that we are only afraid of what we do not understand. And it is difficult, indeed, to understand why doormen and ushers are so pompous, so supercilious, so majestically rude. And when I read serious articles I feel this same undefined fear. Their extraordinary pomposity, the tone of Olympian waggery, the unceremonious treatment of foreign authors, and their dexterity and dignity in milling the wind—all this intimidates and alarms me, being so utterly unlike the modesty, the tone of gentlemanly restraint, to which I am accustomed when reading the works of naturalists or medical men.

And not only their articles, I even find it oppressive to read works translated or edited by our serious Russian writers. The vainglorious, patronizing tone of the prefaces, the superfluity of translator's notes, that prevent me from concentrating on the text, the bracketed question marks and the *sic!*s profusely scattered throughout the article or book, seem to me like so many violations of the author's personality and my independence as a reader.

I was once asked to appear as an expert in the circuit court; during a recess one of my fellow experts drew my attention to the rudeness of the prosecuting attorney to the defendants, among whom were two cultivated ladies. I believe I did not exaggerate when I told him that this rudeness was no worse than that displayed to one another by our writers of serious articles. In fact, this rudeness is so marked that I cannot speak of it without distress. Either they treat one another, or the authors they are criticizing, with a respect so exaggerated as to be undignified, or they deal with them more ruthlessly than I deal with my future son-in-law in my thoughts and in these notes. Accusations of irresponsibility, of dubious intentions, even of all sorts of crimes, are the customary adornments of these articles. All this, as young medical men are fond of saying in their articles, is the *ultima ratio!*

Such an attitude is inevitably reflected in the morals of the younger generation of writers, and consequently I am not at all surprised to find in the new works that have enriched our literature in the past ten or fifteen years, heroes who drink too much vodka and heroines who are somewhat less than chaste.

I sit reading my French novels, from time to time looking out the open window; I can see the tips of the fence palings, two or three scraggy trees, and beyond the fence a road, a meadow, and a broad strip of pine woods. Sometimes I watch a little boy and girl, both fair-haired and ragged, who clamber up the fence and laugh at my bald head. In their bright little eyes I read: "Look at baldy!" They are almost the only ones who care nothing for my rank and reputation.

People no longer come to see me every day. I will speak only of the visits of Nikolai and Pyotr Ignatyevich. Nikolai usually comes on holidays, ostensibly in connection with work, but in fact only to see me. He is always the worse for drink, which never happens in the winter.

"Well, how's everything?" I ask, going to meet him in the entry.

"Your Excellency!" he says, laying his hand on his heart and gazing at me with the ecstasy of a lover. "Your Excellency! . . . May God punish me! May lightning strike me dead on the spot! *Gaudeamus igitur Juvenestus. . . .*"

And he eagerly kisses me on the shoulder, the sleeve, the coat buttons.

"Everything all right back there?" I ask him.

"Your Excellency! As God is my witness . . ."

He tires me out with his pointless and incessant invocations, and I send him to the kitchen where they give him dinner.

Pyotr Ignatyevich also comes to see me on holidays; he comes not only to see how I am, but for the specific purpose of sharing his thoughts with me. He sits down near my table, modest, neat, circumspect, not venturing to cross his legs or lean his elbow on the table, and in an even, gentle voice and fluent bookish language recounts what to his mind are extremely interesting, piquant items of news, all gleaned from journals and books, and all resembling one another, belonging as they do to a single type: a certain Frenchman makes a discovery; some German denounces him by proving that his discovery had been made in 1870 by an American; a third person—also a German—outwits them both by proving that they both had made fools of themselves in mistaking air bubbles for dark pigment under the microscope.

Even when he wants to amuse me, Pyotr Ignatyevich speaks at great length and in the most minute detail, as if he were defending his dissertation; he enumerates all the literary sources from which his material is drawn, tries to be accurate in citing dates, issues of a journal, and names, giving every name in full—never simply Petit, but Jean Jacques Petit. Sometimes he stays to dinner with us, at which time he recounts the same piquant stories throughout the entire meal, reducing everyone at the table to a state of despair. If Gnekker and Liza turn the conversation to fugues and counterpoint, or Bach and Brahms, he lowers his eyes in modest confusion, embarrassed that such trivial subjects should be discussed in the presence of serious persons like myself and him.

In my present state of mind five minutes with him is enough to make me feel as if I had been looking at him and listening to him for an eternity. I detest the poor fellow. I simply wither under the steady sound of his soft voice and bookish language, and his anecdotes stupefy me. . . . He has nothing but the kindest feelings for me, talks for the sole purpose of giving me pleasure, and I repay him by staring at him as if I wanted to hypnotize him, all the while thinking: "Go, go, go. . . ." But he is not susceptible to mental suggestion and continues to stay, stay, stay. . . .

And as he sits before me I cannot rid myself of the thought: "When I die, it is quite possible that he will be appointed in my place"; then my poor lecture hall appears before my eyes as an oasis in which the spring is dry, and I am as ungracious, silent, and morose as if he, not I, were guilty of these thoughts. When he begins, as usual, to laud German scientists, instead of laughing at him good-naturedly, as I used to, I glumly mutter:

"A pack of asses, your Germans. . . ."

I know I am being like the late Professor Nikita Krylov, who, when bathing at Revel with Pirogov, was furious with the water for being cold, and burst out with: "These blasted Germans!" I behave badly with Pyotr Ignatyevich, and only when he has gone and I catch a glimpse of his gray hat on the other side of the garden fence do I have an impulse to call out to him and say: "Forgive me, my dear fellow!"

Our dinners are even more boring than in winter. Gnekker, whom I now loathe and despise, dines with us almost every day. Formerly I bore his presence in silence, now I direct caustic remarks at him, making my wife and Liza blush. Carried away by feelings of anger, I often say things that are simply stupid, without even knowing why I say them. Thus it happened on one occasion that I fixed my scornful gaze on him, and for no reason whatsoever blurted out:

"The eagle lower than the chick may fly,
But never will the chick soar upward to the sky. . . ."

And what I find most vexatious of all is that the chick-Gnekker shows himself to be much cleverer than the eagle-professor. Knowing that my wife and daughter are on his side, he holds to such tactics as responding to my gibes with a condescending silence (the old man's balmy—no use arguing with him) or making amiable fun of me. It is astounding to see how petty a man can become. I am capable of dreaming throughout an entire meal of how Gnekker will turn out to be an adventurer, how my wife and daughter will come to see their mistake, and how I will taunt them—this and other such absurd dreams when I have one foot in the grave!

There are now misunderstandings besides, which in the old days were known to me only by hearsay. Much as I am ashamed, I will describe one that occurred the other day after dinner.

I was sitting in my room smoking my pipe. My wife came in, as usual, sat down, and began talking about how nice it would be, now that the weather is warm and I am free, if I would go to Kharkov and find out what sort of man our Gnekker is.

"Very well, I'll go," I agreed.

Pleased with me, my wife got up and went to the door, but immediately turned back and said:

"Oh, and another thing . . . I know you'll be cross with me, but it is my duty to warn you. . . . Forgive my saying so, Nikolai Stepanych, but all our friends and neighbors have begun talking about how often you go to see Katya. She's an intelligent, educated girl, and I don't deny that she may be pleasant company, but, you know, it looks rather odd for a man of your age and social position to find pleasure in her society. . . . Besides, she has such a reputation that——"

All the blood suddenly left my brain, my eyes flashed, I sprang up, clutching my head, stamping my feet, and shouting:

"Leave me alone! Leave me alone! Leave me!"

My face must have looked awful, and my voice no doubt was strange, for all at once my wife turned pale and in a loud, unnatural voice uttered a desperate shriek. Hearing our cries Liza and Gnekker came running in, followed by Yegor. . . .

"Leave me alone!" I shouted. "Get out! Go away!"

My legs were numb, as if they no longer belonged to me. I felt myself falling into someone's arms, and was briefly aware of the sound of weeping before I fell into a swoon which lasted for two or three hours.

Now about Katya. She comes to see me every day before nightfall, and this, of course, cannot pass unnoticed by our friends and neighbors. She stops only for a minute, then takes me off for a drive with her. She has her own horse and a new little chaise, bought this summer. Altogether she lives in grand style. She has rented an expensive villa with a large garden, has moved all her furniture into it, and keeps two maids and a coachman. . . . I often ask her:

"Katya, what will you live on when you have run through all your father's money?"

"We shall see when the time comes," she replies.

"That money deserves to be treated more seriously, my dear. A good man worked hard to accumulate it."

"You have told me that before. I know."

First we drive through the meadow, then into the pine woods that I see from my window. Nature seems to me as beautiful as ever, though an evil spirit whispers that these pines and firs, these birds and white clouds overhead, will not even notice my absence, when, in three or four months, I am dead. Katya likes taking the reins; she enjoys the fine weather, and having me at her side, and, being in good spirits, refrains from saying harsh things.

"You are a very good man, Nikolai Stepanych," she says. "You are a rare specimen, the actor doesn't exist who could play you. Even a poor actor could play me, for instance, or Mikhail Fyodorych, but not you. I envy you, envy you terribly! After all, what have I made of myself? What?" She thinks for a minute, then asks: "Nikolai Stepanych, I'm nothing but a negative quantity, isn't that so? Isn't it?"

"Yes, it is," I answer.

"Hm-m. . . . And what can I do about it?"

How am I to answer her? It is easy to say: "Work," or "Give all you have to the poor," or "Know thyself," and just because it is so easy, I have no answer for her.

My colleagues who teach therapeutics advise: "Individualize each particular case." One has only to follow this advice to be convinced that the remedies recommended in textbooks as the best standard treatment prove to be absolutely useless in individual cases. This is no less true in moral disorders.

But I must give her some sort of answer, and I say:

"You have too much free time, dear. It's imperative that you find something to do. Why don't you go on the stage again, since acting is your vocation?"

"I can't."

"Why do you assume such a martyred air? I don't like that, my dear. Remember, it was you who became incensed at the people and the system, but you did nothing to improve either one. You didn't combat the evil, you were merely exhausted by it; you were the victim not of a struggle, but of your own weakness. Of course, you were young then, and inexperienced; now everything might be different. Do go on the stage again. You will be working, serving the sacred cause of art. . . ."

"Don't be so sly, Nikolai Stepanych," Katya interrupts me. "Let us agree once and for all: we will talk about actors, actresses, and writers, but leave art in peace. You are a fine, a rare person, but you do not sufficiently understand art to be able, in all conscience, to call it sacred. You've had no time to cultivate this feeling. In any case, I don't like these conversations about art!" she goes on nervously. "Don't like them at all! It has already been so vulgarized—I've had enough!"

"Who has vulgarized it?"

"Some have vulgarized it by their drinking, the newspapers be being so free with it, and clever people by their philosophy."

"Philosophy has nothing to do with it."

"Oh, yes it has. If anyone has to philosophize, that shows he doesn't understand it."

To avoid sharp words I hasten to change the subject, and then remain silent for some time. Only when we leave the woods and are driving toward Katya's house do I return to the subject and say:

"But you haven't told me why you don't want to go back to the stage."

"Nikolai Stepanych, this is really cruel!" she cries, suddenly blushing all over. "Do you want me to come right out and tell you the truth? Very well, if that's what you want! I have no talent! No talent and . . . and a great deal of vanity! There!"

After making this confession, she turns her face away from me and tugs violently at the reins to conceal the trembling of her hands.

As we drive up to the house we see Mikhail Fyodorovich walking near the gate, impatiently waiting for us.

"That Mikhail Fyodorych again!" Katya says with vexation. "Take him away from me, please! I'm fed up with him . . . such a washout. . . . I've had enough!"

Mikhail Fyodorovich was to have gone abroad some time ago, but he keeps postponing his departure from week to week. Certain changes have come over him lately: he looks drawn, drinks wine till he shows it—something he never did before—and his black eyebrows have begun to turn gray. When our chaise stops at the gate, he cannot conceal his joy and impatience. He makes a great fuss helping Katya and me to get out, bombards us with questions, laughs, rubs his hands, and that gentle, pure, imploring look, which I used to see only in his eyes, now suffuses his entire face. He is joyful, and at the same time ashamed of his joy, ashamed of his habit of spending every evening with Katya, and feels impelled to account for his presence by some such obvious absurdity as:

"I was driving by on business and thought I'd drop in for a minute."

We all go into the house; first we have tea, then the long familiar objects begin to appear on the table—the packs of cards, the big piece of cheese, fruit, the bottle of Crimean champagne. The subjects of our conversation are the same too; we talk about the very things we discussed in the winter. The theater, literature, the university and students all come in for their share; the air grows thick and stifling with malicious talk, only now, unlike the winter, it is poisoned by the breath of three toads instead of two. Besides the velvety baritone laugh and the concertinalike giggle, the maid who waits on us now hears the jarring disagreeable laugh of a stage general: he-he-he!

# V

There are nights made terrible by thunder, lightning, wind and rain—"sparrow nights," the country people call them. I experienced just such a "sparrow night" in my personal life. . . .

I woke up after midnight and instantly leaped out of bed. It suddenly seemed to me that I was about to die. What made it seem so? I experienced no particular bodily sensation that would indicate the end was near, but my soul was as oppressed by horror as if I had just seen a huge ominous glow in the sky.

Hastily lighting the lamp, I drank some water straight from the carafe and rushed to the open window. It was a magnificent night. There was the scent of new-mown hay, and something else that smelled sweet. I saw the tips of the fence palings, the gaunt drowsy trees by the window, the road, and the dark strip of woodland; the moon shone serene and bright in the cloudless sky. It was still; not a leaf stirred. I felt that everything was looking at me, holding its breath, waiting for me to die. . . .

It was sinister. I closed the window and quickly went back to bed. I felt for my pulse, and, unable to find it in my wrist, felt my temples, then my chin, and again my wrist, and wherever I touched my body it was cold and clammy. My breathing became more and more rapid, my whole body trembled, and inside me there was turmoil; I had the sensation there were cobwebs on my face and bald spot.

What should I do? Call my family? No, it would be useless. I could not imagine what my wife and Liza would do if they were to come.

I hid my head under the pillow, closed my eyes, and waited . . . and waited. . . . My back was cold, I felt as if my spine was being drawn inward; it was as if death was definitely creeping up to me from behind. . . .

"Kee-vee! Kee-vee!" a screech suddenly pierced the silence of the night, and I could not tell whether it came from outside or from within my breast.

"Kee-vee! Kee-vee!"

My God, how frightful! I wanted to take another drink of water, but I was afraid to open my eyes, afraid to raise my head. I was in the grip of an unaccountable animal fear, unable to understand what I was afraid of; was it that I wanted to live, or that some new unknown pain was in store for me?

Upstairs, in the room overhead, someone either groaned or laughed. . . . I strained my ears. Soon afterward I heard footsteps on the stairs. Someone hurried down, then went back up. A minute later, again the sound of footsteps descending, and someone stopped outside my door and listened.

"Who's there?" I cried.

The door opened. I intrepidly opened my eyes and saw my wife. Her face was pale and her eyes red from weeping.

"Are you awake, Nikolai Stepanych?" she asked.

"What is it?"

"For God's sake, come and see Liza! Something has happened to her. . . ."

"Very well . . . I'll be glad to . . ." I mumbled, relieved at not being alone. "Very well . . . at once. . . ."

I followed my wife, listening to what she was telling me, but too agitated to understand a word. Spots of light from her candle danced on the stairs and our elongated shadows trembled; it seemed to me that someone was pursuing me, trying to seize me from behind; my feet got caught in the skirts of my dressing gown and I gasped for breath.

"I'm going to die right here on the staircase," I thought. "This very minute. . . ."

But the stairs came to an end and we approached Liza's room along a dark corridor with an Italian window. Liza was sitting on the bed with her legs hanging over the side; she had nothing on but a nightgown and was moaning.

"Oh, my God . . . Oh, my God . . ." she mumbled, squinting at the light of our candles. "I cannot, I cannot. . . ."

"Liza, my child," I said, "what is it?"

When she saw me she gave a cry and flung herself on my neck.

"Papa, my good, kind Papa . . ." she sobbed. "My darling, my dearest Papa. . . . I don't know what's the matter with me . . . I'm so miserable!"

She put her arms around me and kissed me, babbling endearing expressions I had not heard from her since she was a child.

"Calm yourself, little one. God bless you," I said. "There's no need to cry. I am miserable too."

I tried to cover her up and my wife gave her something to drink; as we clumsily jostled each other at the bedside, my shoulder brushing my wife's shoulder, I was reminded of how together we used to give our children their baths.

"Help her, help her!" my wife implored me. "Do something for her!"

What could I do? I could do nothing. The poor girl's heart was burdened with something I did not understand, something I knew nothing about, and I could only murmur:

"Never mind, never mind. . . . It will pass. . . . Go to sleep, go to sleep. . . ."

To make things worse, a dog howled outside; at first it was a subdued uncertain sound, then it grew louder as two dogs commenced howling together. I had never attached any significance to such omens as the howling of dogs or the hooting of owls, but now my heart contracted painfully and I hastened to give myself an explanation of this howling.

"It's nonsense," I thought, "the influence of one organism upon another. My violent nervous tension communicated itself to my wife, to Liza, to the dog, that's all. . . . This sort of transference explains prescience and forebodings."

A little later, when I returned to my room to write a prescription for Liza, I no longer thought about my imminent death, but felt so heavy-hearted, so depressed, that I was sorry not to die then and there. For a long time I stood motionless in the middle of the room trying to think what to prescribe for Liza; the moaning overhead ceased and I decided not to prescribe anything, yet I continued to stand there. . . .

The silence was deathly, a silence which, as some writer has put it, rings in your ears. Time passed slowly, the strips of moonlight on the window sill did not move but seemed frozen there. . . . Dawn would be long in coming.

Suddenly the gate creaked, someone stole toward the house, broke a twig from one of the scraggy trees, and cautiously tapped on the window with it.

"Nikolai Stepanych!" I heard a whisper. "Nikolai Stepanych!"

I opened the window and thought I must be dreaming: huddled against the wall under the window, the moonlight full upon her, stood a woman in black gazing up at me with big eyes. Her face was pale, austere, fantastic in the moonlight, as if carved in marble, but her chin was quivering.

"It is I," she said. "I—Katya!"

All women's eyes look big and black in the moonlight, and everyone looks taller and paler; probably for this reason I had failed to recognize her at first.

"What's the matter?"

"Forgive me," she said. "I suddenly felt unbearably miserable. . . . I couldn't stand it and came here. . . . There was a light in your window and . . . and I decided to knock. . . . Forgive me. . . . Oh, if you only knew how wretched I am! What are you doing up?"

"Nothing . . . I couldn't sleep."

"I had a sort of foreboding. But, of course, it's nonsense."

Her eyebrows were raised, tears glistened in her eyes, and her whole face was radiant with the expression of trustfulness that I knew so well but had not seen for a long time.

"Nikolai Stepanych!" she pleaded, holding out her arms to me. "My darling, I beg you, implore you . . . if you do not scorn my friendship and respect for you, do what I ask of you!"

"What is it?"

"Take my money!"

"Come, now, what an idea! What would I do with your money?"

"You could go away somewhere for your health. You need medical treatment. Will you take the money? Will you? Yes, my darling?"

She gazed eagerly into my face and repeated:

"Yes? Will you take it?"

"No, my dear, I will not take it," I said. "Thank you."

She turned her back to me and bowed her head. No doubt there was something in the tone of my refusal which did not admit of further talk about money.

"Go home to bed," I said. "We'll see each other tomorrow."

"So you don't consider me your friend?" she asked despondently.

"I didn't say that. But your money is of no use to me now."

"I beg your pardon . . ." she said, dropping her voice a whole octave. "I understand. . . . To be indebted to a person like me—a retired actress. . . . Well, good-bye. . . ."

And she went away so quickly that I had no time to say good-bye to her.

## VI

I am in Kharkov.

Since it would have been useless and, indeed, beyond my strength to struggle against my present mood, I have determined that the last days of my life should be irreproachable, at least outwardly. If I have been wrong where my family is concerned, which I am well aware is the case, then I will try to do what they wish. I am asked to go to Kharkov—I go to Kharkov. Besides, I have grown so indifferent to everything of late that it does not matter to me where I go—to Kharkov, to Paris, to Berdichev.

I arrived here at midday and came to this hotel not far from the cathedral. The rocking of the train and cold drafts have left me in such a state that I can do nothing but sit on the side of the bed holding my head and waiting for my tic to begin. I ought to have gone to see some of my acquaintances among the professors today, but I have neither the strength nor the inclination.

An old hall porter comes in and asks whether I have brought my own bed linen with me. I detain him for five minutes and question him about Gnekker, on whose account I have come here. The old man turns out to be a native of Kharkov, knows the town like the palm of his hand, but does not remember any family by the name of Gnekker. I question him about the estate—same answer.

The clock in the corridor strikes one, then two, then three. . . . These last months of waiting for death to come have seemed longer to me than all the rest of my life. And never before have I been so reconciled to the slow passage of time. Formerly, if I had to wait in the station for a train, or sit through the students' examinations, a quarter of an hour seemed an eternity, but now I can sit motionless on the side of my bed all night, thinking with complete indifference that tomorrow will be followed by another such long and dismal night, and the day after tomorrow. . . .

The clock in the corridor strikes five, six. . . . It grows dark.

In order to occupy my thoughts, I try to recover the point of view I had before I became indifferent, and ask myself: why am I, a distinguished man, a privy councilor, sitting in this little hotel room, on the side of this bed with the strange gray blanket? Why am I looking at this cheap tin washstand and listening to the jangling of that wretched clock in the corridor? Is this in keeping with my reputation and high position? My answer to these questions is an ironic smile. It amuses me to think of the naïveté with which, in my youth, I exaggerated the importance of fame and the exceptional position that celebrities are supposed to enjoy. I am famous, my name is pronounced with reverence, my picture has appeared in the *Niva* and the *Illustrated World News*, I have even read my biography in a German magazine—and what of it? Here I sit, utterly alone, in a strange city, on a strange bed, rubbing my aching cheek with the palm of my hand. . . .

Family squabbles, the implacability of creditors, the rudeness of railway employees, the inconvenience of the passport system, the expensive and unwholesome food in station buffets, the universal ignorance and coarseness in human relations—all this and a great many other things which it would take too long to enumerate, concern me no less than the ordinary citizen who is known no further than his own street. Then what is so special about my situation? Let us suppose that I am celebrated a thousand times over, that I am a hero of whom my country is proud; that bulletins on the state of my health appear in all the newspapers, letters of sympathy pour in from colleagues, students, the general public; yet all this will not prevent me from dying in a strange bed, in misery and utter loneliness. . . . No one is to blame for it, of course, but, I am sorry to say, I have no love for my renown. It appears to have betrayed me.

I fall asleep around ten o'clock, sleeping soundly in spite

of my tic, and had I not been awakened should have slept a long time. Shortly after one there is a knock at the door.

"Who's there?"

"A telegram."

"You might have waited till morning," I say angrily, taking the telegram from the hall porter.

"Excuse me. Your light was on, so I thought you were awake."

I open the telegram and look first at the signature: from my wife. What can she want?

"Gnekker and Liza married secretly yesterday. Return."

After reading the telegram I am momentarily alarmed, but what alarms me is not so much what Liza and Gnekker have done as my own indifference to the news of their marriage. They say that philosophers and wise men are indifferent. This is not true. Indifference is a paralysis of the soul, a premature death.

Again I go to bed and try to think of something to occupy my mind. What am I to think about? Everything has been thought over; there seems to be nothing left to arouse my interest.

When daylight comes I sit up in bed, clasping my knees, and try, for want of something better to do, to understand myself. "Know thyself" is excellent and useful advice; it is only a pity that the ancients failed to indicate a method for following it.

In the past when I wanted to understand someone, or even myself, I took into consideration, not actions, which are always conditional, but desires. Tell me what you want and I will tell you what you are.

And now I examine myself. What do I want?

I want our wives, children, friends, and students to love in us, not the fame, the label, the connections, but the ordinary man. What else? I should like to have assistants and successors. What else? I should like to wake up a hundred years from now and have a glimpse of what is going on in science. I should like to have lived another ten years. . . . Anything more?

No, nothing more. I think and think, but can think of nothing further. And no matter how much I may think, nor how far-reaching my thoughts, it is clear to me that there is nothing vital, nothing of great importance, in my desires. In my passion for science, in my desire to live, in this sitting up in a strange bed and trying to know myself, in all the thoughts, feelings, and conceptions that I formulate, there is no common element, nothing that would unify them into a whole. Each thought and feeling exists in isolation, and in all my judgments of science, the theater, literature, and my students, in all the pictures my imagination paints, even the most skillful analyst would be unable to find what is called a general idea, or the god of a living man.

And without this there is nothing.

Given such poverty of spirit, any serious ailment, the fear of death, the influence of circumstances or of people, would be enough to upset and scatter to the winds all that I have been accustomed to regard as an outlook that embodied the joy and meaning of my life. It is consequently no wonder that the last months of my life are darkened by thoughts and feelings worthy of a slave and a barbarian, and that I now am indifferent and take no heed of the dawn. When that which is higher and stronger than all external influences is lacking in a man, a good head cold is enough to upset his equilibrium and make him see an owl in every bird and hear the howl of a dog in every sound. At such times all his pessimism or optimism, all his thoughts both great and small, are significant only as symptoms, nothing more.

I am defeated. This being so, it is useless to go on thinking, useless to talk. I will sit and wait in silence for what is to come.

In the morning the porter brings me tea and a copy of the local newspaper. I mechanically read through the advertisements on the first page, the leading article, extracts from other newspapers and magazines, the news of the day. . . . Among the news items I find the following: "The celebrated scientist, Honored Professor Nikolai Stepanovich So-and-So arrived in Kharkov yesterday by express train, and is staying at the Such-and-Such Hotel."

Great names are apparently created to live a life of their own, apart from those who bear them. At this moment my name is nonchalantly parading about Kharkov; in another three months, set out in gold letters on my tombstone, it will blaze like the sun itself—while I shall be covered with moss.

A light tap on the door. Somebody to see me.

"Who's there? Come in."

The door opens, I step back in astonishment, hastily drawing my dressing gown around me. Before me stands Katya.

"How are you?" she says, out of breath from having climbed the stairs. "You weren't expecting me, were you? I too . . . I too . . . have come. . . ."

She sits down, stammering and not looking at me.

"Why don't you say something? I just arrived . . . found out you were in this hotel . . . and came to see you."

"I am very happy to see you," I say, shrugging my shoulders, "but I am surprised. . . . It's as if you had dropped from the sky. What have you come for?"

"Oh . . . I just thought . . . I'd come. . . ."

Silence. All at once she jumps up and impulsively comes to me.

"Nikolai Stepanych!" she says, turning pale and pressing her hands to her breast. "Nikolai Stepanych! I cannot go on living like this! I cannot! In God's name, tell me quickly, this very minute: what am I to do? Tell me, what am I to do?"

"What can I say?" I am perplexed. "There's nothing I can say."

"Tell me, I implore you!" she goes on breathlessly, trembling from head to foot. "I swear I cannot go on like this! It's too much for me!"

She sinks into a chair and begins sobbing. Throwing back her head, she wrings her hands and stamps her feet; her hat slips off her head and dangles by its elastic, her hair is disheveled.

"Help me! Help me!" she pleads. "I can't go on any longer!"

She takes a handkerchief out of her traveling bag and with it pulls out several letters, which fall from her lap to the floor. As I pick them up, I accidentally catch sight of the word "passiona–" on one of them, and recognize Mikhail Fyodorovich's handwriting.

"There is nothing I can tell you, Katya," I say.

"Help me!" she sobs, seizing my hand and kissing it. "After all, you are my father, my only friend! And you are wise, educated, you have lived a long time! You have been a teacher! Tell me: what am I to do?"

"Honestly, Katya, I do not know. . . ."

I am utterly at a loss, bewildered, touched by her sobs, and barely able to stand on my feet.

"Come, let's have some breakfast, Katya," I say with a forced smile. "No more crying."

And then I add in a sinking voice:

"I shall soon be gone, Katya. . . ."

"Just one word, even a word!" she weeps, stretching out her hands to me. "What shall I do?"

"What a queer girl you are, really . . ." I mutter. "I don't understand. . . . Such a sensible girl, and suddenly you . . . go off into tears!"

Silence. Katya arranges her hair, puts on her hat, crumples up the letters and stuffs them into her bag—all very deliberately and without a word. Her face, the front of her dress, and her gloves are wet with tears, but her expression is cold and austere. . . . Looking at her I feel ashamed of being happier than she is. I have discovered in myself the absence of what my philosophic colleagues call a general idea only recently, in my decline, and in the face of death, but the soul of this poor creature has never found and never in her life will find refuge . . . never in her life!

"Come, Katya, let us have breakfast," I say.

"No, thank you," she replies coldly.

Another minute passes in silence.

"I don't like Kharkov," I say. "It's so gray here. . . . Such a gray town."

"Yes, I suppose it is. . . . It's ugly. . . . I shan't be here for long. . . . I'm only passing through. I leave today."

"Where are you going?"

"To the Crimea—to the Caucasus, I mean."

"Oh! For long?"

"I don't know."

Katya gets up, smiling coldly, and without looking at me holds out her hand.

I feel like saying: "So you won't be at my funeral?" But she does not look at me; her hand is cold, like the hand of a stranger. I accompany her to the door in silence. . . . Now she has left me, and walks down the long corridor without glancing back. She knows that I am watching her and will probably look back when she reaches the turn. . . .

No, she did not look back. Her black dress has disappeared from sight for the last time, the sound of her footsteps dies away. . . . Farewell, my precious!

1889

# MY LIFE

## (The Story of a Provincial)

### I

The director said to me: "I only keep you out of respect for your esteemed father; otherwise you would have been sent flying long ago." I replied: "You flatter me, Your Excellency, in assuming that I am capable of flying." And then I heard him say: "Take that gentleman away, he gets on my nerves."

Two days later I was discharged. And thus, to the great chagrin of my father, the municipal architect, in the time that I have been considered an adult I have changed my position nine times.

I have served in various government departments, but all nine of those jobs were as identical as drops of water: I had to sit, write, listen to inane or rude remarks, and wait to be discharged.

When I approached my father he was buried in an armchair with his eyes closed. His gaunt, dry face, with a bluish cast where it was shaved (he had the face of an old Catholic organist), expressed humility and resignation. Without responding to my greeting or opening his eyes, he said:

"If my dear wife, your mother, were alive, your life would be a source of constant grief to her. I see the hand of Divine Providence in her untimely death. Tell me, you unfortunate boy," he continued, as he opened his eyes, "what am I to do with you?"

In the past, when I was younger, my friends and relations knew what to do with me: some advised me to volunteer for the army, others to go into a pharmacy, others into the telegraph service; but now that I am over twenty-five and even growing gray at the temples, and have already been in the army, in a pharmacy, and in the telegraph service, every earthly possibility, it would seem, has been exhausted, and they have given up advising me and merely sigh or shake their heads.

"What do you think of yourself?" my father continued. "At your age young men already have an established social position, and just look at you: a proletarian, a beggar, living on your father!"

And, as usual, he went on to say that the young people of today are going to ruin through lack of faith, materialism, and an inordinate self-conceit, and that amateur theatricals ought to be prohibited because they divert young people from duty and religion.

"Tomorrow we'll go together and you shall apologize to the director and promise him that you will do your work conscientiously," he concluded. "You must not remain a single day without a position in society."

"Please listen to me," I said glumly, though I did not expect anything to come of this conversation. "What you call a position in society is the privilege of capital and education. People who are poor and uneducated have to earn their daily bread by manual labor, and I can see no reason why I should be an exception."

"When you start talking about manual labor it sounds stupid and banal!" said my father irritably. "Understand, you idiot, and get it into your brainless head, that in addition to brute physical strength you have the divine spirit, the sacred fire, which to the very highest degree distinguishes you from the ass or the reptile and brings you nearer to the Deity! For thousands of years this fire has been kept burning by the best of mankind. Your great-grandfather, General Polozniev, fought at Borodino; your grandfather was a poet, an orator, and a Marshal of the Nobility; your uncle, a pedagogue; and lastly, I, your father, am an architect! All the Poloznievs have kept the sacred fire burning—for you to put it out!"

"One must be just," I said. "Millions of people endure physical labor."

"Let them! They don't know how to do anything else! Anyone, any abject fool or criminal, can do physical work; it is the mark of the slave and the barbarian, while the sacred fire is vouchsafed only to the few!"

It was useless to go on with this conversation. My father worshiped himself, and to him nothing was convincing unless he himself had said it. Besides, I knew very well that his supercilious attitude toward manual labor was based not so much on any regard for the sacred fire as on a secret dread that I might become a workingman and set the whole town to talking about me; but the chief thing was that all my contemporaries had graduated from the university long ago and were getting on in the world—the son of the manager of the State Bank was already a collegiate assessor—while I, an only son, was nothing! To pursue the conversation was futile and unpleasant, but I continued to sit there, making feeble rejoinders, hoping that in the end I might be understood. The whole problem, of course, was clear and simple, and concerned nothing except how I was to earn a living, but he could not see the simplicity of it and went on talking to me in mawkish, fulsome phrases about Borodino, the sacred fire, my uncle, and the forgotten poet who had once written worthless, artificial verses, and he kept rudely calling me a brainless fool. And how I longed to be understood! In spite of everything, I loved my father and my sister, and from childhood it has been my habit to consider them, a habit so deeply rooted that I shall probably never get rid of it; whether I am right or wrong, I am constantly afraid of hurting them, afraid that my father's thin neck will turn red with agitation, that he might have a stroke.

"To sit in a stuffy room copying papers," I said, "competing with a typewriter, is shameful and degrading to a man my age. How can there be any question of the sacred fire!"

"At least it's intellectual work," my father said. "But that's enough, let us drop this conversation. And in any case, I warn you: if you persist in your contemptible inclinations and refuse to go back to your office, then I and my daughter will deprive you of our love. And I shall cut you out of my will—I swear by the living God!"

With absolute sincerity, in order to show the complete purity of the motives by which I hoped to be guided throughout my life, I said:

"The question of inheritance is of no importance to me. I renounce everything in advance."

For some quite unexpected reason my father was deeply offended by my words. He turned purple.

"Don't you dare talk to me like that, you fool!" he shouted in a high, shrill voice. "Good-for-nothing!" And with a quick, dexterous, and accustomed gesture, he slapped me twice across the face. "You are forgetting yourself!"

When my father used to beat me as a child, I was required to stand erect, hands at my sides, and look him straight in the face. And now when he struck me I was confused, and, as though still a child, drew myself up and tried to look him in the eye. My father was old and very thin, but his spare muscles must have been as strong as a strap for his blows were very painful.

I stepped back into the hall and there he snatched up his umbrella and struck me several times over the head and shoulders; at that moment my sister opened the drawing-room door to see what the noise was, and immediately drew back, looking horrified and full of pity, but without having said a word in my defense.

My intention not to return to the government office but to begin a new life as a workingman was unshakable. It only remained for me to choose the kind of work—and this presented no particular difficulty, as it seemed to me that I was strong, hardy, and capable of the very heaviest kind of labor. I was facing a monotonous workingman's life with its hunger, stench, and rough surroundings, its constant preoccupation with wages and food. And—who knows?—returning from work along Bolshaya Dvoryanskaya Street, I might occasionally envy Dolzhikov, the engineer, who makes his living by intellectual work; but at the moment, thinking about all these future hardships made me feel cheerful. At one time I had dreamed of intellectual activity, imagining myself a teacher, a doctor, or a writer, but my dreams remained dreams. The predilection for intellectual pleasures—the theater, for example, and reading—developed into a passion with me, but whether I had the capacity for intellectual work I do not know. At school I had an invincible aversion for Greek, so much so that they had to take me out of school when I was in the fourth grade. I was tutored for a long time in preparation for the fifth grade. Later I served in various government offices where I spent a large part of the day in complete idleness, and this, I was told, was intellectual work. My activity in scholastic and official spheres required neither mental effort, nor talent, nor personal qualifications, nor any creative impulse; it was me-

chanical, and that kind of intellectual work I consider lower
than manual labor; I despise it and do not think that even
for a minute it can justify an idle, carefree life, because it
is nothing but a sham, another aspect of that selfsame idleness. In all probability I have never known genuine intellectual work.

Evening was approaching. We lived on Bolshaya Dvoryanskaya Street—the main street of the town—and in the evening, since we lacked a decent public park, it served as a
promenade for our *beau monde*. This charming street did
to some extent take the place of a park, lined as it was on
either side with poplars that smelled sweet, particularly after
a rain, and with its acacias, tall lilac bushes, black alders,
and apple trees behind the fences and palings. The May
twilight, the tender young foliage, the scent of lilac and
the hum of insects, the warmth and stillness—how new,
how wondrous it is, although it recurs every year! I stood
at the gate watching the strollers. I had grown up with most
of them, they had been my playmates, but now any familiarity with me would have embarrassed them, for I was
poorly and unfashionably dressed; people used to talk about
my narrow trousers and big, clumsy boots, saying that they
looked like macaroni stuck on gunboats. Moreover, I had a
bad reputation in the town because I had no social position and often played billiards in low taverns; also, perhaps,
because on two occasions I had been hauled up before the
police, for no particular reason.

In the large house opposite, where the engineer Dolzhikov
lived, someone was playing the piano. It was beginning to
grow dark, stars glimmered in the sky. My father, in an old
top hat with a broad curling brim, walked slowly by with
my sister on his arm, bowing in response to greetings.

"Look up!" he said to my sister, pointing to the sky with
the same umbrella he had used to beat me that afternoon.
"Look at the sky! Those stars, even the very smallest of
them, are all worlds! How insignificant is man in comparison
with the universe!"

And he said this in a tone which suggested that he found
it extremely flattering and pleasant to be so insignificant.
What an untalented man he was! Unfortunately he was
our only architect, and within my memory—the last fifteen
to twenty years—not a single decent house had been built.
When anyone commissioned him to draw a plan he usually

began with the reception hall and drawing room; just as in the old days young ladies in boarding schools were unable to dance unless they could start from the beginning, so his artistic ideas could originate and develop only from a reception hall and drawing room. Then he tacked on the dining room, nursery, and study, connecting them all by doors, so that they inevitably turned out to be passages, and every room had two or three superfluous doors. His ideas must have been vague, limited, and extremely muddled; and in every instance, as though sensing that something was lacking, he would resort to all kinds of outbuildings, planting them one on top of the other, and I can see now the cramped little entries and narrow passages, the crooked stairways leading up to mezzanines where it was impossible to stand upright, and where, instead of a floor, there would be three huge steps like shelves in a bathhouse; and the kitchen, without fail, would be under the house with a vaulted ceiling and brick floor. The façade of the house wore an obdurate, forbidding expression, with its stiff timorous lines, its low squat roof, and fat bun-shaped chimneys invariably topped with wire chimneypots and black, squeaky weather vanes. And for some reason all these houses built by my father—and all resembling one another—vaguely reminded me of his top hat and the back of his stiff, stubborn neck. In the course of time our town grew accustomed to my father's lack of talent; it took root and became the local style.

My father introduced this style into my sister's life. To begin with, he named her Kleopatra (just as he called me Misail). When she was still a little girl he used to frighten her with tales about the stars, the wise men, and our forefathers, expounding at length the nature of life and duty; and now, when she was twenty-six, he went on in the same way, allowing her to walk arm in arm with no one but himself, and imagining that sooner or later a suitable young man would appear and want to marry her out of respect for her father's personal qualities. Yet she adored my father; she feared him and was convinced of his extraordinary intelligence.

It was now quite dark and before long the street was empty. In the house opposite, the music stopped; the gates were thrown open, and, with a light jingling of bells, a

troika careened out into our street. It was the engineer and
his daughter going for a drive. Time to go to bed.

I had my own room in the house, but I lived in the yard
in a hut that shared a roof with the brick shed and had
probably been built as a harness room—there were large
spikes driven into the walls—but was no longer needed; for
the last thirty years my father had used it for storing his
newspapers, which, for some reason, he had bound half-
yearly and allowed no one to touch. Living here I was less
apt to be seen by my father and his guests, and I felt that
if I did not live in a real room and did not go to the house
for dinner every day, my father's reproach that I was living on him lost some of its sting.

My sister was waiting for me. Unknown to my father,
she had brought me supper: a small piece of cold veal and
a slice of bread. In our house such sayings as: "Money
loves an account," "A kopeck saves a ruble," and so on,
were repeated regularly, and my sister, weighed down by
such platitudes, did her utmost to cut down expenses; as a
consequence we were badly fed. She set the plate on the
table, then sat down on my bed and began to cry.

"Misail," she said, "what are you doing to us?"

She did not cover her face, and the tears dropped on her
bosom and hands and her expression was mournful. She
fell onto the pillow and gave way to her tears, her whole
body shuddering with sobs.

"You have left your job again," she said. "Oh, how awful
it is!"

"But try to understand, sister, try to understand," I said,
overcome with despair because of her tears.

As if by design the kerosene in my little lamp gave out
and it commenced smoking and guttering, and the old spikes
in the walls glared ominously, their shadows flickering.

"Have mercy on us!" said my sister, sitting up. "Father is
terribly distressed, and I am ill—I shall go out of my mind.
What will become of you?" she asked, sobbing and holding
out her hands to me. "I beg you, I implore you, for the
sake of our dear mother: go back to the office!"

"I cannot, Kleopatra!" I said, feeling that it would not
take much more to make me give in. "I cannot!"

"Why not?" my sister insisted. "Why not? If you can't get
along with the head of the office, then look for another
place. Why shouldn't you work on the railroad, for instance?

I have just been talking to Anyuta Blagovo, and she assured me they would take you on, she even promised to do what she could for you. For God's sake, Misail, think about it. Think, I implore you!"

We talked a little longer and I gave in. I told her that the thought of working on the railroad which was now being constructed had never occurred to me and that if she liked I was willing to try.

She smiled happily through her tears and clasped my hand, but afterward continued crying because she could not stop, and I went to the kitchen for kerosene.

## II

Among the town's devotees of amateur theatricals, concerts, and *tableaux vivants* which were given for charity, the Azhogins, who had their own house in Bolshaya Dvoryanskaya Street, were the leaders; they always provided the place, and took upon themselves all the necessary trouble and expense. They were a rich landowning family with some nine thousand acres and a magnificent estate in the district, but, not caring for the country, they lived in town summer and winter. The family consisted of the mother, a tall, thin, delicate lady who wore her hair short and dressed in the English fashion in a straight skirt and short jacket, and her three daughters, who were never referred to by name, but simply as the eldest, the middle one, and the youngest. They all had sharp, ugly chins, were nearsighted, round-shouldered, dressed like their mother, and lisped most unattractively, in spite of which they invariably took part in every performance and were always doing something for charity—acting, reciting, singing. They were exceedingly serious, never smiled, and even in comic sketches performed without the least gaiety, but with a businesslike air, as though engaged in bookkeeping.

I loved our theatricals, especially all the noisy and somewhat confused rehearsals, after which we were always given supper. I had no hand in choosing the plays or assigning the parts; my place was behind the scenes. I painted the scenery, copied out the parts, prompted, and made up the actors; and I was also entrusted with the various stage effects, such as thunder, the singing of nightingales, and so on. Because I had no social position and no decent clothes, I kept to myself at rehearsals, staying in the shadow of the wings and maintaining a bashful silence.

I painted the scenery in the Azhogins' yard or coach house, and was assisted by a house painter, or, as he called himself, a painting contractor, Andrei Ivanov, a tall, pale, extremely thin man of about fifty, with a hollow chest, sunken temples, and blue rings under his eyes—quite dreadful-looking. He suffered from a consuming disease of some sort, and every spring and autumn people would say he could not last, but after spending some time in bed he would get up and say: "Well, I didn't die this time!"

The townspeople called him Radish and said it was his real name. He loved the theater as much as I, and no sooner did he hear that a performance was being planned than he dropped his work and went to the Azhogins' to paint scenery.

The day after my talk with my sister I worked from morning till night at the Azhogins'. The rehearsal was set for seven o'clock in the evening, and an hour before it was time to begin all those taking part had gathered in the reception hall, and the eldest, the middle one, and the youngest were walking about the stage reading their parts. Radish, in a long rust-colored overcoat, with a scarf wound around his neck, stood leaning his head against a wall, gazing at the stage with a reverent expression. Madam Azhogin went from one guest to another, saying something pleasant to everyone. She had a way of peering intently into one's face and speaking in a hushed voice, as though confiding a secret.

"It must be difficult to paint scenery," she said softly, as she came up to me. "I was just talking to Madam Mufke about superstitions when I saw you come in. My goodness, all my life I have been waging war against superstition! To convince the servants that all these terrors of theirs are nonsense, I always light three candles, and I begin all my important affairs on the thirteenth."

The daughter of Dolzhikov, the engineer, came in, a beautiful, plump blonde, dressed, as they say, in a completely Parisian style. She did not act, but a chair was put on the stage for her at rehearsals, and a performance never began until she had appeared in the front row, dazzling and astounding everyone with her finery. As a belle from the capital she was allowed to make comments during the rehearsals, which she did with a sweet, condescending smile; it was obvious that she regarded our performances as a childish pastime. She was said to have studied singing at the Petersburg Conservatory, and to have sung for a whole winter in a private opera company. I was very much taken with her, and generally during rehearsals or performances never took my eyes off her.

I had just picked up the script to begin prompting when my sister unexpectedly appeared. Without taking off her cloak and hat she came up to me and said:

"Please, come!"

I went with her. In the doorway behind the stage stood Anyuta Blagovo, also wearing a hat and a dark veil. She was the daughter of the vice-president of the court, a man who had held that office in our town for years, almost from the time the circuit court had been established. Being tall and having a good figure, she was considered indispensable for the *tableaux vivants,* and when she impersonated a fairy or Glory her face burned with shame; but she took no part in the dramatic performances and only dropped in at rehearsals on some errand, never coming into the hall. And now it was apparent that she had come only for a moment.

"My father was speaking about you," she said dryly, not looking at me and blushing. "Dolzhikov has promised to find you a place with the railroad. Go and see him tomorrow, he'll be at home."

I bowed and thanked her for her trouble.

"And you can give this up," she said, pointing to my script.

She and my sister went up to Madam Azhogin and began whispering and looking at me. They were discussing something with her.

"Indeed," Madam Azhogin said softly, as she came toward me, peering intently into my face, "indeed, if this distracts you from serious pursuits," and she drew the script out of my hands, "you can hand it over to someone else. Don't worry, my friend, go along, it will be all right."

I said good-bye to her and left, very much embarrassed. As I went down the stairs I saw my sister and Anyuta Blagovo hurrying away, talking animatedly about something, probably about my working for the railroad. My sister had never been to a rehearsal before, and now she was probably conscience-stricken and afraid my father would find out that she had gone to the Azhogins' without his permission.

The next day I went to Dolzhikov's around one o'clock. The footman showed me into a very beautiful room which was both a drawing room and the engineer's study. Everything was soft and elegant, and for a man as unaccustomed to luxury as I, it seemed strange. There were costly rugs, huge armchairs, bronzes, pictures in gold and velvet frames; the photographs strewn over the walls were of beautiful women in leisurely attitudes, with charming, intelligent faces; from the drawing room a door led straight into the garden, and on the veranda I could see lilacs and a table set for lunch on which stood several bottles and a bowl of roses; there was a fragrance of spring and of expensive cigars, a fragrance of happiness—and everything seemed to say: here lives a man who has worked and won the highest happiness possible on earth. At the writing table the engineer's daughter sat reading a newspaper.

"Have you come to see my father?" she asked. "He's taking a shower, he'll be here presently. Won't you sit down meanwhile?"

I sat down.

"I believe you live across the street, don't you?" she asked, after a brief silence.

"Yes."

"I look out the window every day, from boredom, and, you must forgive me," she said, glancing at her newspaper, "I often see you and your sister. She always has such a kind, thoughtful expression."

Dolzhikov came in. He was rubbing his neck with a towel.

"Papa, Monsieur Polozniev," said his daughter.

"Yes, yes, Blagovo spoke to me," he turned to me briskly, without offering his hand. "But listen, what do you think I can do for you? What kind of jobs have I got? A strange lot, you people!" he went on in a loud voice, as though reprimanding me. "You come to me at the rate of twenty a day— you must think I'm head of a department! I'm building a railroad, my friends, I hire men for heavy labor, I need mechanics, fitters, excavators, carpenters, well drillers, and you people can do nothing but sit and write—that's all! You're all clerks!"

And the same air of happiness emanated from him as

from his rugs and armchairs. A stout, lusty man with broad shoulders and ruddy cheeks, his scrubbed face, calico shirt, and wide trousers made him look like a porcelain figurine of a coachman. He had a round, curly beard—not a single gray hair—a hooked nose, and bright, guileless, dark eyes.

"What can you do?" he continued. "You don't know how to do anything! I'm an engineer, I'm a successful man, but before they gave me this railroad I was in harness for years. I was a locomotive engineer, and for two years I worked in Belgium as an ordinary oiler. Judge for yourself, my dear fellow: what kind of work can I offer you?"

"It's true, of course . . ." I mumbled, in extreme embarrassment, unable to meet his bright, guileless eyes.

"Can you handle a telegraph apparatus, at least?" he asked after a moment's thought.

"Yes, I've worked as a telegraph clerk."

"Hm. . . . Well, we'll see then. Meanwhile, go to Dubechnya. I've already got a fellow there, but he's absolutely worthless."

"And what will my duties consist of?" I asked.

"We shall see. Go there, meanwhile I'll make arrangements. Only, please—don't get drunk, and don't bother me with any requests, or I'll kick you out."

He walked away from me without even a nod. I bowed to him and to his daughter, who was reading the newspaper, and left. My heart was so heavy that when my sister asked me how the engineer had received me, I was unable to utter a single word.

I got up early in the morning, at sunrise, to go to Dubechnya. There was not a soul in the street, everyone was still sleeping, and my footsteps echoed with a solitary, hollow sound. The dew-covered poplars filled the air with a soft fragrance. I felt sad and did not want to go away. I loved my native town. It seemed so beautiful to me, so warm! I loved the vegetation, the still, sunny mornings, the chiming of our bells; but the people I lived among were boring, alien to me, sometimes even abhorrent. I neither liked nor understood them.

I did not understand what these sixty-five thousand people lived for, or how they lived. I knew that in Kimry people lived from the manufacture of boots, that in Tula they made samovars and guns, that Odessa was a seaport, but what our town was and what it did—I did not know. Bolshaya

Dvoryanskaya and the other two decent streets lived on investments and official salaries; but what supported the other eight streets which ran parallel for about three versts and then disappeared behind the hill—this had always been an insoluble riddle to me. And I hate to say how these people lived! No park, no theater, no decent orchestra; the town and club libraries were used only by Jewish youths, so that magazines and new books lay uncut for months; rich and educated people slept in close, stuffy rooms on bug-ridden beds, their children were kept in disgustingly filthy rooms called nurseries, and the servants, even those who were old and respected, slept on the floor in the kitchen covered with rags. On ordinary days the houses smelled of borscht, and on fast days of sturgeon cooked in sunflower oil. The food was unsavory and the water unwholesome. They had been talking for years in the town council, at the governor's, at the bishop's, everywhere in fact, about the lack of a good and cheap water supply and of the need to borrow two hundred thousand rubles from the treasury for a water system; very rich people, of whom there were about three dozen in the town—people who on occasion would lose a whole estate at cards—also drank the water, and all their lives talked heatedly about the loan, and this I could never understand; it seemed to me it would have been simpler for them to take the two hundred thousand out of their own pockets.

In the whole town I did not know a single honest man. My father took bribes and imagined they were given out of respect for his intellectual qualities; high-school boys, in order to be promoted from one class to the next, boarded with their teachers, who charged them exorbitant sums; the wife of the military commander took bribes from recruits when they were called up, even allowing them to treat her to drinks, and on one occasion she was so drunk in church she was unable to rise from her knees; the doctors, too, accepted bribes during recruiting, and the municipal doctor and veterinary surgeon levied a tax on butcher shops and taverns; the district school conducted a trade in certificates assigning boys to the third category for military service; the higher clergy took from the lower clergy and the church elders; in the town council, the citizens' council, the medical board, and every other board, a petitioner was pursued with the cry: "One expects to be thanked!"—and would turn back and give thirty or forty kopecks. And those who did not take bribes, such as officials in the Department of Justice, were overbearing, offered two fingers instead of shaking hands, and were distinguished by the coldness and narrowness of their judgments; they spent a great deal of time at cards, drank to excess, married rich women, and undoubtedly had a pernicious, corrupting influence on those around them. It was only the young girls who radiated any moral purity, most of them having exalted aspirations and pure, honest souls, but no understanding of life; they believed that bribes were given out of respect for spiritual qualities, and, when they married, aged rapidly, let themselves go, and were hopelessly engulfed in the mire of a vulgar, bourgeois existence.

# III

A railroad was being constructed in our district. On the eve of a holiday the town was filled with crowds of ragged-looking men whom the people called "railers," and of whom they were afraid. More than once I had seen one of these men, with a bloody face and no cap, being dragged off to the police, while a samovar or some linen still wet from the wash was carried after him as material evidence. The "railers" generally congregated near the taverns and bazaars; they drank, ate, cursed horribly, and whistled at every loose woman who passed. To entertain this rabble our shopkeepers used to make cats and dogs drink vodka, or tie a kerosene can to a dog's tail; a hue and cry would be raised and the dog, yelping with terror, would tear through the street with the can clanking behind him; he probably thought some monster was after him and would run far out of town and into the fields where he fell exhausted; we had several dogs in town that went around constantly trembling, their tails between their legs, and people used to say it was because they could not bear such tricks and had gone mad.

The station was being built five versts from town. It was said that the engineers had asked for a bribe of fifty thousand rubles to bring the line up to the town, but the town council would give only forty; they could not come to an agreement about the difference, which the townspeople now regretted, as they were obliged to build a road to the station which, according to the estimate, would cost more. The ties and rails had been laid the whole length of the line, service

trains were running, carrying building materials and laborers, and they were only waiting for the bridges that
Dolzhikov was building and for a station here and there to be
completed.

Dubechnya, as our first station was called, was seventeen
versts from town. I went there on foot. Bathed in early morning sunshine the winter crops and spring corn were bright
green. It was flat, cheerful country, and clearly outlined in
the distance were the station, some ancient burial mounds,
and remote manor houses. . . . How good it was to be out
in the open! And how I longed to be pervaded with a sense
of freedom, if only for this one morning, in order not to
think about what was going on in town, not to think of my
own needs, not to feel hungry! Nothing has been such an
obstacle to me in my life as the acute feeling of hunger,
when, strangely mingled with my finest thoughts, there arise
images of buckwheat porridge, cutlets, and baked fish. Here
I stand alone in a meadow, gazing up at a lark hovering
miraculously in the air and trilling hysterically, and I think:
"It would be good to have a piece of bread and butter!" Or
I sit down by the roadside to rest, closing my eyes and listening to the marvelous murmur of a May day, and I suddenly
recall the smell of hot potatoes. Being tall and solidly built
and as a rule having but little to eat, my chief sensation
throughout the day was hunger; perhaps that was why I
could very well understand why so many people who work
for a bare living talk of nothing but food.

At Dubechnya they were plastering the inside of the station
and building a wooden upper story to the pump house. It
was hot and smelled of shavings and rubbish; the switchman
was asleep near his sentry box with the sun blazing full in
his face. There was not a single tree. Here and there hawks
were perched on the faintly humming telegraph wire. I, too,
commenced wandering among the heaps of rubbish, not
knowing what to do, and I remembered the engineer's reply
to my question about what my duties would be: "We shall
see." But what was there to see in this wilderness? The
plasterers spoke of a foreman and a certain Fedot Vassiliev,
but, not understanding them, I gradually was overcome by
depression, a physical depression in which you become conscious of your hands and feet, of your whole big body, and
do not know what to do with them.

After walking around for at least a couple of hours, I

noticed that there were telegraph poles running from the station off to the right of the line for one or two versts and ending at a white stone wall; the men told me the office was there, and at last I decided that that was where I ought to go.

It was a very old, long-abandoned estate. The white porous stone wall was weathered and crumbling in places, and the roof of one wing, the blank wall of which faced a field, had a rusty roof with patches of tin glittering on it. Through the gates I could see a spacious courtyard overgrown with tall weeds and an old manor house with Venetian blinds on the windows and a high roof red with rust. To the right and left of the house were two identical wings; the windows of one were boarded up, but near the other, where the windows were open, there were calves browsing and some washing on a line. The last telegraph pole was in the courtyard, the wire passing through the window of the wing whose blank wall faced the field. The door stood open and I walked in. A man with dark curly hair and wearing a duck jacket sat at the telegraph apparatus; he gave me a sullen, mistrustful look, then immediately smiled and said:

"Hello, Better-than-nothing!"

It was Ivan Cheprakov, an old schoolmate of mine, who had been expelled from the second class for smoking. In the autumn we used to catch goldfinches, greenfinches, and siskins together and sell them in the market early in the morning while our parents were still sleeping. We would lie in wait for flocks of migrating starlings and fire small shot at them, then pick up those we had wounded, some of which died in terrible agony (to this day I can remember how they moaned in the cage at night); those that recovered we sold, brazenly swearing they were all cocks. On one occasion I had only one starling left, which I had been trying for a long time to get rid of; at last I sold it for a kopeck. "Anyway, it's better than nothing!" I said to console myself as I put the kopeck in my pocket; and from that day schoolboys and street urchins called me "Better-than-nothing," and even now shopkeepers and small boys sometimes mock me with this nickname, though no one but me remembers how it came about.

Cheprakov was not a robust man; he was narrow-chested, round-shouldered, and long-legged. He wore a piece of cord for a tie, no waistcoat at all, and boots worse than mine—

worn down at the heels. He hardly ever blinked his eyes and
his face had a strained expression, as if he were on the verge
of grasping something, and he was continually fidgeting.

"But wait a minute," he would say fussily. "Now listen
. . . What in the world was I just saying?"

We began talking and I learned that the estate on which I
now found myself had belonged to the Cheprakovs and only
the previous autumn had become the property of Dolzhikov,
who considered it more profitable to put his money into
land than into securities and had bought up three sizable estates in our district, including the mortgages; at the time of
the sale Cheprakov's mother had stipulated for the right to
live in one of the wings for two years and a place for her
son in the office.

"No wonder he can buy!" Cheprakov said of the engineer. "He takes enough from the contractors alone! He gets
something from every one of them!"

He invited me for dinner, having decided in his fussy way
that I should live in the wing with him and board with his
mother.

"She's a skinflint," he said, "but she won't charge you
much."

It was very cramped in the little rooms where his mother
lived; even the entry and passage were jammed with old-
fashioned mahogany furniture that had been taken from the
house after the sale.

Madam Cheprakova, a stout middle-aged lady with slanting
Chinese eyes, was sitting in a large armchair by the window
knitting a stocking. She received me with ceremony.

"This is Polozniev, Mama, he's going to work here."

"Are you a nobleman?" she asked in a strange, unpleasant
voice that sounded as if she had fat bubbling in her throat.

"Yes," I replied.

"Sit down."

The dinner was poor. There was nothing but a bitter-
tasting curd pie and milk soup. Elena Nikiforovna, my hostess, was continually blinking, first one eye then the other, in
a very odd way. She talked and ate, but there was something
deathlike about her whole aspect, and she seemed to exude
a cadaverous odor. There was only a glimmer of life in her,
a glimmer of consciousness that she had once been the lady
of the manor with her own serfs, that she was the widow of
a general, whom the servants were obliged to address as

"Your Excellency"; and when these pitiable remnants of life momentarily flickered up in her, she would say to her son:

"Jean, that's not the way to hold your knife!"

Or she would draw a deep breath, and, with the mincing air of a hostess trying to entertain a guest, say to me:

"We have sold our estate, you know. It's a pity, of course, we had grown so used to it here, but Dolzhikov has promised to make Jean stationmaster at Dubechnya, so we shan't have to go away, we shall live here at the station, which is the same as being on our own estate. The engineer is such a kind man! And very handsome, don't you think?"

Until recently the Cheprakovs had lived affluently, but with the general's death everything changed. Elena Nikiforovna commenced quarreling with the neighbors, going to law, and not paying her stewards and laborers; she was in perpetual fear of being robbed—and in less than ten years Dubechnya had become unrecognizable.

Behind the great house was an old garden, run wild and overgrown with tall weeds and bushes. I walked along the veranda, which was still unimpaired and beautiful; through the glass door I could see a room, probably the drawing room, with a parquet floor, an old-fashioned piano, and some engravings in wide mahogany frames—nothing more. All that remained in the old flower beds were the peonies and poppies, lifting their white and scarlet heads above the grass; young elms and maples, now stripped by the cows, grew in clumps along the paths. The garden was densely overgrown and seemed impenetrable, but this was only near the house where there were still poplars, fir trees, and old lime trees, all of one age, survivors of former avenues; farther on, the garden had been cleared for hayfields, and here it was no longer like a jungle where one got spiderwebs in one's eyes and mouth, and a light breeze was stirring. The farther one walked the more open it was, and soon there appeared cherry trees, plum trees, and spreading apple trees disfigured by props and canker, as well as pear trees that were so tall it was hard to believe they were pear trees. This part of the garden was let to the market women of the town and was guarded from thieves and starlings by a feeble-minded peasant who lived here in a shack.

The orchard grew more and more sparse till it became a real meadow, sloping down to a river overgrown with reeds and willows; near the milldam was a pool, deep and full of fish; a small thatched mill made an angry clamor and frogs croaked furiously. From time to time circles appeared on the glassy surface of the water, and water lilies, perturbed by playful fish, trembled. On the other side of the river was the little village of Dubechnya. The still, azure pool beckoned with a promise of coolness and peace. And now all this—the pool, the mill, the inviting river banks—belonged to the engineer!

And so my new work began. I received and forwarded telegrams, kept various records, made clean copies of requisitions, claims, and reports, which were sent into the office by illiterate foremen and contractors; but most of the day I did nothing but pace the room waiting for telegrams, or else left a boy sitting there and went for a walk till he came running to tell me that the apparatus was clicking. I ate dinner at Madam Cheprakova's. Meat was rarely served, most of the time we were given dairy dishes; Wednesdays and Fridays were fast days and the food was served on pink plates which were called Lenten plates. Madam Cheprakova blinked incessantly—it was a constant habit with her, and I always felt ill at ease in her presence.

As there was not enough work even for one, Cheprakov did nothing but sleep or go off to the pool with his gun to shoot ducks. In the evenings he got drunk in the village or at the station, and before going to bed he would stare into the mirror and shout:

"How are you, Ivan Cheprakov?"

He was very pale when he was drunk, and would continually rub his hands and laugh with a whinnying sound: "He-he-he!" Or he would strip to the skin and run through the field stark naked, out of sheer insolence. And he used to eat flies and say they were rather sour.

## IV

One day after dinner he came running into the office and breathlessly announced:

"Go along, your sister has come to see you!"

I went out. There at the entrance to the big house stood a hired droshky from town. My sister had come, and with her Anyuta Blagovo and a gentleman in a military tunic. As I approached I recognized him: it was Anyuta's brother, an army doctor.

"We've come for a picnic," he said. "Is it all right?"

My sister and Anyuta had intended to ask me how I was getting on, but they both remained silent and only stared at me. I, too, was silent. They saw that I did not like it here and tears came to my sister's eyes and Anyuta blushed. We went into the garden. The doctor walked ahead of us, enthusiastically exclaiming:

"What air! Holy Mother, what air!"

He was exactly like a student in appearance. He walked and talked like a student, and the expression in his gray eyes was as lively, frank, and artless as that of a nice boy. Beside his tall, handsome sister he seemed weak, frail; his beard was thin, as was his voice—a light but rather agreeable tenor. He was attached to a regiment somewhere and had come home on leave; he said he was going to Petersburg in the autumn to take an examination for his medical degree. He already had a family—a wife and three children; he had married young, in his second year at the university; it was said he was unhappily married and not living with his wife.

"What time is it?" my sister asked uneasily. "We must go back soon. Papa gave me permission to visit my brother only till six o'clock."

"Oh, that papa of yours!" sighed the doctor.

I made tea. We drank it sitting on a rug in front of the veranda of the big house, the doctor on his knees, drinking from a saucer and saying it was sheer bliss. Then Cheprakov came with the key and unlocked the glass door and we all went into the house. It was dusky, mysterious, and smelled of mushrooms, and our footsteps made a hollow sound as though there were a vault under the floor. The doctor stood at the piano running his fingers over the keys; they responded with a faint, tremulous, somewhat rasping but still melodious sound; he tried his voice and commenced singing a song, frowning and impatiently stamping his foot when a key was mute. My sister no longer talked of going home, but animatedly walked about the room saying:

"I'm so happy! I am very, very happy!"

There was a note of surprise in her voice, as though she found it inconceivable that she, too, could feel lighthearted. It was the first time in my life I had seen her so gay. She actually looked prettier. Her profile was not good: her nose and mouth seemed to jut out and make her look as if she were always pouting, but she had beautiful dark eyes, a pale, very delicate complexion, and a kind, melancholy expression that was touching; when she spoke she seemed attractive and even beautiful. We both took after our mother; we were broad-shouldered, strong, and had great stamina, but she had an unhealthy pallor and coughed frequently, and I sometimes caught a look in her eyes that one sees in people who are seriously ill but for some reason trying to hide it. There was something naive, childish, in her present gaiety, as though all the joy that had been suppressed and stifled in our childhood by a strict upbringing had suddenly awakened in her soul and burst forth into freedom.

But when evening came and the horses were brought around, my sister grew very quiet; her face was drawn, and she sat in the droshky looking as if she were on the prisoner's bench.

Then they were gone, the noise died away. . . . I realized that Anyuta Blagovo had not said a word to me the whole day.

"An amazing girl!" I thought. "An amazing girl!"

St. Peter's fast came and we had nothing but Lenten fare every day. I was weighed down by a physical depression caused by idleness and the uncertainty of my position, and, dissatisfied with myself, I loitered about the estate, listless, hungry, and only waiting for the right frame of mind to leave.

One day toward evening when Radish was sitting with us in the wing, Dolzhikov unexpectedly appeared, sunburned and gray with dust. He had spent three days on his land and, after coming to Dubechnya by rail, had walked from the station. While waiting for the carriage which was to come for him from town, he went over the estate with his steward, giving orders in a loud voice, afterward sitting in our wing for a whole hour writing letters; telegrams came for him and he tapped out the answers himself. We three stood silent, at attention.

"What a mess!" he said with a contemptuous glance at the records. "In two weeks I'm going to transfer the office to the station, and then I don't know what I shall do with you, gentlemen."

"I do my best, Your Honor," said Cheprakov.

"Exactly. I can see that. The only thing you know how to

do is draw your salary." The engineer looked at me and went on. "You rely on patronage to *faire la carrière* as quickly and as easily as possible. Well, I don't care much for patronage. Nobody ever did anything for me. Before I got this line I ran an engine, and I worked in Belgium as an ordinary oiler. And you, Pantelei, what are you doing here?" he asked, turning to Radish. "Drinking with them?"

For some reason he called all simple people Pantelei, and men like Cheprakov and me, whom he despised, he called drunkards, beasts, and scum to their faces. In general he was hard on minor employees and either fined them or coldly dismissed them without an explanation.

At last the carriage came for him. In parting he promised to dismiss us all within two weeks, called his steward a blockhead, then stretched out comfortably in the carriage and drove away.

"Andrei Ivanych," I said to Radish, "take me on as a laborer."

"Why not?"

And we set off together in the direction of town. When the station and the estate were far behind us, I asked:

"Andrei Ivanych, why did you come out to Dubechnya today?"

"First, because my boys are working on the line, and second, to pay the interest to the general's widow. I borrowed fifty rubles from her last summer, and now I pay her a ruble a month interest."

The painter stopped and buttonholed me.

"Misail Alekseich, my angel," he said, "the way I see it is this: if any man, whether he be a commoner or a gentleman, takes interest, even the smallest per cent, he is a wrongdoer. The truth is not in him."

Gaunt, pale, and dreadful-looking, Radish shut his eyes, shook his head, and philosophically proclaimed:

"Lice consume grass, rust consumes iron, and lies consume the soul. Lord have mercy on us sinners!"

## V

Radish was not a practical man and was not good at making an estimate; he took more work than he could

do, and when computing became agitated, lost his head, and
as a result was almost always out of pocket. He was a painter,
a glazier, a paper hanger, and would even undertake roofing; I
remember how he used to run around for days at a time
trying to find roofers for the sake of some petty job. He was
an excellent workman, sometimes earning as much as ten
rubles a day, and had it not been for his desire to be an
employer at all costs and to call himself a contractor, he
no doubt would have made plenty of money.

He was paid by the job, but he paid me and the other men
by the day, from seventy kopecks to a ruble a day. While the
weather was hot and dry we did various outside jobs, chiefly
roof painting. Not being used to it my feet burned as if I were
walking on a red-hot stove, and when I wore felt boots it
made my feet swelter. But this was only in the beginning;
later I grew accustomed to it and things went swimmingly. I
now lived among people for whom work was obligatory, inevitable, people who worked like draft horses often without
realizing the moral significance of labor, and who never even
used the word "labor." Among them I too felt like a draft
horse; I became more and more imbued with the necessity and inevitability of what I was doing, and this made
my life easier, ridding me of all doubt.

At first everything interested me, everything was new; it
was like being born again. I could sleep on the ground and
go barefoot—and this was extremely pleasant; I could stand
in a crowd of simple people without inhibiting them, and if
a cab horse fell down in the street I could run and help to
lift it without being afraid of soiling my clothes. But the
chief thing was that I was supporting myself and was not a
burden to anyone!

Roof painting, especially when we used our own oil and
paint, was considered a very profitable business, and therefore even such a good workman as Radish did not scorn this
rough, tedious work. In short pants, with his wasted,
purplish legs, he looked like a stork walking over the roof,
and I could hear him, breathing heavily as he plied his
brush, and saying:

"Woe, woe to us miserable sinners!"

He walked on a roof as freely as on a floor. Although he
was ill and pale as a corpse, his agility was extraordinary; he
would paint a cupola or the dome of a church without a
scaffold, using nothing but a ladder and rope, and it was

rather terrible when, standing high above the earth, he would draw himself up to his full height and declaim to the world at large:

"Lice consume grass, rust consumes iron, and lies consume the soul!"

Or, perhaps thinking about something, he would answer his thoughts aloud:

"Anything can happen! Anything can happen!"

When I went home after work the people sitting on benches at their gates, all the shopkeepers, the shopboys, and their employers, used to shout various jeering, spiteful remarks after me, and at first this upset me and seemed simply monstrous.

"Better-than-nothing!" I heard on every side. "House painter! Yellow ocher!"

And no one treated me so unmercifully as those who had recently been in a humble position, earning their living by manual labor. One day as I was passing an ironmonger's in the shopping arcade, water was poured over me as if by accident, another time a stick was thrown at me. A certain fishmonger, a gray-haired old man, once blocked my way and, with a malicious look, said to me:

"It's not you I'm sorry for, you idiot! I'm sorry for your father!"

And my acquaintances, for some reason, were embarrassed when they met me. Some regarded me as an eccentric, a buffoon, some felt sorry for me, others did not know how to treat me; it was hard to understand them. One day I met Anyuta Blagovo in a side street off Bolshaya Dvoryanskaya; I was on my way to work and was carrying two long brushes and a bucket of paint. When she recognized me she blushed.

"Please don't bow to me in the street," she said nervously, austerely; her voice trembled and she did not offer me her hand. Suddenly there were tears gleaming in her eyes. "If, to your mind, all this is necessary, then . . . then so be it, but I beg you not to greet me!"

I no longer lived in Bolshaya Dvoryanskaya Street, but in the suburb of Makarikha with my old nurse Karpovna, a kindhearted but morose old woman who always had premonitions of evil, was frightened by all dreams, and even saw a bad omen in every bee and wasp that flew into her room. In her opinion the fact that I had become a workman boded no good.

"You're done for!" she would say mournfully, shaking her head. "Done for!"

With her in the little house lived her adopted son, Prokofy the butcher, a huge, lumbering fellow of thirty with red hair and a bristling mustache. When he met me in the passage he would silently and respectfully make way for me, and if he was drunk he would give me a five-finger salute. When he had supper in the evenings I could hear him through the wooden partition, snuffing and snorting as he downed one glass after another.

"Mamasha!" he would call to her in a low voice.

"Well?" Karpovna would reply—she was passionately fond of her adopted son—"What is it, sonny?"

"I'll do you a good turn, Mamasha. I'll feed you in your old age, while you're still in this vale of tears, and when you die I'll bury you at my own expense. I've said it—and you can count on it."

I got up every morning before sunrise and went to bed early. We painters ate heavily and slept soundly; but for some reason, during the night I would feel my heart pounding. I never quarreled with my comrades. All day long there was an endless stream of abuse and desperate oaths, such as "Blast your eyes" or "Plague take you"; nevertheless we got on well together. The men suspected me of being a religious dissenter and made good-natured jokes at my expense, saying that even my own father had disowned me, that they themselves rarely set foot in the house of God, many of them not having been to confession for ten years, and they justified this laxness by saying that the painter among men is like the jackdaw among birds.

The men had a good opinion of me and treated me with respect; they evidently liked it that I did not drink or smoke and led a quiet, steady life. They were only shocked that I took no part in stealing oil or going with them to ask for tips from our clients. Stealing oil and paint from those who employed them was customary among house painters and was not regarded as theft, and it was remarkable that a man as upright as Radish never left work without carrying off a little white lead and oil. Even respectable old men who owned houses of their own in Makarikha were not ashamed to ask for tips, and to see the men go in a body at the beginning or completion of a job and make up to some nonentity, then humbly thank him on being given a ten-kopeck piece, made me feel vexed and ashamed.

They behaved like wily courtiers with the clients, and almost every day I was reminded of Shakespeare's Polonius.

"There'll probably be rain today," a client would say, gazing up at the sky.

"There's sure to be rain, without fail," the painters would agree.

"On the other hand, those clouds are not rain clouds. Perhaps it won't rain."

"It won't, Your Honor. It certainly won't rain."

But behind their backs they regarded their patrons with irony, and when, for example, they saw a gentleman sitting on his veranda reading a newspaper, they would remark:

"He has a newspaper to read, but I'll bet he has nothing to eat."

I never went home to my family. When I returned from work I often found brief, anxious little notes in which my sister wrote about my father that he had been somewhat preoccupied at dinner and had eaten nothing; that he had been unsteady on his feet; that he had locked himself in his room and had not come out for a long time. Such news upset me, I could not sleep, and sometimes would even walk by our house in Bolshaya Dvoryanskaya Street at night and peer into the dark windows, wondering whether all was well within. On Sundays my sister came to see me in secret, pretending to visit our nurse. And when she came into my room she was always very pale, her eyes red with weeping, and she would immediately begin crying.

"Father cannot bear this!" she would say. "If—God forbid—anything should happen to him, it would be on your conscience for the rest of your life. It is awful, Misail! For the sake of our dear mother, I implore you to reform!"

"My darling sister," I would say to her, "how can I reform when I am convinced that I am acting according to my conscience? Try to understand!"

"I know you are obeying your conscience, but perhaps it could be done in some other way, so no one would be hurt."

"Oh, Holy Saints!" the old woman would sigh behind the door. "You're done for! There's going to be trouble, my dears, there's going to be trouble!"

# VI

One Sunday Dr. Blagovo unexpectedly appeared. He was wearing a military tunic over a silk shirt, and high patent-leather boots.

"I have come to visit you!" he began, gripping my hand in his hearty, undergraduate fashion. "I keep hearing about you every day, and I've been meaning to come and have a heart to heart, as they say. It's a dreadful bore in town, not a single living soul, no one worth talking to. Holy Mother, it's hot!" he continued, taking off his tunic and leaving on only his silk shirt. "My dear fellow, do let me talk to you!"

I was feeling bored myself, and had been longing for the companionship of someone other than house painters. I was genuinely glad to see him.

"I'll begin by saying that I sympathize with you from the bottom of my heart," he said, sitting down on my bed, "and I have a profound respect for your present way of life. They don't understand you there in town, and, of course, there is no one to understand you, since, as you yourself know, with very few exceptions they are all a lot of Gogol-esque pig snouts. But I saw from the first what you were—the day of the picnic. You are a noble soul, an honest, high-minded man! I respect you and consider it an honor to shake your hand!" he went on enthusiastically. "To change your life so abruptly and so radically, as you have done, you must have gone through a very complex spiritual experience, and to continue in this way of life, constantly living up to your highest convictions, must be a continual strain on both your mind and heart. Now, to begin with, tell me, don't you think that if you had expended all this will power, effort, and potential on something else, on becoming a great scientist, say, or an artist, that your life would have attained a greater breadth and depth, would have been in every respect more productive?"

We talked, and when we got on the subject of physical labor I expressed this thought: it is imperative that the strong should not enslave the weak, that the minority should not be parasites on the majority, like a sipunculus perpetually sucking up its vital sap; in other words, it is necessary that everyone without exception—the strong and the weak, the rich and the poor—should participate equally in the struggle for existence, each for himself, and that there is no better means of leveling than physical labor in the form of compulsory service for all.

"Then you believe that everyone, without exception, ought to be engaged in physical labor?" asked the doctor.

"Yes."

"But don't you think that if everyone, including the best men, the thinkers and great scientists, were to take part in the struggle for existence, each on his own account, and were to spend his time breaking stones and painting roofs, that this might be a serious, a very dangerous threat to progress?"

"Where's the danger?" I asked. "You see, progress lies in deeds of love, in the fulfillment of the moral law. If you don't enslave anyone and are not a burden to anyone, what further progress do you need?"

"But, look here!" said Blagovo, suddenly losing his temper and getting up. "But, look here! If the snail in its shell is occupied with self-improvement and dabbles in the moral law, do you call that progress?"

"Why dabbles?" I took umbrage. "If you don't compel your fellow man to feed and clothe you, to cart you around and protect you from your enemies, surely in a life that is based entirely on slavery, this is progress, isn't it? In my opinion it's the most genuine kind of progress, perhaps the only progress possible and necessary for man!"

"The limits of universal human progress lie in infinity, and to speak of some 'possible' progress confined to our needs and our temporal conceptions is, if you will forgive me, positively strange."

"If the limits of progress lie in infinity, as you say, it follows that its aims are indeterminate," I replied. "Which means living without definitely knowing what you are living for!"

"That may be! But this 'not knowing' is not so dull as your 'knowing.' I am climbing a ladder known as progress, civilization, culture, I go on and on, not knowing definitely where I am going, but, truly, it's worth living just for the sake of this marvelous ladder; you, meanwhile, know what you are living for: so that some should not enslave others, so that the artist and the man who grinds his colors for him should dine equally well. But that's the bourgeois, the gray, kitchen side of life, and to live for that alone—that really would be disgusting, now wouldn't it? If certain insects enslave others, to hell with them, let them devour one another! There's no need to think about them—they'll die and rot no matter what you do to save them from slavery—you have to think about that great unknown quantity which awaits all mankind in the distant future."

Blagovo argued heatedly with me, but it was apparent that he was troubled by some extraneous thought.

"I expect your sister is not coming," he said, looking at his watch. "She was at our house yesterday and said she would be here. . . . You keep harping on slavery—slavery," he went on, "but that's a special problem; little by little all such problems are automatically solved by mankind."

We began talking about progressive change. I said that everyone decides the question of good and evil for himself, without waiting for mankind to solve it by means of gradual development. Moreover, evolution is a two-edged sword. Along with the gradual development of humanitarian ideas, the gradual growth of ideas of another order may be seen. Serfdom no longer exists, but on the other hand capitalism is growing. And with the ideas of liberalism at their very height, the majority, just as in the days of Baty, feeds, clothes, and defends the minority, while itself remaining hungry, ill-clothed, defenseless. Such a state of affairs harmonizes beautifully with any trend or tendency you like, because the art of enslaving is gradually being cultivated as well. We no longer flog our servants in the stables, we give slavery more refined forms; at any rate we are able to find a justification for it in each individual case. With us ideas are —ideas, but if now, at the end of the nineteenth century, it were possible to saddle the working class with our most unpleasant physiological functions, we should do so, afterward, of course, justifying ourselves by saying that if the best people, the thinkers and great scientists, were to waste their precious time on these functions, progress might be seriously jeopardized.

Just then my sister arrived. When she saw the doctor, she became flustered and excited and immediately commenced saying it was time for her to go home to father.

"Kleopatra Alekseyevna," said Blagovo persuasively, pressing both hands to his heart, "what will happen to your papa if you spend half an hour or so with your brother and me?"

He was openhearted and capable of communicating his high spirits to others. After thinking for a moment my sister burst out laughing, suddenly and unpredictably becoming very gay, just as she had done at the picnic. We went out into the field, sat down on the grass, and continued our talk as we looked toward the town, where all the windows facing west reflected the bright gold of the setting sun.

From that day Blagovo appeared every time my sister came to see me, and they would greet each other as if their meeting in my room was accidental. While the doctor and I argued, my sister listened with a joyous, rapt expression full of tenderness and curiosity, and it seemed to me that little by little a new world was being discovered before her eyes, a world that she had never even dreamed of, and which she was trying to fathom. When the doctor was not there she was quiet and melancholy, and if she sometimes shed tears as she sat on my bed, now it was for reasons of which she did not speak.

In August Radish told us to get ready to go out on the line. A couple of days before we were "exiled" from the town, my father came to see me. He sat down and, without looking at me, unhurriedly wiped his red face, then took out of his pocket our local *Messenger* and deliberately, with emphasis on every word, read aloud the news that the son of the director of the State Bank, one of my contemporaries, had been appointed head of the Department of the Exchequer.

"And now, look at you," he said, folding up the newspaper, "a beggar, a ragged good-for-nothing! Even people of the working class, and peasants, get an education in order to make something of themselves, while you, a Polozniev, with noble, distinguished forebears, aspire only to the gutter. But I did not come here to talk to you—I've washed my hands of you," he continued as he got up. "I came to find out where your sister is, you good-for-nothing. She left the house after dinner, and here it is nearly eight o'clock and she is not back. She has taken to going out without telling me, she's becoming less respectful—and I see your evil, corrupting influence at work. Where is she?"

In his hands he held the umbrella I knew so well; I became confused and stood at attention like a schoolboy, expecting my father to start beating me, but he saw the look I cast at the umbrella and this probably deterred him.

"Live as you like," he said. "You'll not have my blessing!"

"Holy Saints!" my old nurse muttered behind the door.
"Poor, unfortunate child! Oh, I have a foreboding in my
heart, I have a foreboding!"

I was working on the railroad line. It rained continually
the whole month of August and was cold and damp; the
grain had not been carted from the fields, and on the big
farms, where the mowing was done by machine, the wheat
lay, not in sheaves, but in heaps, and I remember how those
mournful heaps grew darker each day, and the grain commenced sprouting in them. It was hard to work; the heavy
downpour ruined everything we managed to get done. We
were not permitted to live or even sleep in the station buildings and took refuge in filthy damp mud huts where the
"railers" had lived in the summer, and at night I could not
sleep for the cold and the wood lice crawling over my face
and arms. And when we worked near the bridges, the
"railers" used to come in a gang in the evening to beat up the
painters—it was a form of sport with them. They used to
beat us, steal our brushes, and in order to harass us and
provoke a fight, sometimes spoiled our work, as when they
smeared the signal boxes with green paint. To add to our
troubles, Radish took to paying us very irregularly. All the
painting on the line was given to one contractor, who sub-
contracted it to another, who in turn gave it to Radish, keeping twenty per cent for himself. The job in itself was unprofitable, and the rain made it more so; time was lost, we
could not work, and Radish was obliged to pay the men by
the day. The hungry painters almost came to blows with
him, called him a swindler, a bloodsucker, a Judas Christ-
seller, while he, poor fellow, sighed, raising his hands to
heaven in despair, and was continually going to Madam
Cheprakova for money.

# VII

Then came a dark rainy muddy autumn. A slack period
set in when I sat at home for three days at a stretch without
work, or did various jobs other than painting, such as hauling
earth for ballast, for which I was paid twenty kopecks a day.
Dr. Blagovo had gone to Petersburg. My sister no longer

came to see me. Radish lay at home ill, expecting to die from one day to the next.

And my mood, too, was autumnal. Perhaps because of having become a workman I now saw our town life only from the seamy side, and almost every day made fresh discoveries which reduced me to a state of despair. Those of my fellow citizens about whom I formerly had no opinion at all, or who outwardly had seemed quite decent, now turned out to be base, cruel, and capable of every sort of vile trick. We common people were deceived, defrauded, kept waiting for hours on end in cold entrances or kitchens, insulted and treated with the utmost harshness. During the autumn I papered the walls of the reading room and two other rooms in the club; I was paid seven kopecks a strip and told to give a receipt for twelve, and when I refused to do so a fine-looking gentleman with gold-rimmed spectacles, probably one of the club stewards, said to me:

"If you say another word, you scoundrel, I'll punch your face for you!"

And when a flunky whispered to him that I was the son of the architect Polozniev, he was embarrassed and turned red, but instantly recovered himself and said:

"Damn him, anyway!"

In the shops they palmed off on us workmen tainted meat, moldy flour, and used tea leaves; in church the police shoved us; in the hospitals the feldshers and nurses fleeced us, and if we were too poor to bribe them they took their revenge by bringing us food on dirty plates; in the post office the most insignificant clerk considered himself justified in treating us like animals, roughly and insolently shouting: "You wait! Where do you think you're going?" Even the yard dogs were unfriendly and rushed at us with a particular viciousness. But what struck me above everything in my new position was the total absence of justice, what the people call "forgetting God." Rarely did a day pass without some swindle. The merchants who sold us oil, the contractors, our own men, the people who employed us, all cheated. Needless to say, there could be no question of our rights; we even had to ask for the money we earned as if it were charity, and stand waiting for it at a back door, cap in hand.

I had been papering one of the rooms adjoining the reading room in the club, and in the evening, as I was getting ready to leave, the daughter of the engineer Dolzhikov walked in with a bundle of books under her arm.

I bowed to her.

"Oh, how do you do?" she said, instantly recognizing me and holding out her hand. "I'm very glad to see you."

She smiled, and with a puzzled, inquisitive expression, looked at my smock, the bucket of paste, and the paper spread out on the floor; I was embarrassed and she too felt awkward.

"You must excuse my looking at you like this," she said. "I have heard so much about you, especially from Dr. Blagovo—he's simply crazy about you. And I have met your sister, too; she is a sweet, appealing girl, but I can't convince her that there is nothing so awful in your choosing the simple life. On the contrary, you've become the most interesting man in town."

Once more she glanced at the bucket of paste and said:

"I asked Dr. Blagovo to make me better acquainted with you, but he either forgot or hadn't the time. Well, now we've met anyway, and I should be much obliged if you would come and see me. I want so much to have a talk with you! I am a very simple person," she said, holding out her hand to me, "and I hope you won't stand on ceremony. My father is away, in Petersburg."

She went into the reading room with a rustling of skirts, and for a long time after I got home I was unable to sleep.

It was during that cheerless autumn that some kind soul, evidently wanting to make my life a little easier, from time to time sent me tea and lemons, pastry, or roast woodcock. Karpovna said they were always brought by a soldier, but who they came from she did not know; and the soldier always asked whether I was well, whether I ate dinner every day, and whether I had warm clothing. When the frosts set in he appeared in the same way, when I was out, and left a soft knitted scarf; it had a faint, elusive fragrance, and I guessed who my good fairy was. The scarf smelled of lily of the valley, Anyuta Blagovo's favorite scent.

As winter approached there was more work and things became more cheerful. Radish recovered and we went to work in the cemetery church applying a ground coat to the iconostasis, which was to be gilded. It was clean, quiet work, and, as our men said, it paid. We could get a lot done in a day, and the time passed quickly, imperceptibly. There was no cursing, no laughing, no loud talk. The place itself imposed quiet and decorum and was conducive to tranquil, serious thoughts. Absorbed in our work, we stood or sat motionless, like statues; there was the dead silence befitting a cemetery, so that if a tool fell, or the flame spluttered in an icon lamp, it made a sharp, resonant sound that made us look round. After a long silence, we might hear a hum like the swarming of bees, and from the church porch would come the slow, hushed chanting of a requiem for a dead infant; or the artist who was painting a dove encircled by stars on the cupola might begin to whistle softly, then, recollecting himself with a start, would instantly fall silent; or Radish, answering his own thought, could be heard sighing: "Anything can happen! Anything can happen!" or overhead the slow, mournful tolling of the bell made the painters remark that it must be for the funeral of some rich man. . . .

My days were spent in this stillness, in the twilight of the church, and during the long evenings I played billiards or sat in the gallery of the theater wearing the new serge suit I had bought out of my earnings. Concerts and performances had already begun at the Azhogins'; Radish was painting the scenery alone now. He used to give me a summary of the plays and *tableaux vivants* he saw there and I would listen to him with envy. I had a great longing to attend the rehearsals, but I could not bring myself to go to the Azhogins'.

A week before Christmas Dr. Blagovo arrived. We resumed our arguments and played billiards in the evenings. He would take off his coat when he played, unbutton his shirt over his chest and, in general, try to give himself the air of a desperate rake. He drank little but he made a great show of it and would somehow manage to go through twenty rubles an evening even in so poor and cheap a tavern as the Volga.

My sister began visiting me again; each time they met, both looked surprised, but from her happy, guilty expression it was obvious that these meetings were not accidental. One evening when we were playing billiards Dr. Blagovo said to me:

"Look here, why don't you call on Dolzhikov's daughter? You don't know Marya Viktorovna; she's clever, charming, and a good, simple soul."

I told him how her father had received me in the spring.

"That's nothing!" he laughed. "The engineer is one thing
—she's another. Really, my dear fellow, you mustn't offend
her, drop around and see her sometime. Let's go tomorrow
evening, for instance. Shall we?"

He persuaded me. The following evening I put on my new
serge suit and set off for the Dolzhikovs' in a state of agitation. The footman did not seem so arrogant and formidable
nor the furniture so luxurious as on the morning when I
had come with a request. Marya Viktorovna was expecting
me and greeted me like an old friend, warmly and firmly
shaking my hand. She was wearing a gray dress with full
sleeves and her hair was done in a style which, when it became the fashion in our town a year later, was called "dog-
ears." The hair was combed down from the temples and over
the ears, which made Marya Viktorovna's face look broader,
and this time she seemed to resemble her father, with his
broad, rather coachmanlike face. She was beautiful and elegant, but not youthful; she looked about thirty, though in
fact she was not more than twenty-five.

"Dear doctor, how grateful I am to him!" she said, making
me sit down. "If it were not for him you would never have
come to see me. I am bored to death! My father went away
and left me alone, and I don't know what to do with myself
in this town."

Then she began asking me where I was working, how much
I earned, where I lived.

"And you spend nothing on yourself but what you earn?"
she asked.

"Yes."

"Fortunate man!" she sighed. "All the evil in life, it seems
to me, comes from idleness, boredom, and spiritual emptiness, which, of course, is inevitable if one is in the habit of
living at someone else's expense. Don't think I'm showing off,
I'm being sincere when I say: it is neither interesting nor
pleasant to be rich. Make to yourself friends of the mammon
of unrighteousness, it is said, because as a rule there is not
and cannot be righteous wealth."

She considered the furniture with a cold, serious expression, as if she were about to make an inventory of it, and
went on:

"Comfort and convenience possess a magic power; little
by little they drag you down, even if you have a strong
will. My father and I used to live modestly, simply, and

now look how we live. It's unheard of," she said, shrugging her shoulders. "We spend twenty thousand a year! In the provinces!"

"Comfort and convenience have come to be regarded as the inevitable privilege of capital and education," I said, "but it seems to me that the conveniences of life can be combined with any sort of labor, even the heaviest and dirtiest. Your father is rich, and yet, as he says, he was obliged to spend some time both as a mechanic and a common oiler."

She smiled and shook her head skeptically.

"Papa sometimes eats bread dipped in kvass," she said. "A whim, a prank."

At that moment the bell rang and she got up.

"The rich and educated ought to work like everyone else," she continued, "and if there is to be any comfort, it should be the same for everyone. There should be no privilege. Well, that's enough philosophy. Tell me something cheerful. Tell me about painters. What are they like? Amusing?"

The doctor came in. I commenced telling them about the painters, but being unaccustomed to talking I felt constrained and spoke in a dull, solemn way, like an ethnologist. The doctor told a few anecdotes about workingmen. He staggered, cried, fell on his knees, and even lay on the floor in imitation of a drunkard. It was as good as a play, and Marya Viktorovna laughed till the tears came to her eyes watching him. Then he played the piano and sang in his light, rather pleasant tenor, and Marya Viktorovna stood by him selecting the songs and correcting him when he made a mistake.

"I hear that you sing, too," I said.

"Sing, too!" cried the doctor, horrified. "She's marvelous, an artist! And you talk of her 'singing, too!' What a way to put it!"

"At one time I studied seriously," she said, in reply to my question, "but now I've given it up."

She sat down on a low stool and told us about her life in Petersburg, and did imitations of the famous singers, mimicking their voices and mannerisms. She made sketches in her album, first of the doctor, then of me, and though she did not draw well, both sketches were good likenesses. She was full of fun, laughing and making delightful faces, and this suited her much better than talking about the mammon of unrighteousness. I began to feel that when she had talked to me about wealth and comfort she was not in earnest but imitating someone. She was a superb comedienne. I mentally compared her to our other young ladies, and even the handsome, dignified Anyuta Blagovo suffered by comparison; the difference was enormous: it was the difference between a beautiful, cultivated rose and sweetbrier.

We stayed to supper. The doctor and Marya Viktorovna drank red wine, champagne, and coffee with cognac. They touched glasses and drank to friendship, wit, progress, and freedom, and while they did not get drunk, they were flushed and frequently laughed till they cried, for no reason. To avoid seeming dull, I, too, drank some red wine.

"Talented, richly endowed natures know how to live," said Marya Viktorovna. "They go their own way; the average person, like me, for instance, knows nothing and can do nothing himself; the only thing for him to do is to look to some deep social trend and float with the stream."

"How can you look to something that isn't there?" asked the doctor.

"It's there, but we don't see it."

"Is that so? Social trends—an invention of the new literature. They don't exist here."

An argument began.

"We have no deep social trends and never have had," said the doctor in a loud voice. "And what hasn't our new literature invented! It concocted the intellectual village toiler, but you can search the entire countryside and you'll find, at most, one country bumpkin in a jacket or black frock coat who'll make four mistakes with one three-letter word. Our cultural life hasn't even begun. There's still the same barbarity, the same everlasting vulgarity, the same pettiness, there was five hundred years ago. Trends and movements, yes—but it's all so puerile, so pitiful, so bent on vulgar, mercenary little interests. Can one possibly see anything serious in them? If you think you have discerned some deep social trend, and, in following it, devote your life to such fashionable problems of the day as the liberation of insects from slavery, or the abstinence from beef cutlets, I congratulate you, Madam. We must study, study, study, but let us wait a bit for the deep social trends; we haven't grown up to them yet and, in all seriousness, we understand absolutely nothing about them."

"You don't understand them, but I do," said Marya Viktorovna. "You really are such a bore today!"

"Our business is to go on studying and studying, to try to accumulate as much knowledge as possible, because serious social trends arise where there is knowledge, and the future happiness of mankind lies only in knowledge. I drink to learning!"

"One thing is certain: one must arrange one's life somehow differently," said Marya Viktorovna, after a moment of reflection. "Life as it has been up to now is not worth living. Let's not even talk about it."

When we left her the cathedral clock was striking two.

"Did you like her?" asked the doctor. "Charming, isn't she?"

We had dinner at Marya Viktorovna's on Christmas Day and went to see her almost every day during the holidays. There was never anyone there but ourselves, and she was right when she said that she had no friends in the town but the doctor and me. We spent most of the time in conversation; occasionally the doctor would bring a book or a magazine and read aloud to us. He was, in fact, the first cultivated man I had ever met. I cannot judge whether he knew much, but he was continually displaying his knowledge as if he wanted others to share it. When he talked about anything relating to medicine he was not like any of our local doctors, but created a fresh and rather singular impression, and it seemed to me that, had he wanted to, he could have become a real scientist. He was perhaps the only person who had a serious influence on me at that time. Seeing him, and reading the books he gave me, little by little I began to feel a need for knowledge in order to give spiritual meaning to my joyless work. It now seemed to me strange that I had never known, for instance, that the whole world is composed of sixty elements, that I had not known what oil is, or paint, and that somehow I had got along without this knowledge. My acquaintance with the doctor elevated me morally, too. I often argued with him, and though I generally stuck to my own opinions, thanks to him I gradually began to perceive that everything was not clear to me, and I commenced trying to work out convictions that were as definite as possible, so that the dictates of my conscience should be definite and have nothing vague about them. Nevertheless, this man, the finest, most cultivated man in the town, was far from perfect. In his manners, his habit of turning every conversation into an argument, his pleasant tenor voice, even in his affability, there was something coarse, something of the seminarian, and every time he took off his coat and sat in his silk shirt, or flung a tip to a waiter in a tavern, it seemed to me that with all his culture a Tartar still stirred in him.

At Epiphany he went back to Petersburg. He left in the morning, and after dinner my sister came to see me. Without taking off her fur coat or hat she sat down, silent, extremely pale, her eyes fixed on one spot. She shivered, apparently fighting some illness.

"You must have caught cold," I said.

Her eyes filled with tears, as though I had hurt her feelings, and without a word she got up and went out to Karpovna. A little later I heard her say in a tone of bitter reproach:

"Nurse, what have I been living for till now? For what? Tell me: haven't I thrown my youth away? All the best years of my life to have known nothing but keeping accounts, pouring tea, counting kopecks, entertaining visitors—and thinking there was nothing better in the world! Nurse, try to understand me! You see, I, too, have human needs, I want to live, but I've been made into some kind of housekeeper. It's awful, awful!"

She flung her keys against the door and they landed in my room with a clatter. They were the keys to the sideboard, the kitchen cupboard, the cellar, and the tea chest—the same keys my mother had carried.

"Oh, oh, Blessed Saints!" cried the old woman in horror. "Holy Saints above!"

As she was leaving to go home, my sister came to my room to pick up the keys and said:

"Forgive me. Something strange has been happening to me lately."

# VIII

Late one evening, on returning home from Marya Viktorovna's, I found a young police inspector in a new uniform sitting in my room; he was leafing through a book on the table.

"At last!" he said, getting up and stretching himself. "This is the third time I've been here. The governor orders you to appear before him tomorrow morning at nine o'clock sharp. Without fail."

He took a signed statement from me saying that I would comply with His Excellency's order, and left. This late visit of the police inspector and the unexpected order to appear before the governor had a most depressing effect upon me. From early childhood I have had a fear of gendarmes, policemen, magistrates, and now I was tormented by anxiety, as though I were actually guilty of something. It was impossible for me to sleep. Nurse and Prokofy were upset, too, and they could not sleep. Nurse, moreover, had an earache; she moaned and several times cried out with pain. Hearing that I was awake, Prokofy cautiously came into my room with a little lamp and sat down at the table.

"You ought to drink some pepper brandy," he said, after a moment's thought. "In this vale of tears you take a drink, and you don't mind things. If Mamasha would pour a little pepper brandy in her ear, it would do her a lot of good."

Between two and three o'clock he got ready to go to the slaughterhouse for his meat. I knew I should not fall asleep before morning, so in order to make the hours till nine pass more quickly, I went with him. We walked, carrying a lantern, while his shopboy, Nikolka, a boy of thirteen with blue splotches on his face from frostbite—a thorough ruffian, judging by his expression—drove after us in the sledge, urging the horse on in a raucous voice.

"They're probably going to punish you at the governor's," Prokofy said to me on the way. "There are rules for governors, rules for the clergy, officers' rules, doctors' rules, every class has its own rules. But you don't stick to yours, and they're not going to allow that."

The slaughterhouse stood behind the cemetery; I had seen it only from a distance till then. It consisted of three gloomy sheds surrounded by a gray fence, and on hot summer days, when the wind blew from that quarter, there was an overwhelming stench. Now, entering the yard in the dark, I did not see the sheds; I kept coming upon horses and sledges, some empty, some already loaded with meat; men walked about with lanterns, cursing horribly. Prokofy and Nikolka cursed just as foully, and the air was thick with oaths and the incessant snorting and neighing of horses.

There was a smell of carcasses and offal. The snow was thawing, turning into mud, and in the darkness I felt as though I were walking in pools of blood.

Having filled the sledge with meat, we set off for the butcher shop in the market. It began to grow light. Cooks carrying baskets and elderly ladies in cloaks walked by, one after the other. Prokofy, a meat ax in his hand and wearing a white, blood-spattered apron, swore terrifically, crossed himself facing the church, and could be heard all over the market saying that he was selling his meat at cost and even taking a loss. He gave short weight and short change; the cooks saw what he was doing, but, deafened by his shouts, made no protest and only called him a hangman. He assumed picturesque attitudes as he raised and brought down his formidable ax, accompanying each blow with the savage cry: "Hack!" And I was afraid he might in fact chop off somebody's head or hand.

I spent the whole morning in the butcher's shop, and when at last I went to the governor's my overcoat smelled of meat and blood. I felt as if someone had sent me out to meet a bear, spear in hand. I remember a long staircase with a striped carpet, a young official in a frock coat with gleaming buttons who mutely indicated the door with both hands, then ran ahead to announce me. I went into a reception hall, luxuriantly but coldly and tastelessly furnished; I was particularly struck by the ugliness of the tall, narrow pier glasses and the bright yellow hangings at the windows. One could see that, although governors changed, the furnishings remained the same. The young official again mutely motioned me with both hands to the door and I went toward a big green table, behind which stood a general with the Order of Vladimir on his breast.

"Mr. Polozniev, I have asked you to appear here," he began, holding a letter in his hand and opening his mouth so wide it looked like an O, "I have asked you to appear here in order to make known to you the following: your esteemed father has applied verbally and in writing to the provincial Marshal of Nobility, appealing to him to summon you, and to lay before you the thorough inconsistency of your conduct with the station of nobility to which you have the honor to belong. His Excellency, Aleksandr Pavlovich, justly assuming that your conduct might serve to lead others astray, and, having found mere persuasion on his part to have been insufficient, has concluded that grave intervention on the part of the authorities is now required, and has set forth in this letter to me his considerations, which I share."

He said this quietly, respectfully, standing erect, as if I were his superior officer, and looking at me without a trace of severity. He had a worn, flabby face covered with wrinkles and had pouches under his eyes; his hair was dyed and it was impossible to tell from his appearance whether he was forty or sixty.

"I trust," he continued, "that you appreciate the esteemed Aleksandr Pavlovich's delicacy in appealing to me in a private rather than in an official capacity. In the same way I have invited you unofficially to come here—not as the governor, but as a sincere admirer of your father. Therefore, I ask you either to alter your conduct and resume the obligations proper to your station, or, to avoid leading others astray, to move to a place where you are not known and where you can do as you please. Otherwise I shall have to take extreme measures."

He stood for half a minute in silence, looking at me with his mouth open.

"Are you a vegetarian?" he asked.

"No, Your Excellency, I eat meat."

He sat down and drew a document of some sort toward him; I bowed and left.

It was not worth while going to work before dinner. I went home and tried to sleep, but it was impossible because of a disagreeable, sickly feeling brought on by the slaughterhouse and my conversation with the governor. I waited till evening and then, feeling out of sorts and gloomy, went to see Marya Viktorovna. I told her about my visit to the governor and she looked at me in bewilderment, as if she did not believe it; and all at once she began to laugh, merrily, loudly, irrepressibly, in a way that only goodhearted, laughter-loving people know how to laugh.

"If I could tell that in Petersburg!" she cried, leaning on the table and nearly dropping with laughter. "If I could tell that in Petersburg!"

# IX

We saw each other often now, sometimes twice a day. She drove to the cemetery almost every day after dinner and would read the epitaphs on the crosses and tombstones while waiting for me; occasionally she came into the church and stood by me, watching me work. The silence, the ingenuous work of the artists and gilders, Radish's pronouncements, and the fact that outwardly I did not differ from the other men, working as they did in a vest and old worn-out shoes, and that they addressed me familiarly—all this was new and touching to her. One day when she was there the artist who was painting the dove overhead called down to me:

"Misail, hand up the whiting!"

I took him the whiting and as I came down the frail scaffolding she looked at me, moved to tears, and smiled.

"How nice you are!" she said.

I remembered from childhood how a green parrot belonging to one of our rich citizens escaped from its cage; for a whole month this beautiful bird drifted through the town, aimlessly flitting from garden to garden, solitary and homeless. Marya Viktorovna reminded me of this bird.

"There's absolutely no place for me to go now except the cemetery," she said to me with a laugh. "The town bores me to distraction. At the Azhogins' they're still reciting, singing, lisping, and I can't bear them lately; your sister is unsociable, Mademoiselle Blagovo for some reason hates me, and I don't care for the theater. Tell me, what am I to do with myself?"

When I went to see her I smelled of paint and turpentine, and my hands were stained—and this pleased her; she even wanted me to come in my ordinary working clothes, but it embarrassed me to wear them in her drawing room. I felt awkward, as if I were in uniform, so I always put on my new serge suit when I went there. And this she did not like.

"You must confess that you are not entirely at home in your new role," she once said to me. "Workman's clothes embarrass you, you feel awkward in them. Tell me, isn't this because you lack conviction and are dissatisfied? The very nature of the work you have chosen, this painting of yours—can that really give you any satisfaction?" she asked, laughing. "I know paint makes things look better and last longer, but after all, these things you paint belong to the rich, and, in the final analysis, are luxuries. Besides, you yourself have said more than once that everyone ought to earn his bread with his own hands, yet you are earning money, not bread. Why not stick literally to your words? One must earn bread, real bread; that is, one must plow, sow, reap, thresh, or do something that has a direct relation to agriculture, such as tending cows, digging in the earth, building huts. . . ."

She opened a pretty little cupboard that stood near her writing table and said:

"The reason I'm saying all this is that I want to share my secret with you. *Voilà!* This is my agricultural library. Here they all are—plowland, vegetable garden, orchard, cattle yard, apiary. I read them avidly, and I've studied all the theories down to the smallest detail. My dream, my dearest wish, is to go to our Dubechnya just as soon as March begins. It's marvelous there, wonderful, isn't it? The first year I shall familiarize myself with everything and grow accustomed to it, but the second year I shall start working in earnest, putting my back into it, as they say. Father has promised to give me Dubechnya, and I'm to do whatever I like with it."

Flushed and excited, between laughter and tears, she dreamed aloud of how she would live at Dubechnya, of what an interesting life it would be. I envied her. March would soon be here, the days were growing longer; on bright sunny days the snow melted, dripped from the roofs, and there was a smell of spring in the air. I, too, longed for the country.

When she talked of living at Dubechnya, I had a vivid picture of myself in town alone, and I felt jealous of her books and her farming. I neither knew nor cared anything about farming, and I was on the verge of saying to her that working the land is a slavish occupation, when I remembered my father having said something of the sort on more than one occasion, and I remained silent.

It was the beginning of Lent. The engineer, Viktor Ivanych, whose existence I had almost forgotten, arrived from Petersburg. He came unexpectedly, without even a telegram announcing his arrival. When I called as usual in the evening, there he was, freshly washed and shaved and looking

ten years younger, walking up and down the drawing room
relating some story to his daughter, who was on her knees
on the floor removing boxes, bottles, and books from his
trunks and handing them to the footman, Pavel. On seeing
the engineer I involuntarily stepped back, but he held out
both hands to me and, with a smile that showed his strong
white coachman's teeth, said:

"Here he is! Here he is! Very glad to see you, Mr. Painter!
Masha's been telling me all about it, singing your praises.
I understand you perfectly, and I approve!" he went on,
taking my arm. "To be a decent workingman is more sensible
and honest than wasting government paper and wearing a
cockade on your head. I myself worked with these two hands
in Belgium, and for two years I was a locomotive engineer. . . ."

He was wearing a short jacket and house slippers and
walked with a shuffling step like a man with gout; he kept
rubbing his hands, humming a tune, and hugging himself
with pleasure at being home again where he could take his
beloved shower.

"There's no disputing it," he said to me at supper, "there's
no disputing it, you are all nice, charming people, but for
some reason, my friends, as soon as you take to physical
work, or go in for saving the peasants, it all comes to nothing but doctrinairism in the end. You're a doctrinaire, aren't
you? Here, you don't drink vodka. What's that if not doctrinaire?"

To satisfy him I took some vodka. I also drank wine. We
tried the cheese, the sausages, pâtés, pickles, and all sorts
of delicacies that the engineer had brought back with him,
as well as the wines sent from abroad in his absence. The
wines were excellent. For some reason he received wine and
cigars from abroad duty free; the caviar and smoked sturgeon
were also sent gratis; he did not pay rent because his land-
lord supplied the railroad with kerosene; and altogether the
engineer and his daughter gave me the impression of having the best of everything in life at their disposal, and all
provided free of charge.

I continued going there, but no longer with the same
eagerness. I felt constrained in his presence, fettered. I could
not bear his clear, guileless eyes, his reasoning sickened and
repelled me; I was also made miserable by the recollection
of being so recently subordinated to this florid, sated man,

and of his having been unmercifully rude to me. True, he would put his arm around me, affably clap me on the shoulder and commend my way of life, but I felt that he despised my insignificance as before and put up with me only to please his daughter; and I was no longer able to laugh or say what I liked, but behaved unsociably, and kept expecting him to call me Pantelei at any moment, as he did his footman Pavel. How my provincial workingman's pride was outraged! I, a proletarian, a house painter, going every day to the home of rich people who were alien to me, whom the whole town regarded as foreigners, every day drinking their expensive wines and eating their exotic food—my conscience refused to be reconciled to it! On my way there I perversely avoided meeting anyone, glowering as if I were in fact a doctrinaire, and when I left their house I was ashamed of my own satiety.

But above all I was afraid of falling in love. Whether walking along the street, or working, or talking with the men, I was always thinking about going to see Marya Viktorovna in the evening; I could think of nothing but her voice, her laugh, the way she walked. When I was getting ready to go and see her I would stand for a long time before Nurse's crooked mirror tying my necktie; my serge suit filled me with disgust, I suffered, and at the same time I despised myself for being so petty. When she would call to me from the next room to say that she was not ready and ask me to wait, I could hear her dressing, and I became so agitated that I felt as if the ground was giving way under me. And when I caught sight of a woman's figure in the street, even at a distance, I made the inevitable comparison, and it seemed to me that all our women and girls were vulgar, absurdly dressed, and did not know how to hold themselves. These comparisons aroused a feeling of pride in me: Marya Viktorovna was better than any of them! And at night I dreamed of her. . . .

Once at supper the engineer and I ate a whole lobster. Afterward, as I was walking home, I recalled that twice during supper he had called me "my dear fellow," and it occurred to me that they treated me very affectionately in that house, as if I were a big, unhappy dog that had been turned out by its master, that they were amusing themselves with me, and when they grew tired of me would drive me away like a dog. I began to feel ashamed and hurt, hurt to the point of tears, and, raising my eyes to the heavens, I vowed to put an end to all this.

The next day I did not go to the Dolzhikovs'. Late in the evening, when it was quite dark and pouring rain, I walked along Bolshaya Dvoryanskaya Street, looking at the windows. Everyone was asleep at the Azhogins'; the only light came from a corner window where Madam Azhogin was sewing by the light of three candles, thinking she was combating superstition. Our house was dark, while across the street at the Dolzhikovs' the windows were lighted up, but it was impossible to see through the flowers and curtains. I kept walking up and down the street, drenched in the cold March rain. I heard my father coming home from the club; he knocked at the gate and a moment later a light appeared in the window and I saw my sister hasten down with a lamp, tidying her thick hair with one hand as she came. Then my father paced the drawing room, talking and rubbing his hands, while my sister sat in an armchair lost in thought, not listening to him.

But soon they left and the light went out. . . . I looked back at the engineer's house: there, too, it was dark. In the darkness and rain I felt myself hopelessly alone, abandoned to a quirk of fate, and I felt that compared with this loneliness of mine, compared with my suffering, both present and yet to come in life, all my work, my desires, everything that I had thought and said till now, were insignificant. Alas, the deeds and thoughts of human beings are not nearly so significant as their suffering! And without clearly realizing what I was doing, I pulled the bell at the Dolzhikovs' gate with all my might, broke it, and ran down the street like a small boy, terrified and thinking they would rush out and instantly recognize me. When I stopped at the end of the street to catch my breath, I heard only the falling rain, and somewhere in the distance a watchman knocking on a sheet of iron.

For a whole week I did not go to the Dolzhikovs'. The serge suit was sold. There were no painting jobs and again I was half-starved, earning ten to twenty kopecks a day wherever I could, doing heavy, disagreeable work. As I floundered in mud up to my knees, straining my chest, I tried to stifle my memories and punish myself for all the cheeses and preserves I had enjoyed at the engineer's; and yet, no sooner did I lie down in bed, wet and hungry, than my wanton imagination evoked marvelous, alluring pictures, and, in wonder, I acknowledged to myself that I was in love, passionately in love, and fell asleep feeling that this life of hard labor only made my body stronger and younger.

One evening, quite unseasonably, it commenced to snow, and the wind blew from the north as if winter had begun again. When I returned from work that evening I found Marya Viktorovna in my room. She was sitting in her fur coat with both hands in her muff.

"Why have you stopped coming to see me?" she asked, looking up at me with her bright, intelligent eyes.

I was overcome with joy and stood stiffly before her as I used to stand before my father when he was about to strike me; she looked me straight in the face and I could see in her eyes that she understood why I was so shaken.

"Why have you stopped coming to see me?" she repeated. "Since you don't want to come, I have come to you."

She stood up and came close to me.

"Don't desert me," she said, and her eyes filled with tears. "I'm alone, utterly alone!"

She began to cry and, covering her face with her muff, murmured:

"I am alone! Life is hard for me, very hard. I have no one in the whole world but you. Don't desert me!"

As she looked for a handkerchief to dry her eyes, she smiled; we were silent for some time, then I took her in my arms and kissed her, scratching my cheek on her hatpin so that it bled.

And we began talking as if we had been close to each other for a long, long time.

# X

Two days later she sent me to Dubechnya, and this made me inexpressibly happy. As I walked to the station, and later, sitting in the train, I laughed for no reason, and people looked at me as if I were drunk. Snow was falling, we still had frost in the mornings, but the roads were beginning to darken under the snow and rooks hovered over them, cawing.

At first I thought of arranging the wing opposite Madam Cheprakova's for Masha and me, but it appeared that pigeons and ducks had been nesting there and it would have been impossible to clean it without destroying countless nests. Like it or not we had to settle for those comfortless rooms with Venetian blinds in the big house. The peasants called it the palace; there were more than twenty rooms, but the only furniture was a piano and a child's armchair, which lay in the attic; if Masha had brought all her furniture from town, we still could not have destroyed the impression of bleak emptiness and coldness. I chose three small rooms with windows looking onto the garden, and worked from early morning till night putting in new windowpanes, papering the walls, filling chinks and holes in the floors. It was easy, pleasant work. Now and then I ran down to the river to see whether the ice was moving; I kept imagining the starlings were returning. And at night, thinking of Masha, I listened with an inexpressibly sweet feeling, with keen delight, to the sound of rats and the whistling and rattling of wind overhead; it sounded like some ancient spook coughing in the attic.

The snow was deep; it was still piling up at the end of March, when suddenly, as if by magic, it melted and the spring floods came with such a tumultuous rush that by the beginning of April the starlings were chattering and yellow butterflies fluttered in the garden. It was wonderful weather. Every day toward evening I walked to town to meet Masha, and what a pleasure it was to go with bare feet along the drying, still soft road! Halfway there I would sit down and look toward the town, unable to make up my mind to go nearer. The sight of it troubled me. I kept wondering how my acquaintances would behave toward me when they learned of my love. What would my father say? But I was particularly disturbed by the thought that my life was becoming complicated, that I had lost all control of it, and it was carrying me off, God knows where, like a balloon. I no longer thought about earning a living, or about how one ought to live, but thought about—I really cannot remember what.

Masha used to come in a carriage; I would get in and sit beside her, and together we drove to Dubechnya, happy and free. Or, after waiting till sunset, I would return home, despondent and weary, wondering why Masha had not come, and then, at the gate or in the garden I would unexpectedly be met by a lovely apparition—she! It would turn out that she had come by train and walked from the station. And then how festive we were! Carrying a modest parasol, and wearing a plain woolen dress with a little neckerchief, but tightly laced, slender, and in expensive imported boots, she was the talented actress playing the little commoner. We inspected our domain and decided which room would be which, where we would have the avenue, the vegetable garden, the apiary. We already had chickens, ducks, and geese, which we loved because they were our own. We also had ready for sowing, oats, clover, timothy, buckwheat, and vegetable seeds, and we were always inspecting them, too, discussing at length what the crops would be like, and everything Masha said seemed to me extraordinarily clever and fine. This was the happiest time of my life.

Soon after Easter we were married in our parish church in the village of Kurilovka, three versts from Dubechnya. Masha wanted everything to be done very modestly; by her wish our "best men" were peasant lads, only the sexton sang, and we returned from the church in a small springless buggy which she herself drove. Our only guest from town was my sister Kleopatra, to whom Masha had sent a note three days before the wedding. My sister wore a white dress and gloves. She was so moved during the ceremony that she quietly wept for joy; her expression was motherly and infinitely kind. Intoxicated with our happiness she smiled as if in a daze, and looking at her, I realized that for her nothing in this world was higher than love, earthly love, that she secretly, timidly, but constantly and passionately dreamed of it. She embraced Masha and kissed her, and, not knowing how to express her rapture, said to her:

"He is good! He is very good!"

Before leaving she changed into her ordinary dress and drew me into the garden to have a talk with me alone.

"Father is very hurt that you have written nothing to him," she said. "You ought to have asked his blessing. But actually he is very much pleased. He says that this marriage will raise you in the eyes of all society, and that under Marya Viktorovna's influence you will begin to take a more serious attitude toward life. In the evenings now we talk of nothing but you, and yesterday he even spoke of you as 'our Misail.' That delighted me. Apparently he has something in mind, and I believe he intends to set you an example of magnanimity by being the first to speak of a reconciliation. It's quite possible that one of these days he may come here to see you."

She quickly made the sign of the cross over me several times and said:

"Well, God bless you. Be happy. Anyuta Blagovo is a very wise girl; she says of your marriage that God has sent you a new trial. To be sure—married life is not made up of joy alone, but suffering, too. It's bound to be."

Masha and I accompanied her for about three versts; we walked back slowly and in silence, as if we had come to rest. Masha held my hand, we were at peace, and there was no need to talk of love; after the wedding ceremony we were closer, dearer to each other, and we felt that nothing could separate us now.

"Your sister is a dear," said Masha, "but she looks as though she had lived in a torment for a long time. Your father must be a dreadful man."

I began telling her how my sister and I had been brought up, how, in fact, our childhood had been a torture and absurd. When she learned that only recently my father had beaten me, she shuddered and drew close to me.

"Don't tell me any more," she said. "It's horrible!"

She never left my side now. We lived in three rooms in the big house, and in the evenings we tightly bolted the door leading into the empty part of the house as if someone we did not know and whom we feared lived there. I got up early, at dawn, and immediately started working. I repaired the carts, laid paths in the garden, cultivated the flower beds, painted the roof of the house. When the time came to sow oats, I undertook the second plowing myself, as well as the harrowing and sowing, and did it all conscientiously, never falling behind our laborer; I was exhausted; the rain and the sharp, cold wind made my face and legs burn for hours afterward, and at night I dreamed of plowed fields. But work on the land did not appeal to me. I neither liked nor understood agriculture, perhaps because my ancestors were not farmers and pure city blood flowed in my veins. I dearly loved nature, loved the fields, meadows, and vegetable gardens, but the peasant turning up the soil with his plow, urging on his pitiful, wet, broken-down and straining horse, was to me an expression of hideous, barbarous, brute strength, and, watching his lumbering movements I could not help thinking of legendary life in the remote past, before men knew the use of fire. The fierce bull running with the herd, or horses stamping their hoofs and rampaging through the village, filled me with terror. And anything that was at all large, powerful, or hostile, whether it was a horned ram, a gander, or a watchdog, was to me a manifestation of that same primitive, brute force. This disposition was particularly strong in me in bad weather, when heavy clouds hung over the dark, plowed fields. And especially when I was plowing and two or three people stood watching me work; then I no longer had a sense of the inevitability and necessity of what I was doing, but felt as though I were amusing myself. I preferred doing something in the yard, and there was nothing I liked so much as painting the roof.

I used to walk through the garden and across the meadow to our mill. It was let to a Kurilovka peasant, Stepan, a handsome, swarthy man with a thick black beard and great physical strength. He disliked the work, which he considered tedious and unprofitable, but stayed at the mill to avoid living at home. He was a harnessmaker, and there was always a pleasant smell of resin and leather about him. He disliked talking, was indolent and sedentary, and would sit in the doorway or on the riverbank softly warbling "oo-loo-loo-loo." His wife and his mother-in-law, both pale, languid, meek women, would sometimes come from Kurilovka to see him; they bowed low and addressed him formally as "Stepan Petrovich." Without a word or a sign of response to their greeting, he continued to sit on the riverbank, softly warbling "oo-loo-loo-loo." An hour or two would pass in silence. His wife and mother-in-law, after whispering together, would get up and stand gazing at him for a while, expecting him to look around, then bow low and in sweet singsong voices say:

"Good-bye, Stepan Petrovich!"

And they would go away. After picking up the bundle of cracknels or a shirt they had left him, he would heave a sigh and, with a wink in their direction, say:

"The female sex!"

The mill, with two sets of millstones, worked day and night. I used to help Stepan; I liked the work, and when he went off somewhere I was glad to take his place.

# XI

After the warm bright weather came the season of bad
roads; throughout May it was cold and rainy. The sound of
mill wheels and of falling rain disposed one to indolence and
sleep. The floor trembled, there was the smell of flour, and
that, too, induced drowsiness. My wife appeared twice a day
in a short fur coat and high peasant galoshes, each time saying the same thing:

"And they call this summer! It's worse than October!"

We would make tea, cook porridge, or just sit for hours at
a time in silence, waiting for the rain to stop. Once when
Stepan had gone away to a fair, Masha spent the night at the
mill. When we got up we could not tell what time it was: the
whole sky was overcast with rain clouds, but sleepy cocks
were crowing in Dubechnya and corncrakes called in the
meadow; it was still very, very early. . . . My wife and I
walked down to the pool and drew up the creel we had seen
Stepan throw in the day before. A big bass was struggling
in it and a crayfish bristled and raised its claws.

"Let them go," said Masha. "Let them be happy, too."

Because of getting up so early and then having nothing to
do, the day seemed exceedingly long, the longest of my entire
life. Stepan returned before evening, and I went home to the
manor house.

"Your father was here today," Masha said to me.

"Where is he?" I asked.

"He's gone. I refused to see him."

When she saw me standing in silence, saw that I was sorry
for my father, she said:

"One must be consistent. I wouldn't receive him and sent
word that he should trouble himself no further, and that he
should not come here to see us."

A minute later I was outside the gate and on my way to
town to explain things to my father. It was muddy, slippery,
cold. For the first time since our wedding I felt suddenly sad,
and there flashed through my mind, exhausted by the long
gray day, the thought that perhaps I was not living as I ought
to live. I was worn out, and gradually, overcome by faint-
heartedness and inertia, I lost all desire to move or think,

and after walking on a little farther, gave it up and turned back.

In the middle of the yard stood the engineer, wearing a leather overcoat with a hood.

"Where's all the furniture?" he was saying in a loud voice. "There was fine furniture here, in the Empire style, there were pictures, vases, and now you could play ball in there! I bought this place with the furniture, damn her!"

Before him, kneading his cap in his hands, stood Moisei, a lanky, pockmarked fellow of twenty-five who was in the service of the general's widow; he had insolent little eyes and one of his cheeks was smaller than the other, as if he had lain on it too long.

"Your Honor was pleased to buy it without the furniture," he said hesitantly. "I recall it, sir."

"Shut up!" shouted the engineer, turning red and beginning to tremble, and the echo in the garden loudly repeated his words.

# XII

Whenever I was doing anything in the garden or the yard, Moisei would stand near me, his hands behind his back, idly staring at me with his insolent little eyes. And this used to irritate me to such a degree that I would drop my work and walk away.

We learned from Stepan that Moisei was Madam Cheprakova's lover. I noticed that when people came to her for money they first addressed themselves to Moisei, and once I saw a peasant, black from head to foot—he must have been a coal heaver—bow down to Moisei's feet. Sometimes, after a whispered exchange, he would hand out money himself without informing his mistress, from which I concluded that he occasionally operated independently, on his own account.

He used to shoot in the garden right under our windows, steal food out of our cellar, and take the horses without asking our permission; we were indignant and no longer felt that Dubechnya was ours. Masha would sometimes turn pale and say:

"Can we really go on living with this rabble for another year and a half?"

Ivan Cheprakov, the widow's son, now worked as a conductor on our railroad. He had grown terribly thin and weak during the winter, so that now a single glass was enough to make him drunk, and he shivered when he stood in the shade. He wore his conductor's uniform with shame and loathing, but he considered his job profitable because he could steal candles and sell them. My new position aroused in him mixed feelings of astonishment, envy, and the vague hope that something of the same sort might happen to him. He used to follow Masha with a rapt look, and ask me what I was having for dinner these days; a sorrowful, mawkish expression would appear on his homely, emaciated face and his fingers moved as if he were touching my happiness.

"Listen, Better-than-nothing," he said fussily, relighting his cigarette every minute—there was always a litter wherever he stood because he used a dozen matches for one cigarette—"listen, my life now couldn't be more revolting. The worst of it is that any little subaltern can shout: 'Hey, conductor! Hey, you!' I've heard all kinds of things, brother, I've heard plenty in the trains, and, you know, I've come to realize that it's a filthy life! My mother ruined me! A doctor in the train told me that if the parents are dissolute the children turn out to be drunkards or criminals. And that's how it is!"

Once he came staggering into the yard, his eyes rolling senselessly, his breathing labored; he laughed, cried, ranted as if he were delirious, and the only words I could catch in his muddled speech were: "My mother! Where is my mother?" which he wailed like a child who has lost his mother in a crowd. I led him into our garden and laid him down under a tree, and Masha and I took turns sitting by him all that day and night. He was very sick, and Masha looked at his pale, wet face with repugnance and said:

"Is it really possible that this rabble is going to go on living on our place for another year and a half? This is horrible! Horrible!"

And how many mortifications the peasants caused us! How many painful disappointments came in the beginning, during those spring months when we so longed to be happy! My wife built a school. I drew the plan of a school for sixty boys, and the zemstvo board approved it but advised us to build the school at Kurilovka, the big village which was only three versts from us; it appeared that the children from four villages, including our Dubechnya, went to the Kurilovka school, and it was old, crowded, and the floor was so rotten it was not safe to walk on. At the end of March, by her own wish, Masha was appointed trustee of the Kurilovka school, and in the beginning of April we called three meetings to persuade the peasants that their school was so old and crowded that it was necessary to build a new one. The public-school inspector and a member of the zemstvo board also came to try to convince them. After every meeting the peasants surrounded us, begging for a pail of vodka; it was hot in the crowd, we were quickly exhausted, and returned home dissatisfied and confused. In the end the peasants allotted a plot of ground for the school and undertook to cart all the building materials from town. And the very first Sunday after they were finished with the spring crops the carts set off from Kurilovka and Dubechnya to fetch bricks for the foundation. They left when it was barely light and came back late in the evening; the peasants were drunk and said they were worn out.

As if to spite us the rain and cold continued all through May. The road was ruined, it was nothing but mud. The carts generally drove into our yard coming back from the town—and what a horror that was! A big-bellied horse would appear, its forelegs straddled, stumbling as it entered the yard; then in crawled a thirty-foot beam on a wagon, wet and slimy-looking; alongside it, wrapped up against the rain, with the skirts of his coat tucked into his belt, strode a peasant, not looking where he was going, splashing through the puddles. Another cart would appear with planks, then a third with a beam, and a fourth . . . and the yard in front of our house was gradually packed with horses, beams, planks. . . . Women with their heads covered and their skirts tucked up stood with the men, staring resentfully at our windows, clamoring for the mistress to come out to them and cursing in loud voices. Moisei, meanwhile, stood on one side, and it seemed to us that he was enjoying our ignominy.

"We're not carting any more!" the peasants shouted. "Let her haul it herself!"

Masha, pale and distraught, thinking they were going to break into the house at any moment, would send out half a pail of vodka, after which the noise would subside, and one after another the long beams slowly crawled out of the yard.

When I decided to go to the building site, my wife became worried and said:

"The peasants are malicious. I'm afraid they might do you some harm. Wait, I'll go with you."

We drove together to Kurilovka, and there the carpenters asked us for a tip. The excavation was ready, it was now time to lay the foundation, but the masons had not come; this caused a delay and the carpenters were grumbling. And when, at last, the masons did appear, it turned out that there was no sand; somehow this requirement had been overlooked. Taking advantage of our predicament, the peasants demanded thirty kopecks a load, though the distance from the building to the river where they got the sand was less than a quarter of a verst, and more than five hundred cartloads were needed. There was no end to the misunderstandings, the wrangling, and begging; my wife grew indignant and the head mason, Tit Petrov, an old man of seventy, took her by the hand and said:

"Have a look at this now! Just have a look! You bring me the sand and I'll set ten men to work instantly, and in two days it will be ready! You'll see!"

Sand was brought and two days passed, four days, a week, and the future foundation was still a gaping hole.

"It's enough to drive you out of your mind!" said my wife growing excited. "What people! What people!"

In the midst of this chaos the engineer Viktor Ivanich came to visit us. He brought sacks of wine and delicacies with him, and after a lengthy meal lay down on the veranda to sleep; he snored so that the workmen shook their heads and said: "What do you think of that!"

Masha took no pleasure in his visits. She had no confidence in him, yet she asked his advice. When, having slept too long after dinner, he got up in a bad mood and spoke disparagingly of the way we managed the place, or expressed his regret at having bought Dubechnya, which had already been such a loss to him, poor Masha looked miserable; but when she complained to him, he yawned and said the peasants ought to be flogged.

He called our marriage and the way we lived play acting, and said it was a caprice, an indulgence.

"She did the same sort of thing once before," he said, speaking of Masha. "She fancied herself an opera singer and ran away from me; it took me two months to find her, and, my dear fellow, I spent a thousand rubles on telegrams alone."

He no longer called me a doctrinaire or Mr. Painter, nor did he speak with approval of my living like a workingman, but said:

"You're a strange person! You're . . . not normal. I won't venture to prophesy, but you'll come to a bad end, sir!"

Masha slept badly at night; she was always sitting at our bedroom window thinking about something. There was no more laughter at supper, no charming grimaces. I suffered; when the rain fell, every drop pierced my heart like small shot, and I was ready to fall on my knees before Masha and ask her to forgive me for the weather. When the peasants made an uproar in the yard, I also felt guilty. I used to sit in one spot for hours at a time thinking only of what a wonderful, what a magnificent, person Masha was. I loved her passionately, and I was fascinated by everything she did, everything she said. She had a penchant for quiet, studious pursuits, and loved to spend long hours reading or studying. She, who knew farming only from books, amazed us all with her knowledge; whatever advice she gave was always practical, and was never followed in vain. And with all that, she had such nobility, such graciousness and good taste—the graciousness one sees only in well-bred people.

For this woman, with her healthy, positive mind, the disorderly environment in which we now lived, with its petty cares and wrangling, was a torment; I saw this and was unable to sleep at night; my brain was in a ferment and I could not choke back the tears. I rushed about not knowing what to do.

I galloped to town and brought her books, newspapers, sweets, and flowers; I went fishing with Stepan, wading up to my neck in cold water for hours in the rain to catch an eelpout to give variety to our fare; I humbly begged the peasants not to make a row, gave them vodka, bribed them, made all sorts of promises. And how many other foolish things I did!

At last the rain stopped; the earth dried. I would get up in the morning, around four o'clock, and go into the garden— the dew sparkled on the flowers, birds and insects twittered and hummed, not a cloud in the sky, the garden, the meadow, and river all so lovely—and then remember the peasants, their carts, the engineer! Masha and I drove out to the fields in the racing droshky to see how the oats were coming. She drove and I sat behind; her shoulders were raised and the wind played in her hair.

"Keep to the right!" she shouted to those passing by.

"You're like a coachman," I said to her once.

"That may be! You know, my grandfather, my father's father, was a coachman. Didn't you know that?" she asked, turning round to me, and immediately began to imitate a coachman shouting and singing.

"Thank God!" I thought as I listened to her. "Thank God!"

And again came recollections of the peasants, the carts, the engineer. . . .

# XIII

Dr. Blagovo arrived on his bicycle. My sister commenced visiting us often. Again we discussed manual labor, progress, and the unknown quantity awaiting man in the distant future. The doctor disliked our farm work because it interfered with these arguments; he said it was unworthy of a free man to plow, reap, and tend livestock, that in time all such crude forms of the struggle for existence would be relegated to animals and machines, and man would apply himself exclusively to scientific investigation. My sister always pleaded to be allowed to go home early, and if she stayed late there was no end to her agitation.

"Good heavens, what a baby you are!" Masha reproached her. "It's positively ridiculous!"

"Yes, it is ridiculous," my sister agreed. "I realize it's ridiculous, but what can I do if I haven't the power to control myself? I keep feeling that I am doing wrong."

During haymaking my whole body ached from the unfamiliar work; in the evening, sitting on the veranda talking with the others, I would suddenly fall asleep, and they all laughed at me. They would wake me up and make me sit down to supper; overcome with drowsiness, I saw the lights, plates, and their faces as though in a dream; I heard voices without understanding what they were saying. As soon as I got up in the morning I took up my scythe or went to the building and worked hard all day.

On holidays, when I remained at home, I noticed that my

wife and sister were concealing something from me, seemed even to be avoiding me. My wife was tender, as always, but she had thoughts of her own which she did not share with me. Undoubtedly her exasperation with the peasants was increasing, and life was growing more and more difficult for her, yet she no longer complained to me. She talked to the doctor more readily than to me, and I could not understand why.

It was the custom in our province during haymaking and harvest for the laborers to come to the manor house in the evening and be treated to vodka, even the girls drank a glass. We did not observe this practice; the reapers and peasant women used to stand in our yard till late in the evening, waiting for vodka, and then go away cursing. Meanwhile Masha would frown grimly and lapse into silence, or irritably mutter to the doctor:

"Savages! Huns!"

In the country newcomers are always received ungraciously, almost with hostility, as they are in school. And that is how we were received. At first we were regarded as stupid, simple-minded people who had bought an estate because they did not know what to do with their money. They laughed at us. The peasants pastured their cattle in our woods and even in our garden; they drove our horses and cows into the village and then demanded money for the damage done. They came in a body into our yard, noisily claiming that in mowing we had encroached on land that did not belong to us, either in Bysheyevka or Semyonikha, and as we did not know the exact boundaries of our land, we took them at their word and paid the fine; later it turned out that we had been in the right. They stripped the lime trees in our wood. One of the Dubechnya peasants, a sharper who sold vodka without a license, bribed our laborers to cheat us in the most insidious ways, substituting old wheels for new on our carts, stealing the yokes of our plows and selling them back to us, and so on. But the most mortifying thing of all was what went on at the construction in Kurilovka; nightly the peasant women stole scantling, bricks, tiles, pieces of iron; the elder made a search of their huts with witnesses, the village council fined them two rubles each, and afterward the whole lot got drunk on the money.

When Masha found out she would indignantly exclaim to the doctor or my sister:

"What beasts! It's awful, awful!"

And more than once I heard her express regret that she had taken it into her head to build a school.

"You must understand," the doctor tried to convince her, "that if you build this school, or undertake any good work, it is not for the peasants but for the sake of culture, for the sake of the future. And the worse the peasants are, the more reason for building the school. You must understand this!"

His voice lacked conviction, however, and it seemed to me that both he and Masha despised the peasants.

Masha often went to the mill, taking my sister with her; they would laughingly say they were going to have a look at Stepan because he was so handsome. Stepan, it turned out, was sluggish and taciturn only with men; in the company of women he behaved in a free and easy manner and never stopped talking. One day when I went to the river to bathe, I accidentally overheard their conversation. Masha and Kleopatra, both in white dresses, were sitting on the bank under the spreading shade of a willow, and Stepan stood nearby, his hands behind his back, saying:

"But are peasants really . . . people? They're not people but, asking your pardon, wild beasts, frauds. What is a peasant's life? Nothing but eating and drinking, trying to get cheaper victuals, bawling at the top of his lungs in a tavern; no decent conversation, no manners, no politeness, nothing but ignorance! He lives in filth, his wife lives in filth, his children live in filth; what he stands up in he lies down in, he picks the potatoes out of his soup with his fingers, drinks kvass with a cockroach in it—he could at least blow it aside!"

"But it's because of the poverty," my sister protested.

"Poverty! There's want, all right, but, you see, there is more than one kind of want, madam. Now if a man is in irons, or, let us say, blind, or has lost the use of his legs, then he really is in a bad way, God help him, but if he is at liberty, in his right mind, still has his hands and his eyes, has God and his strength, what more does he want? It's coddling, madam, ignorance, not poverty. Now let us suppose that you fine people here, with your education, want to give him some help, out of charity: he'll take your money and drink it up, swine that he is, or, what's worse, he'll open a tavern with your money and start robbing other people. You are pleased to call it poverty. But does the rich peasant live any better? He, too, asking your pardon, lives like a swine.

A brawler, a numskull, a clodhopper, broader than he is long, with a bloated red mug—makes you feel you'd like to let go and send him flying. Take Larion of Dubechnya; he's rich, but I'll bet he strips the bark off your trees like any of the poor ones; and he's foul-mouthed, and his children are foul-mouthed, and when he has drunk too much he falls on his face in a puddle and sleeps there. They are all worthless, madam. Living with them in the village is like living in hell. It sticks in my craw, that village, and I thank the Lord, King of Heaven, that I'm well fed and clothed, that I've served my time in the dragoons, spent three years as village elder, and now I'm a free Cossack; I live where I please. I don't want to live in the village, and nobody has the right to force me. A wife, they say—you're obliged to live in the hut with your wife, they say. And why should I? I'm not hired to her."

"Tell me, Stepan, did you marry for love?" asked Masha.

"What kind of love is there in the village?" replied Stepan with a wry grin. "As a matter of fact, madam, if you want to know, this is my second marriage. I'm not from Kurilovka, but from Zalegoshcho, but after I married they took me as a son-in-law in Kurilovka. You see, my father did not want to divide the land among us—we were five brothers—so I bowed to it and off I went to another village, to my wife's family. But my first wife died young."

"What did she die of?"

"Of foolishness. She used to sit and cry, always crying and crying for no reason, so she pined away. She kept drinking some kind of herb mixtures to make herself prettier; she must have damaged her insides. And my second wife, the Kurilovka woman—what's there to her? A village woman, a peasant, that's all. When they made the match for me, I was taken in: she's young, I think, and fair-skinned, and they live in a clean house. Her mother is like some kind of Flagellant and drinks coffee, but the important thing was: they were clean in their ways. Then I get married; the next day I sit down to dinner, and I tell my mother-in-law to get me a spoon; she gets it for me, and what does she do but wipe it with her finger! So much for you, I think, a fine sort of cleanliness! I lived with them a year and then left. Maybe I should have married a town woman," he went on after a pause. "They say a wife is a helpmate to her husband. What do I want with a helpmate—I help myself. What you want is someone to talk to, not that 'te-te-te-te' all the time, but something in particular, with some feeling in it. Without good conversation—what is life?"

Stepan suddenly fell silent and then I heard his dreary, monotonous "oo-loo-loo-loo," which meant that he had caught sight of me.

Masha went often to the mill, evidently finding pleasure in her conversations with Stepan; he abused the peasants with such sincerity and conviction that she was drawn to him. When she returned from the mill the feeble-minded peasant who looked after the garden used to shout at her:

"Wench Palashka! Hello, wench Palashka!" and he would bark at her like a dog: "Bow-wow!"

And she would stop and look at him attentively, as if in this idiot's barking she found an answer to her thoughts; he very likely had the same fascination for her as Stepan's abuse. At home there would be some such news awaiting her as that the geese from the village had ruined the cabbages in our garden, or that Larion had stolen the reins, and she would shrug her shoulders and say with a smirk:

"What can you expect of these people?"

She was outraged, and resentment was beginning to seethe in her soul, while I, on the other hand, was growing used to the peasants and felt more and more drawn to them. For the most part they were nervous, irritable, humiliated people; they were people whose imaginations had been stifled, who were ignorant, whose outlook on life was meager and drab, with always the same thoughts of gray earth, gray days, and black bread, people whose cunning was like that of birds, which hide only their heads behind trees—and they were incapable of calculating. They did not come to us for the twenty rubles they earned at haymaking, but for their half pail of vodka, though twenty rubles would have bought four pails. They were, indeed, dirty, drunken, foolish, and dishonest, but for all that, one felt that peasant life on the whole was healthy and sound at the core. However crude a peasant might appear as he walked behind his plow, however he might stupefy himself with vodka, still, looking at him more closely, one felt that there was something vital, something great in him, which was lacking, for instance, in Masha and the doctor, namely, his belief that the principal thing on earth was truth, that his salvation and that of all people lay in truth alone; and this made him love justice above all else in the world.

I used to tell my wife that she saw the specks on the glass, but not the glass itself; her only response was silence, or, like Stepan, she started humming "oo-loo-loo-loo. . . ." When this kind, clever woman turned pale with indignation and in a trembling voice talked to the doctor about drunkenness and dishonesty, I was confounded by the shortness of her memory. How could she forget that her father, the engineer, also drank—drank heavily—and that the money with which Dubechnya was bought had been acquired by a whole series of bold, unscrupulous swindles? How could she forget?

# XIV

My sister, too, was living a life of her own, which she carefully hid from me. I frequently found her whispering with Masha. Whenever I came near her she seemed to shrink into herself, and her eyes had a guilty, imploring look; evidently there was something going on in her heart of which she was ashamed. To avoid meeting me in the garden or being left alone with me, she clung to Masha and I rarely had an opportunity to talk to her except at dinner.

One evening I was walking quietly through the garden on my way back from the building. It had already begun to grow dark. My sister, not noticing me or hearing my footsteps, was walking absolutely noiselessly, like a phantom, near an old, spreading apple tree. She was dressed in black and moved rapidly back and forth in a straight line, looking at the ground. An apple fell from the tree and she shuddered at the sound, stood still and pressed her hands to her temples. At that moment I went up to her.

The flood of tender love that suddenly filled my heart for some reason made me think of our mother, our childhood, and with tears in my eyes I put my arm around her shoulder and kissed her.

"What is the matter?" I asked her. "You are suffering, I have seen it for a long time now. Tell me, what's wrong?"

"I am frightened . . ." she said, trembling.

"But what is it?" I insisted. "For God's sake, be open with me!"

"I will, I will be open with you. I'll tell you the whole truth. Hiding it from you is so . . . painful, so agonizing!

Misail, I am in love . . ." she continued in a whisper. "I am in love, in love . . . I am happy, but why am I so frightened?"

There was the sound of footsteps and Dr. Blagovo appeared between the trees in his silk shirt and high boots. Evidently they had arranged to meet here near the apple tree. Seeing him she rushed impetuously to him with an anguished cry, as if he were being taken away from her.

"Vladimir! Vladimir!"

She clung to him, looking eagerly into his face, and only then did I notice how pale and thin she had grown lately. It was especially marked by her lace collar, long familiar to me, which now hung more loosely than ever around her long, delicate neck. The doctor was disconcerted, but immediately recovered himself and, stroking her hair, said:

"There, there, now. . . . Why so nervous? You see, I have come."

We were silent, looking at one another in embarrassment. Then we all walked on together and I heard the doctor saying to me:

"Civilized life has not yet begun for us. The old comfort themselves by saying that if now there is nothing, in the forties, or in the sixties, there was something; that's the old talking, but we are young, our brains have not yet been touched with *marasmus senilis* and we cannot comfort ourselves with such illusions. The beginning of Russia was in 862, but the beginning of civilized Russia, as I understand it, is yet to come."

I was unable to enter into these reflections. For some reason, it was strange, but I could not believe that my sister was in love, that she was walking by the side of this stranger, holding his arm and gazing tenderly at him. My sister—this nervous, frightened, crushed, fettered creature, in love with a man who was already married and had children! I was full of pity—without knowing exactly why; and somehow the doctor's presence was distasteful to me now, and I could not imagine what would come of this love of theirs.

# XV

Masha and I drove to Kurilovka for the dedication of the school.

"Autumn, autumn, autumn . . ." said Masha softly, as she looked about. "Summer is over. No more birds, nothing green but the willows."

Yes, summer was over. There were clear, warm days, but the mornings were cool, the shepherds were already wearing their sheepskins, and in our garden dew remained on the asters the whole day. We kept hearing a plaintive sound but could not tell whether it came from shutters creaking on their rusty hinges or cranes flying overhead—and the soul was at peace and one felt so eager for life!

"Summer is over . . ." said Masha. "Now you and I can balance our accounts. We have done a lot of work, a lot of thinking, and we are the better for it—all honor and glory to us! We have succeeded in improving ourselves, but has this success of ours had any perceptible influence on the life around us, has it benefited anyone whatever? No. The ignorance, physical uncleanliness, drunkenness, the appallingly high infant-mortality rate, have all remained just as they were, and no one is the better for your having plowed and sown or for my having spent money and read books. It is plain to be seen that we have been working only for ourselves, and have broadened our minds only for ourselves."

This sort of reasoning confused me, and I did not know what to think.

"We have been sincere from beginning to end," I said, "and anyone who is sincere is right."

"Who disputes that? We were right, but we were wrong in our way of trying to accomplish what we were right about. First of all, our external methods—aren't they mistaken? You want to be of use to people, but from the start, by the very fact of buying an estate, you cut yourself off from the possibility of doing anything beneficial for them. Then if you work, dress, and eat like a peasant, you sanction, as it were, by your authority, that heavy clumsy clothing, those horrible huts and ridiculous beards of theirs. . . . On the other hand, let us suppose that you work for a long, long time, all your life, and in the end obtain certain practical results—what are they, these results of yours, what can they possibly do against such elemental forces as wholesale ignorance, hunger, cold, degeneration? A drop in the ocean! Other methods of fighting are necessary—strong, bold, quick! If one really wants to be of use, one must get out of the narrow circle of ordinary activity and try to act directly on the mass! First of all, you need vehement, energetic propaganda. Why is it that art—music, for example—is so powerful? Because the musician or the singer has an immediate effect on thousands. Precious, precious art!" she went on, dreamily gazing at the sky. "Art gives wings and carries you far, far away! Anyone who is sick of filth and petty, mercenary interests, who is revolted, wounded, and indignant, can find peace and satisfaction only in the beautiful."

When we drove into Kurilovka the weather was bright and joyous. Somewhere they were threshing: there was a smell of rye straw in the air. Behind the wattle fences the mountain ash glowed crimson, and wherever one looked the trees were russet or golden. Bells were ringing in the church tower as the icon was carried to the school; we could hear them singing "Holy Mother, our Defender." And how transparent the air, how high the doves were flying!

A church service was held in the schoolroom. Afterward the Kurilovka peasants brought Masha the icon and the Dubechnya peasants brought her a large twisted loaf and a gilt salt cellar. Masha broke into sobs.

"If we have said anything out of the way, or done anything not to your liking, forgive us," said an old man, bowing down first to her, then to me.

As we drove home Masha kept looking back at the school; the green roof, which I had painted, glistened in the sun and we could see it for a long time. The look Masha turned on it now I felt was a look of farewell.

# XVI

In the evening she prepared to go to town.

Lately she had often driven to town and spent the night there. I felt helpless in her absence, unable to work; our huge yard seemed to me dreary, a hideous wilderness; there were ominous sounds in the garden, and without her the house, the trees, the horses, were no longer "ours."

I did not go out of the house, but spent the whole time sitting at her table by the bookshelf with her books on farming, those former favorites, no longer wanted, which looked out at me abashed. For hours on end, while it struck seven, eight, nine, while the autumn night, black as soot, crept up to the window, I would examine an old glove of hers, or the pen with which she always wrote, or her little scissors; I did nothing, and I clearly realized that whatever I had done before, plowing, mowing, felling trees, was done because she wanted it. And if she had sent me to clean a deep well where I had to stand up to my waist in water, I should have crawled into the well without considering whether it was necessary or not. And now, when she was not near, Dubechnya, with its debris and disorder, its banging shutters, its thieves by day and by night, seemed to me a chaos in which any work would be useless. And what had I to work for here, why the worry and thought for the future, when I felt the ground slipping away from under me, felt that I had played my role in Dubechnya, felt, in a word, that the same fate awaited me as had befallen the books on agriculture? Oh, what anguish it was at night, in the hours of solitude, when I anxiously listened, as though expecting someone to cry out at any minute that it was time for me to go! I did not grieve for Dubechnya, I grieved for my love, whose autumn apparently had begun. What tremendous happiness it is to love and be loved, and what horror to feel that you are beginning to fall from that high tower!

Masha returned from town the next day toward evening. She was annoyed about something but concealed it, and merely asked why all the storm windows had been put in, adding that it was enough to suffocate one. I took out two of the windows. We sat down to supper, but neither of us felt like eating.

"Go and wash your hands," my wife said, "you smell of putty."

She had brought some new illustrated magazines from town and we looked through them together after supper. There were supplements with fashion plates and patterns. Masha gave them a cursory glance and set them aside for a proper examination later; but one dress, with a smooth, bell-shaped skirt and full sleeves, interested her, and she looked at it seriously and attentively for a moment.

"That's not bad," she said.

"Yes, that dress would be very becoming to you," I said. "Very!"

And I gazed at the dress with emotion, admiring that gray patch of paper only because she liked it, and went on tenderly:

"A wonderful, lovely dress! . . . Beautiful, splendid Masha! My darling Masha!"

And tears fell onto the fashion plate.

"Splendid Masha . . ." I murmured. "Dear, darling Masha . . ."

She went to bed and I sat for another hour looking at the illustrations.

"It's a pity you took out the storm windows," she said from the bedroom. "I'm afraid it's going to be cold. Just hear how it's blowing!"

I read certain parts of the "miscellany"—something about a preparation for cheap ink, about the largest diamond in the world. I came upon the illustration of the dress she had liked, and imagined her at a ball, with bare shoulders and a fan, elegant, dazzling, a connoisseur of music, painting, and literature—and how insignificant and brief my role seemed to me!

Our encounter, this marriage of ours, was only an episode, of which there would be many more in the life of this vital, richly endowed woman. All the best of the world, as I have said, was at her disposal, provided absolutely free of charge; even ideas and fashionable intellectual movements served her pleasure, giving variety to her life, and I was merely the cabman who drove her from one enthusiasm to another. Now she no longer needed me; she would take flight and I should be left alone.

As if in answer to my thoughts, a desperate scream was heard in the yard.

"He-e-elp!"

It was a shrill female voice, and the wind, as though imitating it, whistled in the chimney on the same high note. A moment passed and again it was heard through the noise of the wind, but as though from the other end of the yard.

"He-e-elp!"

"Misail, do you hear that?" my wife asked me softly. "Do you hear?"

She came out of the bedroom in her nightgown with her hair down, and stood looking out the dark window, listening.

"Someone is being strangled!" she said. "That's all we needed!"

I took my gun and went out. It was very dark outside and the wind was so strong I could hardly stand up. I walked to the gate and listened; the trees moaned, the wind whistled, and a dog, probably belonging to the feeble-minded peasant, howled sluggishly. Beyond the gate there was total darkness, not a single light on the railroad. Near the wing where last year the office had been there was a smothered scream.

"He-e-elp!"

"Who's there?" I called.

Two men were struggling, one trying to repulse the other and meeting with stubborn resistance; both men were breathing heavily.

"Let go!" one of them cried, and I recognized Ivan Cheprakov. It was he who had screamed in a shrill feminine voice. "Let go, damn you, or I'll bite your hand off!"

The other man I saw was Moisei. I separated them and could not refrain from twice hitting Moisei in the face. He fell down, got up, and I hit him again.

"He tried to kill me," he muttered. "I caught him breaking into Mamasha's chest of drawers. . . . I want to lock him up in the wing for safety."

Cheprakov was drunk and did not recognize me; he kept drawing deep breaths as though getting ready to call for help again.

I left them and went back to the house; my wife was lying on the bed, fully dressed. I told her what had happened and did not conceal the fact that I had struck Moisei.

"It's dreadful living in the country," she said. "What a long night this is—if only it would end!"

"He-e-elp!"

"I'll go and stop them," I said.

"No, let them gnaw each other's heads off," she said, with an expression of disgust.

She lay staring at the ceiling, listening, and I sat beside her, not daring to speak to her, feeling as if I were to blame for the cries of "help" in the yard and for the night being long.

We remained silent, and I waited impatiently for dawn to appear in the window. And all the time Masha looked as though she had just come out of a faint and was wondering how she, so clever and well-educated, so fastidious, happened to be in this miserable provincial wasteland, among a crew of petty, insignificant people; how she could so far have forgotten herself as to have been carried away by one of them and to have been his wife for more than half a year. It seemed to me that now it was all the same to her whether it was I or Moisei, or Cheprakov; for her everything had merged into that wild, drunken cry "help"—I, and our marriage, our work, the autumn mud; and when she sighed or moved into a more comfortable position I could read in her face:

"Oh, if morning would only come soon!"

In the morning she went away.

I remained at Dubechnya for three days waiting for her, then I put all our things in one room, locked the door, and walked to town. It was evening when I rang the bell at the engineer's house, and the lamps were lighted in Bolshaya Dvoryanskaya Street. Pavel told me there was no one at home: Viktor Ivanych had gone to Petersburg and Marya Viktorovna was probably attending a rehearsal at the Azhogins'. I remember with what emotion I walked to the Azhogins', how my heart pounded then sank as I climbed the stairs and stood waiting for a long time on the landing, not daring to enter that temple of the Muses. In the reception hall there were candles burning everywhere, on a small table, on the piano, on the stage, and always in threes; the first performance had been set for the thirteenth, and this first rehearsal was on Monday—an unlucky day! The battle against superstition! All the devotees of dramatic art were assembled; the eldest, the middle one, and the youngest were walking about the stage reading their parts. Radish stood apart from the rest, motionless, leaning his head against a wall and reverently gazing at the stage as he waited for the rehearsal to begin. All as it used to be!

I was making my way toward the hostess—I had to pay my respects—when suddenly everyone began hissing and motioning me to stand still. A hush fell. The piano lid was raised, a lady sat down, squinted with nearsighted eyes at the music, and my Masha walked up to the piano, elegantly dressed and beautiful, but beautiful in a new and quite special way, and not in the least like the Masha who used to come to me in the spring at the mill. She began to sing:

"Why do I love you, radiant night?"

In all the time I had known her, this was the first time I had ever heard her sing. She had a fine, luscious, powerful voice, and listening to her sing was like eating a ripe, sweet, fragrant melon. She finished the song, the audience applauded, and she smiled, very much pleased, flashing her eyes and smoothing her dress like a bird that at last has escaped its cage and preens its wings in freedom. Her hair was combed over her ears and her face had an unattractive, provocative expression, as if she wanted to challenge us all, or to shout at us as she did to the horses: "Hey, there, my beauties!"

At that moment she probably very much resembled her grandfather, the coachman.

"You here, too?" she said, giving me her hand. "Did you hear me sing? Well, how did you like it?" and without waiting for my answer she went on: "You came just at the right moment. I'm going to Petersburg tonight for a short time. You'll let me go, won't you?"

At midnight I accompanied her to the station. She embraced me tenderly, probably feeling grateful to me for not asking unnecessary questions, and promised to write. I held her hands for a long time, kissing them, barely able to restrain my tears and not saying a word.

And when she had gone I stood watching the receding lights, caressing her in my imagination, and murmuring in a low tone:

"My darling Masha, glorious Masha . . ."

I spent the night in Makarikha at Karpovna's, and the next morning I was again at work with Radish, upholstering the furniture of a rich merchant who was marrying his daughter to a doctor.

# XVII

On Sunday after dinner my sister came and had tea with me.

"I read a great deal now," she said, showing me the books she had taken from the town library on her way to me. "Thanks to your wife and Vladimir: they have awakened me and made me aware of myself. They have saved me, made me feel that I am a human being. I used to lie awake nights with all sorts of worries: 'Oh, too much sugar has been used this week! Oh, I'm afraid the cucumbers may be oversalted!' I still can't sleep, but now I have other thoughts. I am tormented thinking that half my life has been spent in such a stupid, cowardly way. I despise my past, and I now look on

Father as my enemy. Oh, how grateful I am to your wife! And Vladimir—he is such a wonderful person! They have opened my eyes."

"It's not good that you don't sleep at night," I said.

"You think I'm ill? Not at all. Vladimir auscultated me and said that I am perfectly healthy. But it's not a question of health, that's not what is important. . . . Tell me: am I right?"

She needed moral support—that was obvious. Masha had gone away, Dr. Blagovo was in Petersburg, and there was no one left in town but me to tell her she was right. She looked at me intently, trying to read my inmost thoughts, and if I appeared thoughtful or fell silent in her presence, she assumed it was on her account and grew sad. I had to be on my guard continually with her, and when she asked me if she was right, I hastened to assure her that she was and that I had the deepest respect for her.

"Did you know? They have given me a part at the Azhogins'?" she went on. "I want to act on the stage. I want to live—I mean, I want to drain the cup. I have no talent whatever, and my part is only ten lines, but it is infinitely better and more noble than pouring tea five times a day and watching to see that the cook doesn't eat an extra morsel. And even more important—let Father at last see that I, too, am capable of protest."

After tea she lay down on my bed and remained there for some time with her eyes closed, looking very pale.

"What weakness!" she said, getting up. "Vladimir says all city-bred women and girls become anemic from doing nothing. What a clever man Vladimir is! He is right, he is always right. We must work!"

Two days later she came to a rehearsal at the Azhogins', her script in her hands. She wore a black dress with a string of coral round her neck, a brooch which from a distance looked like a little puff pastry, and big earrings sparkling with brilliants. It made me uncomfortable to look at her: I was shocked by her lack of taste. The others also noticed that she was oddly dressed and that her jewelry was out of place; I saw their smiles and heard someone say with a laugh:

"Kleopatra of the Nile."

She was trying to be worldly, unconstrained, at ease, which only made her seem mannered and odd. Her simplicity and sweetness deserted her.

"I told Father just now that I was going to a rehearsal," she began, as she came up to me, "and he shouted at me, saying he would deprive me of his blessing, and he actually came very near to striking me. . . . Just imagine, I don't even know my part," she said, glancing down at the script. "I'm sure to make a mess of it. Well, the die is cast," she went on, intensely excited. "The die is cast. . . ."

She felt that everyone was looking at her, that they were all astounded at the momentous step she had taken and were expecting something special from her, and it was impossible to convince her that nobody paid any attention to such unimportant and uninteresting people as herself and me.

She had nothing to do till the third act; her part, that of a guest, a country gossip, consisted only in standing at the door as though eavesdropping, and then delivering a brief monologue. It was at least an hour and a half before her appearance, and while the others were coming and going on the stage, reading their parts, drinking tea, arguing, she did not leave my side and kept mumbling her lines and nervously crumpling the script; and, imagining that everyone was looking at her and waiting for her appearance, she would smooth her hair with a trembling hand and say to me:

"I'm sure to make a mess of it. . . . If you only knew how awful I feel! I'm as terrified as if I were being led to the scaffold."

At last her turn came.

"Kleopatra Alekseyevna—your cue!" said the director.

She walked to the middle of the stage with an expression of horror on her face, looking stiff and ugly, and for half a minute stood there as if dazed, absolutely motionless except for the big earrings dangling in her ears.

"You can use your script the first time," someone said.

It was clear to me that she was trembling so that she could neither speak nor open her script, and that she was utterly incapable of playing her part. I had just made up my mind to go and say something to her when she suddenly fell to her knees in the middle of the stage sobbing loudly.

There was a general commotion and hubbub. I was standing alone in the wings, leaning against the scenery, dumfounded at what had happened, unable to comprehend it, and not knowing what to do. I saw them lift her up and lead her away, saw Anyuta Blagovo approaching me; I had not seen her in the hall, and now she seemed to have sud-

denly sprung from the earth. She was wearing a hat and
veil and looking, as always, as if she had dropped in only
for a moment.

"I told her she shouldn't take a part," she said angrily,
snapping out every word and blushing. "It's madness! You
ought to have stopped her!"

Madam Azhogin, in a short, sleeveless jacket with cigarette ashes on her thin, flat bosom, rushed up to me.

"This is dreadful, my friend," she said, wringing her hands
and, as usual, peering into my face. "This is dreadful! In
your sister's condition . . . she is with child! Take her away,
I implore you. . . ."

She was breathless with agitation. Her three daughters,
all thin and flat-chested like herself, stood by, huddled together in dismay. They were alarmed, stunned, as if a convict had just been caught in their house. What a disgrace,
how dreadful! And this was the estimable family that spent
its whole life combating prejudice and superstition; evidently they thought that mankind's only superstitions and errors
were to be found in burning three candles, the thirteenth
of the month, and Monday—the unlucky day!

"I implore you . . ." repeated Madam Azhogin, irately
pursing her lips and prolonging the syllable "plore." "I
implore you to take her home!"


# XVIII

My sister and I were soon on our way down the stairs.
I covered her with the skirt of my overcoat, and we hurried
away, choosing back streets where there were no lamps and
avoiding passers-by; it was like a flight. She was no longer crying, but looked at me with dry eyes. It was a twenty minutes'
walk to Makarikha, where I took her, yet strangely, in that brief
time, we succeeded in recalling our whole life; we talked over
everything, speculated on our position, planned. . . .

We decided that it was no longer possible for us to live
in this town, and that when I had earned a little money we
would move to some other place. In some of the houses
we passed, people were already asleep, in others they were
playing cards; we hated these houses, we were afraid of
them, and talked about the fanaticism, the utter coarseness
and pettiness, of these respectable families, these amateurs

of dramatic art whom we had so alarmed; and I wondered in what way these stupid, cruel, lazy, dishonest people were superior to the drunken, superstitious peasants of Kurilovka, or in what way they were better than animals, which also are thrown into a panic when some accident occurs to break the monotony of a life constricted by instincts. What would have happened to my sister now if she had been left to live at home? What moral torments would she have undergone talking with my father and meeting her acquaintances every day? As I pictured it there came to mind all the people I had known who had been slowly hounded to death by those nearest and dearest to them; I was reminded of dogs maddened by torture, of sparrows plucked bare by small boys and thrown into the water, and of a long, long series of dark, protracted sufferings which I had been observing uninterruptedly in this town since my childhood; and it was incomprehensible to me what these sixty thousand people lived for, why they read the Gospels, what they prayed for, why they read books and magazines. What benefit did they derive from all that had been spoken and written if they still were possessed of the same spiritual darkness and aversion to freedom as they had been a hundred or three hundred years ago? A master carpenter spends his whole life building houses in the town and goes to his grave calling a gallery a "galdery"; in the same way these sixty thousand inhabitants have been reading or hearing about truth, mercy, freedom, and yet, to the very day of their death they will go on lying from morning to night, tormenting one another, fearing and hating freedom as an enemy.

"And so, my fate is decided," said my sister when we reached home. "After what has happened I cannot go back *there*. Heavens, how good that is! Now I feel at peace."

She went to bed at once. Tears glistened on her eyelashes, but her expression was happy. She fell into a sweet, sound sleep, and one could see that she really was at peace and resting. It had been a long, long time since she had slept like that!

And so we began our life together. She was always singing, always telling me how happy she was, and I had to return unread the books that I brought her from the library; she was no longer able to read, and wanted to do nothing but dream and talk of the future. She would hum as she mended my linen or helped Karpovna around the stove; or she talked of her Vladimir, of his intellect, his fine manners, his kindness, his extraordinary learning, and I agreed with all she said, though I no longer liked her doctor. She wanted to work, to lead an independent life and support herself, and said she would become a schoolteacher or a doctor's assistant as soon as her health permitted, and that she would do her own washing and scrubbing. She already loved her child passionately, and although he was not yet born she knew what his eyes and his hands would be like, and how he would laugh. She loved to talk about his upbringing, and since the best man in the world was her Vladimir, all her ideas were reduced to making the boy as attractive as his father. There was no end to this talk, and all she said aroused an intense joy in her. Sometimes I myself felt happy without knowing why.

She must have infected me with her dreaminess. I, too, gave up reading and did nothing but dream. In the evenings, in spite of my fatigue, I paced up and down the room with my hands in my pockets, talking of Masha.

"When do you think she will come back?" I would ask my sister. "I think she'll be back by Christmas, no later. What's there for her to do there?"

"If she doesn't write to you, it means she's coming very soon."

"That's true," I would agree, though I knew perfectly well that there was nothing for Masha to come back to.

I missed her intensely and could not help deceiving myself and trying to get others to deceive me. My sister was expecting her doctor and I—Masha, and we both laughed and talked incessantly, without ever noticing that we were preventing Karpovna from sleeping. She would lie on the stove muttering:

"That samovar there was hissing this morning, hissing away! Oh, it bodes no good, my dears, no good at all!"

No one ever came to see us but the postman, bringing letters to my sister from the doctor, or Prokofy, who used to drop in sometimes in the evening; after surveying my sister he would go out without a word, and later could be heard in the kitchen:

"Every class ought to know its own rules, and if you're too proud to understand that, it will be the worse for you in this vale of tears."

He loved the expression "vale of tears." One day—it was in Christmas week—when I was walking by the market, he called me into the butcher's shop and, without shaking hands, announced that he had to speak to me on a very important matter. His face was red from frost and vodka; standing near him behind the counter was Nikolka, with his ruffian's face and a bloody knife in his hand.

"I've got something to say to you," Prokofy began. "This situation cannot go on, because, as you yourself know, in this vale of tears people will have no good to say of us, or you. Mamasha, of course, out of pity, can't say anything disagreeable to you and tell you your sister has to move out on account of her condition, but I won't have it any more, because I don't approve of such behavior."

I understood him and left the shop. That same day my sister and I moved to Radish's place. We had no money for a cab and went on foot. I carried a bundle of our belongings on my back, and although my sister had nothing to carry, she was panting, coughing, and kept asking whether we should get there soon.

# XIX

At last a letter came from Masha.

"Dear, good M.A.," she wrote, "kind, gentle 'angel of ours,' as the old painter calls you—farewell! I am going to America for the Exposition. In a few days I shall see the ocean—so far from Dubechnya it is frightening to think of! It's as remote and boundless as the sky, and I am longing to be there, to be free, I am exultant, mad—you see how incoherent my letter is. Dear, kind Misail, give me my freedom, quickly snap the thread that still binds us, tying us to each other. My meeting you and knowing you was a ray from heaven, lighting up my existence; but becoming your wife was a mistake, you understand that, and the consciousness of this mistake now weighs heavily on me, and I beg you, on my knees, my magnanimous friend, quickly, quickly, before I set out for the sea, to telegraph that you agree to rectify our mutual mistake, to remove this solitary stone from my wings. My father, who will undertake all the arrangements, promises not to overburden you with the formalities. So, I am free to go where I will? Yes?

"Be happy, God bless you, and forgive me, a sinner.

"I am alive and well—squandering money, doing all sorts of foolish things, and I thank God every minute that such a

wicked woman has no children. I am singing, with some
success, but this is not one of my enthusiasms—no, it is
my haven, my cell, to which I now retire for peace. King
David had a ring with the inscription: 'All things pass.'
When sad, these words are cheering, when cheerful, they
make one sad. I had a ring like it made for myself, in-
scribed with Hebrew letters, and this talisman keeps me
from being carried away. All things pass, and life passes,
too, so one needs nothing—unless it is a sense of freedom,
for when a man is free he needs nothing, nothing, absolutely nothing. Snap the thread. I warmly embrace you and
your sister. Forgive and forget your M."

My sister used to lie in one room, and Radish, who had
been ill again and was now getting better, in the other. The
moment I received the letter, my sister quietly went into
the painter's room, sat down beside him, and began reading.
Every day she read Ostrovsky or Gogol to him, and he listened, staring straight ahead, never laughing but shaking his
head and muttering to himself from time to time:

"Anything can happen! Anything can happen!"

If there was anything ugly or improper in the play he would
thump the book with his finger and exclaim as if gloating:

"There you have it, lies! That's what they do, those lies!"

He was fascinated by the content as well as the moral of
the plays, and their skillful, complex construction caused him
to marvel at *him*, though he never referred to *him* by name.

"How cleverly *he* fits it all in place!"

My sister read softly, but she was unable to read more
than a page before her voice would fail her. Radish took
her hand and, speaking through parched lips in a hoarse,
barely audible voice, said to her:

"The soul of the righteous man is white and smooth as
honey, and the soul of the sinner is as pumice. The soul of
the righteous is clear oil, and of the sinner—coal tar. We
must labor, we must sorrow and lament," he continued, "and
he who does not labor and sorrow will not enter the kingdom
of heaven. Woe, woe to those who live in plenty, woe to
the mighty, woe to the rich, woe to the moneylenders! They
will not see the kingdom of heaven. Lice consume grass,
rust consumes iron . . ."

"And lies—the soul," my sister concluded, and laughed.

I read the letter through once more. At that moment the
soldier walked into our kitchen who had been coming twice

a week to bring us tea, French bread, and woodcock; we did not know who they came from, but there was always a smell of scent about them. I had no work and was forced to sit home idle for days at a time; undoubtedly whoever sent us the bread knew we were in need.

I heard my sister talking to the soldier and laughing merrily. Then she lay down and said to me, as she ate some of the bread:

"When you refused to go back into government service and became a house painter, Anyuta Blagovo and I knew from the very beginning that you were right, but we were afraid to speak out and say what we thought. Tell me, what is this power that prevents us from saying what we think? Take Anyuta Blagovo, for instance. She loves you, worships you, and she knows that you are right; she loves me, too, like a sister, and knows that I am right—perhaps she even envies me—but some power prevents her from coming to see us; she avoids us, she's afraid."

My sister folded her hands on her breast and said rapturously:

"How she loves you, if you only knew! She has confessed her love to no one but me, and then secretly, in the dark. She used to lead me into a dark avenue in the garden and tell me in a whisper how dear you were to her. You will see, she'll never marry because of loving you. Are you sorry for her?"

"Yes."

"It's she who sends the bread. She is funny, really. Why be so secretive? I too used to be foolish and absurd, but I've gotten away from that and I'm not afraid of anybody now; I think and say what I like, and I'm happy. When I lived at home I had no conception of happiness, but now I wouldn't change places with a queen."

Dr. Blagovo arrived. He had received his doctor's degree and was now staying in our town with his father; he was taking a rest, he said, and would soon return to Petersburg. He wanted to work on typhus vaccines and, I believe, cholera, and intended to go abroad to advance himself, after which he hoped to be appointed to a university. He had left the army and now wore a loose serge jacket, very full trousers, and magnificent neckties. My sister was in ecstasies over his tie pin, his studs, and the red silk handkerchief he flaunted in his outside breast pocket. Once, having nothing to do, she and I started counting all the suits we remembered seeing him wear, and we came to the conclusion that he had at least ten. It was obvious that he still loved my sister, but never once, even in jest, did he speak of taking her to Petersburg or abroad with him, and I could not clearly picture what would become of her if she were to remain alive, or what would become of her child. She did nothing but dream endlessly and refused to think seriously of the future; she said he might go where he liked, and even abandon her, so long as he was happy; she was content with what had been.

Generally when he came to see us he would auscultate her very carefully and make her drink milk with drops in it while he was there. And this time he did the same. He auscultated her, made her drink a glass of milk, and afterward the room smelled of creosote.

"That's a good girl," he said, taking the glass from her. "You mustn't talk too much now, lately you've been chattering like a magpie. Be quiet, please."

She laughed. Then he came into Radish's room where I was sitting and affectionately clapped me on the shoulder.

"Well, how goes it, old man?" he inquired, bending over the invalid.

"Your Honor," Radish articulated, barely moving his lips, "Your Honor, I make so bold as to state . . . we are all in God's hands, we all have to die. . . . Permit me to tell you the truth. . . . Your Honor will never enter the kingdom of heaven!"

"It can't be helped," the doctor said jokingly, "there has to be somebody in hell."

All at once something happened to my consciousness; I saw myself as in a dream standing in the yard of the slaughterhouse on a winter night with Prokofy beside me, smelling of pepper brandy; I tried to pull myself together, rubbed my eyes, and suddenly I seemed to be on my way to the interview with the governor. Nothing like this has ever happened to me before or since, and I attribute these strange, dreamlike recollections to nervous exhaustion. I relived the scene at the slaughterhouse and the interview with the governor, and at the same time I was dimly aware that it was not real. When I came to myself I saw that I was no longer in the house but standing with the doctor by a lamppost in the street.

"It is sad, sad . . ." he was saying, with tears rolling down his cheeks. "She is gay, continually laughing, full of hope, but her condition is hopeless, my dear boy. Your

Radish hates me and keeps trying to make me feel that I have wronged her. In his way he is right, but I have my point of view, too, and I don't in the least regret what has happened. One must love, we all ought to love—isn't that true? Without love there would be no life; anyone who fears and avoids love is not free."

Little by little he passed to other subjects; he began talking about science and his dissertation, which had been well received in Petersburg. He spoke with enthusiasm, no longer thinking of my sister, of his grief, or of me. He was carried away by life. . . . She has America and her ring with the inscription, I thought, and he has his doctor's degree and his scientific career; only my sister and I are left with the past.

When we parted, I stood under the lamp reading her letter again. And I remembered, vividly remembered, that spring morning when she had come to me at the mill, and had lain down and covered herself with her short fur coat —trying to be like a simple peasant woman; and another time, also in the morning, when we pulled the creel out of the water and the willows on the bank sprinkled us with huge raindrops, and we laughed. . . .

It was dark in our house in Bolshaya Dvoryanskaya Street. I climbed the fence and went into the kitchen by the back way, as I did in the old days, to get a lamp. There was no one in the kitchen; the samovar was hissing next to the stove, waiting for my father. "Who pours Father's tea now?" I wondered. Taking the lamp, I went out to the hut, made up a bed out of old newspapers, and lay down. The spikes in the wall glared ominously as of old and the shadows flickered. It was cold. I felt that my sister would come any minute bringing me supper, and then I remembered that she lay ill in Radish's house, and it seemed strange that I had climbed the fence and was now lying in this unheated hut. My mind was confused and I imagined all sorts of absurd things.

A bell rang. Sounds familiar from childhood: first the whirring of a wire along the wall, then a short, plaintive ring in the kitchen. It was my father returning from the club. I got up and went into the kitchen. On seeing me, Aksinya, the cook, clasped her hands and for some reason burst into tears.

"My child!" she said softly. "My precious! Oh, Lord!"

In her excitement she began crumpling her apron in her hands. On the window sill stood several bottles of vodka with berries soaking in them. I poured myself a teacupful and gulped it down, for I was exceedingly thirsty. Aksinya had scrubbed the table and benches not long before and the kitchen smelled the way bright cozy kitchens always smell when kept by tidy cooks. That smell and the chirping of the cricket used to lure us here to the kitchen when we were children, making us feel like listening to fairy tales and playing at kings and queens. . . .

"And where is Kleopatra?" asked Aksinya in a soft breathless voice. "And where is your cap, my dear? Your wife, they say, has gone to Petersburg. . . ."

She had been with us in my mother's day, and used to bathe Kleopatra and me in the washtub, and to her we were still children who needed guidance. In a quarter of an hour or so she laid before me all the reflections which, with the sagacity of an old servant, she had been storing up in the quiet of this kitchen since last we had seen each other. She said that the doctor could be forced to marry Kleopatra—one had only to scare him a bit, and if a petition were nicely written the bishop would annul the first marriage; that it would be a good thing for me to sell Dubechnya without letting my wife know and put the money in the bank in my own name; that if my sister and I were to bow down at my father's feet and ask him nicely he might forgive us; that we ought to have a Te Deum sung to the Queen of Heaven. . . .

"Now go along, my dear, and talk to him," she said when she heard my father's cough. "Go on, speak to him, bow down, your head won't fall off."

I went in. My father was sitting at a table working on the plan of a summer villa with Gothic windows and a squat turret that resembled a fire tower—an extraordinarily rigid, tasteless thing. As I entered the study I stood where I could not help seeing the plan. I did not know why I had come to see my father, but I remember that when I saw his gaunt face and red neck, his shadow on the wall, I wanted to throw my arms around him and, as Aksinya had enjoined me, bow down at his feet; but the sight of the villa with its Gothic windows and thick turret stopped me.

"Good evening," I said.

He glanced at me and instantly lowered his eyes to his drawing.

"What do you want?" he asked, after a pause.

"I have come to tell you . . . my sister is very ill. She will die before long," I added dully.

"Well," sighed my father, taking off his spectacles and laying them on the table. "Whatsoever a man soweth, that shall he also reap. Whatsoever a man soweth," he repeated, getting up from the table, "that shall he also reap. I want you to remember how you came to me two years ago, and on this very spot I asked you, begged you, to give up your delusions; I reminded you of your duty, of your honor, and your obligations to your forebears, whose traditions ought to be held sacred. Did you listen to me? You spurned my advice and obstinately persisted in your erroneous views; moreover, you dragged your sister into your erring ways, forcing her to lose her morals and all sense of shame. Now you are both in a bad way. Well? Whatsoever a man soweth, that shall he also reap!"

He paced up and down the study as he spoke. He probably thought I had come to acknowledge my mistake, and no doubt expected me to plead for myself and my sister. I was cold; I shook as though in a fever, and spoke with difficulty, in a hoarse voice.

"And I must ask you to remember," I said, "how on this very spot I begged you to understand me, to reflect and determine along with me how and to what end we should live, and your answer was to talk about your ancestors, about my grandfather who wrote verses. Now you are told that your daughter is hopelessly ill, and again you go on about ancestors and traditions. . . . What folly in your old age, when death is not far off and you have only five or ten years left to live!"

"Why did you come here?" my father asked sternly, obviously offended at my reproaching him for his folly.

"I don't know. I love you, I am inexpressibly sorry that we are so far apart—that is why I came. I still love you, but my sister has broken with you forever. She does not forgive you, and never will. Your very name arouses in her an aversion for the past, for her life."

"And who is to blame?" my father shouted. "It is you who are to blame, you good-for-nothing!"

"And suppose I am to blame," I said. "I admit that I am to blame for many things, but why is it that this life of yours—which you consider obligatory for us, too—why is it so dreary, so fruitless; why is it that in all these houses you have been building for the past thirty years there has not been a single person from whom I could learn how to live so as not to be guilty? In this whole town there is not one honest man! These houses of yours—they are infernal nests which are death for the mothers and daughters and a torment for the children. . . . My poor mother!" I went on in despair. "My poor sister! You have to stupefy yourself with vodka, cards, scandal, you have to cringe, play the hypocrite, or go on year after year drawing plans in order not to notice all the horrors that lie hidden in these houses. Our town has been in existence for hundreds of years, and in all that time it has not given our country one useful man—not one. You have strangled in embryo everything that was in the least bright or vital. It's a town of shopkeepers, saloonkeepers, clerks, hypocrites, a useless, unnecessary town, which not a soul would regret if it suddenly were to sink through the earth."

"I don't want to listen to you, you good-for-nothing!" my father said, picking up a ruler from the table. "You're drunk! Don't dare to appear before your father in such a state! I'm telling you for the last time, and you can tell it to your shameless sister, you will get nothing from me. I have torn my disobedient children out of my heart, and if they suffer for their disobedience and obstinacy, I have no pity for them. You can go back where you came from! It has pleased God to chastise me with you, and I'll bear this trial with resignation and, like Job, find consolation in suffering and ceaseless toil. You are not to cross my threshold until you have reformed. I am a just man, everything I say is for your benefit, and if you have any regard for your own well-being you ought to remember all your life what I have said to you, and what I am saying now."

I gave up in despair and left. I cannot remember what happened that night or the next day.

I am told that I went staggering through the streets, bareheaded and loudly singing, with crowds of little boys following me and shouting:

"Better-than-nothing! Better-than-nothing!"

If I had wanted to have a ring made for myself, I should have chosen the inscription: "Nothing passes." I believe that nothing passes without leaving a trace, and that the slightest step we take is of consequence for both our present and our future life.

What I have lived through has not been in vain. My great misfortunes and my endurance have touched the hearts of the people of the town, and they no longer call me "Better-than-nothing," nor laugh at me and throw water on me when I walk by the shopping arcade. They have grown used to my being a workingman and see nothing strange in my carrying a pail of paint or putting in windowpanes, though I am a nobleman; on the contrary, they are glad to give me orders, and I am now considered a good worker and the best contractor after Radish, who, though he has recovered and still paints the cupolas of belfries without a scaffold, no longer has the strength to manage the men; it is I now, instead of him, who run about the town looking for orders; I hire the men and pay them, and borrow money at a high rate of interest. And having become a contractor, I understand why it is necessary to spend days at a time trying to find roofers for some paltry job. People are polite to me, address me with respect, and in the houses where I work they offer me tea and send to inquire whether I would care to have dinner. Children and young girls often come and watch me with sad, curious eyes.

One day I was working in the governor's garden, painting a summerhouse to look like marble. The governor, who was taking a walk, came up to the summerhouse and, having nothing better to do, began talking to me. I reminded him of how he had once summoned me to an interview with him. He stared into my face for a moment, then opened his mouth so that it looked like an O, threw up his hands, and said:

"I don't remember!"

I have aged and grown silent, stern, austere; I rarely laugh and they say I have become like Radish, that like him I bore the men with my useless admonitions.

Marya Viktorovna, my former wife, now lives abroad, and her father, the engineer, is constructing a railroad somewhere in the eastern provinces, where he is buying up estates. Dr. Blagovo also lives abroad. Dubechnya is again in the possession of Madam Cheprakova, who bought it after haggling with the engineer till she got the price knocked down twenty per cent. Moisei now goes about in a bowler hat; he often comes into town on business of some sort, driving a racing droshky and stopping near the bank. It is said that he has bought up a mortgaged estate and is continually making inquiries at the bank about Dubechnya, which he also intends to buy. Poor Ivan Cheprakov hung about town for a long time, doing nothing, and drinking. I tried to get him into our work, and for a time he painted roofs and put in windowpanes, and even seemed to take to it, stealing oil, asking for tips, and drinking like a regular painter. But he got tired of it, work bored him, and he went back to Dubechnya. Some time later the men confessed to me that he had tried to persuade them to go with him one night to murder Moisei and rob Madam Cheprakova.

My father has grown very old and bent; in the evening he walks up and down near his house. I never visit him.

During an epidemic of cholera Prokofy doctored the shop-keepers with pepper brandy and tar, and, as I learned from the newspaper, was flogged for sitting in his shop and maligning the doctors. His shopboy, Nikolka, died of cholera. Karpovna is still alive and still loves and fears her Prokofy. Whenever she sees me she shakes her head sadly and says with a sigh:

"You're done for!"

On weekdays I am busy from morning till night. And on holidays in fine weather I take my tiny niece in my arms (my sister expected a boy, but gave birth to a girl) and slowly walk to the cemetery, where I stand or sit for a long time looking at the grave that is so dear to me; and I tell the little girl that her mother lies there.

Sometimes I find Anyuta Blagovo at the grave. We greet each other and stand in silence, or talk of Kleopatra, of her child, of how sad life is in this world. Then, leaving the cemetery, we walk in silence, and she purposely slackens her pace in order to prolong her walk with me. The child, gay and happy, squinting in the bright sunlight, laughingly stretches out her arms to her, and we both stop and caress the dear little girl.

When we reach the town, flushed and agitated, Anyuta Blagovo says good-bye to me and sedately, austerely, walks on alone. And looking at her, no one she passes would think she had just been walking by my side and fondling the child.

1896

# THE NAME-DAY PARTY

## I

After dinner, with its eight courses and endless conversation, Olga Mikhailovna, whose husband's name day was being celebrated, went out into the garden. The obligation to smile and talk continuously, the stupidity of the servants, the clatter of dishes, the long intervals between courses, and the corset she had put on to conceal her pregnancy from her guests, had wearied her to the point of exhaustion. She longed to get away from the house, to sit in the shade and rest in thoughts of the child that was to be born to her in two months. She was accustomed to these thoughts coming to her as she turned to her left from the big avenue into a narrow path; here, in the deep shade of plum and cherry trees, where dry branches scratched her neck and shoulders and spiderwebs lighted on her face, when the image of a little person of indeterminate sex and obscure features would rise in her mind, it seemed to her that it was not a spiderweb caressingly tickling her face and neck, but this little creature, and when, at the end of the path, the sparse wattle hedge came into view, and beyond it paunchy beehives with tiled roofs, when the still stagnant air began to smell of hay and honey and the urgent buzzing of bees could be heard, then the little person took complete possession of Olga Mikhailovna. She would sit down on the bench near a hut of woven branches and sink into a reverie.

This time too she went as far as the bench, sat down, and commenced thinking, but instead of the little person, it was the big persons she had just left who came to her mind. She was deeply perturbed that she, the hostess, had deserted her guests, and she recalled how her husband, Pyotr Dmitrich, and her uncle, Nikolai Nikolaich, had argued at dinner about trial by jury, the press, and education for women—her husband, as usual, arguing partly to flaunt his conservatism before his guests, but chiefly for the sake of disagreeing with her uncle, whom he disliked, while her uncle contradicted him and caviled at every word he uttered so that the company should see that he, in spite of his fifty-nine years, had retained his youthful freshness of spirit and freedom of thought. And toward the end of dinner Olga Mikhailovna could no longer contain herself and she too began making an awkward defense of university education for women—not that higher education was in need of her support, but she wanted to annoy her husband, who, to her mind, was unfair. The guests grew tired of the dispute, but that did not prevent them from intervening and talking a great deal, although none of them had the slightest interest in either trial by jury or the education of women. . . .

Olga Mikhailovna was sitting on the hither side of the wattle hedge near the hut. The sun was hidden behind clouds and the atmosphere and trees lowered as before rain; nevertheless it was hot and sultry. The hay, which had been cut under the trees on St. Peter's Eve, lay ungathered, looking sadly wilted and discolored, and giving off a heavy cloying smell. It was still. From behind the hedge came the monotonous buzzing of bees. . . .

Suddenly there was the sound of voices and footsteps. Someone was coming along the path toward the apiary.

"It's sultry!" said a feminine voice. "What do you think—will it rain or not?"

"It will rain, my charmer, but not before evening," a very familiar male voice answered languidly. "And it will be a good rain."

Olga Mikhailovna decided that if she quickly hid in the hut, they would pass by without seeing her, and she would not have to talk and force herself to smile. She picked up her skirts and bent down to enter the little hut. Instantly she felt a wave of hot steamy air on her face, neck, and arms. Had it not been for the closeness, the suffocating smell of rye bread, fennel, and brushwood, this would have been the perfect place to hide from her visitors, here under a thatched roof in the dusk, and to think about the little person. It was quiet and cozy.

"What a charming spot!" said the feminine voice. "Let's sit down here, Pyotr Dmitrich."

Olga Mikhailovna peeped through a crack between two branches. She saw her husband, Pyotr Dmitrich, and Lyubochka Sheller, a seventeen-year-old girl not long out of boarding school. Pyotr Dmitrich, with his hat on the back of his head, indolent and sluggish from having drunk too much at dinner, shambled along by the hedge, then stopped and raked some hay into a heap with his foot; Lyubochka, rosy from the heat, and extremely pretty as always, stood with her hands behind her back watching the languid movements of his big handsome body.

Olga Mikhailovna knew that her husband was attractive to women and she did not enjoy seeing him with them. There was nothing out of the way in Pyotr Dmitrich's raking the hay together so he could sit there and chat about trivialities with Lyubochka, nor was there anything out of the way in pretty little Lyubochka's sweetly gazing at him, and yet Olga Mikhailovna felt annoyed with her husband, and both frightened and pleased that she could listen to them.

"Sit down, enchantress," said Pyotr Dmitrich, sinking down onto the hay and stretching. "That's right. . . . Well, tell me something."

"Oh, yes! As soon as I start telling you anything, you'll fall asleep!"

"I? . . . Fall asleep? Allah forbid! How could I fall asleep with eyes like yours looking at me?"

And there was nothing out of the way in what her husband said or the fact that he was lolling with his hat on the back of his head in the presence of a lady. He was spoiled by women, knew that they found him attractive, and always adopted a special tone with them that everyone said was becoming to him. He was behaving with Lyubochka exactly as he did with all women. Nevertheless, Olga Mikhailovna was jealous.

"Tell me, please," Lyubochka began, after a brief silence, "is it true that you are being prosecuted?"

"I? Yes, it's true. . . . I am now ranked with the villains, my charmer."

"But what for?"

"For nothing . . . just . . . oh, it's chiefly because of politics," yawned Pyotr Dmitrich. "The struggle between the Right and Left. I, an obscurantist, a reactionary, made so bold as to use an expression in an official paper that is offensive to such impeccable Gladstones as Vladimir Pavlovich Vladimirov and our district justice of the peace, Kuzma Grigorevich Vostryakov."

Pyotr Dmitrich again yawned and continued:

"We have a system in which you can speak disparagingly of the sun, the moon, of anything you please, but Heaven preserve you from touching the Liberals! Heaven preserve you! A Liberal is exactly like one of those nasty dried toad-stools that sprays you with a cloud of dust if you accidentally touch it with your finger."

"But what happened to you?"

"Nothing much. The whole thing was a case of much ado about nothing. A certain schoolteacher, a detestable individual of parochial background, presents Vostryakov with a petition against a tavernkeeper, accusing him of contumely and assault and battery in a public place. Everything points to the fact that both the schoolteacher and the tavernkeeper were drunk as shoemakers and that they behaved equally abominably. If there was any offensive behavior, it undoubtedly was mutual. Vostryakov ought to have fined them both for disturbing the peace and thrown them out of court—and that would have been that! But instead what do we do? As usual, what's always in the foreground with us is never the individual, never the facts, but the trademark, the label. A teacher, no matter how great a scoundrel he may be, is always right just because he's a teacher; and a tavernkeeper is always guilty because he's a tavernkeeper and a kulak. Vostryakov gave him a jail sentence, and he appealed to the circuit court. The circuit court triumphantly upheld Vostryakov's decision. Well, I stuck to my opinion. . . . Got a little hot, that's all."

Pyotr Dmitrich spoke calmly, with nonchalant irony. In reality the impending trial worried him intensely. Olga Mikhailovna remembered how on his return from the unfortunate session he had tried to conceal from the entire household how troubled he was and how dissatisfied with himself. As an intelligent man he could not help feeling that he had gone too far in expressing his personal opinion. And how many lies had been required to conceal this feeling from others and himself! How many futile conversations, how much grumbling and insincere laughter at what was not in the least laughable! On learning that he was going to be prosecuted, he immediately felt harassed and depressed; he began to sleep badly, and more and more often stood at a window drumming on the pane with his fingers. And he was ashamed to admit to his wife that he was worried, and this vexed her. . . .

"I heard that you were in the province of Poltava," said Lyubochka.

"Yes, I was," replied Pyotr Dmitrich. "I just got back the day before yesterday."

"It must be nice there."

"It is. Really very nice. I arrived just in time for hay-making, and, I can tell you, haymaking in the Ukraine is the most poetic time of year. Here we have a big house, a big garden, a lot of servants and commotion, and you don't see the mowing; it all passes unnoticed here. But there at the farm I have a level meadow of forty-five acres spread out before me: you can see the mowers from any window. They are mowing in the meadow, mowing in the garden—no visitors, no fuss, nothing to prevent your seeing, hearing, and feeling only the haymaking. Outdoors and indoors there's the smell of hay. From sunrise to sunset the clang of scythes. Altogether my dear Little Russia is a lovely country. Would you believe it, when I was drinking water at old wells with shadoofs, or filthy vodka in those Jewish taverns, when, on quiet evenings, I could hear the sound of Ukrainian fiddles and tambourines, I was tempted by a fascinating idea—to settle down on my farm and live there the rest of my life, far from these circuit courts, clever conversations, philoso-phizing women, and lengthy dinners. . . ."

Pyotr Dmitrich was not lying. He felt oppressed and really longed to rest. And he had gone to Poltava simply to avoid looking at his study, his servants, his acquaintances, and everything that could remind him of his wounded pride and his mistakes.

Lyubochka suddenly jumped up, waving her arms about in fright.

"Oh, a bee, a bee!" she screamed. "It will sting!"

"Nonsense, it won't sting," said Pyotr Dmitrich. "What a coward you are!"

"No, no, no!" cried Lyubochka, looking back at the bee as she hurried off.

Pyotr Dmitrich followed her with a tender melancholy gaze. He was probably thinking of his farm as he looked at her, of solitude, and (who knows?) perhaps even of how warm and cozy life on his farm would be if this girl were his wife—young, pure, fresh, uncorrupted by higher education and not pregnant. . . .

When their voices and footsteps had died away, Olga Mikhailovna came out of the hut and walked toward the house. She felt like crying. By now she was terribly jealous. She could understand that her husband was exhausted, dissatisfied with himself, and ashamed; that people are aloof when they feel ashamed, especially from those nearest to them, and confide in strangers; she also realized that she had nothing to fear from Lyubochka or from any of those women who were drinking coffee in the house. But it all seemed so inconceivable, so dreadful, and Olga Mikhailovna almost felt that Pyotr Dmitrich only half belonged to her.

"He has no right!" she muttered, trying to comprehend her jealousy and vexation. "He has absolutely no right! And I'm going to tell him so right now!"

She made up her mind to find her husband at once and to speak plainly and tell him what she thought: it was disgusting the way he appealed to women, seeking their admiration as if it were manna from heaven; it was unjust, dishonorable, that he should give to others what by right belonged to his wife, that he should hide his soul and conscience from her only to reveal them to the first pretty face that came along. What harm had his wife done him? What was she guilty of? After all, she was fed up with his lying; he was constantly showing off, flirting, saying things he didn't mean, trying to appear different from what he was and what he ought to be. Why this deceit? Was it becoming in a decent man? When he lied he was dishonoring himself and those to whom he lied, and showing disrespect for what he lied about. Didn't he understand that if he gave himself airs and was captious at the judicial table, or held forth at the dinner table on the prerogatives of the authorities merely to provoke her uncle, didn't he realize that this showed he hadn't the least respect for the court, for himself, for those who were listening to him and watching him?

As she turned into the big avenue, Olga Mikhailovna tried to look as if she had just gone off to attend to some household matter. On the veranda the gentlemen were drinking liqueur and eating berries. One of them, the examining magistrate, a stout elderly man, a humorist and wit, must have been telling a vulgar story, for, seeing his hostess, he suddenly clapped his hand over his fat lips, goggled his eyes, and sat down. Olga Mikhailovna did not like the local officials. Nor did she care for their awkward ceremonious wives, their backbiting, their frequent visits, and their flattery of her husband, whom they all hated. And now, after having eaten their fill, as they sat drinking and showing no sign of leaving, their presence was acutely irksome to her, but not wishing to appear impolite, she smiled cordially at the examining magistrate and shook a finger at him. She crossed the hall and drawing room, smiling and looking as if she had gone to give an order or to make some arrangement. "God grant no one stops me!" she thought, but then forced herself to pause in the drawing room and listen politely to a young man who was playing the piano; after a moment she cried: "Bravo! Bravo, Monsieur Georges!" and, clapping her hands twice, went on.

She found her husband in his study. He was sitting at the table lost in thought. His expression was austere, preoccupied, guilty. This was not the Pyotr Dmitrich who had been arguing at dinner and whom his guests knew, but a different man—exhausted, guilty, dissatisfied with himself, whom no one but his wife knew. He must have come to his study for cigarettes. Before him lay an open cigarette case full of cigarettes, and his hand was still in the drawer of the table. As he was taking out the cigarettes he had become absorbed in his thoughts.

Olga Mikhailovna felt sorry for him. It was as clear as day that the man was tormented and could find no peace, and was, perhaps, undergoing a struggle with himself. Olga Mikhailovna went up to the table without a word; in a desire to show her husband that she had forgotten the argument at dinner and was no longer angry with him, she shut the cigarette case and put it in his side pocket.

"What shall I say to him?" she wondered. "I'll say that lying is like a forest—the farther one goes into it the more difficult it is to get out. I'll say: you were carried away by the fictitious role you were playing and went too far; you have offended people who were attached to you and who have done you no harm. Go now and apologize to them, laugh at yourself, and you will feel better. And if you want peace and solitude, we will go away together."

Meeting his wife's eyes, Pyotr Dmitrich's face instantly

assumed the expression it had worn at dinner and in the garden—indifferent and slightly ironical; he yawned and stood up.

"It's after five," he said, looking at his watch. "If our guests mercifully leave us by eleven, that still leaves another six hours. A cheerful prospect, I must say!"

And, whistling, he unhurriedly walked out of the study with his usual self-assured gait. She heard him cross the hall and drawing room with a sedate step, heard his sedate laugh as he called: "Bra-a-o! Bra-a-o!" to the young man at the piano. Then the footsteps died away; he must have gone into the garden.

And now it was not jealousy, not vexation, but genuine hatred of his walk, his insincere voice and laugh, that took possession of Olga Mikhailovna. She went to the window and looked out into the garden. Pyotr Dmitrich was walking along the avenue with one hand in his pocket, snapping the fingers of his other hand; he swung along, head thrown back, looking as if he were well satisfied with himself, his dinner, his digestion, and with nature. . . .

Two little schoolboys, the sons of Madam Chizhevskaya, having just arrived, now appeared in the avenue; they were accompanied by their tutor, a student wearing a white tunic and very narrow trousers. When they reached Pyotr Dmitrich, they stopped, probably to congratulate him on his name day. With a graceful movement of his shoulders, he patted the children on their cheeks and negligently offered his hand to the student without looking at him. The student must have commended the weather and compared it to the climate of St. Petersburg, for Pyotr Dmitrich said in a loud voice—not as if he were speaking to a guest but in a tone he might have taken with a court bailiff or a witness:

"How's that, sir? Cold in Petersburg? And here, my dear sir, we have the most salubrious air and fruits of the earth in abundance. Eh? What?"

And thrusting one hand into his pocket and snapping the fingers of his other hand, he walked on. Olga Mikhailovna continued to gaze at the back of his head in perplexity till he disappeared behind the nut grove. How had a man of thirty-four come by that sedate military bearing? Where had he acquired that ponderous, elegant manner, the authoritative resonance in his voice, all those *How's that, sir*'s, *To be sure*'s, and *My dear sir*'s?

Olga Mikhailovna recalled how in the first months of her marriage, to relieve the boredom of staying home alone, she had driven to town, to the circuit court where Pyotr Dmitrich sometimes presided in place of her godfather, Count Aleksei Petrovich. In the presidential chair, wearing his uniform and a chain on his breast, he was completely changed. Imposing gestures, a thunderous voice, *How's that, sir? To be sure*, the patronizing tone. . . . All that was ordinary, human, and characteristic of him, everything, in fact, that Olga Mikhailovna was accustomed to seeing in him at home, had vanished in grandeur, and there in the presidential chair sat, not Pyotr Dmitrich, but some other man whom everyone called Mr. President. His consciousness of being a power made it impossible for him to sit still, and he seized every opportunity to ring his bell, look sternly at the public, and shout. . . . Where had he acquired that shortsightedness and deafness, when all at once he would find it difficult to see and hear, and, frowning majestically, would demand that people speak louder, and come closer to the table? From the height of his grandeur he had trouble distinguishing faces and sounds, so that if Olga Mikhailovna herself had approached him, he no doubt would have shouted: "What's your name?" He addressed peasant witnesses familiarly, roared at the public in a voice that could be heard in the street, and was absolutely impossible in his treatment of lawyers. If an attorney addressed him, Pyotr Dmitrich sat half turned away, squinting at the ceiling, hoping by this to show that an attorney was utterly superfluous here, that he neither acknowledged him nor listened to him; but when a poorly dressed local lawyer spoke to him, then Pyotr Dmitrich was all ears and measured the man with a derisive, withering glance, as if to say: "You see what we have for lawyers these days!"

"Just what are you trying to say?" he would interrupt.

If an oratorical attorney tried to use some foreign word and said "factitious" instead of "fictitious" Pyotr Dmitrich instantly became very animated: "How's that, sir? Eh? Factitious? What does that mean?" And then he remarked admonishingly: "Don't use words you can't understand." And when the attorney had finished his speech, he would walk away from the table red and perspiring, while Pyotr Dmitrich, with a self-satisfied smile, leaned back in his chair exulting over his victory. In his treatment of lawyers he was to some extent imitating Count Aleksei Petrovich, but when, for instance, the Count would say: "Counsel for the defense, keep quiet for a while!" it sounded paternally good-natured and natural, while when Pyotr Dmitrich said it, it was rude and forced.

# II

The sound of applause reached her. The young man had finished playing. Olga Mikhailovna was reminded of her guests and hurried to the drawing room.

"I have so enjoyed your playing," she said, going up to the piano. "I was listening to you with delight. You have a remarkable talent! But don't you think our piano is out of tune?"

At that moment the two schoolboys came into the room with the student.

"Good heavens! Mitya and Kolya?" Olga Mikhailovna drawled joyously as she went to meet them. "How you have grown! I hardly recognized you! Where is your mama?"

"I congratulate you on the name day," the student began, rather unceremoniously. "I wish you all the best. Yekaterina Andreyevna sends her congratulations and begs you to excuse her. She's not feeling very well."

"How unkind of her! I've been looking forward to seeing her all day. How long is it since you left Petersburg? What's the weather like there now?" And without waiting for an answer, she looked tenderly at the little boys and again said: "How they have grown! It wasn't so long ago that they were coming here with their nurse, and now they are in school! The old grow older and the young grow up. . . . Have you had dinner?"

"Oh, please don't trouble!" said the student.

"Then you haven't had dinner?"

"For heaven's sake, don't trouble!"

"But you are hungry, aren't you?" Olga Mikhailovna asked in a rude harsh tone, fraught with impatience and annoyance; the words had slipped out unintentionally, and she instantly blushed and commenced coughing and smiling. "How they have grown!" she said softly.

"Please don't trouble," said the student once more.

The student begged her not to trouble and the children remained silent; obviously all three were hungry. Olga Mikhailovna led them into the dining room and ordered Vasily to set the table.

"Your mama is unkind!" she said, seating them at the table. "She has quite forgotten me. Unkind, unkind, unkind. . . . You must tell her so. And what are you studying?" she asked the student.

"Medicine."

"Oh, I'm very partial to doctors. I'm sorry my husband isn't a doctor. What courage it must take to perform operations and dissect corpses! Dreadful! Aren't you afraid? I think I should die of fear! You'll have vodka, of course?"

"Please don't trouble."

"You must have something to drink after your journey. I'm a woman, but even I drink sometimes. And Mitya and Kolya will drink Malaga. Don't worry, it's not a strong wine. What fine young men they are, really! They'll soon be thinking of getting married."

Olga Mikhailovna talked without a pause. She knew from experience that it is far easier and less tiring to talk than to listen. When you talk you don't have to strain your attention, try to think of answers, or even change your facial expression. But she inadvertently asked the student a serious question, to which he was answering at great length, and she was obliged to listen. The student knew that she had gone to the university and made an effort to appear earnest as he talked to her.

"And what are you studying?" she asked, forgetting that she had already put the question to him.

"Medicine."

Olga Mikhailovna remembered that she had been away from the ladies for a long time.

"Really? So you are going to be a doctor?" she said, getting up. "That's splendid. I regret that I didn't take up medicine. Now, you have your dinner, gentlemen, and then come out to the garden. I'll introduce you to the young ladies."

She glanced at her watch as she went out; it was five minutes to six. She was amazed that the time passed so slowly and thought with dread that there were still six hours until midnight, when her guests would leave. How would she get through those six hours? What could she think of to say? How should she behave toward her husband?

There was not a soul in the drawing room or on the veranda. The guests had all wandered off into the garden.

"I shall have to suggest a walk to the birch grove before tea, or else boating," thought Olga Mikhailovna, hurrying to the croquet lawn where she heard laughter and talking. "And the old people can play vint. . . ."

On her way she met Grigory the footman coming back with empty bottles.

"Where are the ladies?" she asked.

"They have gone to the raspberry patch. The master is there too."

"Oh, good Lord!" someone on the croquet lawn shouted in exasperation. "But I've told you the same thing a thousand times already! You have to see Bulgarians to understand them! You can't go by the papers!"

Either because of this outburst or for some other reason, Olga Mikhailovna suddenly felt terribly weak all over, especially in her legs and shoulders. All at once she felt she did not want to speak, to listen, or to move.

"Grigory," she said listlessly, and with an effort, "when you serve tea or anything, please don't look to me, don't ask me anything, don't even speak to me about it. . . . See to everything yourself and . . . and don't make a clatter with your feet. I implore you . . . I can't, because . . ."

She continued on her way to the croquet lawn without finishing what she was saying, then, remembering the ladies, she turned toward the raspberry patch. The sky, the air, and trees, still sullen, promised rain; it was hot and sultry; a great flock of crows, anticipating the storm, flew over the garden cawing. The closer the paths came to the kitchen gardens the more narrow, dark, and overgrown they were; on one of them, hidden in a thicket of wild pears, sorrel, young oaks and hops, clouds of tiny black flies enveloped her. She covered her face with her hands and forced herself to think of the little person. . . .

Through her imagination coursed the figures of Grigory, Mitya, Kolya, and the faces of the peasants who had come with their congratulations in the morning. . . .

Hearing footsteps, she opened her eyes. Her uncle, Nikolai Nikolaich, was coming rapidly toward her.

"It's you, dear! I'm glad . . ." he began, out of breath, "a word with you. . . ." He mopped his red, clean-shaven chin with his handkerchief and, stepping back abruptly, clasped his hands and opened his eyes wide. "My dear, how long can this go on?" he spluttered. "I ask you: is there no limit? Not to speak of the demoralizing effect of his martinet views, and the fact that he offends all that is sacred, all that is best in me and in every honest, thinking man—I say nothing of that, but he could at least behave decently! What is all this, anyhow? He shouts, snarls, gives himself airs, acts like some sort of Bonaparte, never lets anyone else say a word. . . . What the devil's the matter with him? Those lordly gestures, laughing like a general, that patronizing tone! And permit me to ask you: who is he? I am asking you: just who is he? His wife's husband, that's who he is; a titular councilor with a small estate who has had the good luck to marry wealth! An upstart and a *Junker*, like so many others! A character out of Shchedrin! I swear to God, either he is suffering from megalomania, or that senile old rat Count Aleksei Petrovich is right when he says that children and young people today develop late and go on playing at being cab drivers and generals till they're forty!"

"It's true, true," agreed Olga Mikhailovna. "Please let me go. . . ."

"Now just think: what is all this leading to?" continued her uncle, barring her way. "How will this playing at being a conservative and a general end? He's already being prosecuted! Prosecuted! And I'm very glad! All his bluster and hullabaloo has landed him right in the prisoners' dock. And it's not as if it were in the circuit court or anything like that—it's in a higher court! I can't conceive of anything worse! And furthermore he has quarreled with everyone! Today is his name day and, look, Vostryakov's not here, nor Vladimirov, nor Shevud, nor the Count. . . . There's no one more conservative than Count Aleksei Petrovich, but even he hasn't come. And he'll never come again! You'll see, he won't come!"

"Oh, good Lord! But what has all this to do with me?" asked Olga Mikhailovna.

"What has it to do with you? You're his wife! You are a clever woman, you've had a university education, and it is in your power to make an honest worker of him!"

"The courses I took didn't teach me how to influence diffi-cult people. It seems I ought to apologize to everyone for having gone to the university," said Olga Mikhailovna sharply. "You know, Uncle, if you had to listen to the same tune over and over again all day long you wouldn't be able to sit still, you'd get up and run away. I hear the same thing day in and day out the whole year. It's time you took pity on me!"

Her uncle made a very solemn face, gave her a quizzical look, and curled his lip in a mocking smile.

"So that's how it is!" he crooned like an old woman. "Excuse me!" he said with a courtly bow. "If you yourself have fallen under his influence and have betrayed your convictions, you should have said so before. I beg your pardon!"

"Yes, I have betrayed my convictions!" she cried. "Now crow over that!"

"I beg your pardon!" he made a final ceremonious bow, turning a little to one side and shrinking into himself, then with a click of his heels, went on his way.

"Idiot!" thought Olga Mikhailovna. "I hope he goes home."

She found the ladies and young people in the kitchen gardens among the raspberry bushes. Some were eating raspberries, others, who had had their fill, were sauntering through the strawberry beds or rifling the sugar peas. A little to one side of the raspberry patch, near a spreading apple tree propped up by stakes pulled out of an old fence, Pyotr Dmitrich was mowing grass. His hair hung over his forehead, his necktie was untied, and his watch chain dangled from his buttonhole. In every step and swing of the scythe one sensed his skill and an enormous physical strength. Near him stood Lyubochka and Natalya and Valentina, or Nata and Vata, as they were called, two anemic, unhealthily stout blond girls of sixteen or seventeen, the daughters of Colonel Bukreyev, a neighbor, both in white dresses and looking amazingly alike. Pyotr Dmitrich was teaching them to mow.

"It's very simple," he said. "You have only to know how to hold the scythe and not get too hot about it; that is, don't use any more force than necessary. Like this. . . . Would you like to try now?" He offered the scythe to Lyubochka. "Here you are!"

Blushing and laughing, Lyubochka awkwardly took hold of the scythe.

"Don't be afraid, Lyubov Aleksandrovna!" called Olga Mikhailovna in a voice loud enough for all the ladies to hear that she was among them. "Don't be afraid! You'd better learn! If you marry a Tolstoyan he will make you mow."

Lyubochka lifted the scythe, but again burst into laughter and helplessly let it fall. She felt ashamed, yet pleased at being talked to as if she were grown-up. Nata, neither shy nor smiling, but with a cold serious expression, took up the scythe and with one sweep got it tangled in the grass; Vata, also unsmiling, as cool and solemn as her sister, without a word took the scythe and plunged it into the earth. This accomplished, they linked arms and walked off to the raspberry bushes without a word.

Pyotr Dmitrich laughed and capered about like a boy, and this childishly frolicsome mood, in which he became extravagantly good-natured, was far more becoming to him than any other. Olga Mikhailovna loved him when he was in such a mood. But this boyishness generally did not last long. And now, having diverted himself with the scythe, he found it necessary to introduce a note of seriousness.

"You know, when I'm mowing, I feel healthier and more normal," he said. "If I were forced to limit myself to only an intellectual life, I believe I'd go out of my mind. I feel that I wasn't born to be a man of culture! I ought to mow, plow, sow, drive the horses. . . ."

And Pyotr Dmitrich and the ladies began to discuss culture, the advantages of physical labor, and the evils of money and property. Listening to her husband, for some reason Olga Mikhailovna thought of her dowry.

"The time will come, I suppose, when he won't forgive me for being richer than he," she thought. "He is proud and vain. He will probably conceive a hatred for me because of all he owes me."

She stopped near Colonel Bukreyev, who was eating raspberries and also taking part in the conversation.

"Come," he said, making room for her. "The ripest ones are here. . . . And, of course, according to Proudhon," he raised his voice and went on, "property is theft. But, I must confess, I don't consider him a philosopher. For me, the French are not authorities—I've washed my hands of them!"

"Well, as far as your Proudhons and Buckles and all the rest of them are concerned—I'm not up on them," said Pyotr Dmitrich. "When it comes to philosophy, you'll have to deal with my wife. She took courses in all your Schopenhauers and Proudhons, and knows them inside out."

Olga Mikhailovna began to feel weary again. She walked

back through the garden, along the narrow path by the apple and pear trees, looking once more as if she had something very important to do. She came to the gardener's cottage. . . . Varvara, the gardener's wife, was sitting in the doorway with her four little children, all with large shaven heads. She too was pregnant and expected to be confined by St. Elijah's Day. After greeting her, Olga Mikhailovna stood silently gazing at her and the children, then asked:

"Well, how do you feel?"

"Oh, all right. . . ."

A silence fell. The two women seemed to understand each other without words.

"It's terrifying to give birth for the first time," said Olga Mikhailovna after a moment's thought. "I keep feeling I won't get through it, that I shall die."

"That's how I felt, but here I am, alive. . . . You imagine all sorts of things. . . ."

Varvara, now about to have her fifth child and feeling slightly superior because of her experience, took a somewhat didactic tone with her mistress, and Olga Mikhailovna could not help feeling her authority; she would have liked to talk to her of the child, of her fears and sensations, but she was afraid it might seem trivial and naive to Varvara. She waited in silence for her to say something.

"Olga, we're going back to the house!" Pyotr Dmitrich called to her from the raspberry patch.

Olga Mikhailovna enjoyed being silent, watching Varvara and waiting for her to speak. She would have been willing to stand there till nightfall, without speech or obligation. But she had to go. She had hardly left the cottage when Lyubochka, Vata, and Nata came running to catch up with her. All at once the sisters stood rooted to the spot a couple of yards from her, while Lyubochka ran up and flung herself on her neck.

"Darling! Beautiful! Precious!" she babbled. "Do let us have tea on the island!"

"On the island! The island!" chorused the doubles Vata and Nata unsmilingly.

"But it's going to rain, my dears."

"It isn't, it isn't!" cried Lyubochka with a rueful expression. "They've all agreed to go! Dearest! Darling!"

"They've all decided to go to the island for tea," Pyotr Dmitrich said as he joined them. "You arrange things. . . .

We'll all go in the boats and the samovars and the rest of it must be sent by carriage with the servants."

He walked beside his wife, slipping his arm through hers.

Olga Mikhailovna had a desire to say something disagreeable to her husband, something caustic, even to mention her dowry perhaps—the crueler the better, she felt. After thinking for a moment, she said:

"Why is it Count Aleksei Petrovich hasn't come? What a pity!"

"I'm very glad he hasn't come," lied Pyotr Dmitrich. "I'm fed up with that old idiot, sick to death of him."

"And yet before dinner you couldn't wait to see him!"

# III

Half an hour later the guests were crowded together on the bank near a piling to which the boats were tied. There was a great deal of talking and laughing, and so much unnecessary bustling about that they were unable to get settled in the boats. Three of the boats were overflowing with passengers, and two stood empty. The keys for these boats were nowhere to be found and people kept running back and forth from the river to the house looking for them. Some said that Grigory had the keys, others that the steward had them, while a third group advised sending for the blacksmith to break the locks. They all talked at once, interrupting and shouting one another down. Pyotr Dmitrich impatiently strode up and down the bank shouting:

"What's the meaning of this? The keys are supposed to be left in the hall window! Who has dared to take them from there? The steward can get a boat of his own if he wants one!"

At last the keys were found. Then it turned out that two sculls were missing. Again there was a great hubbub. Pyotr Dmitrich, having grown tired of striding up and down, jumped into a long narrow skiff hollowed out of a poplar, rocking it so that he almost fell into the water, and pushed off. One after another the boats followed him, amid loud laughter and the squeals of the ladies.

The white cloudy sky, the trees on the riverside, the reeds, and the boats with their passengers and sculls, were all reflected in the water as in a mirror; under the boats, far below the bottomless depths, was another sky with birds flying across it. The bank on which the house stood was high, steep, and covered with trees; the other bank was sloping and green with broad water-meadows and shimmering coves. The boats had gone a hundred yards when from behind a melancholy, drooping willow on the slope of the bank some huts and a herd of cows came into sight; singing, drunken shouts, and the strains of a concertina were heard.

Fishing boats darted here and there on the river as the men cast their nets for the night. In one boat sat a group of music lovers drunkenly playing homemade violins and cellos.

Olga Mikhailovna sat at the tiller. She smiled affably and talked a great deal to entertain her guests, all the while looking askance at her husband. He was standing up in the first boat, sculling. The light sharp-prowed skiff, which his guests called the *Corsair* and Pyotr Dmitrich for some reason of his own called the *Penderaklia,* sped along; it had an agile, crafty look, as if it resented the burdensome Pyotr Dmitrich and was just waiting for the right moment to slip out from under him. Olga Mikhailovna kept glancing at her husband; she loathed his good looks, loathed the back of his neck, his posture, his familiar manner with women; she hated all those women sitting in his boat, was jealous of them, and at the same time was constantly trembling with fear that the unsteady craft might overturn and cause some mishap.

"Careful, Pyotr!" she called, her heart sinking with fear. "Sit down in the boat! We are convinced of your valor without that!"

She was also disturbed by the people who were in her boat. They were all perfectly nice ordinary people, like so many others, but now they seemed to her extraordinary and evil. She saw nothing but falsity in every one of them. "That young man with the brown hair, handsome beard, and gold spectacles, who is rowing," she thought, "is nothing but a very fortunate, rich, well-fed, mother's darling, whom everyone considers an honest, freethinking, progressive man. It's hardly a year since he graduated from the university and took up life here in the district, but he already speaks of himself as 'we zemstvo workers.' In another year he will be bored, like so many others, and go off to Petersburg, and to justify his desertion, he will tell everyone that the zemstvo is absolutely useless, that it was a disappointment to him. And from the other boat his young wife doesn't take her eyes off him; she believes that he is a 'zemstvo worker,' just as next year she will believe that the zemstvo is useless. And then there is that stout carefully shaven gentleman in the straw hat with a wide ribbon and an expensive cigar in his mouth. One who likes to say: 'Time to drop the fantasy and get to work!' He has Yorkshire pigs, Butler hives, pineapples, rapeseed oil, an oil press, a cheese dairy, and Italian double-entry bookkeeping. But every summer he sells his timber and mortgages part of his land in order to spend the autumn with his mistress in the Crimea. And there's Uncle Nikolai Nikolaich, who is furious with Pyotr Dmitrich and yet, for some reason, doesn't go home."

Olga Mikhailovna glanced at the other boats and saw in them only odd, uninteresting people who were either pretentious or not very intelligent. She thought of all the people she knew in the district and was unable to recall a single one of whom she could say or think anything good. They all seemed to her untalented, insipid, stupid, narrow, false, and hardhearted; they all said what they did not think, and did what they did not want to do. Boredom and despair were stifling her; she wanted to stop smiling at once, to spring up and shout: "I am sick of you!" and then jump out of the boat and swim to shore.

"Friends, let's take Pyotr Dmitrich in tow!" someone shouted.

"Tow him! Tow him!" the others chimed in. "Olga Mikhailovna, take your husband in tow."

In order to do this, Olga Mikhailovna, who was at the tiller, had to seize the right moment and deftly catch hold of the *Penderaklia* by the chain in the prow of the boat. When she leaned over to reach for it, Pyotr Dmitrich frowned and looked at her in alarm.

"I hope you won't catch cold out here!" he said.

"If you're so worried about me and the child," she thought, "why do you torment me?"

Pyotr Dmitrich acknowledged his defeat, and, not wanting to be towed, jumped from the *Penderaklia* into the boat that was already overcrowded, and so recklessly that it careened violently and everyone screamed in terror.

"Now he has jumped to please the ladies," thought Olga Mikhailovna. "He knows how splendid it looks. . . ."

Her hands and feet began to tremble, from ill humor and vexation as she thought, from the strain of smiling and the discomfort she felt all through her body. To conceal the trembling from her guests, she tried to talk louder, to laugh and keep moving. . . .

"If I should suddenly burst into tears," she thought, "I'll say I have a toothache. . . ."

But at last the boats reached the "Isle of Good Hope," as they called the peninsula formed by the river bending at an acute angle; it was covered with a grove of old birch trees, oaks, willows, and poplars. Tables had already been set under the trees, smoke rose from the samovars, and Vasily and Grigory, in dress coats and white knitted gloves, were busy with the tea things. On the other bank, opposite the "Isle of Good Hope," stood the carriages that had brought the provisions. The baskets and parcels had been ferried to the island in a little boat very much like the *Penderaklia*. The footmen, the coachmen, and the peasant who was sitting in the boat had the festive, holiday expression seen only in children and servants.

While Olga Mikhailovna was brewing the tea and filling the first glasses, the guests were busy with liqueurs and sweetmeats. Then began the customary commotion of drinking tea at picnics, which is so tiresome and exhausting for hostesses. Grigory and Vasily hardly had time to carry the glasses around before empty glasses were being held out to Olga Mikhailovna. One asked for it without sugar, another wanted it stronger, another weak, a fourth declined. Olga Mikhailovna had to remember, then to call: "Ivan Petrovich, is it without sugar for you?" or "Gentlemen, which of you wanted it weak?" But whoever had asked for it weak or without sugar had forgotten about it by then, and, carried away by a pleasant conversation, took the first glass that came to hand. Disconsolate figures wandered like shadows off to one side of the table, pretending to look for mushrooms in the grass, or reading the labels on boxes—they were the ones for whom there were no glasses. "Have you had tea?" Olga Mikhailovna kept asking. And whoever she asked would beg her not to trouble, adding: "I'll wait," though it would have suited her better if her guests had not waited but made haste.

Some, engrossed in conversation, drank their tea slowly,

keeping their glasses for half an hour, while others, especially those who had drunk a great deal at dinner, did not leave the table, and drank glass after glass, so that Olga Mikhailovna scarcely had time to keep them filled. One young wag sipped his tea through a piece of sugar and kept saying: "Sinner that I am, I love to indulge myself in the Chinese herb!" From time to time, sighing deeply, he would ask: "One more tiny little dish of tea, if you please!" He drank continually, bit noisily into pieces of sugar, and thought it all very amusing and original and that he was giving a perfect imitation of a merchant. No one realized how agonizing all these trifles were to the hostess, and, indeed, it would have been hard to tell, as Olga Mikhailovna went on smiling amiably and talking nonsense.

She began to feel ill. . . . She was irritated by the crowd, the laughter, the questions, the jocular young man, the stupefied footmen who had run their legs off, the children hanging around the table; irritated by Vata looking like Nata, and Kolya like Mitya, so that it was impossible to tell which of them had had tea and which had not. She felt that her forced smile of cordiality was turning into an angry expression, and that she would burst into tears at any minute.

"Rain, my friends!" someone cried.

Everyone looked at the sky.

"Yes, it really is rain," Pyotr Dmitrich affirmed, and wiped his cheek.

The sky let fall only a few drops; the real rain had not begun, but everyone forsook his tea and made haste to leave. At first they all wanted to drive back in the carriages, but then changed their minds and made for the boats. On the pretext that she had to get home as soon as possible to make arrangements for supper, Olga Mikhailovna asked to be excused for leaving the company and went home in a carriage.

The first thing she did when she was seated in the carriage was to let her face rest from smiling. With an angry expression she drove through the village, with an angry expression acknowledged the bows of the peasants she passed. When she got home she went by the back way to the bedroom and lay down on her husband's bed.

"Merciful God!" she whispered. "What is all this drudgery for? Why do all those people crowd in here and pretend they are enjoying themselves? Why do I smile and lie? I don't understand, I don't understand!"

She heard footsteps and voices. Her guests had come back. "Let them come," she thought, "I shall go on lying here." A maidservant came in and said:

"Madam, Marya Grigoryevna is leaving."

Olga Mikhailovna jumped up, tidied her hair, and hurried out of the room.

"Marya Grigoryevna, what is the meaning of this?" she began in a hurt tone as she went to meet her. "Where are you off to in such a hurry?"

"I must go, darling, I really must! I've stayed too long as it is. My children are expecting me home."

"What a shame! Why didn't you bring the children with you?"

"If you will let me, dear, I'll bring them on an ordinary day, but today——"

"Oh, please do," Olga Mikhailovna interrupted. "I'll be delighted! Your children are such darlings! Kiss them all for me. . . . But really, I'm hurt! I don't understand why you are in such a hurry!"

"I must go, I really must. . . . Good-bye, dear. Take care of yourself. In your condition, you know . . ."

They kissed each other. After seeing her to her carriage, Olga Mikhailovna went to the ladies in the drawing room. The lamps were lighted and the gentlemen were sitting down to cards.

# IV

After supper, at a quarter past twelve, everyone began to leave. Seeing her guests off, Olga Mikhailovna stood on the porch saying:

"You really ought to take a shawl. . . . It's getting a little cool. I hope you won't catch cold!"

"Don't worry, Olga Mikhailovna," someone called back, getting into a carriage. "Well, good-bye! Don't forget, we are expecting you! Don't disappoint us!"

"Who-a!" a coachman cried, curbing his horses.

"Go ahead, Denis! Good-bye, Olga Mikhailovna!"

"Kiss the children for me!"

The carriage set off and instantly disappeared into the darkness. In the red circle of light cast by a lamp on the road, another pair or trio of impatient horses would appear and the silhouette of a coachman with his arms stretched out before him. And once more there were kisses, reproaches, entreaties to come again, or to take a shawl. Pyotr Dmitrich kept running out and helping the ladies into their carriages.

"Now you go by Yefremovshchina," he directed the coachman. "It's shorter by way of Mankino, but the road is worse. If you don't watch out you might overturn. . . . Good-bye, my charmer! *Milles compliments* to your artist!"

"Good-bye, darling Olga Mikhailovna! Go into the house, or you'll catch cold! It's damp."

"Whoa! You're a frisky one!"

"Where did you get these horses?" asked Pyotr Dmitrich.

"They were bought from Khaidarov in Lent," replied the coachman.

"Splendid horses. . . ."

And Pyotr Dmitrich clapped the trace horse on the haunch. "Well, go ahead! God give you luck!"

At last everyone had gone. The red circle of light on the road wavered, floated off to the side, diminished, and went out, as Vasily carried away the lamp from the entrance. Generally after seeing their visitors off Pyotr Dmitrich and Olga Mikhailovna would dance about the drawing room, face to face and clapping their hands as they sang: "They've gone! They've gone!" But this time Olga Mikhailovna was not equal to it. She went to the bedroom, undressed, and got into bed.

She felt as if she would fall asleep instantly and sleep soundly. Her legs and shoulders ached painfully, her head felt leaden from so much talk, and, as before, she had a sensation of discomfort all through her body. She covered her head and lay still for a few minutes, then peeped out from under the blanket at the icon lamp, and, listening to the silence, smiled.

"Lovely, lovely . . ." she whispered, curling up her legs, which felt as if they had grown longer from so much walking. "Sleep, sleep. . . ."

Her legs would not stay still, and she turned over on her other side. A huge fly darted about the room, buzzing and thumping against the ceiling. She also heard Grigory and Vasily in the drawing room, stepping cautiously as they cleared the tables; it seemed to her that she could not be at ease and fall asleep till these sounds had ceased. And again she impatiently turned over. She heard her husband's voice in the drawing room. Someone must be staying the night, for Pyotr Dmitrich was addressing whoever it was in a loud voice, saying:

"I don't say that Count Aleksei Petrovich is a hypocrite. But he necessarily appears to be one because all of you gentlemen attempt to see in him something other than what he actually is. His madness is regarded as originality, his condescension as kindheartedness, his complete lack of convictions as conservatism. Let us suppose that he is, in fact, a conservative of the stamp of '84. But what, essentially, is conservatism?"

Pyotr Dmitrich, angry at Count Aleksei Petrovich, at his guests, and at himself, was unburdening his mind. He abused the Count and his visitors, and in his vexation with himself was ready to hold forth and say what he thought. After seeing his visitor to his room, he paced the drawing room, walked through the dining room, down the corridor, into his study, back to the drawing room, and into the bedroom. Olga Mikhailovna lay on her back with the blanket only up to her waist (by now she felt hot), and with an infuriated expression watched the fly thumping against the ceiling.

"Is someone staying overnight?" she asked.

"Yegorov."

Pyotr Dmitrich undressed and got into his bed. Without speaking, he lit a cigarette, and he too fell to watching the fly. His face looked troubled and austere. Olga Mikhailovna gazed at his handsome profile for five minutes in silence. It seemed to her that if her husband were to turn to her suddenly and say: "Olya, I'm so miserable!" she would burst into tears or laugh, and she would feel better. She thought that the aching of her legs and the discomfort of her whole body was a result of the tension in her soul.

"Pyotr, what are you thinking about?" she asked.

"Oh, nothing . . ." replied her husband.

"You've been having secrets from me lately. It's not right."

"Why isn't it right? We all have our own personal life, and consequently are bound to have our secrets."

"Personal life . . . our secrets. . . . Those are just words! Can't you understand that you are hurting me?" said Olga Mikhailovna, sitting up in bed. "If you are troubled, why do you conceal it from me? Why is it you find it more convenient to confide in other women instead of your wife? I

heard you today at the apiary, opening your heart to Lyubochka!"

"Well, I congratulate you. I'm very glad you heard me."

This meant: leave me alone, don't bother me when I'm
thinking! Olga Mikhailovna was outraged. The irritation,
hatred, and anger that had been accumulating in her during
the whole day suddenly boiled over; she felt impelled to
speak her mind to her husband at once instead of waiting till
the next day; she wanted to wound him, to have her revenge.
. . . With an effort to control herself, to keep from screaming,
she said:

"You may as well know that all this is revolting—revolting
—revolting! I've hated you all day—you see what you've
done!"

Pyotr Dmitrich sat up in bed.

"Revolting, revolting, revolting!" Olga Mikhailovna went on,
trembling all over. "Don't congratulate me! You'd better
congratulate yourself! It's shameful, a disgrace! You've lied
so much you're ashamed to be alone in a room with your
wife! You're a deceitful man! I see through you—I understand every step you take!"

"Olya, I wish you would give me warning when you're
out of sorts so I can sleep in my study."

And Pyotr Dmitrich picked up his pillow and walked out
of the room. Olga Mikhailovna had not forseen this. For several minutes she sat in silence, open-mouthed, trembling, staring at the door through which her husband had escaped, trying to understand what it meant. Was this one of the devices
used by deceitful people when they are in the wrong, or
was it an insult deliberately aimed at her pride? How was
she to take it? She recalled her cousin, a jolly young officer,
who had often told her that when "my spouse starts picking
on me" at night, he generally took his pillow and went
whistling into his study, leaving his wife in a foolish,
ludicrous position. This officer was married to a rich, capricious, silly woman whom he did not respect but merely put
up with.

Olga Mikhailovna jumped out of bed. To her mind there
was only one thing left for her to do: to dress as quickly
as possible and leave the house forever. The house belonged
to her, but so much the worse for Pyotr Dmitrich. Without
considering whether it was necessary or not, she rushed
to the study to inform her husband of her decision ("Fem-

inine logic!" flashed through her mind), and, in farewell, to say something biting and wounding. . . .

Pyotr Dmitrich was lying on the sofa, pretending to read a newspaper. Near him stood a lighted candle on a chair. His face was hidden behind the newspaper.

"Will you kindly tell me the meaning of this? I'm asking you!"

"I'm asking you . . ." Pyotr Dmitrich mimicked her, not showing his face. "It's sickening, Olya. I give you my word, I'm exhausted, I'm not up to this now. . . . We can do our quarreling tomorrow."

"No. I understand you perfectly," she went on. "You hate me. Yes—yes! You hate me for being richer than you! You will never forgive me for it, and you will always lie to me!" ("Feminine logic!" again flashed through her mind.) "I know you're laughing at me right now. . . . I'm absolutely convinced that you married me so you would have property rights . . . and those wretched horses. . . . Oh, I'm so miserable!"

Pyotr Dmitrich dropped his newspaper and sat up. The unexpected insult had stunned him. He looked at his wife in confusion, a childishly helpless smile on his face, his hands outstretched as if to ward off a blow.

"Olya!" he cried beseechingly.

And expecting her to say something more that was awful, he shrank against the back of the sofa, his huge figure looking as childishly helpless as his smile.

"Olya, how could you say it?" he whispered.

Olga Mikhailovna came to herself. She was suddenly conscious of her passionate love for this man, and realized that this was her husband, Pyotr Dmitrich, without whom she could not live for one day, and who passionately loved her too. She sobbed loudly in an unnatural voice, and putting her hands to her head, ran back to the bedroom.

She threw herself onto the bed and the room resounded with her spasmodic, hysterical sobbing; it choked her and caused her arms and legs to contract. Remembering the guest who was sleeping three or four rooms away, she buried her head under the pillow, and tried to stifle her sobs, but the pillow slipped to the floor, and she herself all but fell in her effort to retrieve it. She reached for the blanket to pull it up to her face, but her hands refused to obey her and tore convulsively at everything she touched.

She felt that all was lost, that the lie she had spoken to wound her husband had shattered her life into a thousand pieces. He would never forgive her. The insult she had hurled at him was not the sort that could be smoothed over with caresses, with vows. . . . How could she convince her husband that she herself did not believe what she had said?

"It's all over! All over!" she cried, not noticing that the pillow had slipped to the floor again. "For God's sake, for God's sake!"

Her cries, no doubt, had by now roused the guest and the servants, and tomorrow the whole district would know that she had had hysterics, and everyone would blame Pyotr Dmitrich. She made an effort to restrain herself, but her sobs grew louder and louder every minute.

"For God's sake!" she cried in a strange voice, not knowing why she kept repeating this. "For God's sake!"

It seemed to her that the bed was heaving under her, that her legs were entangled in the blanket. Pyotr Dmitrich came into the room in his dressing gown carrying a candle.

"Olya, hush!" he said.

She raised herself to her knees in bed, and squinting at the light said through her sobs:

"Try to understand . . . understand . . ."

She wanted to tell him that she had been worn out by their visitors, by his lying and her own, that it was seething inside her, but all she could say was:

"Understand . . . understand . . ."

"Here, drink this," he said, giving her some water.

She took the glass obediently and began drinking, but the water splashed and spilled over her hands, her breast, her knees. . . .

"I must look hideous," she thought.

Pyotr Dmitrich put her back into bed without a word, covered her with the blanket, took the candle, and went out.

"For God's sake!" Olga Mikhailovna cried. "Pyotr, understand . . . understand . . ."

All at once something gripped her below the stomach and in the lower part of the back with such violence that it silenced her wailing and made her bite the pillow in agony. But the pain abated and she commenced sobbing again.

The maid came in, arranged the blanket over her, and anxiously asked:

"Mistress, darling, what is the matter?"

"Get out of here!" said Pyotr Dmitrich sternly, as he went up to the bed.

"Understand . . . understand . . ." Olga Mikhailovna kept saying.

"Olya, I beg you to calm yourself!" he said. "I didn't mean to hurt you. I wouldn't have left the room if I had known it would affect you in this way. I was simply depressed. I tell you, in all honesty . . ."

"Understand. . . . You were lying. . . . I was lying. . . ."

"I understand. . . . Come now, that's enough. I understand . . ." he said tenderly, and sat down on the bed beside her. "You spoke in anger, it's natural. . . . I swear to God, I love you more than anything on earth, and when I married you I never once thought of your being rich. I loved you infinitely, and that was all. . . . Believe me. I have never been in need of money or known the value of it, consequently I've never been conscious of the difference between your means and mine. It has always seemed to me that we were equally well off. As for my being deceitful in little things . . . it's true, of course. Till now my life has not been arranged in a very serious way, and it somehow seemed impossible to avoid lying. I feel depressed by it now myself. Let's not talk about it any more, for heaven's sake! . . ."

Olga Mikhailovna again felt a sharp pain, and clutched at her husband's sleeve.

"I am in such pain, pain, pain!" she said rapidly. "Oh, such pain!"

"Damn all those visitors!" muttered Pyotr Dmitrich, getting up. "You ought not to have gone to the island today!" he cried. "What an idiot I am—why didn't I stop you? Oh, good Lord!"

He scratched his head in exasperation, threw up his hands, and left the room.

After that he kept coming back, sitting on the bed beside her, and talking a great deal, now tenderly, now angrily; but she hardly heard him. Her sobs alternated with terrible pains, each more violent and prolonged than the last. At first she held her breath and bit the pillow when the pains gripped her, but later she uttered shameless, harrowing screams. At one moment, seeing her husband near her, she remembered that she had insulted him, and without quite knowing whether she was delirious or whether it really was Pyotr Dmitrich, she seized his hand in both of hers and began kissing it.

"You were lying . . . I was lying . . ." she wanted to justify herself. "Understand . . . understand. . . . They have worn me out . . . driven me out of my wits. . . ."

"Olya, we are not alone," said Pyotr Dmitrich.

Olga Mikhailovna raised her head and saw Varvara on her knees before a chest, opening the bottom drawer. The top drawers were already open. Then she stood up, flushed from her exertions, and with a cold, solemn expression, tried to unlock a little chest.

"Marya, I can't unlock it!" she said in a whisper. "Unlock it, will you?"

Marya, the maid, was digging a candle end out of the candlestick in order to put a fresh one in. She went to Varvara and helped her to unlock the chest.

"There should be nothing locked," whispered Varvara. "Open this basket, my dear. . . . Master," she turned to Pyotr Dmitrich, "you should send to Father Mikhail to unlock the holy gates. You must!"

"Do whatever you like," said Pyotr Dmitrich, breathing heavily, "only, for God's sake, hurry—get the doctor or the midwife! Has Vasily gone? Send someone else as well. Send your husband!"

"I am giving birth . . ." thought Olga Mikhailovna. "Varvara," she moaned, "but he won't be born alive!"

"It's going to be all right, all right, mistress," whispered Varvara. "God willing, he'll be alive! He'll be alive!"

When Olga Mikhailovna came to herself after a pain, she was no longer sobbing or tossing from side to side, but was moaning. She could not help moaning, even in the intervals between pains. The candles were still burning, but daylight was coming in through the blinds. It was probably about five o'clock in the morning. A modest-looking woman in a white apron, someone she did not know, was sitting at a little round table in the bedroom. From the way she sat, it appeared that she had been sitting there for some time. Olga Mikhailovna surmised that this was the midwife.

"Will it be over soon?" she asked, and detected an odd, unfamiliar note, never before heard in her voice. "I must be dying in childbirth," she thought.

Pyotr Dmitrich came cautiously into the bedroom, dressed

for the day, and stood at the window with his back to his wife. He raised the blind and looked out the window.

"What rain!" he said.

"What time is it?" asked Olga Mikhailovna, in order to hear her own unfamiliar voice once more.

"A quarter to six," answered the midwife.

"And what if I really am dying?" thought Olga Mikhailovna, looking at her husband's head and at the window-panes on which the rain was beating. "How will he live without me? With whom will he have tea and dinner . . . talk to in the evening . . . sleep?"

And he seemed to her like a little orphaned child; she felt sorry for him and wanted to say something nice, something loving and consoling. She remembered how in the spring he had wanted to buy himself hounds, but because she found hunting a cruel and dangerous sport, she had prevented him from buying them.

"Pyotr, buy yourself hounds . . ." she moaned.

He lowered the blind and went to the bed; he was about to say something to her when there was another pain and she uttered a piercing, heart-rending scream.

The pains, the repeated screaming and moaning, had stupefied her. She heard, saw, and sometimes spoke, but she understood very little and was conscious only of the pain, or that she was going to be in pain again. It seemed to her that the name-day party had taken place, not the day before, but a long long time ago, a year perhaps; and that her new, agonizing life had gone on longer than her childhood, her schooldays at the institute, her university years, her married life . . . and would go on and on, endlessly. She saw them bring tea to the midwife, summon her to the midday meal, and later to dinner; she saw Pyotr Dmitrich grow accustomed to coming in, standing at the window for some time, and going out again; saw strange men, the maid, Varvara . . . Varvara saying nothing but: "He will be, he will," and looking angry when anyone closed the drawers of the chest. Olga Mikhailovna watched the light change in the windows and in the room: at one time it was twilight, then it turned murky, like fog, then bright daylight, as it had been the day before at dinner, and again twilight. . . . And each of these changes lasted as long as her childhood, her schooldays at the institute, her years at the university. . . .

In the evening two doctors—one bald and bony with a

broad red beard, the other with a swarthy Jewish face and
cheap spectacles—performed some sort of operation on her.
She was completely indifferent to these strange men handling
her body. By now she had no shame, no will, and anyone
might do with her as he pleased. If someone had rushed at
her with a knife, had insulted Pyotr Dmitrich, or had deprived her of her right to the little person, she would not
have said a word.

She was given chloroform for the operation. When she
came to the pain was still there and unbearable. It was
night. And Olga Mikhailovna remembered another such night
—the same stillness, the icon lamp, the midwife sitting motionless near the bed, the drawers of the chest pulled out,
and Pyotr Dmitrich standing at the window—but that was a
long long time ago. . . .

## V

"I am not dead . . ." thought Olga Mikhailovna when the
pain was over and she began to be aware of her surroundings.

A bright summer day looked in at both wide-open windows; outside in the garden the sparrows and magpies kept
up an incessant chatter.

The drawers of the chest were shut now, and her husband's bed had been made. The midwife, the maid, and
Varvara were no longer in the bedroom; only Pyotr Dmitrich, as before, stood motionless at the window, looking into
the garden. But there was no sound of an infant's cry, no
congratulations and rejoicing; it was evident that the little
person had not been born alive.

"Pyotr!" Olga Mikhailovna called to her husband.

Pyotr Dmitrich turned to her. A great deal of time must
have passed since the last guest had departed and Olga
Mikhailovna had insulted her husband, for Pyotr Dmitrich
was perceptibly thinner and looked very drawn.

"What is it?" he asked, going to her.

He looked away; his lips twitched and his face wore a
childishly helpless smile.

"Is it all over?" she asked.

Pyotr Dmitrich tried to answer her, but his lips began to

quiver, and his mouth twisted into a grimace, like an old man, like her toothless old uncle Nikolai Nikolaich.

"Olya!" he said, wringing his hands, and great tears suddenly fell from his eyes. "Olya! I don't care about property qualifications, or circuit courts" (he sobbed) "or about any particular views, or those guests, or your dowry. . . . I don't care about anything! Why didn't we take care of our child? Oh, what's the use of talking!"

And with a gesture of despair, he went out of the room.

But nothing mattered to Olga Mikhailovna now. Her mind was hazy from the chloroform, her soul was empty. . . . The dull indifference to life that she felt when the two doctors performed the operation had not yet left her.

1888

# IN THE RAVINE

# I

The village of Ukleyevo lay in a ravine, so that only the belfry and the chimneys of the cotton mills could be seen from the highway and the railroad station. When passers-by would ask what village it was, they were told:

"That's the one where the sexton ate up all the caviar at the funeral."

It had happened at a funeral repast at the millowner Kostyukov's that the old sexton caught sight of some large-grained caviar among the appetizers and greedily fell to eating it; people nudged him, tugged at his sleeve, but it was as if he was stupefied with pleasure: he felt nothing and simply went on eating. He ate all the caviar, and there were some four pounds in the jar. And although years had passed, and the sexton had long been dead, the caviar was still remembered. Whether it was the poverty of life here, or the inability of people to notice anything besides this unimportant incident that had taken place ten years before, nothing else was ever told about the village of Ukleyevo.

The village was never free from fever, and there was swampy mud in summer, especially under the fences over which hung old willow trees that gave a deep shade. Here there was always a smell of factory waste and acetic acid, which was used in the manufacture of cotton print. The factories—three cotton mills and a tanyard—were not in the village proper but at the edge of it and a little way off. They were small factories, together employing about four hundred workmen, not more. The tanyard often made the water in the little river stink; the waste contaminated the meadows, the

339

peasants' cattle suffered from anthrax, and orders were given that it be closed. It was considered to be closed, but went on working in secret with the knowledge of the local police officer and the district doctor, each of whom was paid ten rubles a month by the owner. In the entire village there were only two decent houses, brick with iron roofs; one was occupied by the district government office, and the other, a two-story house just opposite the church, by Grigory Petrovich Tsybukin, a petit bourgeois from Epifan.

Grigory kept a grocery, but that was only for the sake of appearances; in reality he sold vodka, cattle, hides, grain, and pigs—he traded in whatever came to hand. When, for instance, magpies were wanted abroad for ladies' hats, he made thirty kopecks on every pair; he bought timber for felling, lent money at interest, and altogether was a resourceful old man.

He had two sons. The elder, Anisim, served with the police as a detective and was rarely at home. The younger, Stepan, had gone in for trade and helped his father, but no real help was expected of him as he was in poor health and deaf; his wife, Aksinya, was a handsome woman with a good figure who wore a hat and carried a parasol on holidays, got up early and went to bed late, and ran about the whole day, picking up her skirts and jingling her keys, going from barn to cellar to shop, and old Tsybukin would gaze at her jovially, his eyes glowing; at such moments he regretted that she was not married to his elder son instead of the younger, who was deaf and obviously no judge of female beauty.

The old man had always had a fondness for family life; he loved his family more than anything on earth, especially his elder son, the detective, and his daughter-in-law. Aksinya had no sooner married the deaf son than she revealed an extraordinary gift for business, and in no time knew who could be allowed to run up a bill and who could not; she kept the keys herself, not trusting them even to her husband, rattled away at the abacus, looked at a horse's teeth like a peasant, and was always either laughing or shouting and no matter what she said or did the old man was moved and would mutter:

"Well done, little daughter-in-law! Well done, my beauty, my dear. . . ."

He had been a widower, but a year after his son's wedding

he could not resist getting married himself. A girl was found for him who lived thirty versts from Ukleyevo, Varvara Nikolayevna by name, no longer young but good-looking, presentable. No sooner was she installed in a little room in the upper story than everything in the house brightened up, as though new panes had been put into all the windows. The icon lamps gleamed, the tables were covered with snow-white cloths, flowers with red buds appeared in the windows and front garden, and at dinner, instead of all eating from one bowl, a plate was set before each person. Varvara Nikolayevna smiled pleasantly, sweetly, and it seemed as though the whole house were smiling. Beggars and pilgrims began to drop into the yard, a thing which had never happened in the past; the plaintive singsong voices of the Ukleyevo peasant women and the apologetic coughs of feeble, hollow-cheeked men who had been dismissed from the factory for drunkenness, were heard under the windows. Varvara helped them with money, with bread, and old clothes, and later, when she felt more at home, began taking things out of the shop. One day the deaf man saw her take four ounces of tea, and that confused him.

"Here, Mama's taken four ounces of tea," he afterward informed his father. "Where is that to be entered?"

The old man made no reply, but stood still for a moment thinking and moving his eyebrows; then he went upstairs to his wife.

"Varvarushka," he said affectionately, "if you want anything in the shop, take it and welcome; don't hesitate."

And the next day the deaf man called to her as he ran across the yard:

"If there's anything you need, Mama, take it."

There was something fresh, something lighthearted and gay, about her almsgiving, just as there was in the icon lamps and the red flowers. When, on the eve of a fast day or a church festival that lasted three days, they palmed off on the peasants tainted salt meat that smelled so awful one could hardly stand near the barrel; when they took scythes, caps, their wives' kerchiefs, in pledge from the drunken men; when the factory hands, stupefied with bad vodka, lay rolling in the mud, and sin seemed to thicken and hang like a fog in the air, then it was some sort of relief to think that there in the house was a gentle, tidy woman who had nothing to do with salt meat or vodka; in those oppressive, murky days her charity had the effect of a safety valve.

The days were spent in bustling activity in Tsybukin's house. Before the sun had risen Aksinya was heard snorting as she washed in the entry, and in the kitchen the samovar boiled with a hiss that boded no good. Old Grigory Petrovich, a dapper little figure dressed in a long black coat, cotton trousers, and shiny top boots, walked back and forth through the house tapping his heels like the father-in-law in the well-known song. The shop was opened. At daybreak a racing droshky was brought to the entrance and the old man jauntily climbed in and pulled his big cap down to his ears; looking at him, nobody would have said he was fifty-six. His wife and daughter-in-law saw him off, and at such times, when he had on a good clean coat, and the huge black stallion that had cost him three hundred rubles was harnessed to the droshky, the old man did not want the peasants to approach him with their petitions and complaints; he detested the peasants and was contemptuous of them, and if he saw a peasant waiting at the gate he would angrily shout:

"Why are you standing there? Move on!"

Or, if it were a beggar, he would cry:

"God will provide!"

He would drive off on business, and his wife, in a dark dress and black apron, tidied the rooms or helped in the kitchen. Aksinya tended the shop, and from the yard there was heard the clink of bottles and of money, her laughter and shouting, and the angry voices of the customers she offended; it was also evident that the illicit sale of vodka was already going on in the shop. The deaf man either sat in the shop or walked about the street bareheaded, his hands in his pockets, absent-mindedly gazing now at the huts, now at the sky overhead. Six times a day they had tea in the house; four times a day they sat down to meals. And in the evening they counted the day's receipts, wrote them down, then went to bed and slept soundly.

All three cotton mills in Ukleyevo were connected by telephone to the houses of their owners, the Khrymin Seniors, the Khrymin Juniors, and Kostyukov. A telephone had been installed in the government office too, but it soon stopped working after bedbugs and cockroaches started breeding in it. The district elder was almost illiterate and wrote every word of the official documents in capital letters, but when the telephone went out of order he said:

"Yes, things are going to be a little difficult now without a telephone."

The Khrymin Seniors were continually at law with the Juniors, and sometimes the Juniors quarreled among themselves and started proceedings against one another, and then their mill closed down for a month or two until they were reconciled, and this diverted the inhabitants of Ukleyevo, as there was a great deal of talk and gossip on the occasion of each quarrel. On holidays Kostyukov and the Khrymin Juniors used to go driving, and they would dash about the village and run down calves. Aksinya, dressed to kill and rustling her starched petticoats, used to promenade in the street near her shop; the Juniors would snatch her up and carry her off as if by force. Then old Tsybukin would drive out to show off his new horse, taking Varvara with him.

In the evening after these drives, when people were going to bed, an expensive accordion was played in the Juniors' yard, and if it was a moonlight night the sound of the music disturbed and delighted the soul, and Ukleyevo no longer seemed a miserable hole.

## II

The elder son, Anisim, came home very rarely, only on great holidays, but he often sent by a returning villager presents and letters written in a beautiful hand, always on a sheet of writing paper that looked like a petition. The letters were full of expressions that Anisim never used in conversation: "Dear Papa and Mama, I send you a pound of flower tea for the satisfaction of your physical needs."

At the bottom of every letter was scratched, as though with a broken pen: "Anisim Tsybukin," and under that, again in the same fine hand: "Agent."

The letters were read aloud several times, and the old man, touched, red with emotion, would say:

"Here he didn't want to stay at home, he's gone in for learned work. Well, let him! Every man to his own trade."

It happened that just before Carnival there was a heavy rain with sleet; the old man and Varvara went to the window to look at it, and lo and behold—Anisim came driving up in a sledge from the station! It was entirely unexpected. He came in looking troubled, as if he had been frightened, and remained so for the rest of his stay; but there was something devil-may-care in his manner. He was in no hurry to leave, and it looked as though he had been dismissed from the service. Varvara was glad to see him, and kept glancing at him with a sly expression, sighing and shaking her head.

"How is this, my friends?" she said. "The lad is twenty-eight years old and he's still leading a gay bachelor life . . . tck, tck, tck. . . ."

From the next room her soft, even speech all sounded like: "tck, tck, tck. . . ." She began to whisper with the old man and Aksinya, and their faces, too, took on the sly mysterious expression of conspirators.

It was decided to get Anisim married.

"Tck, tck, tck . . . the younger brother was married long ago," said Varvara, "and here you are still without a mate, like a cock at a fair. What's the meaning of this? Tck, tck, tck. . . . You will be married, please God, then go back to the service if you like, and your wife will stay at home here and help us. There's no order in your life, young man, I see you've forgotten how to live properly. Tck, tck, tck, that's the trouble with you townsfolk."

When the Tsybukins married, as rich men, the most beautiful brides were chosen for them. And for Anisim, too, they found a beautiful girl. He himself had an uninteresting, insignificant appearance: he was of a weak, sickly constitution and short of stature, with full, puffy cheeks that looked as if he were blowing them out, a sharp look in his unblinking eyes, and a sparse red beard that he always stuck into his mouth and gnawed when he was pondering over anything; moreover he drank too much, which could be seen in his face and his walk. But when they told him they had found him a very beautiful bride, he said:

"Well, I'm not so bad myself. All of us Tsybukins are handsome, I must say."

Not far from the town was the village of Torguyevo, one half of which had recently been incorporated into the town, the other half remaining a village. In the former half there lived a widow in her own little house; with her lived a sister who was extremely poor and went out to work by the day, and this sister had a daughter called Lipa, who also worked by the day. Lipa's beauty had already been talked of in Torguyevo, but everyone was put off by her terrible poverty;

some widower or elderly man, they reasoned, would marry her in spite of her poverty, or, perhaps, take her to live with him, and in that way her mother would be taken care of too. Varvara learned about Lipa from the matchmakers and drove over to Torguyevo.

Then a visit of inspection was arranged, as was proper, with wine and a light repast at the aunt's house, and Lipa wore a new pink dress, made especially for the occasion, and a little crimson ribbon gleamed like a flame in her hair. She was thin, frail, wan, with fine, delicate features that were tanned from work in the open air. A timid, mournful smile hovered over her face, and there was a childlike look in her eyes, trustful and curious.

She was young, still a child, her bosom scarcely perceptible, but having reached the legal age she could now be married. And she really was beautiful; the only thing that might be thought unattractive about her was her large, masculine hands, which now hung idle like two big paws.

"There's no dowry—but we don't mind that," the old man said to the aunt. "We took a girl from a poor family for our son Stepan, too, and now we can't say enough for her. In the house and in the shop alike, she has fingers of gold."

Lipa stood in the doorway as if to say: "Do with me as you will, I trust you," while her mother, Praskovya the charwoman, hid in the kitchen, numb with shyness. Once, in her youth, a merchant whose floors she was scrubbing stamped his feet at her in a rage and she was so frozen with terror that for the rest of her life she remained fearful at heart. And this fear made her arms and legs quiver and her cheeks twitch. Sitting in the kitchen she tried to hear what the visitors were saying, and kept crossing herself, pressing her fingers to her forehead and now and then darting looks at the icons. Anisim, slightly drunk, would open the door to the kitchen and in a free-and-easy manner say:

"Why are you sitting in here, precious Mama? We miss you."

And Praskovya, overcome with timidity, would press her hands to her thin, wasted bosom and reply:

"Oh, not at all, sir. . . . It's very kind of you, sir. . . ."

After the visit of inspection the wedding day was set. Then Anisim began to walk about the house whistling or, suddenly thinking of something, he would fall into a reverie and stare at the floor with a fixed, penetrating gaze, as though trying to probe the depths of the earth. He expressed neither pleasure that he was to be married—and married soon, the week after Easter—nor a desire to see his bride, but simply whistled. And it was obvious that he was marrying only because his father and stepmother wished it, and because it was the custom in the village: a son married in order to have a woman to help in the house. When he went away he seemed in no hurry, and altogether behaved as he had not done on his previous visits; he was particularly free-and-easy, saying things he ought not to have said.

# III

In the village of Shikalova lived two dressmakers, sisters, who belonged to the Flagellant sect. The new clothes for the wedding had been ordered from them, and they frequently came for fittings and then stayed a long time drinking tea. For Varvara they made a brown dress trimmed with black lace and bugles, and for Aksinya a dress of light green with a yellow bodice and a train. When the dressmakers had finished their work Tsybukin paid them not in money but in goods from the shop, and they went away dejectedly, carrying parcels of candles and sardines, which they did not in the least need, and when they got out of the village and into the fields, they sat down on a knoll and wept.

Anisim arrived three days before the wedding, dressed all in new clothes. He wore dazzling rubber galoshes, and, instead of a necktie, a red cord with little balls on it, and the overcoat he had flung over his shoulders without putting his arms in the sleeves was new too.

After gravely crossing himself before the icon, he greeted his father and gave him ten silver rubles and ten half rubles; to Varvara he gave the same, and to Aksinya twenty quarter rubles. The chief charm of the present lay in the fact that all the coins, as if carefully selected, were new and glittered in the sun. Trying to appear sober and serious, Anisim screwed up his face and puffed out his cheeks, but he smelled of wine; he must have run out to the refreshment bar at every station. And again there was something devil-may-care and out of place about the man. Then he had a bite and drank tea with the old man, and Varvara kept turning the new coins over in her hands as she inquired about the villagers who had gone to live in town.

"They're all right, thanks be to God, they get on well," said Anisim. "Only something happened in Ivan Yegorov's family: his old woman, Sofya Nikiforovna, died. Of consumption. They ordered the memorial dinner for the peace of her soul from the confectioner's at two and a half rubles a head. And there was wine. Some of the peasants—those from our village—paid two and a half rubles, too. And didn't eat a thing. As if a peasant could appreciate sauces!"

"Two and a half rubles!" said the old man, shaking his head.

"And why not? That's no village there. You go into a restaurant to have a snack, you order one thing and another, others join you, you have a drink—and before you know it it's daybreak, and you've each got three or four rubles to pay. And when you're with Samorodov, he likes to finish off with coffee and cognac—and cognac at sixty kopecks a glass."

"He's making it all up," said the old man delightedly. "He's making it all up!"

"I'm always with Samorodov now. It's Samorodov that writes my letters to you. He writes splendidly. And if I were to tell you, Mama," Anisim went on jovially, addressing Varvara, "the sort of fellow Samorodov is, you wouldn't believe me. We call him Mukhtar, because he's like an Armenian—all black. I can see right through him, Mama, I know all his affairs like the five fingers of my hand, and he feels this, he's always following me around, never leaves me alone, and now we're thick as thieves. He seems kind of scared by this, but he can't get along without me. Where I go, he goes. I've got a good, reliable eye, Mama. I see a peasant selling a shirt at the bazaar—'Stop, that shirt was stolen!' And it really turns out to be so: the shirt was stolen."

"But how can you tell?" asked Varvara.

"I just know it, just have an eye for it. I don't know anything about that shirt, but for some reason I'm drawn to it: it's stolen, that's all. The boys in the department have got a saying: 'Well, Anisim has gone snipe hunting!' That means—looking for stolen goods. Yes. . . . Anybody can steal, but it's another thing to hang onto it! It's a big world, but there's no place to hide stolen goods."

"In our village a ram and two ewes were carried off from the Guntorevs' last week," said Varvara with a sigh. "And there is no one to look for them. . . . Tck, tck, tck. . . ."

"Well? I might have a try. I might, I don't mind."

The day of the wedding arrived. It was a cool but bright, cheerful April day. From early morning people were driving about Ukleyevo in carriages drawn by pairs or teams of three horses, with many-colored ribbons on their yokes and manes, and bells jingling. Alarmed by all this activity, the rooks made a racket in the willows, and the starlings sang incessantly, as though rejoicing that there was a wedding at the Tsybukins'!

In the house the tables were already loaded with long fish, smoked hams, stuffed fowls, boxes of sprats, various salt and pickled dishes, and a great many bottles of vodka and wine; there was a smell of smoked sausage and soured lobster. And the old man walked around the tables, tapping his heels and sharpening the knives against one another. They kept calling Varvara, asking for things, and she would run to the kitchen, breathless and distraught, where the man cook from Kostyukov's and the woman cook from the Khrymin Juniors' had been working since dawn. Aksinya, in a corset but no dress, with hair curled and new squeaky high shoes, flew around the yard like a whirlwind, flashing glimpses of bare knees and bosom. There was a hubbub, oaths and the sound of scolding could be heard, and passers-by stopped at the wide open gates, feeling that something extraordinary was about to take place.

"They've gone for the bride!"

A jingling of bells died away far beyond the village. . . . Between two and three o'clock people came running in: again there was the sound of bells: they were bringing the bride! The church was full, the candelabra were lighted, the choir, just as old Tsybukin had wished, was singing from songbooks. Lipa was dazzled by the glare of lights and the bright-colored dresses; she felt as though the loud voices of the singers were pounding on her head like hammers; her high shoes and corset, which she had put on for the first time in her life, pinched her, and her face looked as though she had just come out of a faint—she gazed about her bewildered. Anisim, in a black coat, and the red cord instead of a necktie, stared at one spot lost in thought, and at every loud burst of song, hastily crossed himself. He was moved, and felt like weeping. This church had been familiar to him since early childhood; there was a time when his dead mother had brought him here to take the sacrament; a time when, along with other little boys, he had sung in the choir; every corner, every icon, held memories for him. And here he was being married; he had to take a wife in the natural course of things, but he was not thinking of that now—somehow he had completely forgotten about his wedding. Tears dimmed his eyes and prevented him from seeing the icons, and he felt heavy at heart; he prayed God that the inevitable misfortunes which threatened him, which were ready to burst upon him tomorrow, if not today, might somehow pass by him, as storm clouds in a drought pass over a village without letting fall one drop of rain. But so many sins had already piled up in the past, so many sins, and all so inescapable, so irreparable, that it seemed senseless even to ask for forgiveness. Yet he not only asked forgiveness but uttered a loud sob; no one took any notice, however, assuming that he had drunk too much.

A fretful childish wail was heard:

"Mama, dear, take me away from here, please!"

"Quiet there!" shouted the priest.

Returning from the church, people ran after them; there were crowds, too, around the shop, at the gates, and in the yard under the windows. Peasant women came to sing songs in their honor. The young couple had scarcely crossed the threshold when the choristers, who were already standing in the entry with their songbooks, burst into loud song; a band, ordered specially from the town, commenced playing. Sparkling Don wine was brought in tall glasses, and Yelizarov, the carpenter-contractor, a tall, gaunt old man with eye brows so bushy his eyes could hardly be seen, addressed the young couple:

"Anisim, and you, my child, love one another, lead a godly life, little children, and the Heavenly Mother will not abandon you."

He fell on the old man's shoulder and sobbed.

"Grigory Petrovich, let us weep, let us weep for joy!" he exclaimed in a thin voice, and immediately burst into laughter and went on in a loud bass: "Ho-ho-ho! This one's a fine daughter-in-law for you, too! She's got everything in the right place, it all runs smoothly, nothing creaks, the whole mechanism is in good working order, plenty of screws."

He was a native of the Yegoryev district, but he had worked in the Ukleyevo mills and in the neighborhood since his youth, and had made it his home. For years he had been a familiar figure, just as old, gaunt, and lanky as he was now, and for years he had been called "Crutch." Perhaps because he had done nothing but repair work in the factories for more than forty years he judged everyone and everything by its soundness, by whether it was in need of repair. And before sitting down to the table he tried several chairs to see if they were steady, and he even touched the fish.

After the sparkling wine they all sat down to the table. The guests talked, moving their chairs about. The choristers sang in the entry, and at the same time peasant women were singing in unison in the yard, and there was a frightful, wild medley of sounds which made one's head spin.

Crutch, alternately laughing and crying, twisted about in his chair, nudged his neighbors with his elbows, and prevented people from talking.

"Children, children, children . . ." he muttered rapidly. "Aksinyushka, my dear, Varvarushka, let us all live in peace and harmony, my dear little hatchets. . . ."

He drank little, and now was drunk from only one glass of English bitters. The revolting bitters, made from nobody knows what, stupefied everyone who drank it; they all appeared to be stunned, and tongues commenced to falter.

The local clergy were present, the clerks from the mills with their wives, tradesmen and tavernkeepers from the other villages. The elder and the clerk of the rural district, who had served together for fourteen years, and who during all that time had never signed a single document or let a single person leave the local government office without cheating and insulting him, were now sitting side by side, both gorged and fat, and it seemed as though they were so steeped in treachery that even the skin of their faces had a somewhat peculiar, fraudulent look. The clerk's wife, an emaciated woman with a squint, had brought all her children with her, and, like a bird of prey, looked out of the corner of her eye at the plates and snatched everything she could lay hands on, stuffing it into her own or her children's pockets.

Lipa sat as though turned to stone, still with the same expression she had worn in church. Anisim had not spoken a word to her since making her acquaintance, so that he did not yet know the sound of her voice; and now, sitting beside her and drinking English bitters, he still remained silent, and when he got drunk began talking to her aunt who sat opposite.

"I've got a friend by the name of Samorodov. A very special kind of person. A most respectable-looking citizen, and he knows how to talk. But I can see right through him, Auntie, and he knows it. Let us drink to his health, Auntie!"

Varvara, worn out and distracted, kept walking around the table urging the guests to eat, evidently pleased that there were so many dishes, and all so lavish—no one could disparage them now. The sun had set, but dinner went on; they no longer knew what they were eating or drinking, it was impossible to distinguish what was said, and only now and then, when the music subsided, could some peasant woman outside be heard shouting:

"You've sucked our blood, you tyrants! A plague on you!"

In the evening there was dancing to the band. The Khrymin Juniors arrived, bringing their own wine, and one of them, when dancing a quadrille, held a bottle in each hand and a wineglass in his mouth, which made everyone laugh. In the middle of the quadrille they suddenly bent their knees and danced in a squatting position; Aksinya passed like a flash of green, raising a wind with her train. Someone trod on her flounce and Crutch shouted:

"Hey, they've torn off the baseboard! Children!"

Aksinya had naive gray eyes that rarely blinked, and a naive smile continually played over her face. In those unblinking eyes, in that little head on its long neck, and in her slenderness, there was something snakelike; dressed in green, with her yellow bodice and that smile on her lips, she looked like a viper lifting its head and stretching itself to peer out of the young rye in spring at a passer-by. The Khrymins behaved very freely with her, and it was quite obvious that she had long been on intimate terms with the eldest of them. But her deaf husband saw nothing; he did not look at her, but sat with his legs crossed eating nuts, cracking them so loudly that it sounded like pistol shots.

All at once old Tsybukin himself stepped into the middle of the room and waved a handkerchief as a sign that he, too, wanted to dance the Russian dance, and all through the house and from the crowd in the yard rose a hum of approval.

"It's *himself* has stepped out. *Himself!*"

Varvara danced and the old man merely waved his handkerchief and kicked up his heels, but the people in the yard, pressing against one another to peep in at the windows, were in raptures, and for the moment forgave him everything—his wealth as well as the wrongs he had done them.

"Well done, Grigory Petrovich!" was heard in the crowd. "Go it! You can still do it! Ha-ha!"

It wasn't over till late, after two in the morning. Anisim, staggering, went around taking leave of the singers and musicians, and gave each of them a new half ruble. The old man, still steady on his feet but limping slightly, said to each of his guests as he saw them off:

"The wedding cost me two thousand."

When the party was breaking up someone took the Shikalova innkeeper's good coat instead of his own old one, and Anisim flew into a rage and began shouting:

"Stop! I'll find it at once! I know who stole it! Stop!"

He ran out into the street in pursuit of someone, but was caught and brought back home, and they pushed him, wet, drunk, and red with anger, into the room where the aunt was undressing Lipa, and locked him in.

# IV

Five days had passed. Anisim, who was ready to leave, went upstairs to say good-bye to Varvara. All the icon lamps were burning, there was a smell of incense in the room, and Varvara was sitting at the window knitting a stocking of red wool.

"You haven't stayed with us long," she said. "You found it dull, I suppose. Tck, tck, tck. . . . We live comfortably, we have plenty of everything, and your wedding was celebrated properly, in good style; the old man says it came to two thousand. In fact, we live like merchants, but it is dull here. And we treat people so badly. My heart aches, dear, we treat them so—oh, my goodness! Whether we barter a horse, or buy something, or hire a laborer—it's cheating in everything. Cheating and cheating. The hempseed oil in the shop tastes bitter, it's rancid, the people have pitch that is better. But isn't it possible, tell me, please, couldn't we sell good oil?"

"Every man to his own trade, Mama."

"But we all have to die, don't we? Oh, oh, you really ought to talk to your father . . . !"

"But you could talk to him yourself."

"Come, come! I did put in a word, but he said just what you say: every man to his own trade. In the next world they're not going to consider what trade a man's been put to! God's judgment is just."

"Of course nobody's going to consider it," said Anisim with a sigh. "There is no God anyhow, you know, Mama, so what considering can there be?"

Varvara looked at him in astonishment and, clasping her hands, burst out laughing. Because she was so genuinely surprised at his words and looked at him as if there was something queer about him, he was embarrassed.

"Maybe there is a God, but no faith," he said. "When I was being married I was not myself. Just as when you take an egg from under a hen and there is a chick peeping in it, so my conscience suddenly piped up, and while I was being married I kept thinking: there is a God! But as soon as I got out of church it was over. And, really, how can I tell if there is a God or not? They never taught us that when we were children; while the babe is still at his mother's breast he's taught just one thing: every man to his own trade. Papa doesn't believe in God either. You were saying that Guntorev had some sheep stolen. . . . I found them: it was a Shikalova peasant who stole them; he stole them, but it was Papa who got the fleeces. . . . That's faith for you!"

Anisim winked and shook his head.

"And the elder doesn't believe in God either," he went on, "nor the clerk, nor the sexton. And as for going to church and keeping the fasts, that's only so people won't speak ill of them, and just in case there really might be a Day of Judgment. Nowadays they're talking as if the end of the world had come because people have grown weaker, don't honor their parents, and so on. That's nonsense. The way I see it, Mama, the whole trouble is that there is so little conscience in people. I see through things, Mama, I know. If a man has stolen a shirt, I see it. A man sits in a tavern, and you think he's just drinking tea, nothing more, but the tea is neither here nor there; I see beyond that, I see that he has no conscience. You can walk around like that the whole day and not find a single man with a conscience. And the only reason is that they don't know whether there's a God or not. . . . Well, good-bye, Mama. Keep alive and well, and think kindly of me."

Anisim bowed down at Varvara's feet.

"I thank you for everything, Mama," he said. "You're a great boon to our family. You're a fine woman, and I'm very appreciative."

Moved, Anisim went out; then he came back and said:

"Samorodov has got me mixed up in something. Either I'll get rich or it'll be the end of me. If anything happens, Mama, you must comfort my father."

"Now, now, what are you saying! Tck, tck, tck . . . God is merciful. And, Anisim, you ought to be more affectionate with your wife, instead of giving each other sulky looks as you do; you might smile at least."

"Yes, she's a queer one . . ." said Anisim with a sigh. "She doesn't understand anything, never talks. She's very young, let her grow up."

The large, sleek, white stallion was already harnessed to the chaise and standing at the entrance. Old Tsybukin hopped in and briskly took up the reins. Anisim kissed Varvara, Aksinya, and his brother. Lipa too was standing on the steps; she stood motionless, looking to one side, as though she had come not to see him off but by chance, not knowing why. Anisim went up to her and just barely touched his lips to her cheek.

"Good-bye," he said.

Without looking at him she smiled somewhat strangely; her face began to quiver, and for some reason everyone felt sorry for her. Anisim jumped in and sat arms akimbo, for he considered himself a handsome fellow.

As they drove up out of the ravine, he kept looking back at the village. It was a clear, warm day. The cattle were being driven out for the first time, and young girls and peasant women in holiday dress were walking by the side of the herd. The dun-colored bull bellowed, glad to be free, and pawed the ground with his forefeet. On all sides, above and below, larks were singing. Anisim looked back at the graceful white church—it had recently been whitewashed— and recalled how he had prayed there five days ago; he looked at the school with its green roof, at the little river where he used to bathe and catch fish, and joy stirred in his breast; and he wished that a wall might rise up from the earth and prevent him from going any farther, that he might be left with only the past.

At the station they went into the refreshment bar and each

drank a glass of sherry. The old man reached into his pocket for his purse.

"I'll stand treat!" said Anisim.

Touched, the old man clapped him on the shoulder and winked at the waiter as if to say: "See what a fine son I've got!"

"You ought to stay at home in the business, Anisim," he said, "you'd be worth any price to me! I'd cover you with gold from head to foot, my son."

"Can't be done, Papa."

The sherry was sour and smelled of sealing wax, but they each drank another glass.

When the old man returned from the station, for the first moment he did not recognize his younger daughter-in-law. Her husband had no sooner driven out of the yard than Lipa was transformed and suddenly grew cheerful. Wearing a shabby old skirt, her feet bare, her sleeves tucked up to her shoulders, she was scrubbing the stairs in the entry and singing in a small, silvery voice; and when she carried out a big washtub of dirty water and looked up at the sun with her childish smile, it seemed as though she too were a lark.

An old laborer who was passing by the door shook his head and rasped:

"Yes, indeed, Grigory Petrovich, your daughters-in-law are a blessing from God!" he said. "Not women, but treasures!"


# V


On Friday, the eighth of July, Yelizarov, known as Crutch, and Lipa were returning from the village of Kazanskoe, where they had gone to a service on the occasion of a church holiday in honor of the Holy Mother of Kazan. Far behind them walked Lipa's mother, Praskovya, who kept falling back, as she was ill and short of breath. It was drawing toward evening.

"Aa-ah!" exclaimed Crutch, listening to Lipa in wonder. "Aa-ah! . . . We-ll!"

"I am very fond of jam, Ilya Makarych," said Lipa. "I sit down in my little corner and I'm always drinking tea with jam, or sometimes I drink tea with Varvara Nikolayevna, and she tells me some sad story full of feeling. She has lots of jam—four jars. 'Have some, Lipa,' she says, 'don't hesitate.' "

"Aa-ah! . . . Four jars!"

"They're rich. They have white bread with their tea; and meat, too—as much as you want. They're rich, only I'm scared of them, Ilya Makarych. Oo-oh, I'm so scared!"

"What are you scared of, child?" asked Crutch, as he looked back to see how far behind Praskovya was.

"Right from the first, as soon as the wedding was over, I was afraid of Anisim Grigorich. He didn't do anything, he never hurt me, only when he comes near me, I feel a cold chill all over me, all through my bones. And I didn't sleep a single night, I was trembling all over, and I kept praying to God. And now I'm afraid of Aksinya, Ilya Makarych. It's not that she does anything, she's always laughing, but sometimes she looks out of the window, and her eyes are so angry and they burn with a green light like the eyes of the sheep in the pen. The Khrymin Juniors are leading her astray. 'Your old man,' they say to her, 'has a piece of land at Butyokino, a hundred acres,' they say, 'and there's sand and water on it, so you, Aksinya,' they say to her, 'build a brickyard for yourself, and we'll go shares with you.' Bricks are now twenty rubles a thousand. It's a profitable business. So yesterday at dinner Aksinya says to the old man: 'I want to build a brickyard at Butyokino,' she says, 'I'm going to go into business on my own.' She said it and laughed. But Grigory Petrovich's face got very dark; you could see he didn't like it. 'As long as I live,' he says, 'the family must not break up. We must stay together.' And she gave him a look and ground her teeth. She didn't eat—and there were fritters for dinner!"

"Aa-ah!" Crutch was amazed. "She didn't eat!"

"And tell me, please, when does she sleep?" Lipa went on. "She sleeps for just half an hour, then jumps up and keeps walking and walking around looking to see if the peasants have maybe set fire to something, or stolen something. . . . I'm scared of her, Ilya Makarych! And after the wedding, the Khrymin Juniors didn't even go to bed; they drove into town to go to law with one another; and now folks are saying it's all on account of Aksinya. Two of the brothers promised to build her the brickyard, and the third doesn't like it at all, and their mill has been at a standstill for a month, and my uncle Prokhor is out of work and goes from house to house to pick up a crust. 'You'd better work on the land for the time being, Uncle, or saw wood,' I tell him. 'Why bring shame on yourself?'—'I've got out of the way of it, Lipynka,' he says, 'I don't know how to do peasant work any more.'"

Near a grove of young aspen trees they stopped to rest and to wait for Praskovya. Yelizarov had long been a contractor, but he kept no horse and went on foot all over the district, striding along, swinging his arms, with only a little bag in which there was bread and onions. It was not easy to walk with him.

At the entrance to the grove stood a milestone. Yelizarov put his hand on it to see if it was steady. Praskovya reached them out of breath. Her wrinkled, perpetually frightened face shone with happiness: today she had gone to church, like other people, then she had gone to the fair, and there had drunk pear kvass! This was so rare that it even seemed to her now that on this day, for the first time in her life, she had lived for her own pleasure.

After resting, all three walked along side by side. The sun had gone down and its rays filtered through the grove, lighting up the tree trunks. There was a faint sound of voices ahead. The Ukleyevo girls had gone on long before but had lingered in the grove, probably gathering mushrooms.

"Hey, wenches!" shouted Yelizarov. "Hey, my beauties!"

There was the sound of laughter in response.

"Here comes Crutch! Crutch! The old horseradish!"

An echo laughed back. And then the grove was left behind. The tops of the factory chimneys came into view, the belfry glittered: this was the village, "the one where the sexton ate up all the caviar at the funeral." Now they were almost home; they had only to go down into that big ravine. Lipa and Praskovya, who had been walking barefoot, sat down on the grass to put on their shoes. Yelizarov sat down with them. Looked at from above, Ukleyevo seemed beautiful, peaceful, with its willow trees, its white church, its little river; the only thing that spoiled it was the factory roofs, which, to save money, had been painted a sullen, somber color. Along the slope on the farther side they could see the rye—some in stacks and sheaves, strewn about here and there as though by a storm, some freshly cut, lying in swaths; the oats, too, were ripe and glistened like mother-of-pearl in the sun. It was harvest time. Today was a holiday, tomorrow they would harvest the rye and cart the hay, and then Sunday, a holiday again. Every day there were rumblings of distant thunder; it was sultry and looked like rain, and now, gazing at the fields, everyone was thinking: "God grant we get the harvest in in time," and they felt at once gay and joyful and anxious at heart.

"Mowers get a lot these days," said Praskovya. "A ruble and forty kopecks a day."

People kept coming by from the fair at Kazanskoe; peasant women, mill hands in new caps, beggars, children. . . . Now a cart would drive by raising the dust, an unsold horse running behind it as if it were glad it had not been sold; now a cow, led along by the horns, obstinately resisting, then another cart, filled with drunken peasants dangling their legs. One old woman was leading a little boy in a big cap and big boots; the boy was tired out from the heat and the heavy boots which prevented him from bending his legs at the knees, but he kept blowing with all his might on a toy trumpet; they had gone on down the slope and turned into the street, but the trumpet could still be heard.

"Our millowners are not quite themselves," said Yelizarov. "It's bad! Kostyukov got angry with me. 'Too many battens have gone into the cornices,' he says. 'Too many? As many have gone into them as were needed, Vassily Danilych. I don't eat them with my porridge,' says I. 'How can you speak to me like that?' he says. 'You blockhead, you so-and-so! You'd better not forget yourself! It was I who made a contractor of you,' he yells. 'Well, there's nothing so wonderful in that,' says I. 'I used to drink tea every day even before I was a contractor.'—'You're all crooks,' he says. . . . I held my peace. 'We're the crooks in this world,' thought I, 'and you'll be the crooks in the next.' Ho-ho-ho! The next day he eased off. 'Don't be angry with me for what I said, Makarych,' says he. 'If I went too far, well, don't forget I'm a merchant of the first guild and your superior—you ought to hold your tongue.'—'You're a merchant of the first guild,' says I, 'and I'm a carpenter, that's correct. And Saint Joseph,' says I, 'was a carpenter too. Ours is a righteous, a godly calling, and if,' says I, 'it pleases you to be my superior, then go right ahead, and welcome, Vassily Danilych.' And later on—after that conversation I mean—I was thinking: now which one is superior? A merchant of the first guild or a carpenter? Why, the carpenter, of course, children!"

Crutch thought for a minute and added:

"That's how it is, children. He who works, he who has patience, is superior."

By now the sun had set and a thick mist, white as milk, was rising over the river, in the church close, and in the clearings around the mills. Now, when darkness was rapidly descending, and lights glimmered below, when it seemed as though the mists were hiding a fathomless abyss, Lipa and her mother, who had been born in poverty and were prepared to live so to the end, giving to others everything except their frightened, gentle souls, may perhaps have fancied for a moment that in this vast, mysterious world, among the endless procession of lives, they too counted for something, they too were superior to someone; they liked sitting up there, and smiled happily, forgetting that, after all, they had to go below again.

At last they reached home. The mowers were sitting on the ground at the gates near the shop. As a rule the Ukleyevo peasants would not work for Tsybukin and he had to hire strangers, and now there seemed to be men with long black beards sitting in the darkness. The shop was open and through the door they could see the deaf man playing checkers with a boy. The men were singing softly, almost inaudibly, or were loudly demanding their wages for the previous day, but they were not paid for fear they should go away before morning. Old Tsybukin, in a waistcoat but no coat, was sitting under the birch tree near the entrance drinking tea with Aksinya; a lighted lamp stood on the table.

"Hey, Grandpa!" one of the mowers cried tauntingly from outside the gates. "Pay us half, anyway! Hey, Grandpa!"

And at once laughter was heard, and again the almost inaudible singing. . . . Crutch sat down to have tea.

"So, we've been to the fair," he said, and began telling them about it. "We had a fine time, children, a very fine time, praise be to God. But an unfortunate thing happened: Sashka the blacksmith bought some tobacco and he gave a half ruble, you see, to the merchant. And the half ruble was no good——" Crutch went on, meaning to speak in a whisper, but speaking in a thick, husky voice that everyone could hear. "The half ruble turned out to be counterfeit. They asked him where he got it. 'Anisim Tsybukin gave it to me,' he says. 'When I was at his wedding,' he says. . . . They called the policeman and took the man away. . . . Watch out, Petrovich, that nothing comes of it, no talk. . . ."

"Grandpa!" came the same taunting voice from outside the gates. "Gra-andpa!"

A silence followed.

"Ah, children, children, children . . ." Crutch rapidly muttered and got up; he was overcome with drowsiness. "Well, thanks for the tea, and for the sugar, children. Time to sleep. I'm beginning to molder, my beams have rotted away. Ho-ho-ho!"

As he walked away he said, "I suppose it's time I was dead." And he gave a sob.

Old Tsybukin did not finish his tea, but just sat there thinking; and his face looked as though he were listening to the footsteps of Crutch, who by now was far down the street.

"Sashka the blacksmith was lying, I expect," said Aksinya, surmising his thoughts.

He went into the house and came back shortly with a parcel; he opened it and there was the glitter of rubles—brand-new ones. He took one, tested it with his teeth, and flung it down on the tray; then he tried another and flung it down. . . .

"The rubles really are counterfeit," he declared, looking at Aksinya completely at a loss. "These are the ones . . . Anisim brought us, his present. Take them, daughter," he whispered, thrusting the parcel into her hands, "you take them and throw them into the well. . . . Away with them! And mind there's no talk of it lest something happen. . . . Take away the samovar, put out the light."

Sitting in the shed, Lipa and Praskovya watched the lights go out one after the other; only upstairs in Varvara's room the blue and red icon lamps continued to gleam, and a feeling of peace, contentment, and innocence seemed to emanate from there. Praskovya never could get used to her daughter's being married to a rich man, and when she came to the house she timidly huddled in the entry with a supplicating smile on her face, and tea and sugar were sent out to her. Lipa could not get used to it either, and after her husband left she no longer slept in her bed, but lay down wherever she happened to be—in the kitchen or in the shed—and every day she scrubbed floors or washed clothes, and felt as though she were hired by the day. And now, after coming back from the church service, they had tea in the kitchen with the cook, then went to the shed and lay down on the

floor between the sledge and the wall. It was dark there and
smelled of harness. The lights around the house went out;
they heard the deaf man locking up the shop and the mowers
settling down in the yard to sleep. In the distance, at the
Khrymin Juniors', they were playing their expensive accordion. . . . Praskovya and Lipa soon dropped off to
sleep.

And when they were awakened by footsteps, it was bright
moonlight; at the entrance to the shed stood Aksinya, her
bedding in her arms.

"Maybe it's cooler here," she said; she came in and lay
down almost in the doorway, and the moonlight fell full
upon her.

She did not sleep, but breathed heavily, tossing from side
to side with the heat and throwing off almost all the bedclothes—and in the bewitching light of the moon, what a
beautiful, proud animal she was! A little time passed, and
again footsteps were heard: the old man appeared, all white
in the doorway.

"Aksinya!" he called. "Are you here?"

"Well?" she replied angrily.

"I told you to throw that money into the well. Did you do
it?"

"What an idea—throwing your property into the water! I
gave it to the mowers. . . ."

"Oh, my God!" cried the old man, alarmed and dumfounded. "You wicked woman. . . . Oh, my God!"

He clasped his hands in dismay and went out, still talking as he walked away.

A little later Aksinya sat up, heaved a sigh of vexation,
and, gathering up her bedclothes, went out.

"Why did you marry me into this family, Mama?"

"You have to be married, daughter. That's how things
are."

A feeling of inconsolable woe almost overwhelmed them.
But it seemed to them that someone was looking down from
high heaven, out of the blue where the stars were, seeing
all that went on in Ukleyevo and watching over them. And
no matter how great the evil, the night was beautiful and
still, and everything on earth was only waiting to be made

one with righteousness, even as the moonlight was one with the night.

And, comforted, they huddled close to each other and fell asleep.

# VI

A long time had passed since the news came that Anisim had been put in prison for making and passing counterfeit money. Months went by, more than half a year; the long winter was over, spring came, and everyone in the house and village had grown used to the fact that Anisim was in prison. And when anyone passed by the house or the shop at night, he would remember that Anisim was in prison; when the bell tolled in the graveyard, for some reason they were also reminded that he was sitting in prison awaiting trial.

A shadow seemed to have fallen upon the house. It looked more somber, the roof had grown rusty, the green paint on the heavy, iron-studded shop door had faded, or, as the deaf man expressed it, "hardened"; and the old man himself seemed to have grown dingy. He gave up cutting his hair and beard and looked shaggy; he no longer sprang into his tarantass nor shouted "God will provide" to beggars. That his strength was waning was apparent in everything he did. People were less afraid of him; the police officer, though he still received his customary bribe, drew up a charge against the shop; three times the old man had been summoned to town to be tried for the illicit sale of spirits, but each time the case was deferred owing to the failure of witnesses to appear, and he was worn out.

He often went to see his son, and was continually hiring someone, submitting a petition, donating a banner; he presented the warden of the prison in which Anisim was confined with a long spoon and a silver holder for a tea glass with the inscription: "The soul knows moderation."

"There is no one, no one to intercede for us," said Varvara. "Tck, tck, tck. . . . You should ask some of the gentry to write to the head officials. . . . At least they might let him out on bail! Why should the poor fellow languish in prison?"

She too was grieved; nevertheless she grew stouter and

whiter. She lighted the icon lamps as before, saw that everything in the house was clean, and regaled the guests with jam and apple confection. The deaf man and Aksinya looked after the shop. They had undertaken a new business—a brickyard in Butyokino—and Aksinya went there almost every day in the tarantass; she drove herself, and when she passed an acquaintance she stretched her neck like a snake in the young rye, smiling naively, enigmatically. And Lipa spent her time playing with the baby which had been born to her before Lent. It was a tiny little baby, thin and pitiful, and it seemed strange that he should look about, cry, and be considered a human being—and even be called Nikifor. He lay in his cradle and Lipa would walk toward the door and say, bowing to him:

"Good day, Nikifor Anisimych!"

And she would rush at him and kiss him. Again she would walk to the door, bow, and say:

"Good day, Nikifor Anisimych!"

And he kicked up his little red legs, and his crying was mixed with laughter, like the carpenter Yelizarov's.

At last the day of the trial was set. The old man went away some five days in advance. They heard that the peasants called as witnesses had been sent for; their old workman, who had received a summons to appear, also left.

The trial was on Thursday. But Sunday passed and still Tsybukin was not back, and there was no news. On Tuesday toward evening Varvara was sitting at the open window listening for the sound of her husband's return. In the next room Lipa was playing with her baby. She would toss him up in her arms and say with delight:

"You will grow up to be big, so-oo big! You'll be a peasant and we'll go out and work by the day together! We'll go out and work by the day!"

"Come, now!" said Varvara, taking umbrage. "Go out to work by the day—what an idea, you little silly! He'll be a merchant, of course!"

Lipa went on singing in a soft voice, but a moment later she had forgotten and began again:

"You'll grow up to be big, so-oo big! You'll be a peasant, and we'll go out and work by the day together!"

"Well, now! She's at it again!"

Lipa, with Nikifor in her arms, stood in the doorway and asked:

"Maminka, why do I love him so? Why am I so sorry for him?" she continued, her voice trembling and her eyes glistening with tears. "Who is he? What is he like? He's light as a feather, or a little crumb, but I love him, love him like a real person. Here he can do nothing, he can't even talk, but I can tell by his little eyes what he wants."

Varvara pricked up her ears; the sound of the evening train coming into the station reached her. Had the old man come? She did not hear nor heed what Lipa was saying, she was unaware of the time passing and trembled all over, not with dread but with intense curiosity. She saw a cart filled with peasants rapidly clatter by. It was the witnesses coming from the station. When the cart passed the shop the old workman jumped out and walked into the yard, where she heard him being greeted and questioned. . . .

"Deprived of rights and all property," he said loudly, "and six years' penal servitude in Siberia."

She saw Aksinya come out of the shop by the back way; she had just been selling kerosene, and was holding a bottle in one hand and a funnel in the other, and there were some silver coins in her mouth.

"Where's Papa?" she asked, lisping.

"At the station," answered the workman. " 'When it gets darker,' he said, 'then I'll come.' "

And when it became known throughout the household that Anisim had been sentenced to penal servitude, the cook in the kitchen suddenly began to wail as though at a funeral, thinking that this was required by the proprieties:

"Who will care for us now you have gone, Anisim Grigorych, our bright falcon. . . ?"

The dogs commenced barking in alarm. Varvara ran to the window, rushing about in her distress, and shouted at the cook with all her might, straining her voice:

"Stop it, Stepanida, stop it! Don't plague us, for Christ's sake!"

They forgot to set the samovar; they were unable to think of anything. Lipa alone could not make out what it was all about and went on playing with her baby.

When the old man arrived from the station they asked him no questions. He greeted them, then walked through the house in silence; he ate no supper.

"There was no one to see to things . . ." Varvara began when they were alone. "I said you should ask some of the gentry, but you wouldn't listen to me then. . . . A petition would——"

"I saw to things!" said the old man with a gesture of despair. "When Anisim was sentenced I went to the gentleman who was defending him. 'It's no use now,' he said, 'it's too late.' And Anisim said the same: too late. But all the same, when I came out of court, I made an arrangement with a lawyer, gave him an advance. I'll wait a week, then I'll go back again. It is as God wills."

Once more the old man walked through all the rooms in silence, and when he went back to Varvara he said:

"I must be sick. My head is in a sort of . . . fog. My thoughts are hazy."

He closed the door so that Lipa could not hear him and went on in a low voice:

"I'm worried about the money. Do you remember, before his wedding, on St. Thomas's Day, Anisim brought me some new rubles and half rubles? One parcel I put away at the time, but the others I mixed with my own money. . . . When my uncle Dmitri Filatych—may the kingdom of heaven be his—was still alive, he used to go to Moscow and the Crimea to buy goods. He had a wife, and this wife—when he was away, that is,—used to take up with other men. She had half a dozen children. And when my uncle had had a drop too much he'd start laughing: 'I can't make out,' he would say, 'which are my children and which are other people's.' —An easygoing nature, to be sure. And in the same way, I can't make out which of my rubles are real and which are false. And they all seem false to me."

"Come now, what are you saying!"

"I buy a ticket at the station, I give the man three rubles, and I keep thinking they're counterfeit. And it scares me. I must be sick."

"There's no denying it, we're all in God's hands. . . . Tck, tck, tck . . ." said Varvara, shaking her head. "You ought to think about that, Petrovich. . . . One can never be sure what might happen, you're not a young man. See that they don't wrong your grandchild when you're dead and gone. Oh, I'm afraid they will wrong Nikifor, I'm afraid they will! He's as good as fatherless now, and his mother is young and foolish. . . . You ought to settle something on him, poor little boy—the land at Butyokino, at least; really, Petrovich, you should! Think about it." Varvara went on to persuade him. "He's such a pretty little boy, it's a shame! Now, you go tomorrow and make out a deed. Why put it off?"

"I'd forgotten about my grandson . . ." said Tsybukin. "I must go and see him. So, you say the boy's all right? Well then, let him grow up. Please God!"

He opened the door and crooked his finger, beckoning to Lipa. She went to him with the baby in her arms.

"If there is anything you want, Lipynka, ask for it," he said. "And eat whatever you like, we don't grudge it, just so you keep healthy. . . ." He made the sign of the cross over the baby. "And take care of my little grandson. My son is gone, but I still have my grandson."

The tears rolled down his cheeks; he sobbed and went out. Soon afterward he went to bed and, after seven sleepless nights, slept soundly.

# VII

The old man went to town for a short time. Someone told Aksinya that he had gone to the notary to make his will, and that he was leaving Butyokino, the very place where she had set up her brickyard, to his grandson Nikifor. She was informed of this in the morning when the old man and Varvara were sitting under the birch tree near the entrance drinking their tea. She locked up the shop, front and back, gathered up all the keys she had, and flung them at the old man's feet.

"I won't work for you any more!" she shouted in a loud voice, and suddenly broke into sobs. "It seems I'm not your daughter-in-law, but a servant! Everyone's laughing at me: 'See what a servant the Tsybukins have found for themselves!' they all say. I didn't hire myself out to you! I'm not a beggar, I'm not some kind of wench, I have a father and mother!"

Without wiping away her tears, she fixed her streaming eyes, vindictive and screwed up with anger, on the old man; her face and neck were tense and red, and she shouted at the top of her voice.

"I don't intend to go on slaving for you!" she continued. "I'm worn out! When it's a matter of work, of sitting in the shop day after day and sneaking out at night for vodka—then it's my share, but when it's giving away land—it's for that convict's wife and that demon of hers! She's mistress here, she's the lady, and I'm her servant! Give her everything, that convict's wife, and may it choke her! I'm going home! Find yourselves another fool, you damned bloodsuckers!"

Never in his life had the old man scolded or punished his children, and it was inconceivable to him that anyone in his family could speak to him rudely or behave disrespectfully, and now he was very much frightened; he ran into the house and hid behind a cupboard. Varvara was so dumfounded she could not get up from her seat, and only waved her hands about as though warding off a bee.

"Oh, Holy Saints! What is the meaning of this?" she muttered in horror. "What is it she's shouting? Tck, tck, tck. . . . People will hear! Do be quiet. . . . Oh, do be quiet!"

"You've given Butyokino to the convict's wife," Aksinya went on screaming; "give her everything now, I don't want anything from you! You can go to the devil! You're all a gang of thieves here! I've seen enough, I'm fed up! You've robbed people coming and going, you brigands, you rob young and old alike! And who's been selling vodka without a license? And the counterfeit money—you've stuffed your coffers with counterfeit money, and now you don't need me any longer!"

By now a crowd had assembled at the open gate and people were staring into the yard.

"Let them look!" bawled Aksinya. "I'll disgrace you! I'll make you burn with shame! You'll crawl at my feet! Hey, Stepan!" she called to the deaf man. "We're going home this very instant! We'll go to my father and mother, I don't want to live with convicts! Get ready!"

Clothes were hanging on lines stretched across the yard; she snatched her still wet petticoats and blouses and flung them into the deaf man's arms. Then, in her fury, she dashed through the yard and tore down everything, throwing what was not hers onto the ground and trampling on it.

"Oh, Holy Saints, make her be quiet!" moaned Varvara. "What is she, anyhow? Give her Butyokino! Give it to her, for Christ's sake!"

"Well! Wh-at a woman!" people were saying at the gate. "Now, that's a wo-man! She really let go—terrific!"

Aksinya ran into the kitchen where the washing was being done. Lipa was washing alone, the cook having gone to the river to rinse the clothes. Steam rose from the trough and from a caldron on the side of the stove, and the air was thick and stifling. There was a heap of unwashed clothing on the floor and Nikifor, kicking up his little legs, lay on a bench beside it, so that if he fell he should not hurt himself. Just as Aksinya came into the kitchen Lipa picked a chemise of hers out of the heap, put it into the trough, and reached for a bucket of boiling hot water that stood on the table.

"Give it here!" cried Aksinya, looking at her with hatred as she snatched her chemise out of the trough. "What right have you to touch my clothes! You're a convict's wife, and you ought to know what you are, and know your place!"

Lipa, taken aback, gazed at her in bewilderment, when suddenly she caught the look Aksinya turned upon the child; she understood instantly and went numb all over. . . .

"You've taken my land, so take this!" and seizing the bucket of boiling hot water Aksinya threw it over Nikifor.

There was a scream such as never before had been heard in Ukleyevo, and no one would have believed that a weak little creature like Lipa could scream like that. It was suddenly silent in the yard. Aksinya walked into the house without a word, but the naive smile was on her lips as before. . . . The deaf man kept walking around the yard with his arms full of clothes, then he began hanging them up again, silently and without haste. And until the cook came back from the river, no one could bring himself to go into the kitchen and see what had happened.

# VIII

Nikifor was taken to the district hospital, and there toward evening, he died. Lipa did not wait for them to come for her, but wrapped the dead baby in his little blanket and carried him home.

The hospital, a new one with large windows, stood high on a hill; it blazed in the sun, looking as if it were on fire inside. There was a hamlet below; Lipa went down the road and before reaching it sat down by a little pond. A woman brought a horse to water but the horse would not drink.

"What more do you want?" said the woman in a low voice, perplexed. "What is it you want?"

A boy in a red shirt, sitting at the water's edge, was washing his father's boots. And there was not another soul to be seen either in the hamlet or on the hill.

"It's not drinking. . . ." said Lipa, gazing at the horse.

Then the woman with the horse and the boy with the boots walked away, and now there was no one to be seen. The sun went to sleep, covering itself with cloth of gold and purple, and long clouds of crimson and lilac stretched across the sky, guarding its rest. Somewhere in the distance a bittern cried, a hollow, melancholy sound, as of a cow shut up in a barn. Every spring they heard the cry of that mysterious bird, but nobody knew what it was like or where it lived. On the hill by the hospital, in the bushes at the edge of the pond, and in the surrounding fields the nightingales warbled. The cuckoo kept counting up somebody's years, then losing count and commencing all over again. In the pond the frogs angrily called to one another, exerting themselves to the utmost, and it was even possible to make out the words: "That's what you are! That's what you are!" What a racket there was! It seemed as though all those creatures were shouting and singing on purpose so that no one should sleep on this spring evening, so that all, even the angry frogs, might appreciate and enjoy every minute: life, after all, is given but once!

A silver half-moon shone in the sky, and there were many stars. Lipa had no idea how long she sat by the pond, but when she got up to go everyone in the little village was asleep and there was not a single light. It was probably a walk of about twelve versts home, but she had not the strength, she could not think how to get there; the moon gleamed now in front of her, now on the right, and the same cuckoo kept calling in a voice grown hoarse but with a chuckle in it, as though teasing her: Oh, watch out, you'll lose your way! Lipa walked rapidly; she lost the kerchief from her head. . . . Looking up at the heavens, she wondered where the soul of her baby was now: was it following her, or floating up there among the stars, no longer thinking of its mother? Oh, how lonely it is in the fields at night, in the midst of that singing when you yourself cannot sing, in the midst of those ceaseless cries of joy, when you yourself cannot be joyful, when the moon, which cares not whether it is spring or winter, whether men live or die, looks down, lonely too. . . . It is hard to be without people when the soul grieves. If only her mother Praskovya, or Crutch, or the cook, or some peasant were with her!

"Boo-oo!" cried the bittern. "Boo-oo!"

Suddenly there was the distinct sound of human speech: "Hitch up, Vavila!"

Ahead of her a campfire burned by the wayside; the flames had died down, only the embers glowed red. She could hear horses munching. In the darkness she made out two carts—one with a barrel on it, the other, a lower one, piled with sacks—and the figures of two men: one leading a horse to put it into the shafts, the other standing motionless by the fire with his hands behind his back. A dog growled near the carts. The man who was leading the horse stopped and said:

"Someone seems to be coming down the road."

"Quiet, Sharik," the other man shouted to the dog.

And from the voice one could tell that he was an old man. Lipa stopped and said:

"God be with you!"

The old man went up to her and after a pause replied: "Good evening!"

"Your dog won't bite, Grandfather?"

"No, come along, he won't touch you."

"I have been at the hospital," Lipa said, then after a moment's silence: "My little son died there. Now I am taking him home."

It must have been unpleasant for the old man to hear this, for he moved away, hurriedly saying:

"Never mind, my dear. It's God's will." Then, to his companion: "You're dawdling, my lad! Look alive!"

"Your yoke isn't here," said the young man. "I don't see it."

"That's just like you, Vavila!"

The old man picked up an ember, blew on it—only his eyes and nose were lighted up—then, when they had found the yoke, he went over to Lipa with the light and looked at her; and his look expressed compassion and tenderness.

"You're a mother," he said. "Every mother grieves for her child."

And he sighed, shaking his head as he spoke. Vavila threw

something on the fire, stamped on it, and instantly it grew very dark; everything vanished, nothing remained but the fields, the sky with the stars, the clamor of birds keeping one another from sleep. And the corncrake called, it seemed, from the very place where the fire had been.

But a minute passed and the two carts, the old man, and the lanky Vavila became visible again. The carts creaked as they moved out onto the road.

"Are you holy men?" Lipa asked the old man.

"No. We're from Firsanova."

"You looked at me just now and my heart was eased. And the young man is gentle. I thought: they must be holy men."

"Have you far to go?"

"To Ukleyevo."

"Get in, we'll take you along as far as Kuzmenki. From there you go straight ahead, and we turn left."

Vavila got into the cart with the barrel, and the old man and Lipa got into the other one. They moved at a walking pace, Vavila in front.

"My little son was in torment the whole day," said Lipa. "He looked at me with his little eyes, not making a sound; he wanted to say something, but he couldn't. Holy Father! Queen of Heaven! I kept falling down on the floor by the bedside. Tell me, Grandfather, why should a little one be tormented before his death? When a grown-up person, a man or a woman, is in torment, his sins are forgiven, but why a little one, when he has no sins? Why?"

"Who can tell?" replied the old man.

They rode on in silence for half an hour.

"We can't know everything, why and how," said the old man. "A bird is not given four wings but two, because it can fly with two; and a man is not given to know everything, but only a half or a quarter. As much as he needs to know in order to live, so much he knows."

"I'd be easier going on foot, Grandfather. Now my heart is all of a tremble."

"Never mind. Sit still."

The old man yawned and made the sign of the cross over his mouth.

"Never mind," he repeated. "Your sorrow is not the worst of sorrows. Life is long, there is good and bad yet to come, there is everything yet to come. Great is Mother Russia!" he said, and he looked around on all sides of him. "I have been all over Russia, I've seen everything in her, and you can believe what I say, my dear. There will be good and there will be bad. I went as a scout from my village to Siberia, and I've been to the Amur River, and the Altai Mountains, and I settled in Siberia; I worked the land there, then I got homesick for Mother Russia and I came back to my native village. We came back to Russia on foot; and I remember we went on a ferry; I was thin as thin can be, all ragged, barefoot, freezing, and gnawing on a crust, and some gentleman traveler who was on the boat—the kingdom of heaven be his if he's dead now—looked at me with pity and tears in his eyes. 'Ah,' he said, 'your bread is black, your days are black. . . .' And when I got back I was without house or home, as they say; I had a wife, but I left her in Siberia, buried there. So, I live as a farm hand. Well, now, I can tell you: since then things have been good, things have been bad. And I don't want to die, my dear, I'd be glad to live another twenty years; so that means there has been more of the good. Great is Mother Russia!" he said, again looking around him.

"Grandfather, when a person dies, how many days does his soul walk the earth?" Lipa asked.

"Now, who can tell! Let's ask Vavila here, he went to school. They teach them everything these days. Vavila!" the old man called.

"Aye?"

"Vavila, when a person dies, how many days does his soul walk the earth?"

Vavila stopped the horse before answering.

"Nine days. When my uncle Kirilla died, his soul lived in our hut for thirteen days."

"How do you know?"

"For thirteen days there was a knocking in the stove."

"Well, all right. Go on," said the old man, and it was obvious that he did not believe a word of it.

Near Kuzmenki the carts turned into the highway and Lipa walked on straight ahead. By now it was growing light. As she went down into the ravine the Ukleyevo huts and the church were hidden in mist. It was cold, and it seemed to her that that same cuckoo still was calling.

When she reached home the cattle had not yet been driven out; everyone was asleep. She sat down on the steps and waited. The old man was the first to come out; he realized at a glance what had happened, and for a long time was unable to utter a word and only smacked his lips.

"Ech!, Lipa," he said, "you didn't take care of my grandson. . . ."

Varvara was awakened. Clasping her hands she broke into sobs and immediately began laying out the baby.

"And he was such a pretty child . . ." she said. "Tck, tck, tck. . . . only the one child, and you failed to take care of him, you silly girl. . . ."

There was a requiem service in the morning and in the evening. He was buried the next day, and after the funeral the guests and the priests ate so much and with such greed that it might be thought they had not tasted food for some time. Lipa waited at table, and the priest said to her, as he lifted his fork with a salted mushroom on it:

"Don't grieve for the babe. For of such is the kingdom of heaven."

And only when they had all left did Lipa fully realize that there was no Nikifor and never would be, and she broke into sobs. But she did not know what room she ought to go into to cry, for she felt that now that her child was dead there was no place for her in the house, that she had no reason to be there, and was in the way; and the others felt this too.

"What are you wailing for?" Aksinya shouted, suddenly appearing in the door; because of the funeral she was dressed in new clothes and had powdered her face. "Shut up!"

Lipa tried to stop but could not, and her sobbing grew louder.

"Do you hear?" screamed Aksinya, stamping her foot in her rage. "Who is it I'm speaking to? Get out of this house and don't you set foot here again, you convict's wife! Get out!"

"There, there, there," the old man spluttered. "Aksinya, don't make such a fuss, my dear. . . . It's only natural she's crying . . . her child is dead. . . ."

"It's only natural," Aksinya mimicked him. "Let her stay the night, and then don't let me see a trace of her here tomorrow! . . . Only natural!" she mimicked again, and bursting into laughter she went into the shop.

Early the next morning Lipa went off to her mother in Torguyevo.

# IX

The roof and the front door of the shop have now been repainted and are as bright as new, gay geraniums bloom in the windows as of old, and all that took place at the Tsybukins' three years ago is almost forgotten.

The old man, Grigory Petrovich, is considered the master, as before, but in reality everything has passed into Aksinya's hands; she buys and sells, and nothing can be done without her consent. The brickyard goes well, and as bricks are needed for the railway, the price has gone up to twenty-four rubles a thousand; peasant women and girls cart the bricks to the station and load them onto cars, and for this they earn a quarter-ruble a day.

Aksinya has gone into partnership with the Khrymins, and the factory is now called Khrymin Junior and Co. They have opened a tavern near the station and now the expensive accordion is played not at the factory but at the tavern, and the postmaster, who is also engaged in some sort of trade, often goes there, as does the stationmaster. The Khrymin Juniors have presented the deaf man with a watch, which he is constantly taking out of his pocket and holding to his ear.

In the village they say of Aksinya that she has acquired great power; and it is true that when she drives to her brickyard in the morning, handsome, happy, the naive smile on her lips, and later when she is giving orders in the factory, her great power can be felt. Everyone is afraid of her in the house, in the village, and in the factory. When she goes into the post office the postmaster jumps to his feet and says to her:

"Be so good as to sit down, Ksenya Abramovna!"

A certain landowner, an elderly dandy in a sleeveless coat of fine cloth and high patent-leather boots, sold her a horse, and was so carried away by his conversation with her that he lowered the price to suit her. He held her hand a long time and, gazing into her merry, sly, naive eyes, said:

.   "I'd do anything for a woman like you, Ksenya Abramovna. Just tell me when we can meet where no one will disturb us."

"Why, whenever you like!"

Since then the elderly dandy drops into the shop every day to drink beer. And the beer is dreadful, bitter as wormwood. The landowner shakes his head, but drinks it. Old Tsybukin no longer takes part in the business. He does not handle any money because he cannot tell good coins from bad, but he keeps silent, never mentioning this weakness to anyone. He has grown forgetful, and if he is not given food he does not ask for it; they have grown used to having dinner without him, and Varvara often says:

"Yesterday he went to bed again without supper."

And she says it unconcernedly because she is used to it. For some reason, summer and winter alike he wears a fur coat, and it is only on very hot days that he does not go out but sits in the house. As a rule he wraps himself up in his fur coat, turns up the collar, and wanders about the village, along the road to the station, or sits from morning till evening on a bench near the church gates. He sits there without stirring. Passers-by bow to him, but he does not respond, disliking the peasants as of old. If he is asked anything he answers quite rationally and politely, but briefly.

There is talk in the village that his daughter-in-law has turned him out of his own house and gives him nothing to eat, and that he seems to live on charity: some people are glad, others are sorry for him.

Varvara has grown even fatter and whiter and, as before, is occupied with good works; Aksinya does not interfere with her. Now there is so much jam that they cannot eat it all before a new crop of berries comes in; it goes to sugar and Varvara is almost in tears, not knowing what to do with it.

They have begun to forget about Anisim. Some time ago a letter came from him, written in verse on a large sheet of paper that looked like a petition, still in the same handwriting. Evidently his friend Samorodov is serving time with him. Under the verses in an execrable, barely legible scrawl there was the single line: "I am ill all the time here, I am miserable, help me, for Christ's sake!"

One day—it was a fine autumn day toward evening—old Tsybukin was sitting near the church gates with the collar of his fur coat turned up so that only his nose and the peak of his cap were visible. At the other end of the long bench sat the contractor Yelizarov, and beside him Yakov the school watchman, a toothless old man of seventy. Crutch and the watchman were talking.

"Children ought to give food and drink to the old. . . . Honor thy father and mother . . ." Yakov was saying fretfully, "but she, this daughter-in-law, has turned her father-in-law out of his own house; the old man is given neither food nor drink—where can he go? It's three days now that he hasn't eaten."

"Three days!" exclaimed Crutch in amazement.

"There he sits, not saying a word. He's grown weak. And why be silent? He ought to bring an action against her—they wouldn't commend her in court."

"Commend who?" asked Crutch, not catching what he had said.

"What?"

"The woman's all right, she does her best. In their business they can't get along without that . . . without sin, that is. . . ."

"Out of his own house," Yakov went on fretfully. "Save up and buy your own house, then you can turn people out of it. A fine one she is! A p-lague!"

Tsybukin listened and did not stir.

"Your own house or another's, it's all one, so long as it's warm and the women don't scold . . ." said Crutch, and he laughed. "When I was young I was very attached to my Nastasya. She was a quiet little woman. It always used to be: 'Buy a house, Makarych! Buy a house, Makarych! Buy a house, Makarych!' She was dying, but she kept saying: 'Buy yourself a racing droshky, Makarych, so you won't have to walk.' And I only bought gingerbread for her, nothing more."

"Her husband's deaf and stupid," continued Yakov, not listening to Crutch, "stupid as can be, just like a goose. Does he understand anything? Hit a goose on the head with a stick —and even then it doesn't understand."

Crutch got up to go back home to the factory. Yakov also got up and they went off together, still talking. When they had gone fifty paces old Tsybukin got up and shuffled after them, walking uncertainly as though on slippery ice.

The village was already sunk in twilight, the sun shone only on the upper part of the road which ran snakelike up the slope. Old women were coming back from the woods, the children with them; they carried baskets of mushrooms. Peasant women and girls came in a crowd from the station where they had been loading the cars with bricks, their noses and the skin under their eyes covered with red brick dust. They were singing. Ahead of them all walked Lipa, gazing up at the sky and singing in a high voice that broke into trills of exultation, as though she were celebrating the fact that the day, praise God, was over, and the time for rest had come. In the crowd, walking with a bundle in her arms, and breathing as always with difficulty, was her mother Praskovya, who went out to work by the day.

"Good evening, Makarych!" said Lipa, catching sight of Crutch. "Good evening, my dear!"

"Good evening, Lipynka!" said Crutch delighted. "Women, girls, love the rich carpenter! Ho-ho! Children, my little children!" (Crutch sobbed.) "My dear little hatchets!"

Crutch and Yakov walked on and could still be heard talking. After them came old Tsybukin and there was a sudden hush in the crowd. Lipa and Praskovya had fallen behind and when the old man was abreast of them, Lipa bowed low and said:

"Good evening, Grigory Petrovich!"

Her mother also bowed. The old man stopped and looked at them both without a word; his lips quivered and his eyes were full of tears. Lipa took a piece of buckwheat pie out of her mother's bundle and gave it to him. He took it and began eating.

By now the sun had set; its glow died away on the road above. It grew dark and cool. Lipa and Praskovya walked on, and for a long time they kept crossing themselves.

1900

# AFTERWORD

Anton Chekhov wrote these stories between 1888 and 1900, years of full artistic maturity, when his fame was secure, when he had begun to write the great plays which crowned his too brief career. He died of tuberculosis in 1904 at the age of forty-four.

In the years between 1880 and 1886, when Chekhov wrote for the gutter weeklies in Moscow and St. Petersburg to support his parents, brothers, and sister, he turned out hundreds of jokes, cartoon captions, mock advertisements, gossip columns, ironic sketches, and harsh little stories about unfaithful spouses, crooked dentists, pompous actors—the full range of vaudeville types. Four of the eleven volumes of creative work in his *Complete Collected Works* (Moscow, 1944–1951) are filled with the output of these years. In 1886, when the guardians of taste recognized him as a writer of unmistakable—if misdirected—gifts, he continued to work at the same hell-rate of production. One hundred ten stories were written and published that year, and half of them were good enough in his own mature judgment to be included in the *Collected Works* he published in 1900.

The many fine stories he produced in this outburst are some of the best known and most anthologized in the West. They are, for the most part, short, spare, swift, brilliantly indirect in statement, ironic in tone, free of unearned emotion and vaudeville cynicism. But a tendentious selection among them—stories like "Vanka" and "Grief," for example —has contributed to a misleading view of Chekhov's sensibility. This view was first formulated by admiring compatriots, including Gorky and Stanislavsky, and was carried abroad by sentimental *emigrés* and institutionalized by uncritical admirers in the West. The subtitle of Nina Toumanova's book, *The Voice of Twilight Russia,* epitomizes all that is wrong and soft-headed in this stereotype. We are asked to

379

look on Chekhov as the wise observer of human "foibles," combining wry humor with an all-forgiving pity: his tender, ephemeral "mood pieces" capture the flutterings of the human soul and gently exhort his fellow man to live better than he does. And we are badly served by recent Russian criticism, which now tells us that he was a very hostile critic of tsarism (by no means untrue) who sensed the approach of revolution (doubtful and irrelevant), and would have welcomed the new Soviet world (preposterous). Only the aged maverick Ilya Ehrenburg has tried to present a reasonably mature version of Chekhov's personality and work.

It would be wrong, of course, to deny that he was wise or compassionate or concerned, but his sensibility was also tough and skeptical, even ruthless, in the sense that it would suppress no evidence about the depth and range of human foolishness, and would report fully the violence, overt and concealed, that blighted the lives of his fellow men. He must be read, in part at least, as a poet of murder and terror whose vision of the pain of existence is heightened by the controlled understating voice in which he tells of it. With this collection of stories we are given the opportunity to escape the stereotype entirely and to sample the full range and power of his mature sensibility.

These late long stories differ in quality from all that preceded them. As they grew in length they grew in depth and complexity. The same swift prose now tells not of that single moment when a life changes direction or when its real direction becomes clear, but of a sequence of moments which plot the full curve of a life or of several entangled lives, or, as it sometimes seems, of the entire community or of Russia itself. With more space to work in, setting becomes a more active part of the story, moral coloration becomes at once more varied and more vivid. A greater number of motifs and symbols thicken and enrich the texture of the narrative. Allowing for Chekhov's extraordinary power to compress, it is reasonable, I think, to see several of the longer works in this collection as novels in miniature.

The first story in point of time, "The Name-Day Party" (1888) (note the bland "factual" quality of all the titles), is played out in the fierce tension between a code of social behavior grounded in the culture, and the authentic human needs of two individuals, expressed in their hidden, elusive love for each other, and in the biological force—the implacable rhythm of approaching childbirth—which carries the story to a disastrous climax. Olga Mikhailovna experiences the faintness and nausea at first as part of the terrible tedium inflicted on her by the power of social convention. When she distinguishes, later, between the true and the false, it is somehow too late.

This play of forces is carefully established in physical and emotional terms in the first paragraphs. The social roles of guest and host at the interminable party constrict movement, stifle feeling, and spread a gloss of falsehood over everyone's behavior. Facial expressions are masks, gesture and utterance respond to the cultural norm, not to human need. Chekhov invokes this inhuman world at regular intervals through the story by citing a frozen smile, an affected remark, a self-serving diatribe, or a partisan political attitude. This aspect of the world is held together by hatred and lies under the surface of party manners.

The anti-human force is established in Olga's first flight from the party. In her hideout, she has been accustomed to sit "in the deep shade of plum and cherry trees," with the summer smell of hay and honey and the sound of bees around her, and summon up her dream of the unborn child she is carrying. A renewed sense of her root attachment to life is her usual reward in this refuge, but as the story begins her refuge and her fantasy are broken in on by her bitter sense of the party she has left, by her guilt as a delinquent hostess, and finally, tangibly, by the languid flirtatious conversation she overhears between her husband and a young thing who has taken a walk with him. In the first confrontation of forces, the advantage already lies with the "enemy." We are prepared for the final outcome in the first page, but we do not realize it fully until the drama is played out in the relationship between Olga Mikhailovna and her husband. Through most of the story they cannot find each other through the masks of their public behavior. His affected drawl and posture, the aggressive statement of his political views, his self-dramatizing account of the trial, the generalized lie of his public self, estrange her from him, generate a slowly mounting rage against him, coinciding with her over-all sense of disgust and with the tension of her approaching physical ordeal.

Several times she glimpses the real man she has known and

loved, but she cannot reach him. Once when she finds him alone and unobserved, she feels strongly the distress he is feeling. But he evades her. "Meeting his wife's eyes, Pyotr Dmitrich's face instantly assumed the expression it had worn at dinner and in the garden—indifferent and slightly ironical; he yawned and stood up." He has snapped back into his social mold. They "miss" each other, talking again through masks. The dialectical process of estrangement from society —as well as from her husband—is accelerated by the first signs of childbirth. Released by fatigue and malaise, her accumulated rage explodes against him in the shocking charge that he has married her for her money. Later, after the pain-dimmed days and nights of labor, when Olga has learned that her baby was born dead, the masks and the falseness between them are gone, but so is much more. The resolution of the tension has the quality of a collapse into an inner emptiness. Olga has lost the capacity to respond to her husband's remorse or to his renewed sense of his love for her. All life-giving connections are broken; a kind of death has taken possession of her.

Dr. Chekhov was always very careful with the medical elements in his stories. Women wrote, he said, that his description of childbirth in this story was flawless. It is possible to read "The Name-Day Party" as a case history: no doubt the long day of tedium and rage may be said to have "caused" the stillbirth, or, contrariwise, the physical strain to have brought on the emotional explosion. But this literal reading would miss the point. The real connections between birth and death, between the flesh and the spirit, between the social occasion and the biological tragedy, are caught in the magnified power of the symbol: death is the only possible issue of lives that are eaten away by lies and hatred.

Another form of death-in-life is the subject of "A Dull Story" (1889). The narrating "I" of the story is dying in the natural course of things, of old age, but he is threatened by a more terrible death of the spirit, before his physical demise occurs. Chekhov has used a special Russian fictional form which presents itself as the confession of an inadequate, crippled, or alienated man. The story's subtitle, "From the Notes of an Old Man," places it squarely in the tradition of Gogol's "Notes of a Madman," Turgenev's "Diary of a Superfluous Man," and Dostoyevsky's "Notes from Underground." Chekhov—with extraordinary ingenuity—has made the borrowed form yield an additional result. In earlier "confessional" stories the narrator undertakes to describe and account for the failure of his life; Chekhov makes the act of description and analysis of the past into a relentless process of further discovery. Describing his life, he destroys it retroactively by uncovering the full extent of its emptiness. At the end of his destructive analysis, when death would be a deliverance, he is left, in the bleakest existential terms, condemned to live a while longer.

If he has taken his form from illustrious predecessors, it may be that he has taken his matter from Tolstoy's brilliant story "The Death of Ivàn Ilyich," published just three years before his own. The two stories are about men approaching and confronting their own deaths, and both use the same double movement through time—forward toward death and backward through reminiscence toward the discovery that the life about to end has not been worth living. Here, again, I think, Chekhov has transcended his model. Tolstoy's Ivan Ilyich discovers, while he is dying, that his life, career, and attachments since childhood have all been inauthentic. But death itself comes as a triumphant return to a higher realm of being. Free of the Tolstoyan pieties, Chekhov has granted the reader no such relief, and has created, therefore, a more terrible—and a greater—story. With the same blighting knowledge of a life mislived, Chekhov's professor is left alive, and when death comes, he knows and we know that he will simply be reabsorbed into the nitrogen cycle.

The story begins with a third-person description of the professor's reputation, rank, and honors. It is the professor himself talking and when he turns to the first person, we are immediately alerted to look for the discrepancy between the public and private man. Indeed, this is one of the governing ideas of the story. We are constantly asked to consider the contrast between the man and his name. Again, as in "The Name-Day Party," the culture corrupts and alienates, this time through the disfiguring mold fame and reputation have imposed on him. Near the end of the analysis of his own past, he recognizes that fame has been a catastrophe. He measures its depredations by the distance he has traveled from simplicity and spontaneity, from all the genuine connections he once had with life through his wife, his children, and his work. The falseness of his private life is marked in one obvious sense by the restrictions of social decorum:

there are no more dogfights under the table, he recalls ruefully, in the smothering respectability his wife has decided is appropriate to his rank.

His reflections are brought on by the sense that he has begun to fail. He first describes a typical day presented in an habitual present tense, which associates the present with the recent past. In this account we are able to fix his position, as it were, with regard to friends, family, work, and colleagues. The survey records significant losses—atrophy of the connections with his family, the decline of their relations into nagging pettiness and hollow routine—but there is still the challenge of lecturing and the great pleasure of meeting that challenge successfully. Suddenly we learn that that has gone, too. In a quick shift of the time perspective, he tells us, "That's the way it used to be." Now fits of panic threaten his control over the material and over the audience. It is time to quit, but he lacks the courage. The static situation in which the story began has given way. Under the new and terrible stimulus, he embarks on a wider and wider examination of his life, of its meaning and of all his relations to the world around him. This process gives the story a special cumulative power. The act of examining his situation in the world accelerates his alienation from it, snapping more and more of his connections with it. The more rot he discovers, the deeper his sense of spiritual death, the more disarmed he becomes against the encroaching terror of physical death.

His sour reflections on his profession, on his colleagues, on the younger generation, on modern literature, on science itself, uncover no source of strength or belief. His private despair is reflected back to him by the world outside. His relationship with Katya, who alone seems to offer connection and hope, provides the central dramatic tension of the story. She stands outside the deadly pantomime of family life; he has known her as a child and recalls the trust and delight on her face when he talked to her. She offers him money and advice—leave the family, quit work, see a doctor—that represents a minimal program for survival. But when she asks him for help—what can she do with her blighted life? —the banality of his first response yields in the final scene in the story to a blank incapacity to respond at all. This failure is the final proof to him and to us that he has died spiritually. But that is not all we know. By that double movement we come to realize that he has not simply lost something precious—he never really possessed it. He was always preoccupied when she came to him as a child; he never shared or even tolerated her interest in the theater; when she was in desperate trouble in Siberia he wrote her long boring letters. A kind of retroactive chain reaction has invalidated the relationship back to its origins, or to that moment when his pursuit of fame, of the culture's image of him, severed his genuine relations with life. Deprived of hope, and of a past as well, he is left to stare at the blank wall of the alien hotel room. Hell, to paraphrase Sartre, is when the last human being on earth leaves without looking back.

The irony and horror of his final situation is prepared for through the story by the controlling metaphor of insomnia. Introduced first as the sign of advancing age, inability to sleep prepares us for his inability to die. Being awake/alive has become the worst of all torments.

When "A Dull Story" was published, one reader thought he had discovered Chekhov's ideas in the professor's reflections. Chekhov denied it flatly: they were the professor's ideas, not his. In some of the later stories, characters argue at length in philosophical language, but we are seldom able to locate Chekhov in the exchanges. Nor are we meant to: "It seems to me that it is not up to writers to solve such questions as God, pessimism, etc. The writer's job is to depict who, how, and under what circumstances people have spoken or thought about God or pessimism." Ideas are a function of character in these "philosophizing" stories, part of an esthetic order. In "The Duel" (1891) the abstract argument and moralizing are part of a complex confrontation between two characters, with a number of observers and commentators stationed around them. They all talk and pass judgment, but Chekhov could not have told us more plainly that no one in the story is right: the refrain "nobody knows the real truth" is repeated four times in the final lines of the story. If Chekhov will not guide us to a true understanding or to his own judgment of events, what is he up to in this story? What is at stake in the duel itself? Is the pointlessness of it all really the point?

"The Duel" reproduces so many stock situations and characters from the Russian literary past, it is hard to believe it was not part of Chekhov's intention to play new variations on familiar themes, to test them in new conditions, perhaps to exorcise them by parody. Lermontov, Pushkin, and later

Tolstoy, "sent" characters on voyages of spiritual discovery to the Caucasus where Russian civilization met the raw grandeur of nature. The fetid love nest Chekhov's Layevsky constructs in the no longer exotic setting may be seen as a parody of his predecessor's Rousseauian experiments. An edge of caricature is strongly felt in the whole account of the conflict between the figures, familiar to us from the Russian literary past, of the discontented liberal (sensitive, alienated, impractical, once known as the man of the 1840's) and the harsh Puritan radical (arrogant, rationalist, activist, known as the man of the 1860's). In reproducing these stereotypes Chekhov has reduced them to caricature. Layevsky is a neurasthenic slob, von Koren a blithering bully. The duel between them suggests the similar scene in Lermontov's *A Hero of Our Time,* and yet always with an edge of parody. The gunplay is deadly serious and yet the entire scene comes through to us as a ghastly comedy. No one knows the rules; the doctor plans to make his profit from the affair; the priest, hiding in the bushes to collect amusing stories, averts an absurd murder when his shout disturbs von Koren's aim. And yet we are relieved and persuaded that Layevsky's life is worth saving. It is a difficult effect, and one that Chekhov often manages: to make us care, without pity or condescension, about the plight of fools. This, I think, is the key to the story's order.

A heightening of effects to the point of caricature is felt in the presentation of all the characters. There is a strong flavor of vaudeville in the early statement of Layevsky's dilemma: how shall he escape the "worse-than-being-married" tedium of his dreary menage at the least risk or expense to himself? He dreams of a brilliant career and quarrels with his woman over cabbage soup; he identifies his problems with Hamlet's and runs off to play cards. Nadya imagines herself light, airy, and charming at the picnic, and we see her fat, drunk and sloppy—and available to the predatory chief of police. Von Koren's ideas echo distantly aspects of Nietzsche, Darwin, and Spencer, but his program to exterminate the unfit in the name of eugenics and the love of Christ shines with the insane glitter of Dostoyevsky's *reductio ad absurdum* paradoxes.

Deception and self-deception accumulate and compound one another, until there seems to be no way out. But Layevsky, surprisingly, begins to change his direction when he reaches a point of absolute self-disgust. He reviews his crimes against others and regards with dismay the mountain of lies ahead of him if he is to escape from Nadya as he had planned. Guilt and compassion are not enough to overcome his moral flabbiness. It is the absurd horror of the duel, we must assume, and the bullet crease in his neck, that persuade him to change his ways. But the point is that he does, and Nadya undergoes a similar metamorphosis brought on by a series of shocks, including the death of the husband she had abandoned. We cannot say they have advanced very far toward self-knowledge or higher standards of human performance, but they have stopped doing what they had been doing. They have come together again, and changed the direction of their lives.

The final confrontation of Layevsky and von Koren still strongly suggests that pointlessness is Chekhov's point. The bully has taught the weakling his lesson, but even he is appalled by the collapsed personality of his victim. Still he is careful not to apologize for the damage he may have done. What are we to conclude? Lazy little sinners, frightened badly enough, become respectable nonentities; victorious bullies learn nothing. Nobody understands anything, we are assured, and yet the final image of the small boat making its halting way against a head sea (another echo from Lermontov) invites us to conclude, I think, that even in the blind working out of small destinies, in the plight of fools, viewed without pity, there is some evidence that forward motion in human affairs is still possible.

The faint flicker of hope in "The Duel"—if we have read it correctly—is entirely absent from "Ward Six." The themes we have encountered in earlier stories are restated with great intensity and brought together in a compelling new way. The culture's power to suffocate through a mechanical code of social behavior—as we first met it in "The Name-Day Party"— is attributed now to the entire social order. It is exerted against any and all deviants from the norm, inflicting a generalized condition of death-in-life upon the entire community. The provincial town—miles from the railroad—is the antagonist in the story. Moral rot spreads outward from its center to blight all signs of restlessness or protest. Nikita, the brutal ex-sergeant, acts for the community as he keeps order in Ward Six, where the lunatics are confined. The community sends its emissaries to trap the doctor when he shows signs of departing from his own passive norm, and Nikita smashes the life out of him when his imprisonment in Ward Six provokes his first—and last—explosion of rage.

A quickening of Chekhov's anger is felt in the vivid, even extravagant coloration he gives to the images of sloth, filth, and breakdown. To gain immediacy, in the opening paragraphs of the story, he addresses us directly and takes us on a personal tour of the godforsaken hospital building where the insane are kept, cataloguing the stinking piles of mattresses and old clothes, describing each of the wretches who is buried alive in the terrible ward. The squalid order Nikita maintains there stands, of course, for the moral condition of the entire community. At the end we are not spared the horror of Ragin's death and the bleak pathos of his burial. The quiet tone of the telling contains but does not conceal Chekhov's anger.

The movement of the story may be described as a complex reversal of values made tangible in one enveloping irony: the two sensitive, intelligent men in the community are locked up as mad; the world of the sane outside is, by any moral or human standard, clearly insane. It is an upside-down world —where doctors ignore the sick, where the filthy hospital *spreads* infection—which would appear to be righted if it were upended. But this world resists overturn, and the doctor's solitary movement toward responsibility and right thinking must inevitably end in his defeat.

The action of the story consists in two case histories which interact in the sense that Gromov, the first victim, "infects" Ragin with the thirst for life that is considered insane. Gromov's case is presented with a deliberate ambivalence. There is evidence enough that his responses are those of a fully developed paranoiac, and yet a parallel case is established that the response of this sensitive, literate man to the stupidity and cruelty around him is morally quite plausible. The final vision that sends him screaming down the street—that of two shackled convicts walking between armed soldiers—might symbolize for any rational man the residual violence in this grim world.

Ragin's convenient pessimism, drawn remotely from Schopenhauer, places everything—duty, the suffering of others, the very sanctity of life—against a million-year perspective which reduces it to insignificance. His one attachment to life, lofty conversation with his intellectual peers, also works as a point of vulnerability, a kind of tragic flaw. The pleasure of exchanging lofty ideas with the mad Gromov—even in bitter argument—conceals the passing of the "infection." Ragin begins the metamorphosis, prefigured by the curve of Gromov's life, that will lead to "irritability," the lowest manifestation of life in the living organism, thence to anger, indignation, and finally to the condition of moral sanity that requires his confinement. The turning point occurs when the sloth-protecting vision of the world a thousand years hence does not hold against the intrusive present. The repellent figures of Khobotov and Mikhail Averyanych appear in the sere landscape of his fantasy. The hot "scum" that has been rising higher and higher in his gorge finally chokes him in a fit of moral apoplexy after he has felt Nikita's fist. His first full response to his new sense of life leads directly to his death.

The story "My Life" (1896), subtitled "The Story of a Provincial," returns us to the same malevolent atmosphere that destroyed Dr. Ragin. The protagonist-narrator of the story professes and tests out a Tolstoyan ideology, and the culture pursues, humiliates, and ostracizes this earnest nonconformist, "a traitor to his class." It does not succeed in destroying him, but his survival is certainly not intended to vindicate Tolstoyanism (Chekhov had repudiated it years before) nor is it meant to mitigate our sense of the brutish evil that dominates the dismal town.

Making suitable allowance for Chekhov's extraordinary power to compress, the twenty chapters—with the last one serving as an epilogue in the manner of Turgenev—the complexity of its entanglements, the number and variety of characters, the detailed report on setting, bring this story as close to the range and density of the novel as anything Chekhov wrote. Mere "coverage" of social types is certainly a primary part of Chekhov's purpose. We meet the governor, the gentry, intelligentsia, the entrepreneur-engineer, the professional class, artisans, and on down the social ladder to the brawling migrants who work on the railroad and the drunken, thieving peasants. Setting extends appropriately from the governor's mansion to the slaughterhouse where the workers wade in pools of blood. The two ends of the social spectrum are brought together when the governor appears in the slaughterhouse in Misail's climactic hallucination. There is little doubt that the catalogue of social types and settings is a catalogue, too, of forms of moral rot, with the slaughter-house looming as the dominant and characterizing image of the community.

Misail, a dogged, earnest man, is persecuted for his deviation from the expected, but he is misfit enough to begin with, it would seem, to suggest that his estrangement from the community is not simply the result of a deliberate decision to reject it on moral grounds. He is a curious mixture of rebellion and submission. (In the midst of his revolt he snaps to attention when his father beats him with an umbrella and when Masha proposes to him!) Through all the slander and hostility he endures, he seeks no more than an adjustment to the world, a personal solution in which he can feel morally at ease about his contribution to and dependence on his fellow men. If his way of life stirs controversy, draws attacks, and attracts the interest of a few sympathetic people, he is not "bearing witness" in a demonstrative way. But in his shy, stubborn, humorless way he sticks to his program for the moral life, despite his father's implacable opposition and his wife's disenchantment and consequent flight.

When we see the man behind his ideology, see him clearly with all his deficiencies, we become aware of a serious fault in the writing. How can this limited, awkward man see his plight so clearly and tell it with such flashing intelligence? And if he understands all the irony of his predicament, how can he endure his situation so stolidly? Chekhov has taken few of the usual precautions to disguise his own vision of the drama behind the narrator's mask, to make the narrator's understanding of events correspond to his intellectual capacity. Our own response to the story is blurred, I think, because of Chekhov's uncharacteristic carelessness on this score.

But when we see the man—not a champion of dissent, not even a well-armed ideologist because of his human limitations—we are better prepared for the central drama, the parallel failure of two loves. Ideology is present in the breakup of Misail's marriage with Masha, in the sense that they draw contrary conclusions from their experience of the raw facts of life in the country—daily contact with the thieving peasantry, climaxed by the howling brawl between Cheprakov and Moisei. But Masha's disgust with the peasants and Misail's undocumented respect for them do not define the break between them. She is merely acting out the drama of commitment, and when the cause fails her the man who has never mattered much is expendable. Misail has no claim on her because he has never had the strength to possess her. Kleopatra, who has a greater impulse toward life beneath her shy, tearful exterior, risks more and loses more. Both have been involved with and exploited by their social and intellectual betters. Masha and Dr. Blagoro dismiss their provincial loves ceremoniously, but cruelly withal, and with no sense of loss or guilt. Both end up in the exciting places of the world far from the provincial desert.

Misail survives his personal defeat, as he survives the full assault of the community, staggering deliriously down the street, pursued by hooting children. He endures in some final kind of accommodation with the society, we learn in the epilogue chapter, too weak to get the best of the community, too passive to flee, too stubborn to give in. The story ends without explicit resolution of the many tensions in it. Time's passage merely softens them. The ending of the story is chordal in the sense that many motifs are evoked simultaneously, with bitter resignation, perhaps, the dominant tonality. The story has plotted the decisive points that describe the curve of Misail's life and we discover at the end the direction it will take. The balance of passivity and defiance in him has not been tipped either way. There is no final decision in the test of Tolstoyan ideas. The resultant of these tensions has placed Misail, rather surprisingly, in a recognized niche in the community: he has taken the place of Radish, the master artisan and lay prophet. He is well liked in the town, at the end, in his new ascetic mien, and yet there is no sense that he has capitulated. Nor is there any revocation of Radish's repeated utterance to the town—both warning and prophecy—"lice eat grass, rust eats iron, lies eat the soul."

In the story "In the Ravine" (1900), the power of evil is beyond challenge. No one can stand against it. The conflict is a dynastic one, wholly within the evil realm of the merchant family; the stakes are control of the business and the terms of the struggle approach the classical in their starkness and clarity of outline. A moral counterweight is present in the story, the perfectly innocent Lipa and her infant, but they are victims, not protagonists. There are gradations of evil in the ruling house: the father sticks at using his son's counterfeit money and shows genuine concern when he is arrested. This exhibition of scruple leads to his downfall, tripped, as it would seem, on a last snag of conscience. Aksinya, the stylized figure of pure evil—"she looked like a viper lifting its head and stretching itself to peer out of the young rye"—has already mixed the tainted with the good money and seizes control from a broken old man. Chekhov's vision of the evil society has reached an apotheosis, with no suggestion of moral redress.

There is, again, a difference between the matter and the telling of it that adds power to the controlling metaphors of the story. It is a mild gossipy voice that tells us about the deacon who ate the entire four-pound jar of caviar at the wedding, opening the story with a casual image of insensate greed. It is a matter-of-fact voice that tells us how the industrial waste has poisoned the meadows and infected the cattle, and how the cockroaches have nested in the telephone. The store sells rancid food and illegal vodka, and outside on payday—the same level voice tells us—the drunks lie in the mud and beg from the passers-by.

When the action begins we are alerted to the squalid reality under the gloss of respectability. The seedy son is a detective with an extraordinary eye for stolen goods. We learn later that he is more criminal than cop, and is about to graduate into a career of professional counterfeiting. He is a man with a very moral mouth who talks a kind of Dostoyevskyan gibberish about sin, morality, and Christ. The dismal wedding feast is conducted with all appropriate ceremony. But the arranged marriage is a travesty of human relationships, reaching a climax of absurdity when he is dragged back from his pursuit of a stolen coat and thrown drunk and blithering into the bridal chamber.

The second and decisive phase of the action begins with his arrest, but not before the counterfeit money has been mixed with the real, and this image of corruption reinforced by all that surrounds it stands forth as the dominant metaphor of the story. Child murder, the central *event* of the story, must approach the unbearable in any esthetic scale. Chekhov balances Lipa's scream, "a scream such as had never been heard before in Ukleyevo," with the lyrical description of her grief under the stars and the reassuring presence of the old wanderer.

Evil triumphs but the innocent survive and assert their countervailing force at the end of the story when Lipa and

"Crutch" take pity on the ruined Tsybukin, turned out, hungry, to wander the streets.

Stanislavsky reports this incident during a production conference on *The Three Sisters*:

> One of the speakers who . . . tried to display his eloquence began to speak of his impressions with pathos and the common vocabulary of a tried orator:
>
> "Although I do not agree with the author in principle, still . . ."
>
> Anton Pavlovich could not survive this "in principle." Confused, hurt, and even insulted, he left the meeting, trying to go out without being noticed. . . . I went at once to his home and found him not only out of spirits and insulted, but angry. I do not remember ever seeing him so angry again.
>
> "It is impossible. Listen—'in principle'!"

Chekhov did not like stereotyped words, or too many words, or other people's words, it would seem, when his own work was under discussion. Gorky reports in his *Reminiscences* that Chekhov once said:

> For twenty-five years I have read criticisms of my stories, and I don't remember a single remark of any value or one word of valuable advice. Only once Skabichevsky wrote something which made an impression on me . . . he said I would die in a ditch, drunk.*

For anyone who knows this, it is hard to write about Chekhov without sensing his disapproving presence.

Time and the history of Chekhov's reputation have disclosed a number of obstacles to the full confrontation of his work. In a sense neither critics nor readers have fully possessed him, and Chekhov himself offers little help in this regard. He does not provide clear moral guidance in many stories that are clearly about the moral side of human behavior. Readers who cannot tolerate ambivalence tend to

* Skabichevsky was wrong, too.

"read in" external or irrelevant values. When Chekhov learned of these mistaken—always oversimplified—readings in his own day, his distress was evident, but only rarely did he offer any clarification, and then only to fight against easy, cliché responses. The story or play spoke for itself. Even when Stanislavsky sentimentalized or vulgarized his work, his reticence seldom gave way.

Despite his contempt for critics, they are almost obliged to rush in to try to guess what he failed to spell out for us. On the basis of many readings, I have tried to point to what I have come to consider the basic order in the story, the relations of its larger working parts to one another. Knowledge of this esthetic order, which contains and organizes the other ingredients, is the surest guide to our understanding. Moral coloration, the element most likely to mislead, is very strong in all these stories—how often death is a consequence of the conflicts and of the choices characters make!—but it takes on its full meaning only as part of an esthetic unity.

The controlling order is made of the most exact balancing of tonalities, in harmony or in discord, or in a movement from one to the other, in the statement, development, and recapitulation of motifs, in the subtle and evocative use of setting. All of this is accomplished without tags, labels, or any other kind of explicit statement. In the talkiest of these stories, "Ward Six," the real story is contained in the connections between the filthy mattresses, the barefooted Jewish lunatic, the hospital bathtub full of potatoes, the doctor's evening bottle of beer, his piles of unread medical literature, the feeling more than the sense of the arguments, the "scum" that rises in his gorge, the moon-made shadows on the floor of the insane ward—to name a few of the ingredients that make up the whole story. Or consider one swift glance we have of Cheprakov in "My Life": we are told without comment that he ran drunk and naked through the meadow and ate flies. This striking vignette tells us about Cheprakov, of course, but it also tells us something about Misail, about the world he inhabits and is willing to endure; it also serves as the final and characterizing note of an important unit in the total narrative structure. The alert reader must be prepared to respond to all the multiple functions of this freighted detail in order to have Chekhov's full effect.

We are used in our day to the implicit story, Hemingway's "iceberg" with seven eighths of the whole invisible beneath the surface of the narrative. But even to our practiced modern eye, Chekhov is very demanding on the reader. Accused once of being too "objective," in the sense that he presented only raw data without "taking sides" or telling the reader how to feel, he answered, "When I write I count upon my reader fully, assuming that he himself will add the subjective elements that are lacking in the story." The reader is challenged to collaborate in the experience of the story, to interpret it in the way an actor interprets the text of a play, or a musician a score. A good "performance" by the reader will yield a very great reward.

RUFUS W. MATHEWSON

# SELECTED BIBLIOGRAPHY

## OTHER WORKS BY ANTON CHEKHOV

*The Confession*, 1883  Story*
*He Understood*, 1883  Story*
*At Sea—A Sailor's Story*, 1883  Story*
*A Nincompoop*, 1883  Story*
*Surgery*, 1884  Story*
*Ninochka—A Love Story*, 1885  Story*
*A Cure for Drinking*, 1885  Story*
*The Jailer Jailed*, 1885  Story*
*The Dance Pianist*, 1885  Story*
*The Milksop*, 1885  Story*
*Marriage in Ten or Fifteen Years*, 1885  Story*
*Sergeant Prishibeyev*, 1885  Story
*Grief*, 1886  Story
*In Spring*, 1886  Story*
*The Kiss*, 1887  Story*
*The Father*, 1887  Story*
*Ivanov*, 1887  Play**
*The Steppe*, 1888  Short novel
*Gusev*, 1890  Story
*In Exile*, 1892  Story*
*Sakhalin Island*, 1893  Travel notes
*A Woman's Kingdom*, 1894  Story
*The Black Monk*, 1894  Story
*Three Years*, 1895  Story*
*The House with the Mansard—An Artist's Story*, 1896
     Story*
*The Sea Gull*, 1896  Play**
*Uncle Vanya*, 1897  Play**
*Peasants*, 1897  Short novel*

  * Available in Signet Classic CW1001
** Available in Signet Classic CW1172

*A Visit to Friends*, 1898   Story
*The Darling*, 1899   Story*
*The New Villa*, 1899   Story
*The Bishop*, 1902   Story
*The Three Sisters*, 1902   Play **
*The Betrothed*, 1903   Story
*The Cherry Orchard*, 1903   Play **

# BIOGRAPHY & CRITICISM

Bruford, W. H. *Chekhov and His Russia*. New York: Humanities Press, Inc., 1963.

Brustein, Robert. *The Theater of Revolt*. Boston: Atlantic-Little, Brown, 1964.

Cole, Toby, ed. *Playwrights on Playwriting*. New York: Hill & Wang, 1961.

Eekman, T., ed. *Anton Čechov: 1860–1960, Some Essays*, Leiden: E. J. Brill, 1960.

Ehrenburg, Ilya. *Chekhov, Stendhal, and Other Essays*. ed. Harrison Salisbury. New York: Alfred A. Knopf, Inc., 1963.

Fergusson, Francis. *The Idea of a Theater*. New York: Doubleday & Company, Inc. (Anchor Books), 1953.

Friedland, Louis S., ed. *Anton Chekhov's Letters on The Short Story, The Drama and Other Literary Topics*. Introduction by Ernest J. Simmons. New York: Benjamin Blom, Inc., 1964.

Gorky, Maxim. *Reminiscences of Tolstoy, Chekhov, and Andreyev*. New York: The Viking Press, Inc. (Compass Books), 1959.

Hellman, Lillian, ed. *Selected Letters of Anton Chekhov*. New York: Farrar, Straus, 1955.

Hingley, Ronald. *Chekhov: A Biographical and Critical Study*. London: George Allen & Unwin, Ltd., 1950; New York: The Macmillan Company, 1950.

Magarshack, David. *Chekhov: A Life*. New York: Grove Press, Inc., 1953.

—— *Chekhov the Dramatist*. New York: Hill & Wang (Dramabooks), 1960.

Saunders, Beatrice. *Tchekhov, The Man*. Chester Springs, Pennsylvania: Dufour Editions; London: Centaur Press, 1961.

Simmons, Ernest J. *Chekhov: A Biography.* Boston: Atlantic-Little, Brown, 1962.

Toumanova, Nina. *Anton Chekhov: The Voice of Twilight Russia.* New York: Columbia University Press; London: Oxford University Press, 1960.

Wilson, Edmund. Preface to *Peasants and Other Stories* by Anton Chekhov. New York: Doubleday & Company, Inc. (Anchor Books), 1956.